凱信企管

用對的方法充實自己，
讓人生變得更美好！

凱信企管

用對的方法充實自己，
讓人生變得更美好！

精準

7000單字

滿分版

初級基礎篇
LEVEL 1 & LEVEL 2

1～2200單字

使用說明

7000 單字滿分元素架構，無縫學習，無懈可擊！
不論是會考、全民英檢初級都能輕鬆過關。

1

收錄單字完整多義，學習滴水不漏

記住拼字的同時，單字的多重意思及不同詞性收錄詳盡，不論怎麼考都不怕，精準答題不誤用，滿分必備因素一次掌握。

fine [faɪn]

形 美好的
副 很好地
名 罰款
動 處以罰金
同 nice 好的

2

英英解釋，協助更精準理解單字

中文直譯常常無法精準地翻譯英文單字的字義。全書每一單字用英英解釋再次完整說明字義，用字能更準確，也能加強單字的深刻記憶。

英英 touch or caress with the lips especially as a sign of love, affection, or greeting

kissed me.

3 生活例句營造感官情境，強化單字記憶

善用感官讓單字自然記憶。利用例句營造情境，完美地理解單字並加深記憶，除能跟上出題方向，同時也能自然地提升生活口語能力。

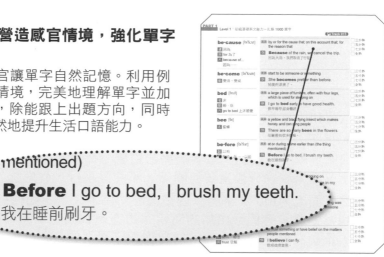

...mentioned)

例 **Before** I go to bed, I brush my teeth.
我在睡前刷牙。

4 特別設計：「熟悉度評量表」，掌握學習成效

單字到底是記得三分熟、七分熟，還是滾瓜爛熟，用評量表檢測最準確。除了促進自我學習動力，還能在考試前，快速針對不熟悉的單字加強複習。

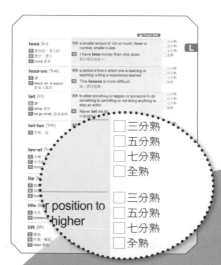

5 單字／例句音檔全收錄，學習隨時都可以

全書單字／例句音檔 MP3 收錄，QR Code 隨手一掃，藉由頻繁地用聲音刷腦記憶，刺激聽覺，單字一定記得住。

Track 106

全書音檔雲端連結

因各家手機系統不同，若無法直接掃描，仍可以至以下電腦雲端連結下載收聽。
（https://tinyurl.com/478t9rvj）

PREFACE
前言

你還再用「死背」的方式來背英文單字？！腦容量真的很有限，若用老方法來記單字，可能會讓你越背越忘，進入單字煉獄的痛苦輪迴中！

每回聽到學生們談到記單字的痛苦經驗，都忍不住替他們覺得辛苦！但英文單字又是考試拿分最重要的關鍵，不背又不行，到底該怎麼辦呢？

其實市面上 7000 單字的學習書已經相當多了，「如何選擇最好、最適合的」也常是學習者們最頭痛的問題；這亦是我們在一開始撰寫這本 7000 單字時，不斷在思量的。「如何能有別與市面上的 7000 單字書」，我們著實想了很久，於是決定讓在台灣有許多教學經驗的 Michael 老師和從小在美國唸書的 Tong 老師聯手撰寫，結合對台灣考情的了解與在地生活英語的應用，讓 7000 單字的選字、例句的編寫，不僅能精準的符合 108 年新課綱注重英文與生活結合，澈底地讓學習者有效記憶單字，更能明確地理解單字及片語如何應用在句子裡，還能同步實際在日常裡發揮口說功能，齊步提升英語力，跨大步朝大考滿分邁進。

《精準 7000 單字滿分版》，我們特別著重三大部分：

一、收錄單字完整多義及不同詞性

單字的多重意思及不同詞性收錄詳盡，不論考題怎麼變化都不怕！答題能更精準，口說不誤用，單字一次學好學滿。

二、用感官情境法學單字

帶你用五感去感受單字。搭配生活例句及英英解釋，在腦海裡營造視覺畫面、創造英文環境，助你強化單字記憶；再利用音檔，刺激聽覺，考試沒問題，溝通也 OK。

三、單字評量表掌握學習成效

單字是三分熟、五分熟還是滾瓜爛熟，用評量檢測最準確！每一個單字特別設計「熟悉度評量表」，除了掌握學習效果，亦能在考試前，快速複習拿高分。

期待這一本《精準 7000 單字滿分版：初級基礎篇 Level 1&Level 2》，能有效並無痛的幫助大家記憶 2200 字，不論是會考、全民英檢初級都能輕鬆過關。

CONTENTS

目錄

Part 1

Level 1：初級基礎英文能力│ 010

▶ 扎根 **1000** 單字

A~Z（Track 001 ～ Track 136）

Part 2

Level 2：初級基礎英文能力│ 148

▶ 邁向 **2200** 單字

A~Z（Track 137 ～ Track 274）

LEVEL 1 音檔雲端連結

因各家手機系統不同，若無法直接掃描，
仍可以至以下電腦雲端連結下載收聽。
（https://tinyurl.com/5bxkzhtp）

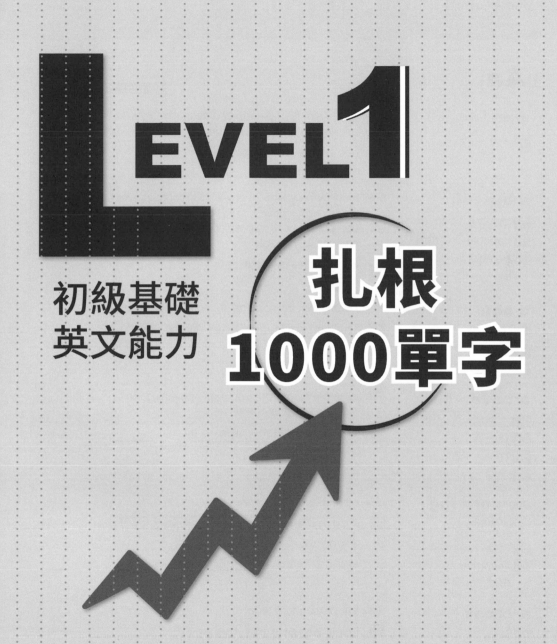

LEVEL1

初級基礎
英文能力

扎根
1000單字

Aa

🎧 Track 001

a/an [ə/æn]

冠 一、一個

英英 one or single; a person or a thing which you're not referring to any particular one; used before a noun

例 Leo has **a** cute dog.
立歐有一隻可愛的狗。

☐ 三分熟
☐ 五分熟
☐ 七分熟
☐ 全熟

---

a·ble [ˋebl̩]

形 能幹的、有能力的
同 capable 有能力的
片 be able to 可以

英英 to have the sufficient physical strength, power, force, mental power, skill, time, money, opportunity or resources of any kind to do something; capable

例 He says he is **able** to fly!
他說他會飛！

☐ 三分熟
☐ 五分熟
☐ 七分熟
☐ 全熟

---

a·bout [əˋbaʊt]

副 大約
介 關於
同 concerning 關於

英英 around, not far from the stated number or amount

例 This pen costs me **about** one hundred dollars.
這枝筆花了我大約一百塊。

☐ 三分熟
☐ 五分熟
☐ 七分熟
☐ 全熟

---

a·bove [əˋbʌv]

形 上面的
副 在上面
介 在……上面
名 上面

英英 in or to a higher position than something, on or over the upper surface

例 There is a rainbow **above** the hill.
山丘上有一道彩虹。

☐ 三分熟
☐ 五分熟
☐ 七分熟
☐ 全熟

---

ac·cord·ing [əˋkɔrdɪŋ]

介 根據……
片 according to...
　　根據……

英英 corresponding to or stated by

例 **According** to the weather report, it will rain tomorrow.
根據氣象報導，明天會下雨。

☐ 三分熟
☐ 五分熟
☐ 七分熟
☐ 全熟

---

a·cross [əˋkrɔs]

副 橫過
介 穿過、橫過
同 cross 越過

英英 from A side to B side

例 I walk **across** this road.
我穿越這條馬路。

☐ 三分熟
☐ 五分熟
☐ 七分熟
☐ 全熟

act [ækt]
名 行為、行動、法案
動 行動、扮演、下判決

英英 process of doing something or do something for a particular purpose
例 She **acts** as Queen Elizabeth in the play.
她在這齣劇中扮演伊莉莎白女王。
☐三分熟 ☐五分熟 ☐七分熟 ☐全熟

A

ac·tion [`ækʃən]
名 行動、活動
同 behavior 行為、舉止

英英 a process or condition of acting, moving or practicing, especially in the situation of dealing with the problem or difficulty
例 His **action** is quick.
他的動作很敏捷。
☐三分熟 ☐五分熟 ☐七分熟 ☐全熟

ac·tor [`æktɚ]
名 男演員
同 performer 演出者

英英 the male person who pretends to be someone else while performing in a performance, film or TV program
例 Leonardo Dicaprio is my favorite **actor**.
李奧納多是我最喜歡的男演員。
☐三分熟 ☐五分熟 ☐七分熟 ☐全熟

ac·tress [`æktrɪs]
名 女演員
同 performer 演出者

英英 the female person who pretends to be someone else while performing in a performance, film or TV program
例 I want to be an **actress** in the future.
以後我想要當一名女演員。
☐三分熟 ☐五分熟 ☐七分熟 ☐全熟

add [æd]
動 增加
反 subtract 減去

英英 to put something into something else for increasing the number or amount or to improve the whole
例 **Add** salt into this soup.
加點鹽到湯裡面。
☐三分熟 ☐五分熟 ☐七分熟 ☐全熟

add·ress [ə`drɛs]
名 住址、致詞、講話
動 發表演說、對……說話
同 speech 演說

英英 the information of the house, name of the road and town where a person lives or works as well as where letters can be sent; speak to, give a speech
例 This is my **address**.
這是我的地址。
☐三分熟 ☐五分熟 ☐七分熟 ☐全熟

a·dult [ə`dʌlt]
形 成年的、成熟的
名 成年人
反 child 小孩

英英 a person, an animal or a plant that has grown to full size and strength; has arrived at maturity
例 I want to be like an **adult**.
我想要像成年人一樣。
☐三分熟 ☐五分熟 ☐七分熟 ☐全熟

a·fraid [ə`fred]
形 害怕的、擔心的
反 brave 勇敢的

英英 not brave enough; fear for someone or something
例 I am **afraid** of spiders.
我怕蜘蛛。
☐三分熟 ☐五分熟 ☐七分熟 ☐全熟

🎧 **Track 003**

af·ter [ˈæftɚ]

形 以後的
副 以後、後來
連 在……以後
介 在……之後
反 before 在……之前

英英 next or later in time, or following in place or order

例 **After** I brush my teeth, I go to bed.
我刷完牙就上床了。

☐ 三分熟
☐ 五分熟
☐ 七分熟
☐ 全熟

---

af·ter·noon
[ˈæftɚˌnun]

名 下午
反 morning 上午

英英 the time period which starts at around noon or after the meal in the middle of the day and ends at about six o'clock or when the sun goes down

例 I read some books in the **afternoon**.
我下午在看書。

☐ 三分熟
☐ 五分熟
☐ 七分熟
☐ 全熟

---

a·gain [əˈɡɛn]

副 又、再

英英 one more time, once more

例 Don't say that **again**.
不要再說了。

☐ 三分熟
☐ 五分熟
☐ 七分熟
☐ 全熟

---

a·gainst [əˈɡɛnst]

介 反對、不同意
同 versus 對抗

英英 in opposition to; on the other side of statement

例 We are **against** this project.
我們反對這計畫。

☐ 三分熟
☐ 五分熟
☐ 七分熟
☐ 全熟

---

age [edʒ]

名 年齡
動 使變老
同 mature 使成熟
片 at the age of...
在……歲

英英 the period of time a person or an animal has been alive or a plant has existed

例 What's your **age**?
你幾歲？

☐ 三分熟
☐ 五分熟
☐ 七分熟
☐ 全熟

---

a·go [əˈɡo]

副 以前
同 since 以前

英英 back in time from now

例 She was fat two years **ago**.
她兩年前很胖。

☐ 三分熟
☐ 五分熟
☐ 七分熟
☐ 全熟

---

a·gree [əˈɡri]

動 同意、贊成
反 disagree 不同意
片 agree with...
認同某人

英英 have the same action or opinion with others, or to accept a suggestion or an opinion from others

例 I can't **agree** with you more!
我完全同意你。

☐ 三分熟
☐ 五分熟
☐ 七分熟
☐ 全熟

A

a·gree·ment
[əˈɡrimənt]

名 同意、一致、協議
反 disagreement
　 意見不一

英英 having the same opinion or ideas on the decision; an exchange of the promises

例 It's hard to have an absolute **agreement**.
很難得到完全的同意。

a·head [əˈhɛd]

副 向前的、在……前面
反 behind 在……後面

英英 have more scores or points than someone in a race or competition; in front or in the future

例 Go **ahead** and you will find the forest in the front.
往前走你就會看到一座森林在前面。

air [ɛr]

名 空氣、氣氛
同 atmosphere 氣氛
片 air pollution 空氣汙染

英英 the gases which surrounds the Earth and provide people, animal or any living creature to survive

例 The **air** pollution here is very serious.
這裡的空氣污染很嚴重。

air·mail [ˈɛrˌmel]

名 航空郵件

英英 to send letters or parcels by aircraft

例 The first airmail from Delhi left on May 20.
第一批的航空郵件於五月二十日由德里寄出。

air·plane/plane
[ˈɛrˌplen]/[plen]

名 飛機

英英 a vehicle designed for air travel, flying through the air, which has wings and engines

例 I am taking an **airplane** to Japan.
我搭飛機去日本。

air·port [ˈɛrˌport]

名 機場

英英 place where aircraft, such as an airplane or helicopter regularly take off and land

例 Do you know how to go to the **airport**?
你知道機場怎麼走嗎？

all [ɔl]

形 所有的、全部的
副 全部、全然
名 全部
同 whole 全部

英英 containing all of things or numbers; the whole

例 **All** you have is money.
你有的只是錢。

al·low [əˈlaʊ]

動 允許、准許
同 permit 允許

英英 to give permission to something and make it possible for someone to do something

例 My mother doesn't **allow** me to buy it.
我媽媽不允許我買這個。

🎧 **Track 005**

al·most [ˋɔl‚most]

副 幾乎、差不多
同 nearly 幾乎、差不多

英英 nearly, not much different

例 You are **almost** as good as he.
你幾乎要跟他一樣強了。

☐ 三分熟
☐ 五分熟
☐ 七分熟
☐ 全熟

a·lone [əˋlon]

形 單獨的
副 單獨地
片 stay alone 獨處

英英 without company or other people

例 Don't walk **alone** in the midnight.
半夜不要一個人走。

☐ 三分熟
☐ 五分熟
☐ 七分熟
☐ 全熟

a·long [əˋlɔŋ]

副 向前
介 沿著
同 forward 向前

英英 next to something; from one part of a street to another; keep moving forward

例 Walk **along** the river.
沿著河走。

☐ 三分熟
☐ 五分熟
☐ 七分熟
☐ 全熟

al·ready [ɔlˋrɛdɪ]

副 已經
反 yet 還（沒）

英英 before now; earlier than the time people expected; by this time

例 I've **already** finished my homework.
我已經寫完作業了。

☐ 三分熟
☐ 五分熟
☐ 七分熟
☐ 全熟

al·so [ˋɔlso]

副 也
同 too 也

英英 too or in addition

例 She thinks the shoes are great and I **also** like them.
她認為那雙鞋子很棒，我也很喜歡。

☐ 三分熟
☐ 五分熟
☐ 七分熟
☐ 全熟

al·ways [ˋɔlwez]

副 總是
反 seldom 不常、很少

英英 every time, more frequently, keep doing something all the time

例 I **always** think he's your Mr. Right.
我總是認為他是你的白馬王子。

☐ 三分熟
☐ 五分熟
☐ 七分熟
☐ 全熟

am [æm]

動 是

英英 form of be, usually used in the first person

例 I **am** a student.
我是學生。

☐ 三分熟
☐ 五分熟
☐ 七分熟
☐ 全熟

a·mong [əˋmʌŋ]

介 在……之中
同 amid 在……之間

英英 mixed or in the middle of other things, surrounded by other things

例 The butterfly flies **among** flowers.
蝴蝶飛在花叢之中。

☐ 三分熟
☐ 五分熟
☐ 七分熟
☐ 全熟

and [ænd]

連 和

英英 as well as; to combine two parts together; join words or related statements together

例 You **and** I are friends.
你和我是朋友。

☐ 三分熟
☐ 五分熟
☐ 七分熟
☐ 全熟

A

an·ger [ˋæŋgɚ]

名 憤怒
動 激怒
同 irritation 激怒
片 in anger 憤怒的

英英 a strong feeling which makes you want to do some damage or be very unpleasant because of something hurtful has happened

例 Jane screamed in **anger**.
珍憤怒地尖叫。

□三分熟
□五分熟
□七分熟
□全熟

an·gry [ˋæŋgrɪ]

形 生氣的
同 furious 狂怒的

英英 strong emotion which makes people feel against someone who has behaved badly, making you want to shout out loud or hurt people

例 The teacher is always **angry** at him.
老師總是對他生氣。

□三分熟
□五分熟
□七分熟
□全熟

an·i·mal [ˋænəml̩]

形 動物的
名 動物
同 beast 動物、野獸

英英 creatures that live and move but is not a human, bird, fish or insect

例 I love **animals**.
我很喜歡動物。

□三分熟
□五分熟
□七分熟
□全熟

an·oth·er [əˋnʌðɚ]

形 另一的、再一的
代 另一、再一

英英 an extra piece or thing, an additional amount

例 Could you please give me **another** shirt?
你可以給我另外一件襯衫嗎？

□三分熟
□五分熟
□七分熟
□全熟

an·swer [ˋænsɚ]

名 答案、回答
動 回答、回報
同 response 回答
片 answer the telephone 接電話
片 answer blows with blows 以牙還牙

英英 to reply to someone or give a reaction to a question or telephone call

例 No one knows the **answer**.
沒人知道答案。

□三分熟
□五分熟
□七分熟
□全熟

ant [ænt]

名 螞蟻

英英 a kind of small insect which lives under the ground in large and stay in groups

例 I don't want to see an **ant** in my room.
我不希望在我房間看到一隻螞蟻。

□三分熟
□五分熟
□七分熟
□全熟

an·y [ˋɛnɪ]

形 任何的
代 仟何一個

英英 some; or the smallest amount or number of something

例 Do you have **any** question?
你有仟何問題嗎？

□三分熟
□五分熟
□七分熟
□全熟

🎧 **Track 007**

an·y·thing
[ˈɛnɪˌθɪŋ]

代 任何事物
片 Anything else
　　其他東西

英英 any action, event, state or object whatever, or something

例 Do you want **anything** else?
你還需要任何的東西嗎？

☐ 三分熟
☐ 五分熟
☐ 七分熟
☐ 全熟

---

ape [ep]

名 猿

英英 an animal like a monkey which has a larger body but no tail, and it uses its arms to swing through trees

例 Gorilla and chimpanzees are **apes**.
大猩猩跟長臂猿都是猿類。

☐ 三分熟
☐ 五分熟
☐ 七分熟
☐ 全熟

---

ap·pear [əˈpɪr]

動 出現、顯得
反 disappear 消失

英英 to become noticeable or to be present; to come or be in sight; to be in view; to become visible

例 The ghost just **appears** in the opera!
有鬼出現在歌劇院！

☐ 三分熟
☐ 五分熟
☐ 七分熟
☐ 全熟

---

ap·ple [ˈæpl̩]

名 蘋果

英英 a round fruit with firm white flesh and a green, red or yellow skin

例 An **apple** a day keeps the doctors away.
一天一蘋果，醫生遠離我。

☐ 三分熟
☐ 五分熟
☐ 七分熟
☐ 全熟

A·pril/Apr. [ˈeprəl]

名 四月

英英 the fourth month of the year

例 We have a mid-term exam in **April**.
我們四月有期中考。

☐ 三分熟
☐ 五分熟
☐ 七分熟
☐ 全熟

---

are [ɑr]

動 是

英英 the plural present indicative of be for second person

例 They **are** my friends.
他們是我的朋友。

☐ 三分熟
☐ 五分熟
☐ 七分熟
☐ 全熟

---

ar·e·a [ˈɛrɪə]

名 地區、領域、面積、
　　方面
同 region 地區

英英 particular part of a place, piece of land or country

例 Stay away from this **area**.
遠離這區域。

☐ 三分熟
☐ 五分熟
☐ 七分熟
☐ 全熟

---

arm [ɑrm]

名 手臂
動 武裝、裝備
片 be armed to the teeth
　　全副武裝

英英 the limb of the human body which extends from the shoulder to the hand

例 I broke my **arm**.
我摔斷了手。

☐ 三分熟
☐ 五分熟
☐ 七分熟
☐ 全熟

ar·my [ˈɑrmɪ]

名 軍隊、陸軍
同 military 軍隊

英英 a particular country's fighting force, a military force that has the training and equipment to fight on land

例 The **army** of this country is stronger and stronger.
這國家的軍隊越來越強壯了。

☐三分熟
☐五分熟
☐七分熟
☐全熟

a·round [əˈraʊnd]

副 大約、在周圍
介 在……周圍

英英 in a position or direction surrounding, or in a direction going along the edge of or from one part to another

例 **Around** the corner, you will see the shop.
在轉角你就會看到這家商店。

☐三分熟
☐五分熟
☐七分熟
☐全熟

art [ɑrt]

名 藝術

英英 the making of objects, images, music, etc. that are beautiful or that express feelings

例 You can find the beauty of life in **art**.
你可以在藝術中尋找人生的美好。

☐三分熟
☐五分熟
☐七分熟
☐全熟

as [æz]

副 像……一樣、如同
連 當……時候
介 作為
代 與……相同的人事物
片 as...as...
   像……一樣……

英英 when; while; used in comparisons to refer to the degree of something; during or at the same time that

例 Jean is **as** pretty as her mother.
吉恩跟她媽媽一樣漂亮。

☐三分熟
☐五分熟
☐七分熟
☐全熟

ask [æsk]

動 問、要求
同 question 問

英英 to put a question to someone, or to request an answer from someone

例 May I **ask** you a question?
我可以問你一個問題嗎？

☐三分熟
☐五分熟
☐七分熟
☐全熟

at [æt]

介 在

英英 primarily, this word expresses the relations of presence, nearness in place or time, or direction toward

例 I will meet you **at** the park.
我將在公園跟你碰面。

☐三分熟
☐五分熟
☐七分熟
☐全熟

Au·gust/Aug.
[ˈɔɡʌst]

名 八月

英英 the eighth month of the year

例 I will finish this work at the end of **August**.
我會在八月底完成這項工作。

☐三分熟
☐五分熟
☐七分熟
☐全熟

A

aunt/aunt·ie/ aunt·y

[ænt]/[ˋænti]/[ˋæntɪ]

名 伯母、姑、嬸、姨

英英 the sister of someone's father or mother, or the wife of someone's uncle

例 I met my **aunt** this morning.
早上我遇到我阿姨。

□三分熟
□五分熟
□七分熟
□全熟

---

au·tumn/fall

[ˋɔtəm]/[fɔl]

名 秋季、秋天

英英 the third season of the year, before winter and comes after summer

例 **Autumn** is my favorite season.
秋天是我最喜歡的季節。

□三分熟
□五分熟
□七分熟
□全熟

---

a·way [əˋwe]

副 遠離、離開
片 stay away 遠離

英英 somewhere else; to or in a different place, position or situation

例 Stay **away** from this man.
遠離這男人。

□三分熟
□五分熟
□七分熟
□全熟

Bb

ba·by [ˋbebɪ]

形 嬰兒的
名 嬰兒
同 infant 嬰兒
片 have a baby 生小孩

英英 a very young child, especially one that has not yet begun to walk or talk

例 My sister is going to have a **baby**.
我姊姊要生小孩了。

□三分熟
□五分熟
□七分熟
□全熟

---

back [bæk]

形 後面的
副 向後地
名 後背、背脊
動 後退
反 front 前面、正面

英英 in, into or towards a previous place or condition, or an earlier time

例 I have pain in my **back**.
我背後好痛。

□三分熟
□五分熟
□七分熟
□全熟

---

bad [bæd]

形 壞的
反 good 好的
片 be bad at...
很不會……

英英 not in a good shape or situation

例 My son is not a **bad** boy.
我兒子不是壞孩子。

□三分熟
□五分熟
□七分熟
□全熟

B

bag [bæg]

名 袋子
動 把……裝入袋中
同 pocket 口袋

英英 a soft container made out of paper, thin plastic, leather, or other material, usually with a handle, in which you carry things that you need for traveling; put sth. into a bag

例 There is no space in my **bag**.
我包包沒有空間了。

☐ 三分熟
☐ 五分熟
☐ 七分熟
☐ 全熟

---

ball [bɔl]

名 舞會、球
同 sphere 球

英英 any object in the shape of a sphere, especially one used as a toy by children or in various sports such as tennis and football

例 Margret went into the **ball**.
瑪格麗特走進舞會。

☐ 三分熟
☐ 五分熟
☐ 七分熟
☐ 全熟

---

bal·loon [bə`lun]

名 氣球
動 如氣球般膨脹、
把……裝入袋中

英英 a bag made of silk or other light material, and filled with hydrogen gas or heated air, so as to rise and float in the atmosphere

例 Give the **balloon** to the girl.
把汽球給那女孩。

☐ 三分熟
☐ 五分熟
☐ 七分熟
☐ 全熟

---

ba·nan·a [bə`nænə]

名 香蕉

英英 a long curved fruit with a yellow skin and soft, sweet white flesh inside

例 **Bananas** are Kevin's favorite fruit.
香蕉是凱文最喜歡的水果。

☐ 三分熟
☐ 五分熟
☐ 七分熟
☐ 全熟

---

band [bænd]

名 帶子、隊、樂隊
動 聯合、結合
同 tie 帶子

英英 a group of musicians who play modern music together; a thin flat piece of cloth, elastic, metal or other material put around something to fasten or strengthen it

例 The Beatles is my father's favorite **band**.
披頭四是我爸爸最喜歡的樂團。

☐ 三分熟
☐ 五分熟
☐ 七分熟
☐ 全熟

---

bank [bæŋk]

名 銀行、堤、岸

英英 an elevation, or rising ground, under the sea; a shoal, shelf, or shallow; an organization where people and businesses can invest or borrow money, change it to foreign money, etc.

例 I need to go to the **bank**.
我要去銀行。

☐ 三分熟
☐ 五分熟
☐ 七分熟
☐ 全熟

---

bar [bɑr]

名 條、棒、橫木、酒吧
動 禁止、阻撓
同 block 阻擋、限制

英英 a straight stick made of metal; a place where especially alcoholic drinks are sold and drunk

例 We went to the **bar** every day.
我們每天都去酒吧。

☐ 三分熟
☐ 五分熟
☐ 七分熟
☐ 全熟

bar·ber [ˋbɑrbɚ]

名 理髮師
同 hairdresser 美髮師

英英 someone who shaves and dress the beard or hair

例 Angela is the best **barber** I've met!
安佐拉是最好的理髮師了！

□ 三分熟
□ 五分熟
□ 七分熟
□ 全熟

---

base [bes]

名 基底、壘
動 以……作基礎
同 bottom 底部

英英 the bottom part of an object, or the lowest part of something

例 The **base** of the company is in the USA.
這家公司的基底在美國。

□ 三分熟
□ 五分熟
□ 七分熟
□ 全熟

---

base·ball

[ˋbesˏbɔl]

名 棒球

英英 a game played by two teams of nine players, in which a player hits a ball with a bat and tries to run around four bases on a large field before the other team returns the ball

例 I watch **baseball** game very often.
我很常看棒球比賽。

□ 三分熟
□ 五分熟
□ 七分熟
□ 全熟

---

bas·ic [ˋbesɪk]

名 基本、要素
形 基本的
同 essential 基本的

英英 providing the base or starting point from which something can develop; simple and not complicated

例 This is a **basic** question.
這是很基本的問題。

□ 三分熟
□ 五分熟
□ 七分熟
□ 全熟

---

bas·ket [ˋbæskɪt]

名 籃子、籃網、得分

英英 a vessel made of osiers or other twigs, cane, rushes, splints, or other flexible materia

例 You need to bring the **basket** to collect the apples.
你需要帶個籃子去撿蘋果。

□ 三分熟
□ 五分熟
□ 七分熟
□ 全熟

---

bas·ket·ball

[ˋbæskɪtˏbɔl]

名 籃球

英英 a team game played by two teams that score points by throwing a large ball through an open net fixed at each court

例 I want to be a **basketball** player in the future.
我想要當籃球員。

□ 三分熟
□ 五分熟
□ 七分熟
□ 全熟

---

bat [bæt]

名 蝙蝠、球棒

英英 a small black animal like a mouse with wings that flies at night; a shaped piece of wood used for hitting the ball

例 There are a lot of **bats** in the cave.
山洞中有很多的蝙蝠。

□ 三分熟
□ 五分熟
□ 七分熟
□ 全熟

---

bath [bæθ]

名 洗澡
動 給……洗澡

英英 the act of washing the body, or part of the body

例 I want to take a **bath** to relax.
我想泡澡放鬆。

□ 三分熟
□ 五分熟
□ 七分熟
□ 全熟

B

bathe [beð]

動 沐浴、用水洗
同 wash 洗

英英 to wash with water

例 The mother **bathes** the baby gently.
媽媽溫柔地幫孩子洗澡。

☐ 三分熟
☐ 五分熟
☐ 七分熟
☐ 全熟

bath·room

[`bæθˌrum]

名 浴室

英英 a space or a room where people take a bath or shower

例 I will go to the **bathroom** to take a shower.
我去浴室洗澡。

☐ 三分熟
☐ 五分熟
☐ 七分熟
☐ 全熟

be [bi]

動 是、存在

英英 which is used to say something about a person, thing or state, to show a permanent or temporary quality, state, job, etc.

例 **Be** nice to your parents.
對你爸媽好一點。

☐ 三分熟
☐ 五分熟
☐ 七分熟
☐ 全熟

beach [bitʃ]

名 海灘
動 拖（船）上岸
同 strand 海濱

英英 the shore of the sea, or of a lake, which is washed by the waves; especially a sandy or pebbly shore; the strand

例 I will go to the **beach** to see the sunset.
我要去海邊看日落。

☐ 三分熟
☐ 五分熟
☐ 七分熟
☐ 全熟

bear [bɛr]

名 熊
動 忍受、負荷、結果實、生子女
同 withstand 禁得起

英英 a large, strong wild mammal with a thick fur coat; to accept or endure especially something unpleasant

例 I can't **bear** the pressure.
我無法忍受這種壓力。

☐ 三分熟
☐ 五分熟
☐ 七分熟
☐ 全熟

beat [bit]

名 打、敲打聲、拍子
動 打敗、連續打擊、跳動
同 hit 打

英英 to hit on someone or something; to defeat someone

例 Her husband **beats** her.
他丈夫打她。

☐ 三分熟
☐ 五分熟
☐ 七分熟
☐ 全熟

beau·ti·ful

[`bjutəfəl]

形 美麗的、漂亮的
反 ugly 醜陋的

英英 pretty, very pleasant looking

例 It was a **beautiful** night.
這是個美麗的夜晚。

☐ 三分熟
☐ 五分熟
☐ 七分熟
☐ 全熟

beau·ty [`bjuti]

名 美、美人、美的東西

英英 the quality of being pleasing, especially to look at, or someone or something that gives great pleasure

例 He loves her because of her **beauty**.
他愛她因為她的美。

☐ 三分熟
☐ 五分熟
☐ 七分熟
☐ 全熟

be·cause [bɪˋkɔz]

連 因為
同 for 為了
片 because of...
　　因為……

英英 by or for the cause that; on this account that; for the reason that

例 **Because** of the rain, we cancel the trip.
因為大雨，我們取消了行程。

☐ 三分熟
☐ 五分熟
☐ 七分熟
☐ 全熟

---

be·come [bɪˋkʌm]

動 變得、變成

英英 start to be someone or something

例 She **becomes** prettier than before.
她變得漂亮了。

☐ 三分熟
☐ 五分熟
☐ 七分熟
☐ 全熟

---

bed [bɛd]

名 床
動 睡、臥
片 go to bed 上床睡覺

英英 a large piece of furniture, often with four legs, which is used for sleeping on

例 I go to **bed** early to have good health.
我早睡早起身體好。

☐ 三分熟
☐ 五分熟
☐ 七分熟
☐ 全熟

---

bee [bi]

名 蜜蜂

英英 a yellow and black flying insect which makes honey and can sting people

例 There are so many **bees** in the flowers.
花叢裡有很多蜜蜂。

☐ 三分熟
☐ 五分熟
☐ 七分熟
☐ 全熟

---

be·fore [bɪˋfor]

副 以前
介 早於、在……以前
連 在……以前
反 after 在……之後

英英 at or during a time earlier than (the thing mentioned)

例 **Before** I go to bed, I brush my teeth.
我在睡前刷牙。

☐ 三分熟
☐ 五分熟
☐ 七分熟
☐ 全熟

---

be·gin [bɪˋgɪn]

動 開始、著手
反 finish 結束、完成

英英 start doing something or working on

例 I **begin** to think about my future in my college years.
在我大學期間，我開始想我的未來了。

☐ 三分熟
☐ 五分熟
☐ 七分熟
☐ 全熟

---

be·hind [bɪˋhaɪnd]

副 在後、在原處
介 在……之後
反 ahead 在前

英英 in the place where someone or something was before; in the back of something or someone

例 There is a lion **behind** me!
我後面有一隻獅子！

☐ 三分熟
☐ 五分熟
☐ 七分熟
☐ 全熟

---

be·lieve [bɪˋliv]

動 認為、相信
同 trust 信賴

英英 to trust something or have belief on the matters people mentioned

例 I **believe** I can fly.
我相信我會飛。

☐ 三分熟
☐ 五分熟
☐ 七分熟
☐ 全熟

bell [bɛl]

名 鐘、鈴
同 ring 鈴聲、鐘聲

B

英英 a hollow metallic vessel, usually shaped somewhat like a cup with a flaring mouth, containing a clapper or tongue, and giving forth a ringing sound on being struck

例 The **bell** rang and everyone ran to their classrooms.
聽到鐘聲，大家都跑回教室裡面。

---

be·long [bəˈlɔŋ]

動 屬於
片 belong to 屬於……

英英 to be in the right or suitable place

例 I don't **belong** to anyone.
我不屬於任何人。

---

be·low [bəˈlo]

介 在……下面、
　　比……低
副 在下方、往下
同 under 在……下面

英英 under or in the low position

例 **Below** the tree, there are so many beautiful flowers.
在樹的下面有好多漂亮的花朵。

---

be·side [bɪˈsaɪd]

介 在……旁邊
同 by 在……旁邊

英英 next to something or someone

例 Her husband stands **beside** her.
她丈夫站在她身邊。

---

best [bɛst]

形 最好的
副 最好地
反 worst 最壞的

英英 having good qualities in the highest degree; most excellent

例 Violet is my **best** friend forever.
費歐蕾是我最好的朋友。

---

bet·ter [ˈbɛtɚ]

形 較好的、更好的
副 更好地
反 worse 更壞的

英英 comparative of good; of a higher standard, or more suitable, pleasing or effective than other things or people

例 You will find a **better** woman.
你會找到更好的女人。

---

be·tween [bɪˈtwin]

副 在中間
介 在……之間

英英 in the middle of something or someone

例 I slept **between** my parents.
我以前睡在爸媽中間。

---

bi·cy·cle/bike

[ˈbaɪsɪkl̩]/[baɪk]

名 自行車
同 cycle 腳踏車

英英 a two wheeled vehicle that you sit on and move by turning the two pedals

例 Everyone in Amsterdam rides a **bike**.
在荷蘭，大家都騎腳踏車。

big [bɪg]

形 大的
反 little 小的

英英 in a large or huge size
例 This shirt is too **big**.
這件襯衫太大了。

☐ 三分熟
☐ 五分熟
☐ 七分熟
☐ 全熟

bird [bɝd]

名 鳥
同 fowl 禽
片 go brid-watching
賞鳥

英英 a creature with feathers and wings, usually able to fly
例 There is a blue **bird**.
那裡有一隻青鳥。

☐ 三分熟
☐ 五分熟
☐ 七分熟
☐ 全熟

birth [bɝθ]

名 出生、血統
反 death 死亡
片 gave a birth to
產下……

英英 the time when a baby comes out of its mother's body
例 Everyone was happy for the baby's **birth**.
大家都對這嬰兒的出生感到開心。

☐ 三分熟
☐ 五分熟
☐ 七分熟
☐ 全熟

bit [bɪt]

名 一點
片 a littlt bit 一點點

英英 small amount of something
例 She's just a **bit** late.
她只不過是晚一點到而已。

☐ 三分熟
☐ 五分熟
☐ 七分熟
☐ 全熟

bite [baɪt]

名 咬、一口
動 咬
同 chew 咬

英英 to seize with the teeth, so that they enter or nip the thing seized; to lacerate, crush, or wound with the teeth
例 The dog once **bit** me.
這隻狗曾經咬了我。

☐ 三分熟
☐ 五分熟
☐ 七分熟
☐ 全熟

black [blæk]

形 黑色的
名 黑人、黑色
動 （使）變黑
反 white 白色

英英 with little or no light; a very dark color
例 The **black** man is good at basketball.
這黑人男人很會打籃球。

☐ 三分熟
☐ 五分熟
☐ 七分熟
☐ 全熟

block [blɑk]

名 街區、木塊、石塊
動 阻塞
反 advance 前進

英英 a large, usually tall building divided into separate parts for use as offices or homes by several different organizations or people; a solid straight-sided piece of hard material; to interrupt the normal function
例 My house is two **blocks** away from here.
我家就在兩個街區之外。

☐ 三分熟
☐ 五分熟
☐ 七分熟
☐ 全熟

blood [blʌd]

名 血液、血統

英英 the fluid which circulates in the principal vascular system of animals, carrying nourishment to all parts of the body

例 Your brother and you have the same **blood**.
你跟你哥哥流著一樣的血。

☐ 三分熟
☐ 五分熟
☐ 七分熟
☐ 全熟

B

---

blow [blo]

名 吹、打擊
動 吹、風吹
同 breeze 吹著微風

英英 to move and make currents of air, or to be moved or make something move on a current of air

例 She **blows** a balloon for the kids.
她吹一個氣球給孩子們。

☐ 三分熟
☐ 五分熟
☐ 七分熟
☐ 全熟

---

blue [blu]

形 藍色的、憂鬱的
名 藍色
片 Monday blue
藍色星期一

英英 the color of the sky without clouds on a sunny day

例 The sky is so **blue** today!
天空好藍喔！

☐ 三分熟
☐ 五分熟
☐ 七分熟
☐ 全熟

---

boat [bot]

名 船
動 划船
同 ship 船
片 in the same boat
同舟共濟

英英 a small open vessel or water craft, usually moved by cars or paddles

例 We row the **boat**.
我們划船。

☐ 三分熟
☐ 五分熟
☐ 七分熟
☐ 全熟

---

bo·dy [ˈbɑdɪ]

名 身體
反 soul 靈魂
片 body shape 體型

英英 the whole physical structure that forms a person or animal

例 The health of **body** and mind are both important.
身心健康都很重要。

☐ 三分熟
☐ 五分熟
☐ 七分熟
☐ 全熟

---

bone [bon]

名 骨
同 skeleton 骨骼

英英 one of the pieces or parts of an animal skeleton

例 The dog loves the **bone** so much.
那隻狗很愛骨頭。

☐ 三分熟
☐ 五分熟
☐ 七分熟
☐ 全熟

---

book [bʊk]

名 書
動 登記、預訂
同 reserve 預訂

英英 a set of pages that have been fastened together inside a cover to be read or written in; to arrange for something in advance

例 My favorite **book** is Jane Eyre.
我最喜歡的書是簡愛。

☐ 三分熟
☐ 五分熟
☐ 七分熟
☐ 全熟

🎧 **Track 017**

born [bɔrn]

形 天生的
同 natural 天生的
片 a born leader
　　天生的領導者

英英 having a natural ability or liking

例 LeBron James is a **born** basketball player.
雷霸龍詹姆士是天生的籃球員。

☐ 三分熟
☐ 五分熟
☐ 七分熟
☐ 全熟

both [boθ]

形 兩、雙
代 兩者、雙方
反 neither 兩者都不

英英 the one and the other; the two or the pair

例 **Both** of our parents like him.
我父母親都很喜歡他。

☐ 三分熟
☐ 五分熟
☐ 七分熟
☐ 全熟

bot·tom [ˈbɑtəm]

名 底部、臀部
形 底部的
反 top 頂部

英英 the lowest part of something

例 There is an ant at the **bottom** of the cup.
杯子的底部有一隻螞蟻。

☐ 三分熟
☐ 五分熟
☐ 七分熟
☐ 全熟

bowl [bol]

名 碗
動 滾動

英英 a round container that is open at the top and is deep enough to hold fruit, sugar, etc.; roll

例 I need a **bowl** for the soup.
我需要一個碗裝湯。

☐ 三分熟
☐ 五分熟
☐ 七分熟
☐ 全熟

box [bɑks]

名 盒子、箱
動 把……裝入盒中、裝箱
同 container 容器

英英 a countainer with square or rectangular shape and sometimes with a lid; to put into a box

例 We need some more **boxes** for moving.
我們需要一些箱子搬家。

☐ 三分熟
☐ 五分熟
☐ 七分熟
☐ 全熟

boy [bɔɪ]

名 男孩
反 girl 女孩

英英 male child or, more generally, a male of any age

例 You used to be a good **boy**.
你以前是個好男孩。

☐ 三分熟
☐ 五分熟
☐ 七分熟
☐ 全熟

brave [brev]

形 勇敢的
同 valiant 勇敢的

英英 showing no fear of dangerous or difficult things

例 He told me not to be **brave** anymore.
他告訴我再也不用勇敢了。

☐ 三分熟
☐ 五分熟
☐ 七分熟
☐ 全熟

bread [brɛd]

名 麵包

英英 an article of food made from flour or meal by moistening, kneading, and baking

例 I bought some **bread** for breakfast.
我買一點麵包當早餐。

☐ 三分熟
☐ 五分熟
☐ 七分熟
☐ 全熟

B

break [brek]

名 休息、中斷、破裂
動 打破、弄破、弄壞
反 repair 修補
片 take a break 下課

英英 rest in the middle; to do some damage on something

例 Let's take a short **break**.
我們下課休息一下吧。

break·fast

[ˋbrɛkfəst]

名 早餐
反 dinner 晚餐
片 have breakfast
　　吃早餐

英英 the first meal at the start of a day

例 I eat **breakfast** every morning.
我每天早上都會吃早餐。

bridge [brɪdʒ]

名 橋

英英 a structure that is built over a river, road or railway to allow people and vehicles to cross from one side to the other

例 London **Bridge** is falling down.
倫敦鐵橋正在降下來。

bright [braɪt]

形 明亮的、開朗的
同 light 明亮的

英英 shinning and full of light; not dark

例 It's a **bright** room.
這是一個很明亮的房間。

bring [brɪŋ]

動 帶來
同 carry 攜帶

英英 to carry someone or something to a place or a person

例 Could you **bring** me home?
你可以載我回家嗎？

broth·er [ˋbrʌðɚ]

名 兄弟
反 sister 姊妹

英英 a man or boy with the same parents as another person

例 He's my **brother**.
他是我哥哥。

brown [braʊn]

形 褐色的、棕色的
名 褐色、棕色

英英 of various shades between black and red or yellow; a dark color

例 You have **brown** hair.
你有褐色的頭髮。

bug [bʌg]

名 小蟲、毛病
同 insect 昆蟲

英英 a very small or tiny insect

例 There is a **bug** in my soup.
在我的湯裡面有一隻小蟲。

build [bɪld]

動 建立、建築
同 construct 建造

英英 to make something by putting bricks or other materials together

例 You need some bricks to **build** a house.
你需要一些磚塊蓋房子。

☐三分熟
☐五分熟
☐七分熟
☐全熟

---

build·ing [ˋbɪldɪŋ]

名 建築物

英英 a structure which is established with a roof and walls

例 Taipei 101 used to be the highest **building** in the world.
臺北 101 曾是世界上最高的建築。

☐三分熟
☐五分熟
☐七分熟
☐全熟

---

bus [bʌs]

名 公車

英英 a large vehicle which drivers are driven to take people from one place to another

例 I go to school by **bus** every day.
我每天早上搭公車上學。

☐三分熟
☐五分熟
☐七分熟
☐全熟

---

bus·y [ˋbɪzɪ]

形 忙的、繁忙的
反 free 空閒的

英英 working very hard; paying all your attention to something and have no time to rest

例 I have been **busy** recently.
我最近很忙。

☐三分熟
☐五分熟
☐七分熟
☐全熟

---

but [bʌt]

副 僅僅、只
連 但是
介 除了……以外
同 however 可是、然而

英英 used to introduce an added statement, usually something that is different from what you have said before

例 I want nobody **but** you.
我只要你。

☐三分熟
☐五分熟
☐七分熟
☐全熟

---

but·ter [ˋbʌtɚ]

名 奶油

英英 a pale yellow solid containing a lot of fat and usually is spread on bread or toast or used in cooking

例 I need some **butter** for the toast.
我需要奶油配吐司。

☐三分熟
☐五分熟
☐七分熟
☐全熟

---

but·ter·fly

[ˋbʌtɚˏflaɪ]

名 蝴蝶

英英 a type of insect with large colored wings

例 There are so many **butterflies** in the garden.
花園中有很多的蝴蝶。

☐三分熟
☐五分熟
☐七分熟
☐全熟

---

buy [baɪ]

名 購買、買
動 買
同 purchase 買

英英 to purchase; to acquire the ownership of property by giving an accepted price

例 Let's buy some **pizza** for the party!
我們去買一些披薩到派對吧！

☐三分熟
☐五分熟
☐七分熟
☐全熟

by [baɪ]

介 被、藉由、
在……之前、
在……旁邊

英英 to show someone does something or something is done

例 I was hit **by** the man.
我被這男人打了。

☐ 三分熟
☐ 五分熟
☐ 七分熟
☐ 全熟

C

Cc

cage [kedʒ]

名 籠子、獸籠、鳥籠
動 關入籠中

英英 a space surrounded by bars or wires to keep animals or birds

例 I bought a cage for the bird.
我買了個鳥籠給小鳥。

☐ 三分熟
☐ 五分熟
☐ 七分熟
☐ 全熟

cake [kek]

名 蛋糕
片 It's a piece of cake.
這很簡單。

英英 a small mass of dough baked, which is sweet and soft with sugar and fat

例 I love to eat cake.
我喜歡吃蛋糕。

☐ 三分熟
☐ 五分熟
☐ 七分熟
☐ 全熟

call [kɔl]

名 呼叫、打電話
動 呼叫、打電話

英英 to telephone someone; to name someone or give someone a name

例 Please **call** me.
請你打電話給我。

☐ 三分熟
☐ 五分熟
☐ 七分熟
☐ 全熟

cam·el [ˈkæml̩]

名 駱駝

英英 an animal with a long neck and big size, that lives in the desert and with one or two humps on its backs

例 I rode a **camel** in a desert.
我在沙漠中騎駱駝。

☐ 三分熟
☐ 五分熟
☐ 七分熟
☐ 全熟

ca·me·ra

[ˈkæmərə]

名 照相機

英英 a device for taking pictures or making films or television programmes

例 I took a picture with a **camera**.
我用相機攝影。

☐ 三分熟
☐ 五分熟
☐ 七分熟
☐ 全熟

camp [kæmp]

名 露營
動 露營、紮營
片 go camping 露營

英英 an activity in which people stay in tents for temporary stay

例 We will go **camping** next week.
我們下周要去露營。

☐ 三分熟
☐ 五分熟
☐ 七分熟
☐ 全熟

Track 021

can [kæn]

動 裝罐
動 能、可以
名 罐頭

英英 to put something into a can; a closed metal container, usually made with cylindrical, in which some types of drink and food are sold
例 I believe I **can** fly.
我相信我可以飛。

☐ 三分熟
☐ 五分熟
☐ 七分熟
☐ 全熟

can·dy/sweet [ˈkændɪ]/[swit]

名 糖果
同 sugar 糖

英英 sweet food made from sugar or chocolate with different shape
例 My mother bought me **candy**.
我媽媽買糖果給我。

☐ 三分熟
☐ 五分熟
☐ 七分熟
☐ 全熟

cap [kæp]

名 帽子、蓋子
動 給……戴帽、覆蓋於……的頂端
同 hat 帽子

英英 a soft, flat hat without a brim which has a curved part sticking out at the front; to cover with a cap
例 A **cap** would be a nice gift for him.
送他帽子當禮物很棒。

☐ 三分熟
☐ 五分熟
☐ 七分熟
☐ 全熟

car [kɑr]

名 汽車

英英 a powered road vehicle with an engine and four wheels for caring a small number of people
例 My brother bought a **car** for his work.
我哥哥為了工作買了一輛車。

☐ 三分熟
☐ 五分熟
☐ 七分熟
☐ 全熟

card [kɑrd]

名 卡片

英英 a piece of card or plastic with your information telling who you are
例 I wrote a **card** for my mother.
我寫張卡片給我媽媽。

☐ 三分熟
☐ 五分熟
☐ 七分熟
☐ 全熟

care [kɛr]

名 小心、照料、憂慮
動 關心、照顧、喜愛、介意
同 concern 使關心
片 take care 照顧

英英 serious attention, especially to a situation, something or someone
例 My girlfriend takes **care** of the dogs.
我女朋友總是照顧狗。

☐ 三分熟
☐ 五分熟
☐ 七分熟
☐ 全熟

care·ful [ˈkɛrfəl]

形 小心的、仔細的
同 cautious 十分小心的

英英 taking very good care to avoid mishap or harm; cautious
例 Be **careful**.
小心點。

☐ 三分熟
☐ 五分熟
☐ 七分熟
☐ 全熟

car·ry [ˈkærɪ]

動 攜帶、搬運、拿
同 take 拿、取

英英 to have something with you wherever you go
例 I will **carry** some gifts to your house.
我會帶禮物去你家。

☐ 三分熟
☐ 五分熟
☐ 七分熟
☐ 全熟

C

case [kes]
名 情形、情況、箱、案例
同 condition 情況
片 just in case 以防萬一

英英 a container or box for putting things in
例 This **case** is so tough.
這案子太難了。

☐ 三分熟
☐ 五分熟
☐ 七分熟
☐ 全熟

cat [kæt]
名 貓、貓科動物
同 kitten 小貓
片 cat nap 打盹、裝睡

英英 a small animal with fur, four legs, a tail and claws, likes chasing after mice
例 I want to keep a **cat** as a pet.
我想要養貓當寵物。

☐ 三分熟
☐ 五分熟
☐ 七分熟
☐ 全熟

catch [kætʃ]
名 捕捉、捕獲物
動 抓住、趕上
同 capture 捕獲

英英 to take hold of objects, especially something that is moving through the air
例 **Catch** the ball.
接住球。

☐ 三分熟
☐ 五分熟
☐ 七分熟
☐ 全熟

cause [kɔz]
動 引起
名 原因
同 make 引起、產生

英英 to bring about; the reason why something happened
例 It is the pressure **causing** his illness.
是壓力引起他的疾病的。

☐ 三分熟
☐ 五分熟
☐ 七分熟
☐ 全熟

cent [sɛnt]
名 分（貨幣單位）

英英 a unit of money worth 0.01 of the US dollar
例 This stamp costs me 1 dollar and nine **cents**.
這郵票花了我一元九分。

☐ 三分熟
☐ 五分熟
☐ 七分熟
☐ 全熟

cen·ter [ˈsɛntɚ]
名 中心、中央
反 edge 邊緣

英英 the middle or central portion of anything
例 The **center** of the world is Seoul.
世界的中心是首爾。

☐ 三分熟
☐ 五分熟
☐ 七分熟
☐ 全熟

cer·tain [ˈsɝtən]
形 一定的
代 某幾個、某些
反 doubtful 不明確的

英英 know something exactly and have no doubts
例 It is a **certain** thing.
這是很確定的事情。

☐ 三分熟
☐ 五分熟
☐ 七分熟
☐ 全熟

chair [tʃɛr]
名 椅子、主席席位
同 seat 座位

英英 a seat with a back and four legs, which is for people to sit down
例 Please sit on the **chair**.
請坐在這張椅子上。

☐ 三分熟
☐ 五分熟
☐ 七分熟
☐ 全熟

Track 023

chance [tʃæns]

名 機會、意外
同 opportunity 機會
片 take a chance
　 冒險、碰運氣

英英 to make something happen possiblely
例 Give me a **chance** to love you.
　 給我一個機會愛你。

☐ 三分熟
☐ 五分熟
☐ 七分熟
☐ 全熟

chart [tʃɑrt]

名 圖表
動 製成圖表
同 diagram 圖表

英英 a drawing using lines and curves to show information in a simple way
例 I am making a **chart**.
　 我正在做表格。

☐ 三分熟
☐ 五分熟
☐ 七分熟
☐ 全熟

chase [tʃes]

名 追求、追逐
動 追捕、追逐
同 follow 追逐

英英 in order to catch someone or something, tend to run or follow after them
例 The dog is **chasing** its tail.
　 這隻狗在追它的尾巴。

☐ 三分熟
☐ 五分熟
☐ 七分熟
☐ 全熟

check [tʃɛk]

名 檢查、支票
動 檢查、核對
片 check up 核對、檢驗

英英 to make sure that something or someone is correct, or something is right or reasonable by examining it or them quickly
例 I want to **check** my account.
　 我要確認我帳戶。

☐ 三分熟
☐ 五分熟
☐ 七分熟
☐ 全熟

chick [tʃɪk]

名 小雞

英英 a baby bird or a young chicken
例 The **chick** was hatched.
　 小雞被孵化出來。

☐ 三分熟
☐ 五分熟
☐ 七分熟
☐ 全熟

chicken

名 雞、雞肉

英英 a type of bird, which its meat is cooked and eaten, usually kept on a farm for its eggs or its meat
例 My mother cooks **chicken** soup.
　 我媽媽燉雞湯。

☐ 三分熟
☐ 五分熟
☐ 七分熟
☐ 全熟

chief [tʃif]

形 主要的、首席的
名 首領
同 leader 首領

英英 mian or most important and cruial
例 The **chief** announced the decision.
　 主席宣告決定。

☐ 三分熟
☐ 五分熟
☐ 七分熟
☐ 全熟

child [tʃaɪld]

名 小孩
同 kid 小孩

英英 a boy or girl from the time of birth until he or she is an adult
例 The **child** is so bad.
　 那小孩好壞。

☐ 三分熟
☐ 五分熟
☐ 七分熟
☐ 全熟

Christ·mas/
Xmas [ˈkrɪsməs]

名 聖誕節

英英 a Christian holy day which celebrates the birth of Jesus Christ, which is on 25, December

例 **Christmas** is coming.
聖誕節快到了。

☐ 三分熟 ☐ 五分熟 ☐ 七分熟 ☐ 全熟

C

church [tʃɝtʃ]

名 教堂

英英 a building for holding Christian religious activities

例 I visited a lot of **churches** in Europe.
我去歐洲拜訪很多教堂。

☐ 三分熟 ☐ 五分熟 ☐ 七分熟 ☐ 全熟

ci·ty [ˈsɪtɪ]

名 城市

英英 a big town

例 Taipei is a beautiful **city**.
臺北是很美的城市。

☐ 三分熟 ☐ 五分熟 ☐ 七分熟 ☐ 全熟

class [klæs]

名 班級、階級、種類
同 grade 階級

英英 a group of students who are gathered together and taught at school, college or university

例 There are fourty **classes** in my school.
我的學校有四十個班。

☐ 三分熟 ☐ 五分熟 ☐ 七分熟 ☐ 全熟

clean [klin]

形 乾淨的
動 打掃
反 dirty 髒的

英英 not dirty, very neat; to make clean

例 Clean the **classroom**.
打掃教室。

☐ 三分熟 ☐ 五分熟 ☐ 七分熟 ☐ 全熟

clear [klɪr]

形 清楚的、明確的、澄清的
動 澄清、清除障礙、放晴
反 ambiguous 含糊不清的
片 crystal clear 十分清楚

英英 very easy to understand, read, hear or see

例 It is **clear**.
這很明顯。

☐ 三分熟 ☐ 五分熟 ☐ 七分熟 ☐ 全熟

climb [klaɪm]

動 攀登、上升、爬

英英 to go up towards the top of something

例 I love to go mountain **climbing**.
我喜歡爬山。

☐ 二分熟 ☐ 五分熟 ☐ 七分熟 ☐ 全熟

clock [klɑk]

名 時鐘、計時器

英英 a device for measuring and showing time, which is usually put in the building or hang on the wall

例 It's twelve **o'clock** now.
現在十二點了。

☐ 三分熟 ☐ 五分熟 ☐ 七分熟 ☐ 全熟

🎧 Track 025

close [klos]/[kloz]

形 靠近的、親近的
動 關、結束、靠近
反 open （打）開
片 close to
　　近的、接近的

英英 dear; familiar; to change something from being open to not being open
例 I feel **close** to you.
　　我覺得跟你很親近。

☐ 三分熟
☐ 五分熟
☐ 七分熟
☐ 全熟

cloud [klaʊd]

名 雲
動 （以雲）遮蔽
片 a cloud of 一大群

英英 a visible mass with gray or white color in the sky
例 The cloud is **gray**.
　　雲朵很灰。

☐ 三分熟
☐ 五分熟
☐ 七分熟
☐ 全熟

coast [kost]

名 海岸、沿岸

英英 the land close or next to sea
例 The hotel near the **coast** is good.
　　海岸邊的那家飯店很棒。

☐ 三分熟
☐ 五分熟
☐ 七分熟
☐ 全熟

coat [kot]

名 外套
同 jacket 外套

英英 an outer piece of clothing with sleeves which keeps people warm
例 We need to buy a new **coat**.
　　我們要買件新的外套。

☐ 三分熟
☐ 五分熟
☐ 七分熟
☐ 全熟

co·coa [ˈkoko]

名 可可粉、可可飲料、可可色

英英 a dark brown powder used to make chocolate and add a chocolate flavor to drink, usually made from cocoa beans
例 I want to have a cup of hot **cocoa**.
　　我想要來一杯熱可可。

☐ 三分熟
☐ 五分熟
☐ 七分熟
☐ 全熟

cof·fee [ˈkɔfɪ]

名 咖啡

英英 a dark brown powder made by coffee beans, with a strong flavor and smell powder
例 I had a cup of **coffee** today.
　　我今天喝了一杯咖啡。

☐ 三分熟
☐ 五分熟
☐ 七分熟
☐ 全熟

co·la/Coke
[ˈkolə]/[kok]

名 可樂

英英 a dark-colored carbonated soft drink flavored with extract of the cola nut
例 My son has a glass of **Coke**.
　　我兒子總是點一杯可樂。

☐ 三分熟
☐ 五分熟
☐ 七分熟
☐ 全熟

cold [kold]

形 冷的
名 感冒
反 warm 暖的

英英 producing or feeling chilliness common infection which often causes a cough or a slight fever and sometimes some pain in the muscles
例 Today is so **cold**.
　　今天好冷。

☐ 三分熟
☐ 五分熟
☐ 七分熟
☐ 全熟

C

co·lor [ˈkʌlɚ]

名 顏色
動 把……塗上顏色

英英 the effect of a bright color or of a lot of colors together

例 I love the **color** of the clothes.
我喜歡這衣服的顏色。

□ 三分熟
□ 五分熟
□ 七分熟
□ 全熟

come [kʌm]

動 來
反 leave 離開

英英 to move or go towards the speaker or with the speaker

例 Dad **comes** home at six.
爸爸六點回家。

□ 三分熟
□ 五分熟
□ 七分熟
□ 全熟

com·mon [ˈkɑmən]

形 共同的、平常的、普通的
名 平民、普通
反 special 特別的
片 commom sense 常識

英英 the same in a lot of places or in many ways for a lot of people

例 It's **common** to have a cell phone now.
現在有手機是很正常的。

□ 三分熟
□ 五分熟
□ 七分熟
□ 全熟

con·tin·ue [kənˈtɪnjʊ]

動 繼續、連續
同 persist 持續
片 to be continued 未完成

英英 something keeps happening, existing or someone keeps doing something

例 **Continue** your work.
繼續工作。

□ 三分熟
□ 五分熟
□ 七分熟
□ 全熟

cook [kʊk]

動 烹調、煮、燒
名 廚師

英英 to prepare for eating by boiling, baking, frying, etc.; one who prepares food

例 I am **cooking** the dinner.
我正在煮晚餐。

□ 三分熟
□ 五分熟
□ 七分熟
□ 全熟

cook·ie/cook·y [ˈkʊkɪ]

名 餅乾

英英 sweet and hard biscuit

例 I am baking some **cookies**.
我正在烤餅乾。

□ 三分熟
□ 五分熟
□ 七分熟
□ 全熟

cool [kʊl]

形 涼的、涼快的、酷的
動 使變涼
反 hot 熱的

英英 slightly cold; of a low temperature

例 It's **cool** tonight.
今晚很涼爽。

□ 三分熟
□ 五分熟
□ 七分熟
□ 全熟

🎧 Track 027

corn [kɔrn]

名 玉米
片 pop corn 玉米

英英 a grain, single seed of certain plants, such as wheat, rye, barley, and maize

例 Feed the pigs some **corns**.
餵豬吃點玉米吧！

□三分熟
□五分熟
□七分熟
□全熟

---

cor·rect [kəˋrɛkt]

形 正確的
動 改正、糾正
同 right 正確的

英英 right and not wrong; to make right

例 Give me a **correct** answer.
給我一個正確的答案。

□三分熟
□五分熟
□七分熟
□全熟

---

cost [kɔst]

名 代價、價值、費用
動 花費、值
反 income 收入、收益

英英 the amount of money needed for buying things, or making something

例 The computer **costs** me a lot.
這臺電腦花了我不少錢。

□三分熟
□五分熟
□七分熟
□全熟

---

count [kaʊnt]

動 計數
名 計數

英英 to calculate the number of people or objects, or to say the names of numbers one after the other in order

例 My little baby can **count** now!
我的小孩現在就會計數了！

□三分熟
□五分熟
□七分熟
□全熟

---

coun·try [ˋkʌntrɪ]

形 國家的、鄉村的
名 國家、鄉村
同 nation 國家

英英 a nation has its own government and armed forces

例 Japan is an amazing **country**.
日本是個讓人驚豔的國家。

□三分熟
□五分熟
□七分熟
□全熟

---

course [kors]

名 課程、講座、過程、路線
同 process 過程

英英 a set of classes or a plan of study on a particular subject

例 English is my favorite **course** this year.
英文是我今年最喜歡的課程。

□三分熟
□五分熟
□七分熟
□全熟

---

cov·er [ˋkʌvɚ]

名 封面、表面
動 覆蓋、掩飾、包含
反 uncover 揭露、發現

英英 to put something over another, or to lie on the surface of something

例 The **cover** of the book is colorful.
這本書的封面很繽紛。

□三分熟
□五分熟
□七分熟
□全熟

---

cow [kaʊ]

名 母牛、乳牛

英英 a large female farm animal kept to produce meat and milk

例 There are lots of **cows** in the farm.
農場裡有很多母牛。

□三分熟
□五分熟
□七分熟
□全熟

cow·boy [ˈkaʊˌbɔɪ]

名 牛仔

英英 a person whose job is to take care of cattle, especially in the western U.S

例 I love the adventure story of **cowboy**.
我喜歡牛仔冒險故事。

☐ 三分熟
☐ 五分熟
☐ 七分熟
☐ 全熟

C

---

crow [kro]

名 啼叫、烏鴉
動 啼叫、報曉

英英 a large black bird with a loud noisy cry

例 The **crow** at night scares me.
晚上烏鴉叫嚇到我了。

☐ 三分熟
☐ 五分熟
☐ 七分熟
☐ 全熟

---

cry [kraɪ]

名 叫聲、哭聲、大叫
動 哭、叫、喊
同 wail 慟哭

英英 a loud high sound that expresses an anxious or unpleasant emotion

例 The baby is **crying**.
這嬰兒在哭。

☐ 三分熟
☐ 五分熟
☐ 七分熟
☐ 全熟

---

cub [kʌb]

名 幼獸、年輕人

英英 a young lion, bear, wolf, fox, etc.

例 Around the **cubs** is their mother.
在幼獸旁邊總是伴隨著牠們的母親。

☐ 三分熟
☐ 五分熟
☐ 七分熟
☐ 全熟

---

cup [kʌp]

名 杯子
同 glass 玻璃杯
片 is not my cup of tea
不是我的菜

英英 a small round container used for drinking tea, coffee and often with a handle

例 Give me a **cup** of tea please.
請給我一杯茶。

☐ 三分熟
☐ 五分熟
☐ 七分熟
☐ 全熟

---

cut [kʌt]

動 切、割、剪、砍、削、刪
名 切口、傷口
同 split 切開
片 clear-cut 清楚的

英英 to break the surface of something; a slice

例 I **cut** the paper.
我把這紙割好了。

☐ 三分熟
☐ 五分熟
☐ 七分熟
☐ 全熟

---

cute [kjut]

形 可愛的、聰明伶俐的
同 pretty 可愛的

英英 describing someone who is pleasant and attractive

例 My girlfriend is **cute**.
我女朋友很可愛。

☐ 三分熟
☐ 五分熟
☐ 七分熟
☐ 全熟

Dd

🎧 **Track 029**

**dad·dy/dad/
pa·pa/pa/pop**

[`dædɪ]/[dæd]/[`pɑpə]/
[pɑ]/[pɑp]

名 爸爸

英英 a father or male parent

例 **Daddy** is always there for me.
爸爸總是在我身邊。

☐ 三分熟
☐ 五分熟
☐ 七分熟
☐ 全熟

---

dance [dæns]

名 舞蹈
動 舞蹈、動、跳舞

英英 to move the body and feet when listening to music

例 I am not good at **dancing**.
我不擅長跳舞。

☐ 三分熟
☐ 五分熟
☐ 七分熟
☐ 全熟

---

danc·er [`dænsɚ]

名 舞者

英英 someone who take dancing as a job or for pleasure

例 The **dancer** is so hot.
那舞者太辣了。

☐ 三分熟
☐ 五分熟
☐ 七分熟
☐ 全熟

---

dan·ger [`dendʒɚ]

名 危險
反 safety 安全

英英 the possibility of putting someone in harm or death

例 There is a **danger** in loving somebody too much.
太愛一個人總是很危險的。

☐ 三分熟
☐ 五分熟
☐ 七分熟
☐ 全熟

---

dark [dɑrk]

名 黑暗、暗處
形 黑暗的
反 light 明亮的

英英 with little or no ligh

例 Everyone has his **dark** side.
人人都有自己的黑暗面。

☐ 三分熟
☐ 五分熟
☐ 七分熟
☐ 全熟

---

date [det]

名 日期、約會
動 約會、定日期
同 appointment 約會

英英 a numbered day in a week, the month and the year

例 What **date** is today?
今天是幾月幾號？

☐ 三分熟
☐ 五分熟
☐ 七分熟
☐ 全熟

---

daugh·ter [`dɔtɚ]

名 女兒
反 son 兒子

英英 your female child

例 My **daughters** are important for me.
我女兒對我來說很重要。

☐ 三分熟
☐ 五分熟
☐ 七分熟
☐ 全熟

---

day [de]

名 白天、日
反 night 晚上
片 day and night
日日夜夜

英英 a period of 24 hours

例 I miss you every **day** and night.
我每個日日夜夜都在想念你。

☐ 三分熟
☐ 五分熟
☐ 七分熟
☐ 全熟

D

dead [dɛd]

名 死者
形 死的
反 live 活的

英英 not now living, without no feeling at all from your body and breathe; all those who have died

例 There is a **dead**.
這裡有名死者。

☐ 三分熟
☐ 五分熟
☐ 七分熟
☐ 全熟

---

deal [dil]

動 處理、應付、做買賣、經營
名 買賣、交易
同 trade 交易
片 a deal is a deal 說話算話

英英 to take action; a business agreement

例 I can't **deal** with that.
我不能處理這狀況。

☐ 三分熟
☐ 五分熟
☐ 七分熟
☐ 全熟

---

dear [dɪr]

形 昂貴的、親愛的
副 昂貴地
感 啊！唉呀！（表示傷心、焦慮、驚奇等）
同 expensive 昂貴的
片 at a dear price 很昂貴的

英英 loved or liked very much; very precious

例 My **dear**, you look great!
親愛的，你看起來好棒喔！

☐ 三分熟
☐ 五分熟
☐ 七分熟
☐ 全熟

---

death [dɛθ]

名 死、死亡
反 life 生命、活的東西

英英 the end of life, without no feelings

例 They are sad for his **death**.
他們為他的死亡感到難過。

☐ 三分熟
☐ 五分熟
☐ 七分熟
☐ 全熟

De·cem·ber/

Dec. [dɪˋsɛmbɚ]

名 十二月

英英 the twelfth and last month of the year, after November and before January

例 Christmas is in **December**.
聖誕節在十二月。

☐ 三分熟
☐ 五分熟
☐ 七分熟
☐ 全熟

---

de·cide [dɪˋsaɪd]

動 決定
同 determine 決定

英英 to choose something after thinking or considering carefully about several possibilities

例 I have **decided**.
我下定決心了。

☐ 三分熟
☐ 五分熟
☐ 七分熟
☐ 全熟

---

deep [dip]

形 深的
副 深深地
反 shallow 淺的

英英 being a long way down from the top or surface

例 The water is so **deep**.
這水很深。

☐ 三分熟
☐ 五分熟
☐ 七分熟
☐ 全熟

🎧 Track 031

deer [dɪr]

名 鹿

英英 a large animal with four legs which eats grass and leaves

例 There were many **deer** in Taiwan.
臺灣以前有很多鹿。

☐ 三分熟
☐ 五分熟
☐ 七分熟
☐ 全熟

desk [dɛsk]

名 書桌

英英 a type of table that you can work at or do the reading, often one with drawers

例 There are books on her **desk**.
在她的桌子上有幾本書。

☐ 三分熟
☐ 五分熟
☐ 七分熟
☐ 全熟

die [daɪ]

動 死
同 perish 死去

英英 to stop living or existing

例 He will **die** soon.
他即將死去。

☐ 三分熟
☐ 五分熟
☐ 七分熟
☐ 全熟

dif·fer·ent
[ˈdɪfərənt]

形 不同的
反 identical 一模一樣的

英英 not the same from the other parts or the other things

例 I am **different** from you.
我跟你不一樣。

☐ 三分熟
☐ 五分熟
☐ 七分熟
☐ 全熟

dif·fi·cult [ˈdɪfəˌkʌlt]

形 困難的
反 easy 簡單的

英英 not easy, needing skill or effort

例 Life is always so **difficult**.
生命中總有很多的困難。

☐ 三分熟
☐ 五分熟
☐ 七分熟
☐ 全熟

dig [dɪg]

動 挖、挖掘
反 bury 埋

英英 to move soil or mud by using a tool, a machine or your hands

例 The dog **dug** a hole.
那隻狗挖了洞。

☐ 三分熟
☐ 五分熟
☐ 七分熟
☐ 全熟

din·ner [ˈdɪnɚ]

名 晚餐、晚宴
同 supper 晚餐
片 have dinner 吃晚餐

英英 the meal you eat in the evening of a day

例 I am going to have **dinner** with Lori.
我要跟洛麗吃晚餐。

☐ 三分熟
☐ 五分熟
☐ 七分熟
☐ 全熟

dir·ect [dəˈrɛkt]

形 筆直的、直接的
動 指示、命令
同 order 命令、指示

英英 going in a straight line towards somewhere without stopping or changing direction; to regulate or instruct

例 The road is **direct**.
這條路很直。

☐ 三分熟
☐ 五分熟
☐ 七分熟
☐ 全熟

D

dirt·y [ˈdɜtɪ]

形 髒的
動 弄髒
反 clean 清潔的

英英 not clean or not neat

例 This room is so **dirty**.
這房間好髒。

☐ 三分熟
☐ 五分熟
☐ 七分熟
☐ 全熟

dis·cov·er

[dɪˈskʌvɚ]

動 發現
同 find 發現

英英 to find information, a place or an object in the first time

例 I have **discovered** the secret.
我發現了祕密。

☐ 三分熟
☐ 五分熟
☐ 七分熟
☐ 全熟

dish [dɪʃ]

名 （盛食物的）盤、碟
同 plate 盤、碟

英英 a container, flatter than a bowl, which can be used for cooking or serveing for food

例 I miss the **dish**.
我好想念這道菜。

☐ 三分熟
☐ 五分熟
☐ 七分熟
☐ 全熟

do [du]

助 （無詞意）
動 做
同 perform 做

英英 to act or take action; to work on something

例 How **do** you **do**?
你最近做得如何？（你最近好嗎？）

☐ 三分熟
☐ 五分熟
☐ 七分熟
☐ 全熟

doc·tor/doc

[ˈdɑktɚ]

名 醫生、博士
同 physician 醫師
片 see a doctor 看醫生

英英 a person with a medical degree whose job is to treat ill people or someone who is hurt

例 I saw a **doctor**.
我去看了醫生。

☐ 三分熟
☐ 五分熟
☐ 七分熟
☐ 全熟

dog [dɔg]

動 尾隨、跟蹤
名 狗
片 keep a dog 養狗

英英 to follow; a common animal with four legs, usually kept by people as a pet at home

例 We want to keep a **dog**.
我想要養狗。

☐ 三分熟
☐ 五分熟
☐ 七分熟
☐ 全熟

doll [dɑl]

名 玩具娃娃
同 toy 玩具

英英 a child's toy in the shape of a small person or baby

例 I bought a **doll**.
我買了娃娃。

☐ 三分熟
☐ 五分熟
☐ 七分熟
☐ 全熟

dol·lar/buck

[ˈdɑlɚ]/[bʌk]

名 美元、錢

英英 the standard unit of money used in the US, Canada, Australia, New Zealand and other countries

例 I spent two **dollars**.
我花了兩塊錢。

☐ 三分熟
☐ 五分熟
☐ 七分熟
☐ 全熟

door [dor]

名 門
同 gate 大門

英英 a flat object which is used to close the entrance of a room or building

例 Open the **door**.
開門。

☐ 三分熟 ☐ 五分熟 ☐ 七分熟 ☐ 全熟

dove [dʌv]

名 鴿子

英英 a white or grey bird, people often take it as a symbol of peace

例 There are so many **doves**.
這裡有很多鴿子。

☐ 三分熟 ☐ 五分熟 ☐ 七分熟 ☐ 全熟

down [daʊn]

形 向下的
副 向下
介 沿著……而下
反 up 在上面

英英 in or towards a low or lower position, from a higher one

例 Go **down** the street.
沿著這條街往下走。

☐ 三分熟 ☐ 五分熟 ☐ 七分熟 ☐ 全熟

down·stairs

[ˌdaʊnˈstɛrz]

形 樓下的
副 在樓下
名 樓下
反 upstairs 在樓上

英英 go to or on a lower floor of a building

例 Go **downstairs**.
下樓去吧。

☐ 三分熟 ☐ 五分熟 ☐ 七分熟 ☐ 全熟

doz·en [ˈdʌzn̩]

名 （一）打、十二個

英英 twelve as a dozen

例 I have a **dozen** of pens.
我有一打筆。

☐ 三分熟 ☐ 五分熟 ☐ 七分熟 ☐ 全熟

draw [drɔ]

動 拉、拖、提取、畫、繪製
同 drag 拉、拖

英英 to pull or drag; to make a picture of someone or some real objects with a pencil or pen

例 I want to **draw** an elephant.
我想要畫一個大象。

☐ 三分熟 ☐ 五分熟 ☐ 七分熟 ☐ 全熟

dream [drim]

名 夢
動 做夢
反 reality 現實
片 dream of/about...
夢見……

英英 something that you want to happen very much or something you want to have but that is not very likely

例 I **dream** a **dream**.
我做了個夢。

☐ 三分熟 ☐ 五分熟 ☐ 七分熟 ☐ 全熟

E

drink [drɪŋk]

名 飲料
動 喝、喝酒

英英 liquid which is taken into the body through the mouth
例 I **drink** tea every day.
我每天喝茶。

☐ 三分熟
☐ 五分熟
☐ 七分熟
☐ 全熟

---

drive [draɪv]

名 駕車、車道
動 開車、驅使、操縱（機器等）
同 move 推動、促使

英英 to move or trek on land in a motor vehicle
例 Dad **drives** me to school.
爸爸開車載我去學校。

☐ 三分熟
☐ 五分熟
☐ 七分熟
☐ 全熟

---

driv·er [ˈdraɪvɚ]

名 駕駛員、司機

英英 someone who drives a car or truck, etc.
例 The bus **driver** is very nice.
那公車司機人很好。

☐ 三分熟
☐ 五分熟
☐ 七分熟
☐ 全熟

---

dry [draɪ]

形 乾的、枯燥無味的
動 把……弄乾、乾掉
同 thirsty 乾的、口渴的

英英 describes something without water or other liquid in it; to free from moisture
例 The air in desert is so **dry**.
沙漠的空氣很乾燥。

☐ 三分熟
☐ 五分熟
☐ 七分熟
☐ 全熟

---

duck [dʌk]

名 鴨子

英英 a bird that lives in a group by water, has webbed feet
例 **Ducks** swim in the pond.
池塘中有鴨子在游泳。

☐ 三分熟
☐ 五分熟
☐ 七分熟
☐ 全熟

---

duck·ling [ˈdʌklɪŋ]

名 小鴨子

英英 a young duck
例 Many **ducklings** are hatched.
好多小鴨子孵出來了。

☐ 三分熟
☐ 五分熟
☐ 七分熟
☐ 全熟

---

dur·ing [ˈdjʊrɪŋ]

介 在……期間

英英 from the beginning to the end of a particular period
例 **During** the war, her father died.
在戰爭期間,他父親過世了。

☐ 三分熟
☐ 五分熟
☐ 七分熟
☐ 全熟

Ee

each [itʃ]

形 各、每
代 每個、各自
副 各、每個

英英 every piece of object, every thing or every person, etc., usually in a group of two or even more, considered separately
例 I love **each** of my kids.
我愛我每一個孩子。

☐ 三分熟
☐ 五分熟
☐ 七分熟
☐ 全熟

🎧 Track 035

ea·gle [ˈigl̩]

名 鷹

英英 a large bird with a curved beak which eats meat and has excellent eyesight

例 **Eagles** fly in the sky.
老鷹在空中飛著。

☐ 三分熟
☐ 五分熟
☐ 七分熟
☐ 全熟

---

ear [ɪr]

名 耳朵

英英 either of the two organs, one on each side of the head, for people or animals to hear sounds

例 The movie star has big **ears**.
那電影明星有雙大耳朵。

☐ 三分熟
☐ 五分熟
☐ 七分熟
☐ 全熟

---

ear·ly [ˈɝlɪ]

形 早的、早期的、及早的
副 早、在初期
反 late 晚的

英英 at the beginning of time, or before the expected or planned time

例 I came home **earlier**.
我昨天比較早回家。

☐ 三分熟
☐ 五分熟
☐ 七分熟
☐ 全熟

---

earth [ɝθ]

名 地球、陸地、地面
同 globe 地球
片 on earth 到底、究竟

英英 the world we're living on, the planet between Venus and Mars, the third in order of distance from the Sun

例 We live on the **Earth**.
我們住在地球上。

☐ 三分熟
☐ 五分熟
☐ 七分熟
☐ 全熟

---

ease [iz]

動 緩和、減輕、使舒適
名 容易、舒適、悠閒
同 relieve 緩和、減輕

英英 become less serious or severe, make more comfortable

例 The pain killer can **ease** my pain.
止痛藥可以減輕疼痛。

☐ 三分熟
☐ 五分熟
☐ 七分熟
☐ 全熟

---

east [ist]

形 東方的
副 向東方
名 東、東方
反 west 西方

英英 the direction where the sun rises at the equinoxes, on the back side of a person facing west

例 She's from the **east**.
她來自東方的國度。

☐ 三分熟
☐ 五分熟
☐ 七分熟
☐ 全熟

---

eas·y [ˈizɪ]

形 容易的、不費力的
反 difficult 困難的
片 take it easy 慢慢來

英英 achieving something without great effort or strength

例 Forgiving is not so **easy**.
原諒不是那麼簡單。

☐ 三分熟
☐ 五分熟
☐ 七分熟
☐ 全熟

---

eat [it]

動 吃
同 dine 用餐

英英 put food or fruit into the mouth and chew and swallow it

例 You **ate** my chicken soup!
你吃了我的雞湯！

☐ 三分熟
☐ 五分熟
☐ 七分熟
☐ 全熟

E

edge [εdʒ]

名 邊、邊緣
同 border 邊緣
片 at the edge of
在……邊緣

英英 the outside limit of a place, area or object

例 I am at the **edge** of the small bed.
我已經在這張小床的邊緣了。

☐ 三分熟
☐ 五分熟
☐ 七分熟
☐ 全熟

egg [εg]

名 蛋

英英 an oval or round object laid by a fish or female bird, with an ovum which if fertilized can develop into a new organism

例 I like to eat **eggs**.
我喜歡吃雞蛋。

☐ 三分熟
☐ 五分熟
☐ 七分熟
☐ 全熟

eight [et]

名 八

英英 one more than seven, one less than nine

例 There are **eight** people there.
那邊有八個人。

☐ 三分熟
☐ 五分熟
☐ 七分熟
☐ 全熟

eigh·teen [ˈeˈtin]

名 十八

英英 one more than seventeen, one less than nineteen

例 She's like **eighteen** years old.
她就像十八歲一樣。

☐ 三分熟
☐ 五分熟
☐ 七分熟
☐ 全熟

eight·y [ˈeti]

名 八十

英英 ten less than ninety, ten more than seventy

例 My grandmother is **eighty** years old.
我的奶奶八十歲了。

☐ 三分熟
☐ 五分熟
☐ 七分熟
☐ 全熟

ei·ther [ˈiðɚ]

形 （兩者之中）任一的
代 （兩者之中）任一
副 也（不）

英英 usually used before the first of two alternatives listed

例 **Either** you or I will leave.
不是你走就是我走。

☐ 三分熟
☐ 五分熟
☐ 七分熟
☐ 全熟

e·le·phant [ˈεləfənt]

名 大象
片 white elephant
無用品、無價值的東西

英英 a very large plant-eating animal, which has a trunk, large ears and long curved tusks, usually native to Africa and southern Asia, such as Thailand

例 I drew an **elephant**.
我畫了一隻大象。

☐ 三分熟
☐ 五分熟
☐ 七分熟
☐ 全熟

e·le·ven [ɪˈlεvn̩]

名 十一

英英 one more than ten, one less than twelve

例 I go to sleep at **eleven**.
我十一點去睡覺。

☐ 三分熟
☐ 五分熟
☐ 七分熟
☐ 全熟

Track 037

else [ɛls]

副 其他、另外
片 or else 否則

英英 used after words to mean other, another, different, extra, such as anyone else, everything else, etc.
例 What **else** can I do?
我還可以做什麼？

□三分熟
□五分熟
□七分熟
□全熟

end [ɛnd]

名 結束、終點
動 結束、終止
反 origin 起源

英英 the final part or the closure of something
例 In the **end**, we lost everything.
最終，我們失去了所有。

□三分熟
□五分熟
□七分熟
□全熟

Eng·lish [ˈɪŋglɪʃ]

形 英國的、英國人的
名 英語

英英 the language of England, or the people from England
例 She loves the **English** man.
她喜歡那英國男人。

□三分熟
□五分熟
□七分熟
□全熟

e·nough [əˈnʌf]

形 充足的、足夠的
名 足夠
副 夠、充足
同 sufficient 足夠的

英英 as much or as many as is necessary or expected
例 I have **enough** money.
我有足夠的錢。

□三分熟
□五分熟
□七分熟
□全熟

en·ter [ˈɛntɚ]

動 加入、參加
反 exit 退出

英英 come or go into some occasions, or begin to get involved in or do
例 I **entered** a haunted house.
我進到一間鬼屋。

□三分熟
□五分熟
□七分熟
□全熟

e·qual [ˈikwəl]

名 對手
形 相等的、平等的
動 等於、比得上
同 parallel 相同的

英英 a person or thing that is equal to another; being the same in amount, measure, size, degree, value, or status
例 One plus one **equals** two.
一加一等於二。

□三分熟
□五分熟
□七分熟
□全熟

e·ven [ˈivən]

形 平坦的、偶數的、
　相等的
副 甚至
同 smooth 平坦的

英英 very flat and smooth, level; equal in quantity, size, number, amount, or value
例 The road is **even**.
這條路很平。

□三分熟
□五分熟
□七分熟
□全熟

eve·ning [ˈivnɪŋ]

名 傍晚、晚上

英英 the period of tim e before or at the end of the day
例 In the **evening**, we take a walk.
我們在傍晚散步。

□三分熟
□五分熟
□七分熟
□全熟

E

ev·er [ˋɛvɚ]

副 曾經、永遠
反 never 不曾

英英 used in comparisons at all times, forever or always

例 Have you **ever** been to Japan?
你曾經去過日本嗎？

☐ 三分熟
☐ 五分熟
☐ 七分熟
☐ 全熟

eve·ry [ˋɛvrɪ]

形 每、每個
反 none 一個也沒

英英 used to refer to all the individual objects or members of a set without exception

例 **Every** child goes to school.
所有的孩子都會去學校。

☐ 三分熟
☐ 五分熟
☐ 七分熟
☐ 全熟

ex·am [ɪgˋzæm]

名 考試

英英 a test of knowledge or proficiency in a subject or skill, which is usually held in a formal occasion

例 The **exam** is very easy.
那考試很簡單。

☐ 三分熟
☐ 五分熟
☐ 七分熟
☐ 全熟

ex·am·ine

[ɪgˋzæmɪn]

動 檢查、考試
同 test 考試

英英 to investigate carefully; to test

例 You'd better **examine** the contract carefully before singing.
你最好在唱歌前檢查合約。

☐ 三分熟
☐ 五分熟
☐ 七分熟
☐ 全熟

ex·am·ple

[ɪgˋzæmpl]

名 榜樣、例子
同 instance 例子

英英 a person's behavior when considered for their suitability to be copied

例 Please give me an **example**.
請給我個例子。

☐ 三分熟
☐ 五分熟
☐ 七分熟
☐ 全熟

ex·cept/ ex·cept·ing

[ɪkˋsɛpt]/[ɪkˋsɛptɪŋ]

介 除了……之外
同 besides 除……之外

英英 not including or aside from something; other than

例 **Except** Mary, everyone likes her.
除了瑪莉，大家都喜歡她。

☐ 三分熟
☐ 五分熟
☐ 七分熟
☐ 全熟

eye [aɪ]

名 眼睛
片 cast an eye on 粗略的看一下

英英 the organ of sight in humans and animals

例 You have beautiful **eyes**.
你有雙漂亮的眼睛。

☐ 三分熟
☐ 五分熟
☐ 七分熟
☐ 全熟

Ff

🎧 Track 039

face [fes]

名 臉、面部
動 面對
同 look 外表

英英 the fore or the front part of a person's head

例 I washed my **face**.
我洗了臉。

☐ 三分熟
☐ 五分熟
☐ 七分熟
☐ 全熟

---

fact [fækt]

名 事實
反 fiction 虛構
片 in fact 事實上

英英 a thing that is undoubted and true

例 Could you please tell me the **fact**?
你可以告訴我事實嗎？

☐ 三分熟
☐ 五分熟
☐ 七分熟
☐ 全熟

---

fac·to·ry [ˈfæktərɪ]

名 工廠
同 plant 工廠

英英 a building where manufactures goods chiefly with machines

例 The **factories** are in Vietnam.
那些工廠現在在越南。

☐ 三分熟
☐ 五分熟
☐ 七分熟
☐ 全熟

---

fall [fɔl]

名 秋天、落下
動 倒下、落下
同 drop 落下、降下

英英 the third season of a year, comes before winter; to move quickly and without control from a higher to a lower level

例 **Fall** is coming.
秋天就要來了。

☐ 三分熟
☐ 五分熟
☐ 七分熟
☐ 全熟

---

false [fɔls]

形 錯誤的、假的、虛偽的
反 correct 正確的

英英 untrue or incorrect

例 It is a **false** assumption.
這是錯誤的假設。

☐ 三分熟
☐ 五分熟
☐ 七分熟
☐ 全熟

---

fa·mi·ly [ˈfæməlɪ]

名 家庭
同 relative 親戚、親屬

英英 a group contains two parents and their children living together as a unit

例 I have a happy **family**.
我有個幸福的家庭。

☐ 三分熟
☐ 五分熟
☐ 七分熟
☐ 全熟

---

fan [fæn]

名 風扇、狂熱者
動 搧、搧動

英英 a hand-held device, typically folding and circular, that is waved so as to cool the user or the environment; a person who is very into someone or something; to drive a current of air upon

例 I am a **fan** of NBA.
我是 NBA 的粉絲。

☐ 三分熟
☐ 五分熟
☐ 七分熟
☐ 全熟

F

fa·nat·ic [fəˋnætɪk]

名 狂熱者
形 狂熱的

英英 a person filled with excessive enthusiasm, especially for an extreme political or religious events
例 She's so **fanatic** for the singer.
她對那歌手很狂熱。

☐ 三分熟
☐ 五分熟
☐ 七分熟
☐ 全熟

---

far [fɑr]

形 遙遠的、遠（方）的
副 遠方、朝遠處
同 distant 遠的

英英 situated at a long distance in space or distant from the middle
例 Now, I am **far** from you.
現在我離你很遠。

☐ 三分熟
☐ 五分熟
☐ 七分熟
☐ 全熟

---

farm [fɑrm]

名 農場、農田
動 耕種
同 ranch 大農場

英英 an area of land and its buildings used for planting crops and raising animals
例 I have a **farm**.
我有一座農場。

☐ 三分熟
☐ 五分熟
☐ 七分熟
☐ 全熟

---

farm·er [ˋfɑrmɚ]

名 農夫

英英 a person who owns or manages a farm
例 The **farmer** plants rice.
那位農夫種米。

☐ 三分熟
☐ 五分熟
☐ 七分熟
☐ 全熟

---

fast [fæst]

形 快速的
副 很快地
反 slow 緩慢的

英英 moving at high speed or acting rapidly
例 He comes **fast**.
他很快就來了。

☐ 三分熟
☐ 五分熟
☐ 七分熟
☐ 全熟

---

fat [fæt]

形 肥胖的
名 脂肪
反 thin 瘦的

英英 plump; a natural oily substance in animal bodies, placed under the skin or around certain organs
例 He is too **fat**.
他太胖了。

☐ 三分熟
☐ 五分熟
☐ 七分熟
☐ 全熟

---

fa·ther [ˋfɑðɚ]

名 父親
反 mother 母親

英英 a male parent
例 My **father** is tall.
我的爸爸很高。

☐ 三分熟
☐ 五分熟
☐ 七分熟
☐ 全熟

---

fear [fɪr]

名 恐怖、害怕
動 害怕、恐懼
同 fright 恐怖

英英 an unpleasant or awful emotion caused by the threat of danger, pain, or harm; to be in dread
例 The **fear** makes her cry.
那種恐懼讓她哭了。

☐ 三分熟
☐ 五分熟
☐ 七分熟
☐ 全熟

🎧 **Track 041**

Feb·ru·ar·y/
Feb. [ˈfɛbruˌɛrɪ]
名 二月

英英 the second month of a year, comes after January
例 Chinese New Year is in **February**.
農曆過年通常在二月。

☐ 三分熟
☐ 五分熟
☐ 七分熟
☐ 全熟

feed [fid]
動 餵
同 nourish 滋養

英英 give food to or furnish an adequate supply of food for somebody
例 Don't feed the dog chocolate.
不要餵狗吃巧克力。

☐ 三分熟
☐ 五分熟
☐ 七分熟
☐ 全熟

feel [fil]
動 感覺、覺得
同 experience 經歷、感受

英英 be aware of through physical sensation or awareness
例 I can **feel** you.
我可以感覺到你。

☐ 三分熟
☐ 五分熟
☐ 七分熟
☐ 全熟

feel·ing [ˈfilɪŋ]
名 感覺、感受
同 sensation 感受

英英 an emotional state or emotional responses or tendencies to respond
例 I didn't think about your **feeling**.
我沒有想到你的感受。

☐ 三分熟
☐ 五分熟
☐ 七分熟
☐ 全熟

feel·ings [ˈfilɪŋz]
名 感情、敏感

英英 emotions that someone feels, such as anger, sadness, or happiness, especially those influenced by other people
例 Her **feelings** to him are ambiguous.
她對他的感情很曖昧。

☐ 三分熟
☐ 五分熟
☐ 七分熟
☐ 全熟

few [fju]
形 少的
名 （前面與 a 連用）少數、幾個
反 many 許多

英英 not many, just a small number of
例 **Few** people know about the event.
很少人知道這活動。

☐ 三分熟
☐ 五分熟
☐ 七分熟
☐ 全熟

fif·teen [ˈfɪfˈtin]
名 十五

英英 one more than fourteen, one less than sixte
例 I had **fifteen** dollars.
我本來有十五塊錢。

☐ 三分熟
☐ 五分熟
☐ 七分熟
☐ 全熟

fif·ty [ˈfɪftɪ]
名 五十

英英 ten less than sixty; ten more than forty
例 What will we become in **fifty** years?
五十年後的我們會變成怎樣？

☐ 三分熟
☐ 五分熟
☐ 七分熟
☐ 全熟

F

fight [faɪt]

名 打仗、爭論
動 打仗、爭論
同 quarrel 爭吵

英英 take part in a violent struggle involving physical power or weapons

例 I don't want to **fight** with you.
我不想跟你爭論。

☐ 三分熟
☐ 五分熟
☐ 七分熟
☐ 全熟

fill [fɪl]

動 填空、填滿
反 empty 倒空

英英 make full in an empty space; become full

例 Please **fill** the blanks.
請填好表單。

☐ 三分熟
☐ 五分熟
☐ 七分熟
☐ 全熟

fi·nal [ˈfaɪn!]

形 最後的、最終的
反 initial 最初的

英英 coming at the end of a series or event or approached as the outcome of a process

例 The **final** exam is coming.
期末考要來了。

☐ 三分熟
☐ 五分熟
☐ 七分熟
☐ 全熟

find [faɪnd]

動 找到、發現

英英 discover by chance or easily; recognize or discover to be present or to be the case

例 I will **find** you.
我會找到你。

☐ 三分熟
☐ 五分熟
☐ 七分熟
☐ 全熟

fine [faɪn]

形 美好的
副 很好地
名 罰款
動 處以罰金
同 nice 好的

英英 of very excellent quality; in good health and feeling well; money paid as a penalty; to punish by imposing a fine

例 I am **fine**.
我沒事。

☐ 三分熟
☐ 五分熟
☐ 七分熟
☐ 全熟

fin·ger [ˈfɪŋgɚ]

名 手指
反 toe 腳趾

英英 each of the four slender or five (if the thumb is included) jointed parts attached to either hand

例 Her **fingers** are long.
她的手指很長。

☐ 三分熟
☐ 五分熟
☐ 七分熟
☐ 全熟

fin·ish [ˈfɪnɪʃ]

名 完成、結束
動 完成、結束
同 complete 完成

英英 bring or come to an end or to complete something

例 I will **finish** my work soon.
我很快就要完成我的工作了。

☐ 三分熟
☐ 五分熟
☐ 七分熟
☐ 全熟

fire [faɪr]

名 火
動 射擊、解雇、燃燒
同 dismiss 解雇
片 build a fire 生火

英英 the state of burning, in which substances combine chemically with oxygen from the air; to discharge from employment

例 Animals are afraid of **fire**.
動物怕火。

☐ 三分熟
☐ 五分熟
☐ 七分熟
☐ 全熟

🎧 Track 043

first [fɝst]

名 第一、最初
形 第一的
副 首先、最初、第一
反 last 最後的

英英 1st, earliest or faster; coming or finishing before all others in time or order

例 I got the **first** prize.
　　我得到第一名。

☐ 三分熟
☐ 五分熟
☐ 七分熟
☐ 全熟

fish [fɪʃ]

名 魚、魚類
動 捕魚、釣魚

英英 a limbless cold-blooded animal lives in water, usually with a backbone, gills and fins; to catch fish

例 I love to eat **fish**.
　　我喜歡吃魚。

☐ 三分熟
☐ 五分熟
☐ 七分熟
☐ 全熟

five [faɪv]

名 五

英英 one more than four, one less than six

例 My grandparents have **five** children.
　　我祖父母有五個小孩。

☐ 三分熟
☐ 五分熟
☐ 七分熟
☐ 全熟

floor [flor]

名 地板、樓層
反 ceiling 天花板

英英 a story of a building, the lower surface in a room

例 We live on the second **floor**.
　　我們住在二樓。

☐ 三分熟
☐ 五分熟
☐ 七分熟
☐ 全熟

flow·er [ˋflaʊɚ]

名 花

英英 the seed-bearing part of a plant, which is brightly colored with a delightful smell

例 He gave her a bouquet of **flowers**.
　　他給了她一束花。

☐ 三分熟
☐ 五分熟
☐ 七分熟
☐ 全熟

fly [flaɪ]

名 蒼蠅、飛行
動 飛行、飛翔

英英 a small disgusting insect with two wings; to move through the air under control

例 There are two **flies** on the meat.
　　這塊肉上面有兩隻蒼蠅。

☐ 三分熟
☐ 五分熟
☐ 七分熟
☐ 全熟

fog [fɑg]

名 霧

英英 a weather condition in which very small droplets of water come together to form a thick cloud in the atmosphere, or to the land or sea, making it difficult to see

例 There is always **fog** in London.
　　倫敦總是有霧。

☐ 三分熟
☐ 五分熟
☐ 七分熟
☐ 全熟

fol·low [ˋfɑlo]

動 跟隨、遵循、聽得懂
同 trace 跟蹤

英英 move behind or go after someone for observing or monitoring them

例 Just **follow** me.
　　跟著我就是了。

☐ 三分熟
☐ 五分熟
☐ 七分熟
☐ 全熟

food [fud]

名 食物

英英 any nutritious substance that people or animals eat or drink to maintain life and growth

例 Please give me some **food**.
請給我一些食物。

☐ 三分熟
☐ 五分熟
☐ 七分熟
☐ 全熟

---

foot [fʊt]

名 腳

英英 the lower extremity of the leg below the ankle for people to walk

例 I hurt my **foot**.
我傷到了腳。

☐ 三分熟
☐ 五分熟
☐ 七分熟
☐ 全熟

---

for [fɔr]

介 為、因為、對於
連 因為
同 as 因為

英英 because of something; due to

例 This gift is just **for** you.
這禮物只給你一個人的。

☐ 三分熟
☐ 五分熟
☐ 七分熟
☐ 全熟

---

force [fors]

名 力量、武力
動 強迫、施壓
同 compel 強迫

英英 physical strength, energy or power as an action or movement; to overpower by strength

例 Don't **force** me!
不要強迫我。

☐ 三分熟
☐ 五分熟
☐ 七分熟
☐ 全熟

---

for·eign [ˈfɔrɪn]

形 外國的
反 native 本土的

英英 language or the characteristic belong to a country, which is not your own

例 I love to visit **foreign** countries.
我喜歡去外國。

☐ 三分熟
☐ 五分熟
☐ 七分熟
☐ 全熟

---

for·est [ˈfɔrɪst]

名 森林
同 wood 森林

英英 a large area covered with trees, plants and undergrowth

例 It is dangerous to go to the **forest**.
去森林很危險。

☐ 三分熟
☐ 五分熟
☐ 七分熟
☐ 全熟

---

for·get [fɚˈgɛt]

動 忘記
反 remember 記得

英英 fail to remember, absently neglect to do something

例 I **forgot** to bring my key.
我忘記帶鑰匙了。

☐ 三分熟
☐ 五分熟
☐ 七分熟
☐ 全熟

---

fork [fɔrk]

名 叉

英英 an implement used for lifting or holding food, which usually has two or more prongs

例 I prefer to use a **fork**.
我比較想要用叉子。

☐ 三分熟
☐ 五分熟
☐ 七分熟
☐ 全熟

---

for·ty [ˈfɔrtɪ]

名 四十

英英 ten less than fifty, ten more than thirty

例 We have **forty** people on this bus.
這輛公車上有四十個人。

☐ 三分熟
☐ 五分熟
☐ 七分熟
☐ 全熟

four [for]

名 四

英英 one more than three, one less than five

例 We have walked for **four** hours.
我們已經走了四個小時了。

☐ 三分熟
☐ 五分熟
☐ 七分熟
☐ 全熟

four·teen [ˈforˈtin]

名 十四

英英 one more than thirteen, one less than fifteen

例 I have known him since I was **forteen**.
我從十四歲就認識他。

☐ 三分熟
☐ 五分熟
☐ 七分熟
☐ 全熟

free [fri]

形 自由的、免費的
動 釋放、解放
同 release 解放
片 for free 免費

英英 totally not under the control or in the power of another

例 You are **free** now.
你現在自由了。

☐ 三分熟
☐ 五分熟
☐ 七分熟
☐ 全熟

fresh [frɛʃ]

形 新鮮的、無經驗的、淡（水）的
反 stale 不新鮮的

英英 not previously known or used; new, original or different; the food recently made or obtained; not preserved

例 I need some **fresh** air.
我需要一點新鮮的空氣。

☐ 三分熟
☐ 五分熟
☐ 七分熟
☐ 全熟

Fri·day/Fri.

[ˈfraɪˌde]

名 星期五

英英 the day of the week before Saturday and coming after Thursday

例 On **Friday**, we usually go shopping.
星期五我們通常會去血拼。

☐ 三分熟
☐ 五分熟
☐ 七分熟
☐ 全熟

friend [frɛnd]

名 朋友
反 enemy 敵人
片 make friends 交朋友

英英 a person with whom one has a bond of mutual affection, who you know very well or like very much

例 I made a lot of **friends** in college.
我在大學交了很多朋友。

☐ 三分熟
☐ 五分熟
☐ 七分熟
☐ 全熟

frog [frɑg]

名 蛙

英英 a tailless amphibian which has a short squat body and very long hind legs for leaping

例 The **frogs** sing loudly.
青蛙大聲地唱歌。

☐ 三分熟
☐ 五分熟
☐ 七分熟
☐ 全熟

from [frɑm]

介 從、由於

英英 used to show the place where someone or something starts or the thing you start at

例 I am **from** Taiwan.
我來自臺灣。

☐ 三分熟
☐ 五分熟
☐ 七分熟
☐ 全熟

front [frʌnt]

名 前面
形 前面的
反 rear 後面、背後

英英 the side of an object that shows itself to view or that is normally seen first

例 Open the **front** door.
打開前門。

□ 三分熟
□ 五分熟
□ 七分熟
□ 全熟

fruit [frut]

名 水果

英英 the sweet and fleshy product of a tree that usually holds seed and can be eaten as food

例 My favorite **fruit** is durian.
我最喜歡的水果是榴槤。

□ 三分熟
□ 五分熟
□ 七分熟
□ 全熟

full [fʊl]

形 滿的、充滿的
反 empty 空的
片 full of 充滿

英英 containing or holding as much or as many as possible

例 The family is **full** of love.
這是一個充滿愛的家庭。

□ 三分熟
□ 五分熟
□ 七分熟
□ 全熟

fun [fʌn]

名 樂趣、玩笑
同 amusement 樂趣

英英 light-hearted amusement, full of pleasure

例 Learning English can be **fun**.
學英文可以很有趣的。

□ 三分熟
□ 五分熟
□ 七分熟
□ 全熟

fun·ny [ˈfʌnɪ]

形 滑稽的、有趣的
同 humorous 滑稽的

英英 very amusing or causing laughter or amusement

例 Your joke is not **funny** at all.
你的笑話一點也不好笑。

□ 三分熟
□ 五分熟
□ 七分熟
□ 全熟

Gg

game [gem]

名 遊戲、比賽
同 contest 比賽
片 see through sb.'s game
看穿某人的詭計

英英 taking part in an activity for amusement; a form of competitive activity or sport played according to a set of rules

例 The **game** is over.
遊戲結束了。

□ 三分熟
□ 五分熟
□ 七分熟
□ 全熟

gar·den [ˈɡɑrdn̩]

名 花園
片 botanical garden
植物園

英英 a piece of ground belonging to a house, typically containing a lawn and flowerbeds

例 Children playing in the **garden**.
孩子們在花園玩。

□ 三分熟
□ 五分熟
□ 七分熟
□ 全熟

🎧 **Track 047**

gas [gæs]

名 汽油、瓦斯
片 gas up 加汽油

英英 a fluid substance that is air-like which expands freely to fill any space available, regardless of its quantity

例 We are running out of **gas**.
我們快要沒有油了。

☐ 三分熟
☐ 五分熟
☐ 七分熟
☐ 全熟

gen·er·al [ˈdʒɛnərəl]

形 大體的、一般的
名 將軍
反 specific 特定的
片 in general 大致上

英英 affecting or concerning the majority, all, or most people or things; not specialized or limited to; a commander of an army, or an army officer ranking above the lieutenant general

例 Generally speaking, your project is good.
大體而言，你的計畫很好。

☐ 三分熟
☐ 五分熟
☐ 七分熟
☐ 全熟

get [gɛt]

動 獲得、成為、到達
同 obtain 獲得

英英 to pick up, move, deal with, or bring

例 I want to **get** a good grade.
我想要取得好成績。

☐ 三分熟
☐ 五分熟
☐ 七分熟
☐ 全熟

ghost [gost]

名 鬼、靈魂
同 soul 靈魂

英英 the spirit of a dead person which is believed to appear to the living

例 I am afraid of **ghost**.
我怕鬼。

☐ 三分熟
☐ 五分熟
☐ 七分熟
☐ 全熟

gift [gɪft]

名 禮物、天賦
同 present 禮物

英英 something given willingly to someone without obtaining payment; a present

例 Thank you for your **gift**.
謝謝你的禮物。

☐ 三分熟
☐ 五分熟
☐ 七分熟
☐ 全熟

girl [gɝl]

名 女孩
反 boy 男孩

英英 a female child; a young or relatively young woman

例 **Girls** are taught to be **girls**.
女孩被教導成一個女孩。

☐ 三分熟
☐ 五分熟
☐ 七分熟
☐ 全熟

give [gɪv]

動 給、提供、捐助
反 receive 接受

英英 to provide or freely transfer the possession of; cause to receive or have

例 I **gave** her my phone number.
我給了她我的手機號碼。

☐ 三分熟
☐ 五分熟
☐ 七分熟
☐ 全熟

glad [glæd]

形 高興的
同 joyous 高興的

英英 pleased; delighted; grateful; causing contentment

例 I am so **glad** to see you here.
很高興在這邊遇到妳。

☐ 三分熟
☐ 五分熟
☐ 七分熟
☐ 全熟

G

glass [ˈglæs]

名 玻璃、玻璃杯
同 pane 窗戶玻璃片

英英 a drinking container made of glass that is used for drinking

例 I need a **glass** of water please.
我要一杯水。

- 三分熟
- 五分熟
- 七分熟
- 全熟

glass·es [ˈglæsɪz]

名 眼鏡

英英 a lens or optical instrument, with two transparent parts worn in front of the eyes to enhance vision

例 My daughter needs a pair of **glasses**.
我女兒她需要一副眼鏡。

- 三分熟
- 五分熟
- 七分熟
- 全熟

go [go]

動 去、走
反 stay 留下

英英 move to or from a place; pass into or be in a specified state

例 I am **going** to school now.
我正在去學校。

- 三分熟
- 五分熟
- 七分熟
- 全熟

god/god·dess

[gɑd]/[ˈgɑdɪs]

名 神／女神

英英 the creator and supreme ruler of the universe

例 She's like a **goddess** to me.
她對我來說就像是個女神。

- 三分熟
- 五分熟
- 七分熟
- 全熟

gold [gold]

形 金的
名 金子

英英 made from or covered with gold; a yellow precious metal, used in jewelry and as a decoration, or as a monetary medium

例 This ring is made of **gold**.
這戒指是金子做的。

- 三分熟
- 五分熟
- 七分熟
- 全熟

good [gʊd]

形 好的、優良的
名 善、善行
同 fine 好的

英英 enjoyable, pleasant, interesting, to be desired or approved of

例 Jonny is a **good** student.
強尼是好學生。

- 三分熟
- 五分熟
- 七分熟
- 全熟

good-bye/good-bye/ good-by/good-by/ bye-bye/bye

[gʊdˈbaɪ]/[gʊdˈbaɪ]/ [gʊdˈbaɪ]/[ˈbaɪˌbaɪ]/[baɪ]

名 再見
片 visit to say goodbye 話別

英英 used to express good wishes or polite words when parting or ending a conversation

例 Never say **goodbye** to me.
不要對我說再見。

- 三分熟
- 五分熟
- 七分熟
- 全熟

Track 049

goose [ɡus]

名 鵝

英英 a large water bird similar to a duck

例 I saw a lot of **geese** in the pond.
我看到池塘中有很多鵝。

□ 三分熟
□ 五分熟
□ 七分熟
□ 全熟

---

grand [ɡrænd]

形 宏偉的、大的、豪華的
同 large 大的

英英 large, special, ambitious, or impressive in scale

例 This building is **grand**.
這座建築物很雄偉。

□ 三分熟
□ 五分熟
□ 七分熟
□ 全熟

---

grand·child

[ˈɡrændˌtʃaɪld]

名 孫子

英英 a child of one's son or daughter

例 She adores her **grandchild**.
她疼愛孫子。

□ 三分熟
□ 五分熟
□ 七分熟
□ 全熟

---

grand·daugh·ter

[ˈɡrændˌdɔtɚ]

名 孫女、外孫女

英英 a daughter of one's son or daughter

例 His **granddaughter** is pretty.
他的孫女很漂亮。

□ 三分熟
□ 五分熟
□ 七分熟
□ 全熟

---

grand·fath·er/ grand·pa

[ˈɡrændˌfɑðɚ]/[ˈɡrændpɑ]

名 祖父、外祖父

英英 the father of one's father or mother

例 I gradually understand what my **grandfather** said.
我漸漸明白祖父所說的。

□ 三分熟
□ 五分熟
□ 七分熟
□ 全熟

---

grand·moth·er/ grand·ma

[ˈɡrændˌmʌðɚ]/[ˈɡrændmʌ]

名 祖母、外祖母

英英 the mother of one's father or mother

例 My **grandmother** always sings a song to me.
我祖母總是唱歌給我聽。

□ 三分熟
□ 五分熟
□ 七分熟
□ 全熟

---

grand·son

[ˈɡrændˌsʌn]

名 孫子、外孫

英英 the son of one's son or daughter

例 She is stricter to her **grandson**.
她對孫子比較嚴格。

□ 三分熟
□ 五分熟
□ 七分熟
□ 全熟

---

grass [ɡræs]

名 草
同 lawn 草坪

英英 a common plant of narrow green leaves grown at ground level, growing wild or cultivated on lawns and pasture

例 The **grass** is so green.
這草很綠。

□ 三分熟
□ 五分熟
□ 七分熟
□ 全熟

gray/grey

[gre]/[gre]

名 灰色
形 灰色的、陰沉的

英英 the color of rain clouds; of the color that is between the colors of black and white

例 The sky is **gray**.
天空好灰。

☐ 三分熟
☐ 五分熟
☐ 七分熟
☐ 全熟

great [gret]

形 大量的、很好的、
　 偉大的、重要的
同 outstanding 突出的、
　 傑出的
片 a great amount 很多

英英 of a large extent, amount, or intensity considerably above those compared to average

例 They made a **great** amount of money.
他們賺很多錢。

☐ 三分熟
☐ 五分熟
☐ 七分熟
☐ 全熟

green [grin]

形 綠色的
名 綠色

英英 of the color between blue and yellow in the spectrum; colored like grass

例 **Green** apples are tasty.
青蘋果很好吃。

☐ 三分熟
☐ 五分熟
☐ 七分熟
☐ 全熟

ground [graʊnd]

名 地面、土地
同 surface 表面

英英 the solid surface of the earth below our feet; land of a specified kind

例 He fell down on the **ground**.
他跌在地板上。

☐ 三分熟
☐ 五分熟
☐ 七分熟
☐ 全熟

group [grup]

名 團體、組、群
動 聚合、成群
同 gather 收集

英英 a number of people or things located, gathered, connected, or classed together in one place; to form into a collection

例 This **group** of people are angry.
這群人很生氣。

☐ 三分熟
☐ 五分熟
☐ 七分熟
☐ 全熟

grow [gro]

動 種植、生長
同 mature 變成熟、長成
片 grow up 成長

英英 undergo natural development by physically changing and increasing in size

例 Some boys never **grow** up.
有些男孩永遠不會長大。

☐ 三分熟
☐ 五分熟
☐ 七分熟
☐ 全熟

guess [gɛs]

名 猜測、猜想
動 猜測、猜想
同 suppose 猜測、認為

英英 estimate or hypothesis (something) without sufficient information to ensure correctness

例 **Guess** what I cooked.
猜看看我煮了什麼。

☐ 三分熟
☐ 五分熟
☐ 七分熟
☐ 全熟

guest [gɛst]

名 客人
反 host 主人、東道主

英英 a person invited into someone's home or take part in a function

例 He is my **guest**.
他是我的客人。

☐ 三分熟
☐ 五分熟
☐ 七分熟
☐ 全熟

---

guide [gaɪd]

名 引導者、指南
動 引導、引領
同 lead 引導

英英 a person who advises or shows the way to others; a directing principle or standard; to lead or direct

例 I need a **guide**.
我需要一個領導者。

☐ 三分熟
☐ 五分熟
☐ 七分熟
☐ 全熟

---

gun [gʌn]

名 槍、砲

英英 a device for shooting something in a required direction

例 People can't use **guns** in Taiwan.
在臺灣，人們不可以使用槍。

☐ 三分熟
☐ 五分熟
☐ 七分熟
☐ 全熟

Hh

hair [hɛr]

名 頭髮

英英 the fine thread-like strands growing from the skin of mammals and other animals, or from the epidermis of plants

例 I love the color of your **hair**.
我喜歡你頭髮的顏色。

☐ 三分熟
☐ 五分熟
☐ 七分熟
☐ 全熟

---

hair·cut [ˈhɛrˌkʌt]

名 理髮

英英 the specific style in which someone's hair is cut into

例 You need to have a **haircut**.
你需要剪頭髮。

☐ 三分熟
☐ 五分熟
☐ 七分熟
☐ 全熟

---

half [hæf]

形 一半的
副 一半地
名 半、一半
片 half of 一半……

英英 when something is divided into two equal or corresponding parts

例 **Half** of my classmates are teachers now.
我有一半的同學現在都是老師。

☐ 三分熟
☐ 五分熟
☐ 七分熟
☐ 全熟

---

ham [hæm]

名 火腿

英英 meat from the back or upper part of a pig's leg salted and dried or smoked

例 I have **ham** for breakfast.
我吃火腿當早餐。

☐ 三分熟
☐ 五分熟
☐ 七分熟
☐ 全熟

H

hand [hænd]

名 手
動 遞交
反 foot 腳

英英 the end part of the arm extending from the wrist; to give to

例 His **hands** are big.
他的手很大。

☐ 三分熟
☐ 五分熟
☐ 七分熟
☐ 全熟

---

hap·pen [ˈhæpən]

動 發生、碰巧
同 occur 發生
片 happen to...
發生在……身上

英英 take place; occur, when a situation exists

例 Something **happened** yesterday.
昨天發生了點事情。

☐ 三分熟
☐ 五分熟
☐ 七分熟
☐ 全熟

---

hap·py [ˈhæpɪ]

形 快樂的、幸福的
反 sad 悲傷的

英英 feeling or showing pleasure or contentment

例 I am so **happy** to see you again.
我好高興可以再見到你。

☐ 三分熟
☐ 五分熟
☐ 七分熟
☐ 全熟

---

hard [hɑrd]

形 硬的、難的
副 努力地
同 stiff 硬的

英英 solid, firm, and stiff not easily broken, bent, or pierced

例 It's **hard** to say goodbye.
說再見很難。

☐ 三分熟
☐ 五分熟
☐ 七分熟
☐ 全熟

---

hat [hæt]

名 帽子
同 cap 帽子

英英 a shaped covering for the head, typically with a brim and a crown, used for fashion, or protection from the sun and natural elements

例 I need to buy a **hat**.
我要買一頂帽子。

☐ 三分熟
☐ 五分熟
☐ 七分熟
☐ 全熟

---

hate [het]

名 憎恨、厭惡
動 憎恨、不喜歡
反 love 愛、愛情

英英 feel intense dislike for or a strong aversion towards something or someone

例 I **hate** to be cheated.
我討厭被欺騙。

☐ 三分熟
☐ 五分熟
☐ 七分熟
☐ 全熟

---

have [hæv]

助 已經
動 吃、有

英英 possession of something

例 I **have** seen you before.
我曾經看過你。

☐ 三分熟
☐ 五分熟
☐ 七分熟
☐ 全熟

---

he [hi]

代 他

英英 used as the subject of the verb when referring to someone male who has been previously mentioned

例 **He** is just a boy.
他只是個男孩。

☐ 三分熟
☐ 五分熟
☐ 七分熟
☐ 全熟

🎧 **Track 053**

head [hɛd]

名 頭、領袖
動 率領、朝某方向行進
同 lead 引導

英英 the upper part of the human body, attached to the neck, or the front or upper part of the body of an animal, containing the brain, mouth, and sensory organs; to lead

例 He hit my **head**.
他打我的頭。

□ 三分熟
□ 五分熟
□ 七分熟
□ 全熟

health [hɛlθ]

名 健康

英英 in the condition of being free from illness or injury

例 **Health** is more important than wealth.
健康比財富重要。

□ 三分熟
□ 五分熟
□ 七分熟
□ 全熟

hear [hɪr]

動 聽到、聽說
同 listen 聽

英英 to be aware of or perceive (a sound) with the ears

例 I **heard** a strange sound.
我聽到一個奇怪的聲音。

□ 三分熟
□ 五分熟
□ 七分熟
□ 全熟

heart [hɑrt]

名 心、中心、核心
同 nucleus 核心
片 heart-broken 心碎的

英英 a hollow muscular organ that pumps the blood to circulate the body

例 My **heart** was broken.
我心都碎了。

□ 三分熟
□ 五分熟
□ 七分熟
□ 全熟

heat [hit]

名 熱、熱度
動 加熱
反 chill 寒氣

英英 the quality of being hot; high in temperature; to make hot

例 The **heat** of the oven is 750 degree.
烤箱溫度是 750 度。

□ 三分熟
□ 五分熟
□ 七分熟
□ 全熟

heav·y [ˈhɛvɪ]

形 重的、猛烈的、厚的
反 light 輕的
片 heavy rain 大雨

英英 of substantial weight; difficult to lift or move

例 The **heavy** rain caused the traffic jam.
這陣大雨造成交通癱瘓。

□ 三分熟
□ 五分熟
□ 七分熟
□ 全熟

hel·lo [həˈlo]

感 哈囉（問候語）、喂
（電話應答語）

英英 used as a greeting, a polite word to say, or to begin a telephone conversation

例 Say **hello** to the guests.
跟客人說哈囉。

□ 三分熟
□ 五分熟
□ 七分熟
□ 全熟

help [hɛlp]

名 幫助
動 幫助
同 aid 幫助

英英 to give assistance to, make it easier for (someone) to do something

例 Could you please **help** me?
你可以幫我嗎？

□ 三分熟
□ 五分熟
□ 七分熟
□ 全熟

her [hɝ]

代 她的

H

英英 the possessive form of she, which means that something belongs to a particular woman or girl

例 **Her** mother is young.
她的媽媽很年輕。

☐ 三分熟
☐ 五分熟
☐ 七分熟
☐ 全熟

---

hers [hɝz]

代 她的東西

英英 used to indicate something or something belong to a female that has just been mentioned

例 The fence divides my land from **hers**.
籬笆將我跟她的地隔開。

☐ 三分熟
☐ 五分熟
☐ 七分熟
☐ 全熟

---

here [hɪr]

副 在這裡、到這裡
名 這裡
反 there 那裡

英英 in, at, or to the current place or position

例 **Here** comes a bus.
有一輛公車來了。

☐ 三分熟
☐ 五分熟
☐ 七分熟
☐ 全熟

---

high [haɪ]

形 高的
副 高度地
反 low 低的

英英 of great distance from top to bottom; of a specified height

例 This mountain is so **high**.
這座山好高。

☐ 三分熟
☐ 五分熟
☐ 七分熟
☐ 全熟

---

hill [hɪl]

名 小山
同 mound 小丘

英英 a naturally raised area of land, of lesser height than a mountain

例 They live on the **hills**.
他們住在山丘上。

☐ 三分熟
☐ 五分熟
☐ 七分熟
☐ 全熟

---

him [hɪm]

代 他

英英 used after a verb or preposition referring to a previously mention male

例 She didn't love **him** anymore.
她不愛他了。

☐ 三分熟
☐ 五分熟
☐ 七分熟
☐ 全熟

---

his [hɪz]

代 他的、他的東西

英英 things that relate to or belong to a previously mentioned male

例 **His** bag is always heavy.
他的包包很重。

☐ 三分熟
☐ 五分熟
☐ 七分熟
☐ 全熟

---

his·to·ry [ˈhɪstərɪ]

名 歷史

英英 the study of past events; the past considered as a whole

例 I studied the **history** of Taiwan.
我讀臺灣史。

☐ 三分熟
☐ 五分熟
☐ 七分熟
☐ 全熟

🔊**Track 055**

---

hit [hɪt]

名 打、打擊
動 打、打擊
同 strike 打、打擊

英英 an instance of one thing coming in contact with another at great force; to direct a blow at (someone or something) with one's hand or a tool or weapon

例 Don't **hit** the dog.
不要打那隻狗。

☐ 三分熟
☐ 五分熟
☐ 七分熟
☐ 全熟

---

hold [hold]

動 握住、拿著、持有
名 把握、控制
同 grasp 抓緊、緊握
片 hold on 等一下

英英 to grasp, carry, or support something or someone

例 **Hold** the pen.
握住筆。

☐ 三分熟
☐ 五分熟
☐ 七分熟
☐ 全熟

---

hole [hol]

名 孔、洞
同 gap 裂口

英英 a hollow space in a solid object or surface

例 There is a **hole** on the wall.
牆上有一個洞。

☐ 三分熟
☐ 五分熟
☐ 七分熟
☐ 全熟

---

hol·i·day [ˈhɑləˌde]

名 假期、假日
反 weekday 工作日、平常日

英英 an extended period of rest and recreation, especially away from home

例 What do you want to do in the **holiday**?
你假日要做什麼呢？

☐ 三分熟
☐ 五分熟
☐ 七分熟
☐ 全熟

---

home [hom]

名 家、家鄉
形 家的、家鄉的
副 在家、回家
同 dwelling 住處

英英 the place where one lives and maintains a family; an institution for people needing professional care

例 I will go **home** this weekend.
我這禮拜要回家。

☐ 三分熟
☐ 五分熟
☐ 七分熟
☐ 全熟

---

home·work

[ˈhomˌwɝk]

名 家庭作業
同 task 工作、作業

英英 school work that a student is required to do at home

例 Do your **homework**.
做你的功課。

☐ 三分熟
☐ 五分熟
☐ 七分熟
☐ 全熟

---

hope [hop]

名 希望、期望
動 希望、期望
反 despair 絕望

英英 a feeling of expectation and want for something to happen

例 I **hope** to see you soon.
我希望趕快看到你。

☐ 三分熟
☐ 五分熟
☐ 七分熟
☐ 全熟

horse [hɔrs]

名 馬

H

英英 a large powerful four-legged mammal with a flowing mane and tail, used for riding, racing, and for pulling heavy loads

例 I rode a **horse** in Mongolia.
我在蒙古騎馬。

☐ 三分熟
☐ 五分熟
☐ 七分熟
☐ 全熟

---

hot [hɑt]

形 熱的、熱情的、辣的
反 icy 冰冷的

英英 having an extreme or high temperature; feeling or producing an uncomfortable sensation of heat

例 It is so **hot** in Taipei.
臺北很熱。

☐ 三分熟
☐ 五分熟
☐ 七分熟
☐ 全熟

---

hour [aʊr]

名 小時

英英 60 minutes; the 24th part of a day

例 I spend an **hour** studying English.
我花一個小時讀英文。

☐ 三分熟
☐ 五分熟
☐ 七分熟
☐ 全熟

---

house [haʊs]

名 房子、住宅
同 residence 房子、住宅

英英 a building for people to live

例 I want to buy a **house**.
我想要買房子。

☐ 三分熟
☐ 五分熟
☐ 七分熟
☐ 全熟

---

how [haʊ]

副 怎樣、如何

英英 in what way or by what means something is done

例 **How** to get to the train station?
請問該如何到火車站？

☐ 三分熟
☐ 五分熟
☐ 七分熟
☐ 全熟

---

huge [hjudʒ]

形 龐大的、巨大的
反 tiny 微小的

英英 extremely large

例 A **huge** sadness is in her mind.
她心中有巨大的傷痛。

☐ 三分熟
☐ 五分熟
☐ 七分熟
☐ 全熟

---

hu·man [ˈhjumən]

形 人的、人類的
名 人
同 man 人

英英 a man, woman, or child; relating to humankind

例 We are all **humans**.
我們都是人類。

☐ 三分熟
☐ 五分熟
☐ 七分熟
☐ 全熟

---

hun·dred [ˈhʌndrəd]

名 百、許多
形 百的、許多的
片 hundreds of 數百個

英英 ten more than ninety and ten less than one hundred and ten

例 I have a **hundred** dollars.
我有一百塊錢。

☐ 三分熟
☐ 五分熟
☐ 七分熟
☐ 全熟

hun·gry [ˈhʌŋgrɪ]

形 饑餓的

英英 feeling or showing hunger

例 He is always **hungry**.
他總是肚子餓。

☐ 三分熟
☐ 五分熟
☐ 七分熟
☐ 全熟

---

hurt [hɝt]

形 受傷的
動 疼痛
名 傷害

英英 to cause pain or injury; a wound

例 I get **hurt**.
我受傷了。

☐ 三分熟
☐ 五分熟
☐ 七分熟
☐ 全熟

---

hus·band

[ˈhʌzbənd]

名 丈夫
反 wife 妻子

英英 a married man considered in relation to his wife

例 Her **husband** is very nice to her.
她的丈夫對她很好。

☐ 三分熟
☐ 五分熟
☐ 七分熟
☐ 全熟

Ii

I [aɪ]

代 我

英英 used to refer to oneself as a speaker

例 **I** like to play basketball.
我喜歡打籃球。

☐ 三分熟
☐ 五分熟
☐ 七分熟
☐ 全熟

---

ice [aɪs]

名 冰
動 結冰
同 freeze 結冰

英英 frozen water; the solid state of transparent crystalline; to change into a frozen state

例 I need some **ice** for the beer.
我需要一點冰塊配啤酒。

☐ 三分熟
☐ 五分熟
☐ 七分熟
☐ 全熟

---

i·de·a [aɪˋdɪə]

名 主意、想法、觀念
同 notion 概念、想法

英英 a thought or suggestion about a course of action; a formulated thought or opinion

例 I have no **idea**.
我完全不知道。

☐ 三分熟
☐ 五分熟
☐ 七分熟
☐ 全熟

---

if [ɪf]

連 如果、是否

英英 used to express that a particular thing or event can or will happen only after another thing happens or comes true

例 What **if** it rains tomorrow?
如果明天下雨怎麼辦？

☐ 三分熟
☐ 五分熟
☐ 七分熟
☐ 全熟

im·por·tant

[ɪmˋpɔrtn̩t]

形 重要的
同 principal 重要的

英英 something or someone of great significance or value or to have high rank or social status

例 Health is **important**.
健康很重要。

☐ 三分熟
☐ 五分熟
☐ 七分熟
☐ 全熟

I

---

in [ɪn]

介 在……裡面、
　　在……之內
反 out 在……外面

英英 within in a space or inside of a container or enclosed by something

例 There is a ball **in** the box.
箱子裡有一顆球。

☐ 三分熟
☐ 五分熟
☐ 七分熟
☐ 全熟

---

inch [ɪntʃ]

名 英吋

英英 a unit of measure that is equal to one twelfth of a foot (2.54 cm)

例 The leaf is one **inch** long.
這草有一英吋這麼長。

☐ 三分熟
☐ 五分熟
☐ 七分熟
☐ 全熟

---

in·side [ˋɪn͵saɪd]

介 在……裡面
名 裡面、內部
形 裡面的
副 在裡面
反 outside 在……外面

英英 the inner side or surface of a thing or the interior part

例 What's **inside** the box?
箱子裡面是什麼？

☐ 三分熟
☐ 五分熟
☐ 七分熟
☐ 全熟

---

in·ter·est

[ˋɪntərɪst]

名 興趣、嗜好
動 使……感興趣
同 hobby 嗜好

英英 to give attention to or wanting to know about something or someone

例 What is your **interest**?
你的興趣是什麼？

☐ 三分熟
☐ 五分熟
☐ 七分熟
☐ 全熟

---

in·to [ˋɪntu]

介 到……裡面

英英 towards the inside or middle of something from outside, entering when a person or thing changes from one condition to another

例 Walk **into** the house.
走進這房子裡。

☐ 三分熟
☐ 五分熟
☐ 七分熟
☐ 全熟

---

i·ron [ˋaɪən]

名 鐵、熨斗
形 鐵的、剛強的
動 熨、燙平
同 steel 鋼鐵

英英 a strong, hard magnetic dark gray metal, used in steel-making, construction, and manufacturing; small amounts found in food and blood; to smooth with an iron

例 Please **iron** the skirt.
請燙好這裙子。

☐ 三分熟
☐ 五分熟
☐ 七分熟
☐ 全熟

🎧 **Track 059**

---

is [ɪz]

動 是

英英 he / she / it form of be, used before a singular object
例 She **is** a teacher. 她是老師。

☐ 三分熟
☐ 五分熟
☐ 七分熟
☐ 全熟

---

it [ɪt]

代 它

英英 used when referring to a thing, animal or situation which has previously been mentioned
例 **It** is the cute cat. 這隻貓很可愛。

☐ 三分熟
☐ 五分熟
☐ 七分熟
☐ 全熟

---

its [ɪts]

代 它的

英英 belonging to a thing, animal or situation which has been previously mentioned
例 The dog is chasing **its** tail. 那隻狗正在追牠的尾巴。

☐ 三分熟
☐ 五分熟
☐ 七分熟
☐ 全熟

Jj

---

jam [dʒæm]

名 果醬、堵塞
片 traffic jam 塞車

英英 a sweet soft food or spread preserved by cooking fruit with sugar; squeezing or packing tightly into a space
例 I need some **jam** for the bread. 我要果醬配麵包。

☐ 三分熟
☐ 五分熟
☐ 七分熟
☐ 全熟

Jan·u·ar·y/Jan.

[ˋdʒænjʊˌɛrɪ]

名 一月

英英 the first month of a year, comes before February
例 It is cold in **January** in Canada. 加拿大的一月很冷。

☐ 三分熟
☐ 五分熟
☐ 七分熟
☐ 全熟

---

job [dʒɑb]

名 工作
同 work 工作

英英 a regular work to earn money or a paid position; a task or bit of work
例 I am looking for a **job** now. 我在找新的工作。

☐ 三分熟
☐ 五分熟
☐ 七分熟
☐ 全熟

---

join [dʒɔɪn]

動 參加、加入
同 attend 參加

英英 to connect to, link, or fasten together to form a whole
例 Would you like to **join** us? 你要加入我們嗎？

☐ 三分熟
☐ 五分熟
☐ 七分熟
☐ 全熟

joke [dʒok]

名 笑話、玩笑
動 開玩笑
同 kid 開玩笑

英英 a funny story, statement, or trick old or done to make people laugh; to make fun of

例 Your **joke** is not funny at all.
你的笑話一點也不好笑。

☐ 三分熟
☐ 五分熟
☐ 七分熟
☐ 全熟

joy [dʒɔɪ]

名 歡樂、喜悅
同 sorrow 悲傷

英英 great happiness, person or thing that causes happiness or a cause of joy

例 My family is filled with **joy**.
我家充滿歡樂。

☐ 三分熟
☐ 五分熟
☐ 七分熟
☐ 全熟

juice [dʒus]

名 果汁

英英 the liquid that comes from fruit or vegetables; a drink originally made from fruits or vegetables

例 I want to have a glass of **juice**.
我想要來一杯果汁。

☐ 三分熟
☐ 五分熟
☐ 七分熟
☐ 全熟

July/Jul. [dʒuˋlaɪ]

名 七月

英英 the seventh month of a year, comes before June

例 We went to the beach in **July**.
我們七月去海邊玩。

☐ 三分熟
☐ 五分熟
☐ 七分熟
☐ 全熟

jump [dʒʌmp]

名 跳躍、跳動
動 跳躍、躍過
片 jump to conclusions 貿然下結論

英英 push oneself off the ground into the air using the muscles in the legs and feet

例 He **jumped** the obstacle easily.
他輕鬆地跳過了障礙物。

☐ 三分熟
☐ 五分熟
☐ 七分熟
☐ 全熟

June/Jun. [dʒun]

名 六月、瓊（女子名）
同 spring 跳、躍

英英 the sixth month of a year, comes after May

例 We graduated in **June**.
我們六月畢業。

☐ 三分熟
☐ 五分熟
☐ 七分熟
☐ 全熟

just [dʒʌst]

形 公正的、公平的
副 正好、恰好、剛才
同 fair 公平的
片 just as it is 照原樣

英英 behaving in a morally, fair, or correct way; appropriate or deserved

例 I **just** heard the news from my mom.
我剛從我媽那邊得知消息。

☐ 三分熟
☐ 五分熟
☐ 七分熟
☐ 全熟

J

Kk

Track 061

keep [kip]

名 保持、維持
動 保持、維持
同 maintain 維持

英英 have or continue to have possession of or retain or reserve for future use

例 Please **keep** it secret.
請守住祕密。

☐ 三分熟
☐ 五分熟
☐ 七分熟
☐ 全熟

---

keep·er [ˋkipɚ]

名 看守人

英英 a person who manages or keeps watch after something or someone

例 The door **keeper** is excellent.
這位守門員很傑出。

☐ 三分熟
☐ 五分熟
☐ 七分熟
☐ 全熟

---

key [ki]

形 主要的、關鍵的
名 鑰匙、關鍵
動 鍵入

英英 main; a person or thing that is very important and having great influence on other people or things

例 Your kindness is the **key**.
你的善良才是關鍵。

☐ 三分熟
☐ 五分熟
☐ 七分熟
☐ 全熟

---

kick [kɪk]

名 踢
動 踢

英英 to use force from the foot or feet; to strike or hit out the foot or feet

例 The boy **kicked** my leg.
那個男孩踢我的腿。

☐ 三分熟
☐ 五分熟
☐ 七分熟
☐ 全熟

---

kid [kɪd]

名 小孩
動 開玩笑、嘲弄
同 tease 嘲弄

英英 a young child or person; making fun of or laugh at someone

例 The **kid** is very naughty.
那個小孩太調皮了。

☐ 三分熟
☐ 五分熟
☐ 七分熟
☐ 全熟

---

kill [kɪl]

名 殺、獵物
動 殺、破壞
同 slay 殺

英英 to cause someone or something to die, create the death of; put something to the end

例 Don't **kill** Formosan bears.
別殺臺灣黑熊。

☐ 三分熟
☐ 五分熟
☐ 七分熟
☐ 全熟

---

kind [kaɪnd]

形 仁慈的
名 種類
反 cruel 殘酷的

英英 describe people who is gentle and friendly; people or things that have similar characteristics

例 The **kind** man helped many people.
那個仁慈的男人幫過很多人。

☐ 三分熟
☐ 五分熟
☐ 七分熟
☐ 全熟

---

king [kɪŋ]

名 國王
同 ruler 統治者

英英 the male ruler of a country or independent state, holding this position by inheriting it from birth

例 The **king** rules the country.
國王統治著整個國家。

☐ 三分熟
☐ 五分熟
☐ 七分熟
☐ 全熟

kiss [kɪs]

名 吻
動 吻

英英 touch or caress with the lips especially as a sign of love, affection, or greeting

例 Tom **kissed** me.
湯姆吻了我。

☐ 三分熟
☐ 五分熟
☐ 七分熟
☐ 全熟

K

---

kitch·en [ˋkɪtʃɪn]

名 廚房

英英 a room or area where food is prepared and cooked

例 I go to the **kitchen** to get food.
我去廚房找點食物。

☐ 三分熟
☐ 五分熟
☐ 七分熟
☐ 全熟

---

kite [kaɪt]

名 風箏
片 fly a kite 放風箏

英英 a flying object consisting of a light frame with thin material stretched over it, flown in the wind at the end of a long string

例 We used to fly the **kite**.
我們以前會一起放風箏。

☐ 三分熟
☐ 五分熟
☐ 七分熟
☐ 全熟

---

kit·ten/kit·ty

[ˋkɪtn̩]/[ˋkɪtɪ]

名 小貓

英英 a young or baby cat

例 The **kitten** was so small.
那隻小貓好小喔。

☐ 三分熟
☐ 五分熟
☐ 七分熟
☐ 全熟

---

knee [ni]

名 膝、膝蓋
片 knee down 下跪

英英 the joint between the thigh and the lower leg allowing a leg to bend; the upper surface of a one's thigh when in a sitting position

例 My grandmother's **knees** hurt.
我祖母的膝蓋會痛。

☐ 三分熟
☐ 五分熟
☐ 七分熟
☐ 全熟

---

knife [naɪf]

名 刀
同 blade 刀片

英英 a tool consisting of a metal blade and handle used for cutting or spreading food

例 There are many **knives** in the kitchen.
廚房裡有很多把刀子。

☐ 三分熟
☐ 五分熟
☐ 七分熟
☐ 全熟

---

know [no]

動 知道、瞭解、認識
同 understand 瞭解

英英 have knowledge or understanding through observation, inquiry, experience, or information

例 I don't **know** his name.
我不知道他的名字。

☐ 三分熟
☐ 五分熟
☐ 七分熟
☐ 全熟

Ll

🎧 Track 063

---

lack [læk]

名 缺乏
動 缺乏
同 absence 缺乏
片 lack of 缺乏

英英 when there is not enough of something if it is not available

例 Some children **lack** food.
有些孩子缺乏食物。

□ 三分熟
□ 五分熟
□ 七分熟
□ 全熟

---

la·dy [ˈledɪ]

名 女士、淑女
反 gentleman 紳士

英英 of referring or talking to a woman in a polife way; a woman of high social position

例 **Ladies** and gentlemen, the train is about to leave.
先生女士們，火車即將離開。

□ 三分熟
□ 五分熟
□ 七分熟
□ 全熟

---

lake [lek]

名 湖
同 pond 池塘

英英 a large area of water surrounded by land.

例 Ducks swam in the **lake**.
鴨子在湖裡面游泳。

□ 三分熟
□ 五分熟
□ 七分熟
□ 全熟

---

lamb [læm]

名 羔羊、小羊

英英 a young sheep or flesh of young sheep consumed as meat

例 The **lamb** is eaten by the tiger.
那隻小羊被老虎吃掉了。

□ 三分熟
□ 五分熟
□ 七分熟
□ 全熟

---

lamp [læmp]

名 燈
同 lantern 燈籠、提燈

英英 an electric, oil, or gas instrument used to give light

例 Please turn off the **lamp**.
請關掉燈。

□ 三分熟
□ 五分熟
□ 七分熟
□ 全熟

---

land [lænd]

名 陸地、土地
動 登陸、登岸
反 sea 海

英英 the part of the earth's surface not covered by water; ground used for farming and building purposes

例 The flight is **landing**.
飛機即將降落。

□ 三分熟
□ 五分熟
□ 七分熟
□ 全熟

---

large [lɑrdʒ]

形 大的、大量的
反 little 小的

英英 of considerable or great amount, size, extent, or capacity

例 We need a **large** bucket.
我們需要一個大的桶子。

□ 三分熟
□ 五分熟
□ 七分熟
□ 全熟

L

last [læst]

形 最後的
副 最後
名 最後
動 持續
同 final 最後的

英英 after or behind everyone or everything else

例 You are the **last**.
你是最後一個。

☐ 三分熟
☐ 五分熟
☐ 七分熟
☐ 全熟

late [let]

形 遲的、晚的
副 很遲、很晚
反 early 早的

英英 arriving, or happening after the planned, proper, usual, or expected time

例 I came home **late** today.
我今天晚回家。

☐ 三分熟
☐ 五分熟
☐ 七分熟
☐ 全熟

laugh [læf]

動 笑
名 笑、笑聲
反 weep 哭泣
片 laugh at 嘲笑

英英 smiling and making sounds with your voice to express happiness and amusement

例 He looked at me and **laughed**.
他看著我大笑。

☐ 三分熟
☐ 五分熟
☐ 七分熟
☐ 全熟

law [lɔ]

名 法律
同 rule 規定、章程

英英 a rule or system usually made by a government in a country or community as regulating the actions of its members and enforced by the imposition of penalties

例 The **law** in Singapore is strict.
新加坡的法律很嚴格。

☐ 三分熟
☐ 五分熟
☐ 七分熟
☐ 全熟

lay [le]

動 放置、產卵
同 put 放置

英英 put down, especially gently or carefully in a flat horizontal position; put down and set in position for use

例 **Lay** the bag on the table.
把包包放在桌上就好。

☐ 三分熟
☐ 五分熟
☐ 七分熟
☐ 全熟

la·zy [ˈlezɪ]

形 懶惰的
反 diligent 勤奮的

英英 unwilling to work or use energy, not putting effort into anything; a lack of effort or care

例 Lucy is very **lazy**.
露西很懶惰。

☐ 三分熟
☐ 五分熟
☐ 七分熟
☐ 全熟

lead [lid]

名 領導、榜樣
動 領導、引領
反 follow 跟隨

英英 cause (a person or animal) to follow with one, especially by drawing them along or by preceding them to a destination

例 You **lead** me to the forest.
你帶領我走向森林。

☐ 三分熟
☐ 五分熟
☐ 七分熟
☐ 全熟

🎧 **Track 065**

lead·er [ˈlidɚ]

名 領袖、領導者
同 chief 首領

英英 a person or thing that leads or controls others; a person or thing in control of a group

例 She is a good **leader**.
她是個好的領導者。

☐ 三分熟
☐ 五分熟
☐ 七分熟
☐ 全熟

leaf [lif]

名 葉

英英 a flattened, typically green, structure of a plant, that is attached to a stem grown from a tree

例 The **leaf** fell on the floor.
那片樹葉掉落在地板上。

☐ 三分熟
☐ 五分熟
☐ 七分熟
☐ 全熟

learn [lɝn]

動 學習、知悉、瞭解
反 teach 教導

英英 attaining knowledge of or skill in (something) through study or experience or by being taught in courses or institution

例 I've **learned** a lot from you.
我跟你學到很多。

☐ 三分熟
☐ 五分熟
☐ 七分熟
☐ 全熟

least [list]

名 最少、最小
形 最少的、最小的
副 最少、最小
同 minimum 最少、最小
片 last but not least...
最後一點……

英英 smallest in amount, number, or significance; less than anything or anyone

例 At **least**, you have done your best.
至少你努力過了。

☐ 三分熟
☐ 五分熟
☐ 七分熟
☐ 全熟

leave [liv]

動 離開
名 准假
同 depart 離開

英英 depart from or to stop living at

例 I have to **leave** now.
我現在要走了。

☐ 三分熟
☐ 五分熟
☐ 七分熟
☐ 全熟

left [lɛft]

形 左邊的
名 左邊
反 right 右邊

英英 on, towards, or relating to the side of a person or of a thing which is to the west when the person or thing is facing north

例 On your **left** side, you will see the bookstore.
在你左手邊會看到書店。

☐ 三分熟
☐ 五分熟
☐ 七分熟
☐ 全熟

leg [lɛg]

名 腿
反 arm 手臂

英英 one of the parts of the body on which a person or animal moves and stands

例 My **leg** hurts.
我的腳好痛。

☐ 三分熟
☐ 五分熟
☐ 七分熟
☐ 全熟

less [lɛs]

形 更少的、更小的
副 更少、更小
反 more 更多

英英 a smaller amount of; not so much; fewer in number, smaller in size
例 I have **less** money than she does.
我的錢比她更少。

☐三分熟
☐五分熟
☐七分熟
☐全熟

L

---

less·on [ˈlɛsṇ]

名 課
片 teach sb. a lesson 給某人教訓

英英 a period of time in which one is learning or teaching; a thing or experience learned
例 This **lesson** is more difficult.
這一課比較難。

☐三分熟
☐五分熟
☐七分熟
☐全熟

---

let [lɛt]

動 讓
同 allow 准許
片 let go of sth. 放掉某物

英英 to allow something to happen or someone to do something by permitting or not doing anything to stop an action
例 Never **let** me go.
不要讓我走。

☐三分熟
☐五分熟
☐七分熟
☐全熟

---

let·ter [ˈlɛtɚ]

名 字母、信

英英 a written message from one individual to another; any of the symbols of an alphabet
例 I wrote a **letter** to my mom.
我寫封信給我媽。

☐三分熟
☐五分熟
☐七分熟
☐全熟

---

lev·el [ˈlɛvḷ]

名 水準、標準
形 水平的
同 horizontal 水準的

英英 a horizontal plane or line with respect to the distance of a given point; on a horizontal plane; on a horizontal plane
例 The students are high-**level**.
這些學生程度很好。

☐三分熟
☐五分熟
☐七分熟
☐全熟

---

lie [laɪ]

名 謊言
動 說謊、位於、躺著
反 truth 實話

英英 be in or assume a horizontal or resting position on an elevated surface or on the ground
例 Don't **lie** to me.
不要對我說謊。

☐三分熟
☐五分熟
☐七分熟
☐全熟

---

life [laɪf]

名 生活、生命
同 existence 生命

英英 the period of time between life and death
例 We'll live a happy **life**.
我們會過得很開心。

☐三分熟
☐五分熟
☐七分熟
☐全熟

---

lift [lɪft]

名 舉起
動 升高、舉起
同 raise 舉起

英英 to move, raise or be raised from a lower position to a higher position or level; to pick up to a higher level
例 I can't **lift** the box.
我無法舉起這箱子。

☐三分熟
☐五分熟
☐七分熟
☐全熟

light [laɪt]

名 光、燈
形 輕的、光亮的
動 點燃、變亮
反 dark 黑暗

英英 the brightness that comes from the sun, moon, fire, and from electrical devices that make things visible; not heavy; to illuminate

例 The box is **light**.
這箱子很輕。

☐ 三分熟
☐ 五分熟
☐ 七分熟
☐ 全熟

---

like [laɪk]

動 喜歡
介 像、如
反 dislike 不喜歡

英英 similar to; in the same way of manner of someone or something

例 I **like** apples.
我喜歡蘋果。

☐ 三分熟
☐ 五分熟
☐ 七分熟
☐ 全熟

---

like·ly [ˈlaɪklɪ]

形 可能的
副 可能地
同 probable 可能的

英英 describes something that is possible, such as well might be the case; probable

例 You are **likely** to pass the exam.
你有可能通過考試。

☐ 三分熟
☐ 五分熟
☐ 七分熟
☐ 全熟

---

lil·y [ˈlɪlɪ]

名 百合花

英英 a large bell shaped flower on a tall, slender stem

例 There are **lilies** here.
這邊有很多百合花。

☐ 三分熟
☐ 五分熟
☐ 七分熟
☐ 全熟

---

line [laɪn]

名 線、線條
動 排隊、排成
同 string 繩、線

英英 a long, narrow mark or band on a surface; a length of cord, wire, etc. serving a purpose; to from a row

例 Draw a **line** here.
在這裡畫一條線。

☐ 三分熟
☐ 五分熟
☐ 七分熟
☐ 全熟

---

li·on [ˈlaɪən]

名 獅子

英英 a large tawny-colored cat originating from Africa and NW India, the male of which has a shaggy mane

例 There are **lions** in the zoo.
動物園裡面有獅子。

☐ 三分熟
☐ 五分熟
☐ 七分熟
☐ 全熟

---

lip [lɪp]

名 嘴唇

英英 either of the two soft, red fleshy parts forming the edges of the mouth opening

例 I bit my **lips**.
我咬到嘴唇了。

☐ 三分熟
☐ 五分熟
☐ 七分熟
☐ 全熟

---

list [lɪst]

名 清單、目錄、列表
動 列表、編目

英英 items or names written in consecutive order; to set forth in order

例 What's on your **list**?
你清單上有什麼？

☐ 三分熟
☐ 五分熟
☐ 七分熟
☐ 全熟

lis·ten [ˈlɪsn̩]

動 聽
同 hear 聽

英英 to give attention to a sound in order to hear it; make an effort to hear something
例 I love **listening** to my mother tell stories.
我喜歡聽媽媽說故事。

□ 三分熟
□ 五分熟
□ 七分熟
□ 全熟

lit·tle [ˈlɪtl̩]

形 小的
名 少許、一點
副 很少地
反 large 大的

英英 small in size, amount, number or degree
例 I know so **little** about him.
我只知道一點點關於他的事。

□ 三分熟
□ 五分熟
□ 七分熟
□ 全熟

live [laɪv]/[lɪv]

形 有生命的、活的
動 活、生存、居住
反 die 死

英英 remain alive; be alive at a specified time; to make a place your home
例 I **live** in Taipei.
我住在臺北。

□ 三分熟
□ 五分熟
□ 七分熟
□ 全熟

long [lɔŋ]

形 長（久）的
副 長期地
名 長時間
動 渴望
反 short 短的

英英 of a great distance or duration; relatively great in extent; great in length
例 **Long** time ago, there was a princess here.
很久以前，這裡有一個公主。

□ 三分熟
□ 五分熟
□ 七分熟
□ 全熟

look [lʊk]

名 看、樣子、臉色
動 看、注視
同 watch 看

英英 to direct your eyes toward certain areas in order to see
例 **Look** at me.
看著我。

□ 三分熟
□ 五分熟
□ 七分熟
□ 全熟

lot [lɑt]

名 很多
同 plenty 很多
片 a lot of 很多

英英 a large number or amount; a great deal
例 I have **lots** of questions.
我有很多問題。

□ 三分熟
□ 五分熟
□ 七分熟
□ 全熟

loud [laʊd]

形 大聲的、響亮的
反 silent 安靜的

英英 producing or capable of making great noise
例 The music is too **loud**.
這音樂太大聲了。

□ 三分熟
□ 五分熟
□ 七分熟
□ 全熟

love [lʌv]

動 愛、熱愛
名 愛
同 adore 熱愛

英英 an intense feeling of deep affection or liking to friends or family; a deep romantic or sexual attachment to another adult

例 I **love** to sing and dance with my best friends.
我熱愛和好朋友唱歌跳舞。

☐ 三分熟
☐ 五分熟
☐ 七分熟
☐ 全熟

low [lo]

形 低聲的、低的
副 向下、在下面
同 inferior 下方的

英英 toward the bottom of something, or close to the ground or at ground-level

例 The temperature in Russia is **low**.
俄國的氣溫很低。

☐ 三分熟
☐ 五分熟
☐ 七分熟
☐ 全熟

luck·y [ˈlʌkɪ]

形 有好運的、幸運的

英英 having, bringing, or resulting from good luck, having good things happen by chance

例 I am so **lucky** to meet you.
與你相遇好幸運。

☐ 三分熟
☐ 五分熟
☐ 七分熟
☐ 全熟

lunch/ lunch·eon

[lʌntʃ]/[ˈlʌntʃən]

名 午餐
片 lunch box 午餐餐盒

英英 a meal eaten in the middle of the day

例 I am having **lunch** with my mom.
我正在跟我媽吃午餐。

☐ 三分熟
☐ 五分熟
☐ 七分熟
☐ 全熟

Mm

ma·chine [məˈʃin]

名 機器、機械

英英 a piece of equipment or an apparatus with moving parts, for performing a particular task

例 We need to buy a washing **machine**.
我們要買一臺洗衣機。

☐ 三分熟
☐ 五分熟
☐ 七分熟
☐ 全熟

mad [mæd]

形 神經錯亂的、發瘋的
同 crazy 瘋狂的

英英 mentally ill; extremely foolish or ill-advised; showing impulsiveness, confusion, or frenzy; to become angry

例 My dad is **mad** at me.
我爸對我發飆。

☐ 三分熟
☐ 五分熟
☐ 七分熟
☐ 全熟

mail [mel]

名 郵件
動 郵寄
同 send 發送、寄

英英 letters and packages sent by post; to send by post

例 Send me a **mail** if you have time.
有空的時候寫信給我。

☐ 三分熟
☐ 五分熟
☐ 七分熟
☐ 全熟

make [mek]

動 做、製造
同 manufacture 製造

英英 to produce something by putting parts together or combining substances; cause to be or come about; force to do something

例 We **made** a card for mom.
我們做了張卡片給媽媽。

□ 三分熟
□ 五分熟
□ 七分熟
□ 全熟

M

man [mæn]

名 成年男人
名 人類（不分男女）

英英 an adult male human being; a male member of a workforce, team

例 The **man** is tall.
那男人很高。

□ 三分熟
□ 五分熟
□ 七分熟
□ 全熟

man·y [ˈmɛnɪ]

形 許多
同 numerous 很多

英英 a great number of

例 I have **many** friends.
我有很多朋友。

□ 三分熟
□ 五分熟
□ 七分熟
□ 全熟

map [mæp]

名 地圖
動 用地圖表示、
　 繪製地圖

英英 a drawing of an area of land or sea showing physical features, cities, roads, etc.; to picture in a chart

例 Don't forget to bring a **map** when travelling.
去旅行時別忘了帶地圖。

□ 三分熟
□ 五分熟
□ 七分熟
□ 全熟

March/Mar.

[mɑrtʃ]

名 三月

英英 the third month of a year, comes after February

例 My birthday is in **March**.
我的生日在三月。

□ 三分熟
□ 五分熟
□ 七分熟
□ 全熟

mar·ket [ˈmɑrkɪt]

名 市場

英英 a place or event for the purchase and sale of food, livestock, or other commodities

例 We go to the **market** in the morning.
我們早上去市場。

□ 三分熟
□ 五分熟
□ 七分熟
□ 全熟

mar·ry [ˈmærɪ]

動 使結為夫妻、結婚
反 divorce 離婚

英英 to legally take as one's wife or husband in an official or religious ceremony; to join (two people) in matrimony

例 Would you **marry** me?
你要跟我結婚嗎？

□ 三分熟
□ 五分熟
□ 七分熟
□ 全熟

mas·ter [ˈmæstɚ]

名 主人、大師、碩士
動 精通

英英 a person who has authority, control, or ownership; acquire complete knowledge or skill in

例 You are a **master** in English.
你是英文大師。

□ 三分熟
□ 五分熟
□ 七分熟
□ 全熟

🎧 Track 071

match [mætʃ]

名 比賽
動 相配
同 contest 比賽

英英 a competition or event in which people or teams compete against each other; correspond or cause to correspond; make or be harmonious

例 You two are **matching**.
你們很相配。

☐ 三分熟
☐ 五分熟
☐ 七分熟
☐ 全熟

mat·ter [ˋmætə]

名 事情、問題
動 要緊
同 affair 事情、事件

英英 physical substance or material in general, which possesses mass in the universe; to be of importance

例 What's the **matter**?
有什麼事情？

☐ 三分熟
☐ 五分熟
☐ 七分熟
☐ 全熟

May [me]

名 五月

英英 the fifth month of a year, comes after April

例 There are many flowers in the garden in **May**.
五月的花園裡有許多鮮花。

☐ 三分熟
☐ 五分熟
☐ 七分熟
☐ 全熟

may [me]

助 可以、可能

英英 used to show possibility

例 **May** I help you?
我可以幫你嗎？

☐ 三分熟
☐ 五分熟
☐ 七分熟
☐ 全熟

may·be [ˋmebɪ]

副 或許、大概

英英 used to express that something is possible or something having the possibility of being true

例 **Maybe** you should try again.
或許你可以再試試看。

☐ 三分熟
☐ 五分熟
☐ 七分熟
☐ 全熟

me [mi]

代 我

英英 usually used after a verb or preposition, or to refer to the person speaking or writing

例 Don't shout at **me**.
不要對我吼叫。

☐ 三分熟
☐ 五分熟
☐ 七分熟
☐ 全熟

mean [min]

動 意指、意謂
形 惡劣的
同 indicate 指出、顯示

英英 to express or represent an idea, thought, or fact; unwilling to give or share; not generous; unkind or unpleasant

例 Don't be so **mean** to me.
不要對我那麼惡劣。

☐ 三分熟
☐ 五分熟
☐ 七分熟
☐ 全熟

meat [mit]

名 （食用）肉
反 vegetable 蔬菜

英英 the flesh of an animal used as food; the main substance or chief part

例 I ate too much **meat** recently.
我最近吃太多肉了。

☐ 三分熟
☐ 五分熟
☐ 七分熟
☐ 全熟

meet [mit]

動 碰見、遇到、舉行集會、開會

同 encounter 碰見

英英 to come together with at the same place and time intentionally; see or be introduced to for the first time

例 Nice to **meet** you.
很高興遇到妳。

□ 三分熟
□ 五分熟
□ 七分熟
□ 全熟

mid·dle [ˈmɪdḷ]

名 中部、中間、在……中間

形 居中的

英英 the central part to something; in between two ends of something

例 She sat in the **middle**.
她坐在中間。

□ 三分熟
□ 五分熟
□ 七分熟
□ 全熟

mile [maɪl]

名 英里（－ 1.6 公里）

英英 a unit of distance equal to 1,760 yards (approximately 1.609 kilometers)

例 It's a **mile** away from here.
離這裡一英里遠。

□ 三分熟
□ 五分熟
□ 七分熟
□ 全熟

milk [mɪlk]

名 牛奶

英英 a white liquid produced by female mammals for the nourishment of their young

例 The cat drank **milk**.
這隻貓喝了牛奶。

□ 三分熟
□ 五分熟
□ 七分熟
□ 全熟

mind [maɪnd]

名 頭腦、思想

動 介意

反 body 身體

英英 a part of a person that makes it possible to think, feel emotions and understand things; a person's intellect or memory; to feel annoyanc

例 Would you **mind**?
你會介意嗎？

□ 三分熟
□ 五分熟
□ 七分熟
□ 全熟

min·ute [ˈmɪnɪt]

名 分、片刻

同 moment 片刻

英英 any of the 60 parts an hour is divided into, consisting of 60 seconds

例 Wait a **minute**.
等我一下。

□ 三分熟
□ 五分熟
□ 七分熟
□ 全熟

Ms./Miss [mɪs]

名 小姐

反 Mr./Mister 先生

英英 a girl or young woman who is not married

例 **Miss** Lee is nice to us.
李小姐對我們很好。

□ 二分熟
□ 五分熟
□ 七分熟
□ 全熟

miss [mɪs]

動 想念、懷念

名 失誤、未擊中

反 hit 擊中

英英 to feel the need of; failure to hit, reach, or make contact with; failure to notice, hear, or understand

例 I **miss** you all the time.
我總是很想你。

□ 三分熟
□ 五分熟
□ 十分熟
□ 全熟

M

Track 073

mis·take [mɪˋstek]

名 錯誤、過失
同 error 錯誤
片 make a mistake 犯錯

英英 an action, decision, or judgment which produces an unwanted or unexpected result

例 Don't make any **mistake**.
不要犯錯。

☐ 三分熟
☐ 五分熟
☐ 七分熟
☐ 全熟

mo·ment

[ˋmomənt]

名 一會兒、片刻
同 instant 頃刻、一剎那
片 in a moment 一會兒

英英 a short or brief period of time; an exact point in time

例 I'll be back in a **moment**.
我一會兒就會回來。

☐ 三分熟
☐ 五分熟
☐ 七分熟
☐ 全熟

mom·my/mom/ mom·ma/ma/ mum·my/ma·ma

[ˋmɑmɪ]/[mɑm]/[ˋmɑmɑ]/ [mɑ]/[ˋmʌmɪ]/[mɑmə]

名 媽咪

英英 one's mother; a female parent

例 The baby is looking for its **mommy**.
那個嬰兒正在尋找媽媽。

☐ 三分熟
☐ 五分熟
☐ 七分熟
☐ 全熟

Mon·day/Mon.

[ˋmʌnde]

名 星期一
片 Monday blue
星期一憂鬱症

英英 the day of the week before Tuesday and following Sunday

例 I saw him this **Monday**.
我這個星期一有看到他。

☐ 三分熟
☐ 五分熟
☐ 七分熟
☐ 全熟

mon·ey [ˋmʌnɪ]

名 錢、貨幣
同 cash 現金

英英 a medium of exchange in the form of coins and banknotes

例 I have no **money**.
我沒有錢。

☐ 三分熟
☐ 五分熟
☐ 七分熟
☐ 全熟

mon·key [ˋmʌŋkɪ]

名 猴、猿

英英 a small to medium-sized primate with a long tail that lives in tropical countries

例 He's like a **monkey**.
他就像隻猴子一樣。

☐ 三分熟
☐ 五分熟
☐ 七分熟
☐ 全熟

month [mʌnθ]

名 月

英英 a period of about four weeks divided into twelve periods of a year

例 I visit my grandmother every **month**.
我每個月都會去看我奶奶。

☐ 三分熟
☐ 五分熟
☐ 七分熟
☐ 全熟

M

moon [mun]

名 月亮
反 sun 太陽

英英 a round object that orbits the earth every 28 days and shines by reflected light from the sun

例 Don't point at the **moon**.
不要用手指月亮。

☐ 三分熟
☐ 五分熟
☐ 七分熟
☐ 全熟

---

more [mor]

形 更多的、更大的
反 less 更少的、更小的

英英 a larger or extra number or amount of something

例 The **more** you read, the **more** you know.
你讀得越多，你知道得越多。

☐ 三分熟
☐ 五分熟
☐ 七分熟
☐ 全熟

---

morn·ing [ˈmɔrnɪŋ]

名 早上、上午
反 evening 傍晚、晚上

英英 the period of time between midnight and noon, especially from when the sun rises to noon

例 He always sleeps at six in the **morning**.
他總是早上六點才睡覺。

☐ 三分熟
☐ 五分熟
☐ 七分熟
☐ 全熟

---

most [most]

形 最多的、大部分的
名 最大多數、大部分
反 least 最少的

英英 the biggest quantity or amount of; more than anything or anyone else

例 **Most** people don't like the weather in Taipei.
大部分的人都不喜歡臺北的天氣。

☐ 三分熟
☐ 五分熟
☐ 七分熟
☐ 全熟

---

moth·er [ˈmʌðɚ]

名 母親、媽媽
反 father 爸爸

英英 a parent of female gender

例 My **mother** is young.
我媽媽很年輕。

☐ 三分熟
☐ 五分熟
☐ 七分熟
☐ 全熟

---

moun·tain [ˈmaʊntṇ]

名 高山

英英 a mass of land rising abruptly from the Earth's surface and to a large height from the surrounding level

例 The **mountain** is high.
這座山很高。

☐ 三分熟
☐ 五分熟
☐ 七分熟
☐ 全熟

---

mouse [maʊs]

名 老鼠
同 rat 鼠

英英 a small rodent with short fur, a pointed snout, relatively large ears and eyes, and a long thin tail

例 I keep a **mouse** as a pet.
我養了一隻老鼠當寵物。

☐ 三分熟
☐ 五分熟
☐ 七分熟
☐ 全熟

---

mouth [maʊθ]

名 嘴、口、口腔

英英 the space between the lips in the body of most animals through which food is taken and sounds are emitted

例 His **mouth** is full of food.
他的嘴裡充滿了食物。

☐ 三分熟
☐ 五分熟
☐ 七分熟
☐ 全熟

🎧 **Track 075**

move [muv]

動 移動、行動
反 stop 停

英英 go or cause to go in a certain direction or manner; change or cause to change position

例 **Move** to the center of the car.
請往車廂內部移動。

☐ 三分熟
☐ 五分熟
☐ 七分熟
☐ 全熟

---

move·ment

[`muvmənt]

名 運動、活動、移動
同 motion 運動、活動

英英 a change of place or position; the process of moving or the state of being moved

例 The **movement** is significant.
這個活動很有代表性。

☐ 三分熟
☐ 五分熟
☐ 七分熟
☐ 全熟

**mov·ie/
mo·tionpic·ture/
film/cin·e·ma**

[`muvɪ]/[`moʃən ˌpɪktʃɚ]/

[film]/[`sɪnəmə]

名 （一部）電影
片 see a movie 看電影

英英 a cinematic film

例 I had a **movie** date with her.
我約她看電影。

☐ 三分熟
☐ 五分熟
☐ 七分熟
☐ 全熟

Mr./Mis·ter

[`mɪstɚ]

名 對男士的稱呼、先生

英英 an informal and often rude form of address for a man whose name you do not know

例 **Mr**. Brown is our neighbor.
布朗先生是我們的鄰居。

☐ 三分熟
☐ 五分熟
☐ 七分熟
☐ 全熟

Mrs. [`mɪsɪz]

名 夫人

英英 a title used a married woman before her family name or full name

例 **Mrs**. Lin went here last night.
林夫人昨晚來過這裡。

☐ 三分熟
☐ 五分熟
☐ 七分熟
☐ 全熟

Ms. [mɪz]

名 女士
（代替 Miss 或 Mrs. 的字，
不指明對方的婚姻狀況）

英英 a title used before a woman's family name or full name, whether she is married or not

例 **Ms**. Chen will take her goods tomorrow.
林女士明天會來拿她的貨物。

☐ 三分熟
☐ 五分熟
☐ 七分熟
☐ 全熟

---

much [mʌtʃ]

名 許多
副 很、十分
形 許多的
（修飾不可數名詞）
反 little 少、不多的

英英 a large amount of something, often more than wanted; indicating that someone or something is a poor specimen

例 How **much** is it?
這多少錢？

☐ 三分熟
☐ 五分熟
☐ 七分熟
☐ 全熟

N

mud [mʌd]

名 爛泥、稀泥
同 dirt 爛泥

英英 a liquid soft, sticky mixture consisting of mixed soil and water

例 The road is covered by the **mud**.
道路上都覆蓋著爛泥。

☐ 三分熟
☐ 五分熟
☐ 七分熟
☐ 全熟

mug [mʌg]

名 帶柄的大杯子、馬克杯

英英 a large cylindrical cup with a handle and straight sides usually used for hot drinks

例 I gave the poor man a **mug** of hot milk.
我給那可憐的男人一杯熱牛奶。

☐ 三分熟
☐ 五分熟
☐ 七分熟
☐ 全熟

mu·sic [ˋmjuzɪk]

名 音樂
片 listen to music
聽音樂

英英 the art of combining a pattern of sounds whether vocal or instrumental

例 I love pop **music**.
我喜歡流行音樂。

☐ 三分熟
☐ 五分熟
☐ 七分熟
☐ 全熟

must [mʌst]

助動 必須、必定

英英 necessary or very important that something happens or gets done in the present or future

例 You **must** go.
你必須要走。

☐ 三分熟
☐ 五分熟
☐ 七分熟
☐ 全熟

my [maɪ]

代 我的

英英 of or belonging or related to the person who is speaking

例 **My** bag is heavy.
我的包包很重。

☐ 三分熟
☐ 五分熟
☐ 七分熟
☐ 全熟

Nn

name [nem]

名 名字、姓名、名稱、名義
同 label 名字、稱號

英英 the word or group of words by which someone or something is known, addressed, or referred to

例 What's in a **name**?
名字有什麼意義？

☐ 三分熟
☐ 五分熟
☐ 七分熟
☐ 全熟

na·tion [ˋneʃən]

名 國家
同 country 國家

英英 a large body of people united by common descent, culture, or language, living in a country

例 We are a strong **nation**.
我們是個很強壯的國家。

☐ 三分熟
☐ 五分熟
☐ 七分熟
☐ 全熟

na·ture [ˋnetʃɚ]

名 自然界、大自然
片 Mother Nature
大自然

英英 all plants, animals, substances, the landscape, and natural phenomena, which are not made by humans

例 I go to the **nature** to relax.
我在大自然中才能放鬆自己。

☐ 三分熟
☐ 五分熟
☐ 七分熟
☐ 全熟

🎧 Track 077

near [nɪr]

形 近的、接近的、近親的、親密的

反 far 遠的

英英 not far away in distance, at or to a short distance in space or time

例 There is a convenient store **near** here.
這附近有家便利商店。

☐ 三分熟
☐ 五分熟
☐ 七分熟
☐ 全熟

---

neck [nɛk]

名 頸、脖子

英英 the part of the body connecting the head to the rest of the body, between the head and shoulders

例 The giraffe has a long **neck**.
長頸鹿有很長的脖子。

☐ 三分熟
☐ 五分熟
☐ 七分熟
☐ 全熟

---

need [nid]

名 需要、必要
動 需要
同 demand 需要、需求
片 in need 需要幫助的

英英 require (something) because it is essential or very important to have or to do

例 I **need** some water.
我需要一些水。

☐ 三分熟
☐ 五分熟
☐ 七分熟
☐ 全熟

---

nev·er [ˈnɛvɚ]

副 從來沒有、決不、永不
反 ever 始終、曾經

英英 not ever; not at any time

例 **Never** say **never**.
永不言敗。

☐ 三分熟
☐ 五分熟
☐ 七分熟
☐ 全熟

---

new [nju]

形 新的
反 old 老舊的

英英 not existing or different from before; recently made, introduced, or discovered for the first time at present or recent

例 I am looking for a **new** job.
我在找新的工作。

☐ 三分熟
☐ 五分熟
☐ 七分熟
☐ 全熟

---

news [njuz]

名 新聞、消息
（不可數名詞）
同 information
消息、報導

英英 the announcement of newly received or noteworthy information about recent events

例 I got the **news** from the radio.
我從廣播上聽到新聞。

☐ 三分熟
☐ 五分熟
☐ 七分熟
☐ 全熟

---

news·pa·per

[ˈnjuzˌpepɚ]

名 報紙

英英 a daily or weekly publication consisting of large, folded sheets of paper, containing news, articles, and advertisements

例 My grandma reads **newspaper** every morning.
我祖母每天都會看報紙。

☐ 三分熟
☐ 五分熟
☐ 七分熟
☐ 全熟

N

next [nɛkst]

副 其次、然後
形 其次的
同 subsequent 後來的

英英 coming immediately after the present one in time, space, or order; the nearest to now

例 See you **next** time.
下次見。

□三分熟
□五分熟
□七分熟
□全熟

---

nice [naɪs]

形 和藹的、善良的、好的
反 nasty 惡意的

英英 pleasant; agreeable; satisfactory; to emphasize positive qualities; kind

例 The teacher is very **nice**.
那老師人很好。

□三分熟
□五分熟
□七分熟
□全熟

---

night [naɪt]

名 晚上
反 day 白天

英英 the time from sunset to sunrise, the time when it is dark and people usually go to sleep

例 She didn't come home last **night**.
她昨晚沒有回家。

□三分熟
□五分熟
□七分熟
□全熟

---

nine [naɪn]

名 九個

英英 one number less than ten and more than eight

例 The fox doesn't have **nine** tails.
狐狸沒有九條尾巴。

□三分熟
□五分熟
□七分熟
□全熟

---

nine·teen

[ˋnaɪnˏtin]

名 十九

英英 one number less than twenty and more than eighteen

例 I have **nineteen** bottles of beer.
我有十九罐啤酒。

□三分熟
□五分熟
□七分熟
□全熟

---

nine·ty [ˋnaɪntɪ]

名 九十

英英 one more than eighty-nine and less than ninety-one

例 My grandfather died in his **ninety**.
我祖父九十歲時候過世。

□三分熟
□五分熟
□七分熟
□全熟

---

no/nope

[no]/[nop]

形 沒有、不、無

英英 not any; not one; not a; give a negative answer

例 I have **no** idea.
我沒有想法。

□三分熟
□五分熟
□七分熟
□全熟

---

noise [nɔɪz]

名 喧鬧聲、噪音、聲音
反 silence 安靜

英英 a sound, often loud, unpleasant, or disturbing

例 Stop making the **noise**.
不要製造噪音。

□三分熟
□五分熟
□七分熟
□全熟

---

nois·y [ˋnɔɪzɪ]

形 嘈雜的、喧鬧的、熙熙攘攘的
反 silent 安靜的

英英 people or things that are full of noise, or making a lot of noise

例 The baby is very **noisy**.
那嬰兒好吵。

□三分熟
□五分熟
□七分熟
□全熟

noon [nun]

名 正午、中午

英英 twelve o'clock in the middle of the day; midday

例 We had a meeting at **noon**.
我們中午時候開會。

☐三分熟
☐五分熟
☐七分熟
☐全熟

---

nor [nɔr]

連 既不……也不、
（兩者）都不
反 or 或是

英英 used after "neither" to introduce the next set of negative possibilities in a sentence

例 Neither he **nor** she will come.
他跟她都不會來。

☐三分熟
☐五分熟
☐七分熟
☐全熟

---

north [nɔrθ]

名 北、北方
形 北方的
反 south 南方、南方的

英英 the direction in which a compass needle normally points, towards the horizon on the left-hand side of a person facing the rising sun

例 **North** Korea is testing their nuclear weapons.
北韓在測試他們的核武。

☐三分熟
☐五分熟
☐七分熟
☐全熟

---

nose [noz]

名 鼻子

英英 the facial part above the mouth, with nostrils used in breathing and smelling

例 Cleopatra's **nose** is pretty.
埃及豔后的鼻子很漂亮。

☐三分熟
☐五分熟
☐七分熟
☐全熟

---

not [nɑt]

副 不（表示否定）

英英 used to form a negative phrase or sentence; gives the next word or group of words a negative meaning

例 I do **not** like the cake.
我不喜歡這蛋糕。

☐三分熟
☐五分熟
☐七分熟
☐全熟

---

note [not]

名 筆記、便條
動 記錄、注釋
同 write 寫下
片 take a note 記筆記

英英 a brief letter or words written to help you remember something

例 Don't forget to take a **note**.
別忘了記筆記。

☐三分熟
☐五分熟
☐七分熟
☐全熟

---

noth·ing [ˈnʌθɪŋ]

副 決不、毫不
名 無關緊要的人、事、物

英英 not anything; something of no importance, concern, or of value; a thing of no value, use, or importance; a nobody

例 There is **nothing** left to say.
沒有什麼好說的。

☐三分熟
☐五分熟
☐七分熟
☐全熟

---

no·tice [ˈnotɪs]

動 注意
名 佈告、公告、啟事
反 ignore 忽略

英英 attention; observation; awareness of something; advanced notification or warning

例 I didn't **notice** what she said.
我沒有注意她說什麼。

☐三分熟
☐五分熟
☐七分熟
☐全熟

O

No·vem·ber/
Nov. [noˋvɛmbɚ]

名 十一月

英英 the eleventh month of the year

例 Let's go hiking in **November**.
十一月來健行吧。

☐ 三分熟
☐ 五分熟
☐ 七分熟
☐ 全熟

---

now [naʊ]

副 現在、此刻
名 如今、目前
反 then 那時、當時

英英 immediately or at the present time; at or from this precise moment

例 **Now**, I know everything.
現在我知道一切了。

☐ 三分熟
☐ 五分熟
☐ 七分熟
☐ 全熟

---

num·ber [ˋnʌmbɚ]

名 數、數字

英英 a quantity or value used in a counting system expressed by a word, symbol, or figure

例 What's the **number** of Kobe?
柯比是幾號？

☐ 三分熟
☐ 五分熟
☐ 七分熟
☐ 全熟

---

nurse [nɝs]

名 護士

英英 a person who is trained to care for the sick or injured people

例 My sister works as a **nurse** in this hospital.
我姐姐在這家醫院工作。

☐ 三分熟
☐ 五分熟
☐ 七分熟
☐ 全熟

Oo

O.K./OK/okay
[ˋoˏke]

名 好、沒問題

英英 to show that you agree with someone to do something

例 **OK**, no problem!.
好的，沒問題！

☐ 三分熟
☐ 五分熟
☐ 七分熟
☐ 全熟

---

o·cean [ˋoʃən]

名 海洋
同 sea 海洋

英英 a very large expanse of sea; one of the five main areas the sea is divided into

例 The Pacific **Ocean** is the largest one.
太平洋是最大的海洋。

☐ 三分熟
☐ 五分熟
☐ 七分熟
☐ 全熟

---

o'clock [əˋklɑk]

副 ……點鐘

英英 used in specifying the hour when telling the time

例 Wake up at 6 **o'clock**.
六點起床。

☐ 三分熟
☐ 五分熟
☐ 七分熟
☐ 全熟

Oc·to·ber/Oct.
[ɑkˋtobɚ]

名 十月

英英 the tenth month of the year, comes after September

例 The National Day of ROC is on **October** 10th.
國慶日在十月十日。

☐ 三分熟
☐ 五分熟
☐ 七分熟
☐ 全熟

🎧 Track 081

of [əv]

介 含有、由⋯⋯製成、關於、從、來自

片 be made of 由⋯⋯製成

英英 to show possession, belonging, relating, or origin

例 The table is made **of** wood.
這桌子是木頭做成的。

☐ 三分熟
☐ 五分熟
☐ 七分熟
☐ 全熟

---

off [ɔf]

介 從⋯⋯下來、離開⋯⋯、不在⋯⋯之上

副 脫開、去掉

英英 away from a place or position, especially the present place, position or time, not on something

例 I will take a day **off** tomorrow.
我明天將休息一天。

☐ 三分熟
☐ 五分熟
☐ 七分熟
☐ 全熟

---

of·fice [ˈɔfɪs]

名 辦公室

英英 a room, set of rooms, or building where people do non-manual work

例 He stayed in the **office** last night.
他昨天晚上待在辦公室。

☐ 三分熟
☐ 五分熟
☐ 七分熟
☐ 全熟

---

of·fi·cer [ˈɔfəsɚ]

名 官員
同 official 官員

英英 a person in a position of authority, especially a member of the armed forces who holds a commission or a member of the police force

例 The **officer** is very mean.
那個官員很苛刻。

☐ 三分熟
☐ 五分熟
☐ 七分熟
☐ 全熟

---

of·ten [ˈɔfən]

副 常常、經常

英英 frequently, occurring many times; in many instances

例 She's **often** late.
她常常遲到。

☐ 三分熟
☐ 五分熟
☐ 七分熟
☐ 全熟

---

oil [ɔɪl]

名 油
同 petroleum 石油

英英 a thick liquid obtained from petroleum, used especially as a fuel or lubricant, or from plants and vegetables, used in cooking

例 You need more **oil** to fry the chicken.
你需要多一點油來炸雞。

☐ 三分熟
☐ 五分熟
☐ 七分熟
☐ 全熟

---

old [old]

形 年老的、舊的
反 young 年輕的

英英 having lived or existed for a long time; no longer young; made or built long ago

例 You are too **old**.
你太老了。

☐ 三分熟
☐ 五分熟
☐ 七分熟
☐ 全熟

---

on [ɑn]

介 （表示地點）在⋯⋯上、在⋯⋯的時候、在⋯⋯狀態中

副 在上

英英 something that is touching something else below it, or that something is moving into such a position

例 The book is **on** the table.
那本書在桌子上。

☐ 三分熟
☐ 五分熟
☐ 七分熟
☐ 全熟

once [wʌns]

副 一次、曾經
連 一旦
名 一次
反 again 再一次

英英 on one single occasion or for one time only

例 I have met her **once**.
我見過她一次。

☐ 三分熟
☐ 五分熟
☐ 七分熟
☐ 全熟

O

---

one [wʌn]

形 一的、一個的
名 一、一個

英英 single, a piece, a particular person in a group

例 I have **one** more thing to say.
我還有一件事要說。

☐ 三分熟
☐ 五分熟
☐ 七分熟
☐ 全熟

---

on·ly [ˈonlɪ]

形 唯一的、僅有的
副 只、僅僅
同 simply 僅僅、只不過

英英 a single one or very few of something, or that there are no others, not more than a certain size or amount

例 I **only** want you to tell me the truth.
我只是要你告訴我實話。

☐ 三分熟
☐ 五分熟
☐ 七分熟
☐ 全熟

---

o·pen [ˈopən]

形 開的、公開的
動 打開
反 close 關
片 open-minded
　　心胸開闊

英英 allowing access, passage, or view; changes to a position that is not closed, fastened, or restricted; to move from closed position

例 **Open** the door, please.
請打開門。

☐ 三分熟
☐ 五分熟
☐ 七分熟
☐ 全熟

---

or [ɔr]

連 或者、否則

英英 to connect different possibilities, before the last in a list of possibilities

例 Which one do you want, juice **or** tea?
你要哪一個，果汁還是茶？

☐ 三分熟
☐ 五分熟
☐ 七分熟
☐ 全熟

---

or·ange [ˈɔrɪndʒ]

名 柳丁、柑橘
形 橘色的

英英 a large round citrus fruit with a tough bright reddish-yellow rind, a color mixture of red and yellow

例 There are **oranges** on the tree.
樹上有橘子。

☐ 三分熟
☐ 五分熟
☐ 七分熟
☐ 全熟

---

or·der [ˈɔrdɚ]

名 次序、順序、命令
動 命令、訂購
同 command 指揮、命令

英英 the arrangement of people or things in sequence or according to a certain method

例 I have **ordered** a meal.
我訂了一個餐點。

☐ 三分熟
☐ 五分熟
☐ 七分熟
☐ 全熟

🎧 **Track 083**

---

oth·er [ˈʌðɚ]

形 其他的、另外的
同 additional 其他的

英英 as well as the thing or person already mentioned or similar to those talked about

例 Do you have some **other** questions?
你有其他問題嗎？

☐ 三分熟
☐ 五分熟
☐ 七分熟
☐ 全熟

---

our(s) [ˈaʊr(z)]

代 我們的（東西）

英英 of or belonging to us

例 This is **our** home.
這是我們的家。

☐ 三分熟
☐ 五分熟
☐ 七分熟
☐ 全熟

---

out [aʊt]

副 離開、向外
形 外面的、在外的
反 in 在裡面的

英英 not inside of a place or container

例 Get **out** of here.
離開這裡。

☐ 三分熟
☐ 五分熟
☐ 七分熟
☐ 全熟

---

out·side [ˈaʊtˌsaɪd]

介 在……外面
形 外面的
名 外部、外面
反 inside 裡面的

英英 not inside; the external side or surface of something

例 There is a dog **outside** the door.
門外有一條狗。

☐ 三分熟
☐ 五分熟
☐ 七分熟
☐ 全熟

---

o·ver [ˈovɚ]

介 在……上方、遍及、超過
副 翻轉過來
形 結束的、過度的

英英 above or higher than something else; one thing covering another on occasion; at the end

例 There is a rainbow **over** the hill.
山丘上有一道彩虹。

☐ 三分熟
☐ 五分熟
☐ 七分熟
☐ 全熟

---

own [on]

形 自己的
代 屬於某人之物
動 擁有
同 possess 擁有

英英 belonging or relating to a specified person; to possess

例 I have my **own** problem.
我有自己的問題。

☐ 三分熟
☐ 五分熟
☐ 七分熟
☐ 全熟

Pp

---

page [pedʒ]

名 （書上的）頁

英英 one side of pages in a book, magazine, or newspaper, or the material written or printed on it

例 Which **page** are you reading?
你在看哪一頁？

☐ 三分熟
☐ 五分熟
☐ 七分熟
☐ 全熟

P

paint [pent]

名 顏料、油漆
動 粉刷、油漆、
　（用顏料）繪畫
同 draw 畫、描繪

英英 a colored liquid which is spread over or cover a surface to give a thin decorative or protective coating

例 I am **painting** the wall.
我在粉刷這面牆。

☐ 三分熟
☐ 五分熟
☐ 七分熟
☐ 全熟

---

pair [pɛr]

名 一雙、一對
動 配成對
同 couple 一對、一雙

英英 something of two parts joined together, or regarded as a unit

例 I wear a **pair** of blue shoes.
我穿一雙藍色的鞋子。

☐ 三分熟
☐ 五分熟
☐ 七分熟
☐ 全熟

---

pants/trou·sers

[pænts]/['traʊzəz]

名 褲子

英英 a piece of clothing that covers the waist to the feet consisting of two cylindrical parts covering each leg and joined at the top

例 I want to buy a pair of **pants**.
我要買一條褲子。

☐ 三分熟
☐ 五分熟
☐ 七分熟
☐ 全熟

---

pa·pa/pop

['papə]/[pap]

名 爸爸

英英 one's father

例 The baby just said **papa**.
那嬰兒剛剛叫爸爸了。

☐ 三分熟
☐ 五分熟
☐ 七分熟
☐ 全熟

---

pa·per ['pepə]

名 紙、報紙

英英 pulp of wood or other fibrous substances manufactured into thin sheets, used for writing or printing on or as wrapping material

例 I need a piece of **paper** to write it down.
我需要一張紙把它寫下來。

☐ 三分熟
☐ 五分熟
☐ 七分熟
☐ 全熟

---

par·ent(s)

['pɛrənt(s)]

名 雙親、家長
反 child 小孩
片 helicopter parents
　直升機家長、怪獸家長

英英 a father or mother of a person or animal; an animal or plant from which younger ones are derived

例 My **parents** are young.
我爸媽很年輕。

☐ 三分熟
☐ 五分熟
☐ 七分熟
☐ 全熟

---

park [park]

名 公園
動 停放（汽車等）

英英 a large area of land, or public garden in a town, used for recreation; stop and leave (a vehicle) temporarily

例 See you at the **park**.
公園見。

☐ 三分熟
☐ 五分熟
☐ 七分熟
☐ 全熟

🎧 **Track 085**

part [pɑrt]

名 部分
動 分離、使分開

英英 a piece or segment of a whole; move apart or divide to leave a space between them

例 A **part** of the apple is eaten.
一部分的蘋果被吃掉了。

☐ 三分熟
☐ 五分熟
☐ 七分熟
☐ 全熟

---

par·ty [`pɑrtɪ]

名 聚會、黨派

英英 a social event of invited guests to meet

例 Are you going to her birthday **party**?
你會去她的生日派對嗎？

☐ 三分熟
☐ 五分熟
☐ 七分熟
☐ 全熟

---

pass [pæs]

名 （考試）及格、通行證
動 經過、消逝、通過
反 fail 不及格

英英 to move or go onward, go past, through, or across

例 I will **pass** the exam.
我會通過那場考試。

☐ 三分熟
☐ 五分熟
☐ 七分熟
☐ 全熟

---

past [pæst]

形 過去的、從前的
名 過去、從前
介 在……之後
反 future 未來的

英英 gone by in time and no longer existing, before and until the present

例 You think too much about the **past**.
你想太多過去的事情。

☐ 三分熟
☐ 五分熟
☐ 七分熟
☐ 全熟

---

pay [pe]

名 工資、薪水
動 付錢

英英 money given for service done, for goods, etc.; to give (someone) money due to work, services provided, goods, or an outstanding debt

例 How much did you **pay**?
你付多少錢？

☐ 三分熟
☐ 五分熟
☐ 七分熟
☐ 全熟

---

pay·ment

[`pemənt]

名 支付、付款

英英 the action of paying or the process of being paid; an amount of money paid or payable

例 The **payment** is reasonable.
支付這價錢很合理。

☐ 三分熟
☐ 五分熟
☐ 七分熟
☐ 全熟

---

pen [pɛn]

名 鋼筆、原子筆

英英 an instrument containing ink used for writing or drawing

例 **Pens** are important for students.
筆對學生來說很重要。

☐ 三分熟
☐ 五分熟
☐ 七分熟
☐ 全熟

---

pen·cil [`pɛnsḷ]

名 鉛筆

英英 an instrument consisting of a thin stick of graphite used for writing or drawing

例 Do the exercises with a **pencil**.
用鉛筆回答習題。

☐ 三分熟
☐ 五分熟
☐ 七分熟
☐ 全熟

P

peo·ple [ˋpip!]

名 人、人們、人民、民族

英英 used in reference to persons in general, or every one considered collectively

例 The **people** of the country are tall.
這國家的人民都很高。

☐三分熟
☐五分熟
☐七分熟
☐全熟

per·haps
[pɚˋhæps]

副 也許、可能
同 maybe 也許

英英 used to express possibility, uncertainty or possibility; used when making a polite request or suggestion

例 **Perhaps** I will stay here.
我可能會待在這裡。

☐三分熟
☐五分熟
☐七分熟
☐全熟

per·son [ˋpɝsn]

名 人

英英 a man, woman, or child regarded as an individual

例 The **person** is strange.
這個人好奇怪。

☐三分熟
☐五分熟
☐七分熟
☐全熟

pet [pɛt]

名 寵物、令人愛慕之物
形 寵愛的、得意的

英英 a domestic or tamed animal kept for companionship or pleasure, and treated kindly; favorite

例 The turtle is my **pet**.
這隻烏龜是我的寵物。

☐三分熟
☐五分熟
☐七分熟
☐全熟

pi·an·o [pɪˋæno]

名 鋼琴
片 play the piano
彈鋼琴

英英 a large keyboard musical instrument with black and white keys, and metal strings, which are struck by hammers when the keys are pressed

例 She is playing the **piano**.
她正在彈鋼琴。

☐三分熟
☐五分熟
☐七分熟
☐全熟

pic·ture [ˋpɪktʃɚ]

名 圖片、相片
動 畫
同 image 圖像
片 take a picture 照相

英英 a painting, drawing, or photograph; to draw

例 Show me the **picture**.
給我看這照片。

☐三分熟
☐五分熟
☐七分熟
☐全熟

pie [paɪ]

名 派、餡餅

英英 a baked dish of savory or sweet ingredients covered with pastry

例 We baked a **pie** for the festival.
我們烤了個派慶祝節慶。

☐三分熟
☐五分熟
☐七分熟
☐全熟

piece [pis]

名 一塊、一片
同 fragment 碎片

英英 a part of a whole, an item used in constructing something or forming part of a set

例 Give me a small **piece** of cake.
給我一小塊蛋糕就好。

☐三分熟
☐五分熟
☐七分熟
☐全熟

🎧 Track 087

pig [pɪg]

名 豬

英英 a domesticated farm animal that is pink, brown, or black, with sparse bristly hair and a flat snout, kept for its meat

例 There are so many **pigs** in the farm.
這座農場裡有好多的豬。

☐ 三分熟
☐ 五分熟
☐ 七分熟
☐ 全熟

place [ples]

名 地方、地區、地位
動 放置
反 displace 移開

英英 a particular position or location; a suitable area occupied by or set aside for someone or something

例 It is a nice **place**.
這是個很棒的地方。

☐ 三分熟
☐ 五分熟
☐ 七分熟
☐ 全熟

plan [plæn]

動 計畫、規劃
名 計畫、安排
同 project 計畫

英英 a detailed and set of decisions for doing or achieving something in the future

例 Do you have any **plan**?
你有任何的計畫嗎？

☐ 三分熟
☐ 五分熟
☐ 七分熟
☐ 全熟

plant [plænt]

名 植物、工廠
動 栽種
反 animal 動物

英英 living thing which grows in earth, in water or on other plants, and usually has a stem, leaves, roots and flowers and produces seeds; to put into the ground for growth

例 It is the tallest **plant**.
這是最高的植物。

☐ 三分熟
☐ 五分熟
☐ 七分熟
☐ 全熟

play [ple]

名 遊戲、玩耍
動 玩、做遊戲、扮演、演奏
同 game 遊戲

英英 engage in games or spend time on other activities for enjoyment rather than for a serious or practical purpose

例 Let's **play** the game together.
一起玩遊戲吧。

☐ 三分熟
☐ 五分熟
☐ 七分熟
☐ 全熟

play·er [`pleɚ]

名 運動員、演奏者、玩家
同 sportsman 運動員

英英 a person taking part in a team sport or game; a person who is involved and influential in an activity

例 Kobe is a **player** in Laker.
柯比是湖人隊的運動員。

☐ 三分熟
☐ 五分熟
☐ 七分熟
☐ 全熟

play·ground [`ple͵graʊnd]

名 運動場、遊戲場

英英 an area designated for children to play outside, especially in schools

例 Go to the **playground** to exercise.
去運動場運動吧。

☐ 三分熟
☐ 五分熟
☐ 七分熟
☐ 全熟

P

please [pliz]
動 請、使高興、取悅
反 displease 得罪、觸怒

英英 cause to feel content and satisfied; wish or desire
例 **Please** follow me.
請跟著我。

☐ 三分熟
☐ 五分熟
☐ 七分熟
☐ 全熟

pock·et [ˈpɑkɪt]
名 口袋
形 小型的、袖珍的

英英 a small bag sewn into or on the outside of clothing, used for carrying small articles; relatively small
例 This vest has lots of **pockets**.
這背心有很多口袋。

☐ 三分熟
☐ 五分熟
☐ 七分熟
☐ 全熟

po·et·ry [ˈpoˌɪtrɪ]
名 詩、詩集
同 verse 詩

英英 collective poems as a form of literature
例 **Poetry** is elegant.
詩很優雅。

☐ 三分熟
☐ 五分熟
☐ 七分熟
☐ 全熟

point [pɔɪnt]
名 尖端、點、要點、（比賽中所得的）分數
動 瞄準、指向
同 dot 點
片 point to 指向

英英 the tapered, sharp end of a tool, weapon, or other object; a particular spot, place, main idea, or moment; to aim
例 That's the **point**.
這就是問題點。

☐ 三分熟
☐ 五分熟
☐ 七分熟
☐ 全熟

po·lice [pəˈlis]
名 警察

英英 a civil force responsible for the prevention and detection of crime and the maintenance of public order
例 The **police** are looking for the girl.
警方正在尋找這女孩。

☐ 三分熟
☐ 五分熟
☐ 七分熟
☐ 全熟

po·lice·man/ cop [pəˈlismən]/[kɑp]
名 警察

英英 a member of a police force
例 He is a **policeman**.
他是警察。

☐ 三分熟
☐ 五分熟
☐ 七分熟
☐ 全熟

pond [pɑnd]
名 池塘

英英 a pool of water smaller than a lake, usually made artificially
例 The ducks are swimming in the **pond**.
鴨子在池塘裡游泳。

☐ 三分熟
☐ 五分熟
☐ 七分熟
☐ 全熟

pool [pul]
名 水池

英英 a small body of water
例 The **pool** is too deep.
這水池太深了。

☐ 三分熟
☐ 五分熟
☐ 七分熟
☐ 全熟

🎧 Track 089

poor [pʊr]

形 貧窮的、可憐的、差的、壞的
名 窮人
反 rich 富有的

英英 lacking sufficient money or possessions to live at a comfortable or normal standard
例 They are **poor**.
他們很窮。

☐ 三分熟
☐ 五分熟
☐ 七分熟
☐ 全熟

pop·corn
[ˋpɑpˏkɔrn]

名 爆米花

英英 seeds of maize that burst open when heated becoming soft and light and are then eaten as a snack
例 Go to the cinema with **popcorn**.
帶著爆米花進戲院。

☐ 三分熟
☐ 五分熟
☐ 七分熟
☐ 全熟

po·si·tion
[pəˋzɪʃən]

名 位置、工作職位、形勢
同 location 位置

英英 the appropriate place or location (of something or someone)
例 I want to apply for the **position**.
我要申請這職位。

☐ 三分熟
☐ 五分熟
☐ 七分熟
☐ 全熟

pos·si·ble
[ˋpɑsəbl̩]

形 可能的
同 likely 可能的

英英 able to exist, happen, or achieved
例 Is it **possible**?
這有可能嗎？

☐ 三分熟
☐ 五分熟
☐ 七分熟
☐ 全熟

pow·er [ˋpaʊɚ]

名 力量、權力、動力
同 strength 力量
片 nuclear power
核能動力

英英 the ability to control people or events, or act in a particular way
例 Germans are against nuclear **power**.
德國人反對核能動力。

☐ 三分熟
☐ 五分熟
☐ 七分熟
☐ 全熟

prac·tice
[ˋpræktɪs]

名 實踐、練習、熟練
動 練習
同 exercise 練習

英英 applying a plan, learned information, or method, as opposed to the theories relating to it; to do something to be proficient
例 You need to **practice** more.
你需要多加練習。

☐ 三分熟
☐ 五分熟
☐ 七分熟
☐ 全熟

pre·pare [priˋpɛr]

動 預備、準備

英英 make ready for use or consideration; make or get ready to do or deal with something in the future
例 I will **prepare** something for you.
我會幫你準備點東西。

☐ 三分熟
☐ 五分熟
☐ 七分熟
☐ 全熟

P

pret·ty [ˋprɪtɪ]

形 漂亮的、美好的
同 lovely 可愛的
片 pretty good 很好

英英 attractive in a delicate way without being truly beautiful, pleasant to look at

例 She is very **pretty**.
她很漂亮。

☐ 三分熟
☐ 五分熟
☐ 七分熟
☐ 全熟

---

price [praɪs]

名 價格、代價
同 value 價格、價值

英英 the amount of money expected, required, or given in payment for something that is sold

例 The **price** is too high.
這價格太高了。

☐ 三分熟
☐ 五分熟
☐ 七分熟
☐ 全熟

---

print [prɪnt]

名 印跡、印刷字體、版
動 印刷

英英 numbers, words, letters, symbols produced on paper with ink

例 Let's **print** it out.
把它印出來。

☐ 三分熟
☐ 五分熟
☐ 七分熟
☐ 全熟

---

prob·lem [ˋprɑbləm]

名 問題
反 solution 解答

英英 an unwelcome harmful matter, situation, or person needing to be dealt with

例 Do you have any **problem**?
你有什麼問題嗎？

☐ 三分熟
☐ 五分熟
☐ 七分熟
☐ 全熟

---

prove [pruv]

動 證明、證實
同 confirm 證實

英英 demonstrate by evidence or argument that something is true or exists

例 **Prove** yourself.
證明你自己。

☐ 三分熟
☐ 五分熟
☐ 七分熟
☐ 全熟

---

pub·lic [ˋpʌblɪk]

形 公眾的
名 民眾
反 private 私人的

英英 of, concerning, or available to the people for use not privately; the people in general

例 The **public** is against the law.
民眾反對這項法律。

☐ 三分熟
☐ 五分熟
☐ 七分熟
☐ 全熟

---

pull [pʊl]

動 拉、拖
反 push 推

英英 to take hold of something and move it to another place

例 **Pull** the door.
拉開門。

☐ 三分熟
☐ 五分熟
☐ 七分熟
☐ 全熟

---

pur·ple [ˋpɝp!]

形 紫色的
名 紫色

英英 the color between red and blue

例 The **purple** flower is pretty.
這朵紫色的花很漂亮。

☐ 三分熟
☐ 五分熟
☐ 七分熟
☐ 全熟

🎧 **Track 091**

pur·pose [`pɝpəs]

名 目的、意圖
同 aim 目的
片 on purpose 故意的

英英 the reason for why something is done or for why something exists

例 What's your **purpose**?
你的目的是什麼？

☐ 三分熟
☐ 五分熟
☐ 七分熟
☐ 全熟

push [pʊʃ]

動 推、壓、按、促進
名 推、推動
反 pull 拉、拖

英英 exert force on (someone or something) in order to move them away from oneself or from the source of the force

例 Don't **push** me.
不要推我。

☐ 三分熟
☐ 五分熟
☐ 七分熟
☐ 全熟

put [pʊt]

動 放置
同 place 放置

英英 move to or place in a particular position

例 Just **put** it aside.
把它放一邊就好。

☐ 三分熟
☐ 五分熟
☐ 七分熟
☐ 全熟

Qq

queen [`kwin]

名 女王、皇后
反 king 國王

英英 the female ruler in some countries, the wife of a king, especially one who inherits the position by right of birth

例 The **queen** is waving her hands.
女王在揮手。

☐ 三分熟
☐ 五分熟
☐ 七分熟
☐ 全熟

ques·tion

[`kwɛstʃən]

名 疑問、詢問
動 質疑、懷疑
反 answer 答案

英英 a sentence worded or expressed to ask for information

例 I have some **questions**.
我有點問題。

☐ 三分熟
☐ 五分熟
☐ 七分熟
☐ 全熟

quick [kwɪk]

形 快的
副 快
同 fast 快

英英 doing something or moving fast; lasting or taking a short time

例 His action was not **quick** enough.
他的動作不夠快。

☐ 三分熟
☐ 五分熟
☐ 七分熟
☐ 全熟

qui·et [`kwaɪət]

形 安靜的
名 安靜
動 使平靜
同 still 寂靜的

英英 without much activity, disturbance, or excitement; making little or no noise; freedom from motion

例 She's very **quiet**.
她很安靜。

☐ 三分熟
☐ 五分熟
☐ 七分熟
☐ 全熟

quite [kwaɪt]
副 完全地、相當、頗

英英 completely, entirely or abousutely
例 The boy is **quite** angry.
那男孩相當生氣。

☐三分熟
☐五分熟
☐七分熟
☐全熟

Rr

race [res]
動 賽跑
名 種族、比賽
同 folk （某一民族的）廣人成員

英英 a competition between people run, ride, drive, etc. to see which one is the fastest
例 We are the same **race**.
我們都是同種族的人。

☐三分熟
☐五分熟
☐七分熟
☐全熟

ra·di·o [ˈredɪo]
名 收音機

英英 a piece of equipment used in broadcasting in sound, music, news broadcasts, etc.
例 Let's listen to the **radio**.
聽聽收音機吧。

☐三分熟
☐五分熟
☐七分熟
☐全熟

rail·road [ˈrelˌrod]
名 鐵路

英英 the metal tracks laid in the ground that trains travel on
例 The **railroad** is very long.
這條鐵路很長。

☐三分熟
☐五分熟
☐七分熟
☐全熟

rain [ren]
名 雨、雨水
動 下雨
同 shower 雨、降雨

英英 the condensed moisture of the atmosphere falling to the earth in separate drops; to fall in drops of rain
例 It's **raining**.
正在下雨。

☐三分熟
☐五分熟
☐七分熟
☐全熟

rain·bow [ˈrenˌbo]
名 彩虹

英英 an arch of colors of seven colors visible in the sky, caused by the sun shining through rain
例 There is a **rainbow** after the rain.
雨後有彩虹。

☐三分熟
☐五分熟
☐七分熟
☐全熟

raise [rez]
動 舉起、抬起、提高、養育
反 lower 下降

英英 to lift or move to a higher position or level; increase in amount or level
例 **Raise** your hands, please.
請舉手。

☐三分熟
☐五分熟
☐七分熟
☐全熟

rat [ræt]

名 老鼠
同 mouse 老鼠

英英 a rodent is large, and long-tailed, typically considered a serious pest

例 I heard a **rat** running.
我聽到老鼠在跑。

☐ 三分熟
☐ 五分熟
☐ 七分熟
☐ 全熟

---

reach [ritʃ]

動 伸手拿東西、到達
同 approach 接近

英英 stretch out an arm to take, touch, or grasp something

例 I can't **reach** the box.
我伸手拿不到那箱子。

☐ 三分熟
☐ 五分熟
☐ 七分熟
☐ 全熟

---

read [rid]

動 讀、看（書、報等）、朗讀

英英 look at and understand the meaning of words (written or printed matter)

例 **Read** it to me.
唸給我聽。

☐ 三分熟
☐ 五分熟
☐ 七分熟
☐ 全熟

---

read·y [ˋrɛdɪ]

形 做好準備的

英英 prepared for an activity, situation, or doing something; made suitable and available for immediate use

例 Are you **ready**?
你做好準備了嗎？

☐ 三分熟
☐ 五分熟
☐ 七分熟
☐ 全熟

---

re·al [ˋriəl]

形 真的、真實的
副 真正的
同 actual 真的、真正的

英英 actually existing or factual; not imagined or supposed

例 Is it **real**?
這是真的嗎？

☐ 三分熟
☐ 五分熟
☐ 七分熟
☐ 全熟

---

rea·son [ˋrizṇ]

名 理由
同 cause 理由、原因

英英 a cause, explanation, justification, facts about why something happens, or why someone does something; good or obvious cause of doing something

例 That's the **reason**!
這就是原因了啊！

☐ 三分熟
☐ 五分熟
☐ 七分熟
☐ 全熟

---

re·ceive [rɪˋsiv]

動 收到
反 send 發送、寄

英英 be given, presented with, or paid; to accept or take delivery of something that has been given to you

例 Did you **receive** her mail?
你有收到她的信嗎？

☐ 三分熟
☐ 五分熟
☐ 七分熟
☐ 全熟

---

red [rɛd]

名 紅色
形 紅色的

英英 of a color at the end of the spectrum next to orange and opposite violet, as of blood, fire, or rubies

例 The **red** coat is not cheap.
那件紅色的外套並不便宜。

☐ 三分熟
☐ 五分熟
☐ 七分熟
☐ 全熟

R

re·mem·ber

[rɪˋmɛmbɚ]

動 記得
同 remind 使記起

英英 something or someone from the past to have come into one's mind

例 Do you **remember** to lock the door?
你有記得鎖門嗎？

□三分熟
□五分熟
□七分熟
□全熟

re·port [rɪˋport]

動 報告、報導
名 報導、報告

英英 to give information about something or something you have done to someone; a spoken or written account of something; a description or information about an event or situation

例 Don't forget to **report** back.
不要忘記回報。

□三分熟
□五分熟
□七分熟
□全熟

rest [rɛst]

動 休息
名 睡眠、休息
同 relaxation 休息
片 take a rest 休息

英英 to take a break from work or activities for getting refreshment; a period of time in which work is ceased in order to relax, sleep, or recover strength

例 I need some more **rest**.
我需要多休息一下。

□三分熟
□五分熟
□七分熟
□全熟

re·turn [rɪˋtɝn]

動 歸還、送回
名 返回、復發
形 返回的
反 depart 出發

英英 come or go back to a place you were before

例 When will you **return** my book?
你何時要還我書？

□三分熟
□五分熟
□七分熟
□全熟

rice [raɪs]

名 稻米、米飯

英英 a swamp grass which is cultivated into small grains as a source of food in many diets

例 Chinese live on **rice**.
中國人以米飯為主食。

□三分熟
□五分熟
□七分熟
□全熟

rich [rɪtʃ]

形 富裕的
同 wealthy 富裕的

英英 having a great deal of money, assets, valuable goods

例 The **rich** man is generous.
那位富裕的男人很慷慨。

□三分熟
□五分熟
□七分熟
□全熟

ride [raɪd]

動 騎、乘
名 騎車或乘車旅行、
騎馬

英英 to travel by sitting on and controlling the movement of (a horse, bicycle, or motorcycle)

例 She **rides** a bike to work.
她騎腳踏車上班。

□三分熟
□五分熟
□十分熟
□全熟

right [raɪt]

形 正確的、右邊的
名 正確、右方、權利
同 correct 正確的

英英 correct; on or towards the side of your body that is to the east when you are facing north

例 You are always **right**.
你總是對的。

☐ 三分熟
☐ 五分熟
☐ 七分熟
☐ 全熟

---

ring [rɪŋ]

動 按鈴、打電話
名 戒指、鈴聲

英英 to ring a bell; to telephone; a small circle of any material, worn on a finger, a circular band, object, or mark

例 When did you hear the bell **ring**?
你何時聽到電話鈴聲？

☐ 三分熟
☐ 五分熟
☐ 七分熟
☐ 全熟

---

rise [raɪz]

動 上升、增長
名 上升
同 ascend 升起

英英 to move upwards, come or go up; get up from lying, sitting, or kneeling

例 The sun **rises** every day.
太陽每天都會升起。

☐ 三分熟
☐ 五分熟
☐ 七分熟
☐ 全熟

---

riv·er [ˈrɪvɚ]

名 江、河
同 stream 小河

英英 a large natural and wide flow of water travelling across the land into the sea, a lake, or joining another river

例 It is the longest **river**.
這是最長的河。

☐ 三分熟
☐ 五分熟
☐ 七分熟
☐ 全熟

---

road [rod]

名 路、道路、街道、路線
同 path 路、道路

英英 a long hard surface made for traveling on between places, especially for use by vehicles

例 Walk along the **road**.
沿著這條路走。

☐ 三分熟
☐ 五分熟
☐ 七分熟
☐ 全熟

---

ro·bot [ˈrobət]

名 機器人

英英 a machine controlled by computers capable of carrying out a complex series of actions automatically

例 The **robot** can do anything.
這機器人可以做任何的事情。

☐ 三分熟
☐ 五分熟
☐ 七分熟
☐ 全熟

---

rock [rɑk]

動 搖晃
名 岩石
同 stone 石頭

英英 to move backward and forward; the hard mineral material of the earth's crust; the dry solid part of the earth's surface

例 There are six **rocks** at the top of the mountain.
山頂上有六顆巨石。

☐ 三分熟
☐ 五分熟
☐ 七分熟
☐ 全熟

R

roll [rol]

動 滾動、捲
名 名冊、捲
同 wheel 滾動、打滾

英英 to move by turning over and over on an axis, or from sided to side; move forward on wheels or with a smooth, undulating motion; a list or register

例 I need a **roll** of tissue paper.
我需要一捲衛生紙。

□三分熟
□五分熟
□七分熟
□全熟

---

roof [ruf]

名 屋頂、車頂
反 floor 地板

英英 a structure which is the upper covering of a building or vehicle

例 He is singing on the **roof**.
他在屋頂上唱歌。

□三分熟
□五分熟
□七分熟
□全熟

---

room [rum]

名 房間、室
同 chamber 房間

英英 space viewed in terms of its capacity to accommodate one's needs

例 The **room** is too dark.
這房間好黑。

□三分熟
□五分熟
□七分熟
□全熟

---

roost·er [ˋrustɚ]

名 雄雞、好鬥者
同 cock 公雞

英英 an adult male domestic fowl; a cocky or vain person

例 The **roosters** are fighting.
公雞們正在打鬥。

□三分熟
□五分熟
□七分熟
□全熟

---

root [rut]

名 根源、根
動 生根
同 origin 起源

英英 a part of a plant normally below ground, which is the plant's support and collects water and nourishment; to plant and fix in the earth

例 The **root** of the tree is long.
這棵樹的根很長。

□三分熟
□五分熟
□七分熟
□全熟

---

rope [rop]

名 繩、索
動 用繩拴住
同 cord 繩索

英英 a length of stout cord made by twisting long threads together; to fasten with a rope

例 Bring some **ropes** when you go camping.
要帶點繩子去露營。

□三分熟
□五分熟
□七分熟
□全熟

---

rose [roz]

名 玫瑰花、薔薇花
形 玫瑰色的

英英 a fragrant flower often brightly colored, (typically red, pink, yellow, or white) growing on a prickly bush or shrub

例 I bought a **rose** for my girlfriend.
我買了朵玫瑰給我女朋友。

□三分熟
□五分熟
□七分熟
□全熟

---

round [raʊnd]

形 圓的、球形的
名 圓形物、一回合
動 使旋轉
介 在……四周

英英 shaped like a circle or ball, curved; shaped like a sphere

例 The Earth is **round**.
地球是圓的。

□三分熟
□五分熟
□七分熟
□全熟

🎧 Track 097

row [ro]

名 排、行、列
動 划船
同 paddle 划船

英英 line of things, number of people in a more or less straight line; to propel by means of oars

例 We **row** the boat.
我們划小船。

☐ 三分熟
☐ 五分熟
☐ 七分熟
☐ 全熟

---

rub [rʌb]

動 磨擦

英英 apply firm pressure to (a surface); to press or be pressed against with a repeated back and forth motion

例 The giraffe **rubs** its neck.
長頸鹿摩擦牠的脖子。

☐ 三分熟
☐ 五分熟
☐ 七分熟
☐ 全熟

---

rub·ber [ˋrʌbɚ]

名 橡膠、橡皮
形 橡膠做的

英英 a tough elastic substance made from the juice of a tropical plant or artificially; made of rubber

例 Tie the bag with **rubber** band.
用橡皮筋綁這袋口。

☐ 三分熟
☐ 五分熟
☐ 七分熟
☐ 全熟

---

rule [rul]

名 規則
動 統治
同 govern 統治、管理

英英 a regulation or principle or instruction stating the way things should be done; governing conduct or procedure within a particular sphere; to govern

例 We should all follow the **rules**.
我們都應該遵守規則。

☐ 三分熟
☐ 五分熟
☐ 七分熟
☐ 全熟

---

run [rʌn]

動 跑、運轉
名 跑

英英 move at a speed faster than walking, taking quick steps and never having both or all feet on the ground at the same time

例 **Running** is a good exercise.
跑步是很好的運動。

☐ 三分熟
☐ 五分熟
☐ 七分熟
☐ 全熟

Ss

sad [sæd]

形 令人難過的、悲傷的
同 sorrowful 悲哀的

英英 feeling sorrow; unhappy, or making you feel unhappy

例 You made me **sad**.
你讓我很難過。

☐ 三分熟
☐ 五分熟
☐ 七分熟
☐ 全熟

---

safe [sef]

形 安全的
反 dangerous 危險的

英英 protected from danger or risk; not dangerous, causing or leading to harm or injury

例 It is not **safe** in the country.
這個國家不太安全。

☐ 三分熟
☐ 五分熟
☐ 七分熟
☐ 全熟

S

---

sail [sel]

名 帆、篷、航行、船隻
動 航行

英英 a piece of material fixed to a mast to catch the wind and propel a boat or ship; to travel in a boat or ship

例 The Titanic **sailed** to America.
鐵達尼號航向美國。

☐ 三分熟
☐ 五分熟
☐ 七分熟
☐ 全熟

---

sale [sel]

名 賣、出售
反 purchase 購買
片 on sale 拍賣

英英 the exchange of a commodity for money; the act of selling goods

例 This house is for **sale**.
這間房子正在出售中。

☐ 三分熟
☐ 五分熟
☐ 七分熟
☐ 全熟

---

salt [sɔlt]

名 鹽
形 鹽的
反 sugar 糖

英英 a white crystalline substance used for seasoning or preserving food; falvored with salt

例 **Salt** was expensive in the past.
在以前，鹽是很貴的。

☐ 三分熟
☐ 五分熟
☐ 七分熟
☐ 全熟

---

same [sem]

形 同樣的
副 同樣地
代 同樣的人或事
反 different 不同的

英英 exactly alike; unchanged; not different

例 You are doing the **same** thing.
你正做一樣的事情。

☐ 三分熟
☐ 五分熟
☐ 七分熟
☐ 全熟

---

sand [sænd]

名 沙、沙子

英英 a substance found on beaches and deserts, consisting of fine particles of eroded rocks

例 The children are playing in the **sand**.
孩子們在玩沙。

☐ 三分熟
☐ 五分熟
☐ 七分熟
☐ 全熟

Sat·ur·day/Sat.

[ˈsætəde]

名 星期六

英英 the day of the week before Sunday and following Friday

例 I went to Kenting on **Saturday**.
我星期六去墾丁。

☐ 三分熟
☐ 五分熟
☐ 七分熟
☐ 全熟

---

save [sev]

動 救、搭救、挽救、儲蓄
反 waste 浪費、消耗

英英 keep safe or rescue from harm or danger; prevent from dying

例 The man **saved** my life.
這男人救了我一命。

☐ 三分熟
☐ 五分熟
☐ 七分熟
☐ 全熟

---

saw [sɔ]

名 鋸
動 用鋸子鋸

英英 a hand tool with a sharp serrated edge used for cutting wood or other hard materials; to cut with saw

例 I **sawed** the log.
我用鋸子鋸木頭。

☐ 三分熟
☐ 五分熟
☐ 七分熟
☐ 全熟

🎧 **Track 099**

say [se]

動 說、講

英英 to speak or utter words so as to convey information, an opinion, an instruction, etc.

例 Did I **say** something wrong?
我說錯了什麼話嗎？

☐ 三分熟
☐ 五分熟
☐ 七分熟
☐ 全熟

---

scare [skɛr]

動 驚嚇、使害怕
名 害怕
同 frighten 使害怕

英英 cause great fear or nervousness in a person or animal; to frighten

例 I was **scared** by you.
我被你嚇到了。

☐ 三分熟
☐ 五分熟
☐ 七分熟
☐ 全熟

---

scene [sin]

名 戲劇的一場、風景
同 view 景色

英英 a place, a view, or picture of a place where a real or fictional incident occurs or occurred

例 The **scene** is beautiful.
這景色好美。

☐ 三分熟
☐ 五分熟
☐ 七分熟
☐ 全熟

---

school [skul]

名 學校

英英 an institution in which children are educated; a day's work at school; lessons

例 She is late to **school** every day.
她每天上學遲到。

☐ 三分熟
☐ 五分熟
☐ 七分熟
☐ 全熟

---

sea [si]

名 海
同 ocean 海洋
片 by the sea 海運

英英 the large area of salt water that covers most of the earth's surface and surrounds its land masses

例 The goods are by the **sea**.
這些貨物是海運的。

☐ 三分熟
☐ 五分熟
☐ 七分熟
☐ 全熟

---

sea·son [ˋsizn̩]

名 季節

英英 each of the four periods of the year (spring, summer, autumn, and winter) marked by particular weather patterns and daylight hours

例 Spring is my favorite **season**.
春天是我最愛的季節。

☐ 三分熟
☐ 五分熟
☐ 七分熟
☐ 全熟

---

seat [sit]

名 座位
動 坐下
同 chair 椅子

英英 a thing made or used for sitting on; the horizontal or flat part of a chair; to fit well on its seat

例 This **seat** is very comfortable.
這個座位很舒服。

☐ 三分熟
☐ 五分熟
☐ 七分熟
☐ 全熟

---

sec·ond [ˋsɛkənd]

形 第二的
名 秒

英英 constituting number two in a sequence; coming immediately after the first; the 60th part of a minute

例 She is **second** to none.
她是首屈一指的。

☐ 三分熟
☐ 五分熟
☐ 七分熟
☐ 全熟

S

see [si]

動 看、理解
同 watch 看

英英 to notice or perceive people and things with the eyes

例 What did you **see**?
你看到什麼了？

☐ 三分熟
☐ 五分熟
☐ 七分熟
☐ 全熟

---

seed [sid]

名 種子
動 播種於

英英 a flowering plant's unit of reproduction; a round object in which other plants can grow out from; to sprinkle with seed

例 The farmer bought **seeds** from me.
那農夫跟我買了些種子。

☐ 三分熟
☐ 五分熟
☐ 七分熟
☐ 全熟

---

seem [sim]

動 似乎

英英 appear to be a particular thing, or give the impression of being; appear to be unable to do, despite having tried

例 It **seems** to be good.
這看起來不錯。

☐ 三分熟
☐ 五分熟
☐ 七分熟
☐ 全熟

---

see·saw [ˋsiˏsɔ]

名 翹翹板

英英 a long board that children play on by pushing off the ground with their feet to make the board up

例 Kids love to play **seesaw**.
小孩子都喜歡翹翹板。

☐ 三分熟
☐ 五分熟
☐ 七分熟
☐ 全熟

---

self [sɛlf]

名 自己、自我
片 take yourself at home
當自己家

英英 the set of someone's characteristics including personality, abilities, etc.

例 Enjoy **yourself**.
請自便。

☐ 三分熟
☐ 五分熟
☐ 七分熟
☐ 全熟

---

self·ish [ˋsɛlfɪʃ]

形 自私的、不顧別人的

英英 mainly concerned with one's own personal benefit, profit or pleasure without consideration for others

例 He is very **selfish**.
他很自私。

☐ 三分熟
☐ 五分熟
☐ 七分熟
☐ 全熟

---

sell [sɛl]

動 賣、出售、銷售
反 buy 買
片 sold out 賣出

英英 hand over something in exchange for money; make a monetary deal in (goods or property); (of goods) attain sales

例 I **sell** you some cakes.
我賣你一些蛋糕。

☐ 三分熟
☐ 五分熟
☐ 七分熟
☐ 全熟

---

send [sɛnd]

動 派遣、寄出
同 mail 寄信

英英 to arrange for something to go, or be taken to a destination; cause to move sharply or in a fast motion

例 **Send** me a letter!
要寄信給我喔！

☐ 三分熟
☐ 五分熟
☐ 七分熟
☐ 全熟

🎧 **Track 101**

sense [sɛns]

名 感覺、意義
片 sense of humor
幽默感

英英 any of the 5 natural abilities of sight, smell, hearing, taste, and touch, by which the body perceives stimulus externally

例 It doesn't make **sense**.
這沒有意義。

☐三分熟
☐五分熟
☐七分熟
☐全熟

---

sen·tence

[ˈsɛntəns]

名 句子、判決
動 判決
同 judge 判決

英英 a group of words usually containing a verb that is complete in itself, conveying a statement, question, exclamation, or command and typically containing a subject and predicate; to condemn by judgment of court

例 The killer is **sentenced** to death.
殺人犯被判死刑。

☐三分熟
☐五分熟
☐七分熟
☐全熟

Sep·tem·ber/

Sept. [sɛpˈtɛmbɚ]

名 九月

英英 the ninth month of the year

例 The kids go to school in **September**.
孩子們九月去上學。

☐三分熟
☐五分熟
☐七分熟
☐全熟

---

serve [sɝv]

動 服務、招待
片 serve as 扮演著……

英英 perform duties or services for; to do work that helps society; be employed in the government or as a member of the armed forces

例 What did they **serve** you?
他們招待你什麼嗎？

☐三分熟
☐五分熟
☐七分熟
☐全熟

---

serv·ice [ˈsɝvɪs]

名 服務

英英 the action or process of serving

例 The **service** of the restaurant is good.
這家餐廳的服務很好。

☐三分熟
☐五分熟
☐七分熟
☐全熟

---

set [sɛt]

名 （一）套、（一）副
動 放、擱置
同 place 放置
片 set up 準備

英英 to put, lay, or stand in a specified place or position; to arrange when something will happen

例 I need a **set** of tableware.
我需要一套餐具。

☐三分熟
☐五分熟
☐七分熟
☐全熟

---

sev·en [ˈsɛvən]

名 七

英英 one more than six and one less than eight

例 I went to school at the age of **seven**.
我七歲上學。

☐三分熟
☐五分熟
☐七分熟
☐全熟

S

sev·en·teen

[ˌsɛvənˈtin]

名 十七

英英 one more than sixteen and one less than eighteen

例 Do fall in love with someone at your **seventeen**.
不要在十七歲愛上一個人。

□三分熟
□五分熟
□七分熟
□全熟

sev·en·ty

[ˈsɛvəntɪ]

名 七十

英英 ten less than eighty; ten more than sixty

例 Her grandma passed away at the age of **seventy**.
她祖母七十歲時過世的。

□三分熟
□五分熟
□七分熟
□全熟

sev·er·al [ˈsɛvərəl]

形 幾個的
代 幾個

英英 some, but not many

例 I have **several** books for you.
我有幾本書要給你。

□三分熟
□五分熟
□七分熟
□全熟

shake [ʃek]

動 搖、發抖
名 搖動、震動

英英 to make quick short movements either side to side or up and down, or to cause something to do this

例 He **shook** his head and said no.
他搖頭說不。

□三分熟
□五分熟
□七分熟
□全熟

shall [ʃæl]

連 將

英英 used instead of will (in the first person) expressing the future tense

例 **Shall** we dance?
我們要跳舞嗎？

□三分熟
□五分熟
□七分熟
□全熟

shape [ʃep]

動 使成形
名 形狀
同 form 使成形

英英 to make into a certain form the physical or external form or appearance of someone or something

例 Look at the stone with the **shape** of heart.
看那有愛心形狀的石頭。

□三分熟
□五分熟
□七分熟
□全熟

shark [ʃɑrk]

名 鯊魚

英英 a long-bodied marine fish with a triangular fin on its back, typically predatory and voracious

例 There are **sharks** in the bay.
這海灣中有鯊魚。

□三分熟
□五分熟
□七分熟
□全熟

sharp [ʃɑrp]

形 鋒利的、刺耳的、尖銳的、嚴厲的
同 blunt 嚴厲的

英英 having a cutting or piercing edge or point with the ability to make a hole in something

例 Be careful for the **sharp** knife.
小心那把鋒利的刀。

□三分熟
□五分熟
□七分熟
□全熟

🎧 **Track 103**

she [ʃi]

代 她

英英 to refer to a woman, girl or female animal that has been previously mentioned

例 **She** is nice to me.
她對我很好。

☐ 三分熟
☐ 五分熟
☐ 七分熟
☐ 全熟

---

sheep [ʃip]

名 羊、綿羊

英英 a domesticated farm animal with a thick woolly coat, kept in flocks for its wool, skin, or meat

例 There are a lot of **sheep** in Australia.
澳洲有很多的綿羊。

☐ 三分熟
☐ 五分熟
☐ 七分熟
☐ 全熟

---

sheet [ʃit]

名 床單

英英 a large thin rectangular piece of cotton or other fabric, especially used on a bed to cover the mattress or as a layer beneath blankets

例 My mom is changing the **sheet** for me.
媽媽在幫我換床單。

☐ 三分熟
☐ 五分熟
☐ 七分熟
☐ 全熟

---

shine [ʃaɪn]

動 照耀、發光、發亮
名 光亮
同 glow 發光

英英 to reflect or send out light; sheen

例 The sun **shines**.
陽光普照。

☐ 三分熟
☐ 五分熟
☐ 七分熟
☐ 全熟

---

ship [ʃɪp]

名 大船、海船
同 boat 船

英英 a large boat for traveling on the sea, especially crossing the sea

例 The **ship** sails to the north.
這艘船航向北方。

☐ 三分熟
☐ 五分熟
☐ 七分熟
☐ 全熟

---

shirt [ʃɝt]

名 襯衫

英英 a garment made of light cloth for the upper body, with a collar and sleeves and buttons down the front

例 The man in blue **shirt** is my dad.
那穿藍色襯衫的男人是我爸。

☐ 三分熟
☐ 五分熟
☐ 七分熟
☐ 全熟

---

shoe(s) [ʃu(z)]

名 鞋

英英 a covering for the feet made of a sturdy sole, strong material such as leather, and not reaching above the ankle

例 The **shoes** fit me well.
這雙鞋很適合我。

☐ 三分熟
☐ 五分熟
☐ 七分熟
☐ 全熟

---

shop/store

[ʃɑp]/[stor]

名 商店、店鋪

英英 a building or part of a building where one can buy goods or services

例 The **store** is near to my house.
這家商店離我家很近。

☐ 三分熟
☐ 五分熟
☐ 七分熟
☐ 全熟

shore [ʃor]

名 岸、濱
同 bank 岸

| 英英 the land lining the edge of a sea, wide river, lake, etc. |
| 例 The villa is on the **shore**.
這別墅在海岸。 |

☐ 三分熟
☐ 五分熟
☐ 七分熟
☐ 全熟

short [ʃɔrt]

形 矮的、短的、不足的
副 突然地
反 long 長的；遠的

| 英英 of a small length, distance, height, or duration; relatively small in extent; suddenly |
| 例 The boy is too **short** to play basketball.
這男孩太矮了，不能打籃球。 |

☐ 三分熟
☐ 五分熟
☐ 七分熟
☐ 全熟

shot [ʃɑt]

名 子彈、射擊
同 bullet 子彈

| 英英 the firing of a gun or cannon |
| 例 Give him a **shot**.
開槍打他。 |

☐ 三分熟
☐ 五分熟
☐ 七分熟
☐ 全熟

shoul·der [ˈʃoldɚ]

名 肩、肩膀

| 英英 the joint between the upper arm or forelimb at each side of the neck, and the main part of the body |
| 例 I pat the blind's **shoulder**.
我拍拍那盲人的肩膀。 |

☐ 三分熟
☐ 五分熟
☐ 七分熟
☐ 全熟

shout [ʃaʊt]

動 呼喊、喊叫
名 叫喊、呼喊
同 yell 叫喊

| 英英 speak or call out very loudly, usually as loud as possible to be heard over a lot of noise |
| 例 The girl is **shouting** for help.
那女孩大聲求救。 |

☐ 三分熟
☐ 五分熟
☐ 七分熟
☐ 全熟

show [ʃo]

動 出示、表明
名 展覽、表演
同 display 陳列、展出

| 英英 to make something visible; exhibit or produce for inspection or viewing |
| 例 Please **show** me your passport.
請出示你的護照。 |

☐ 三分熟
☐ 五分熟
☐ 七分熟
☐ 全熟

shut [ʃʌt]

動 關上、閉上

| 英英 move into position to block an opening; to close something |
| 例 Please **shut** the door.
請關上門。 |

☐ 三分熟
☐ 五分熟
☐ 七分熟
☐ 全熟

shy [ʃaɪ]

形 害羞的、靦覥的
反 bold 大膽的

| 英英 nervous, uncomfortable, or timid in the company of other people |
| 例 She Is very **shy**.
她很害羞。 |

☐ 三分熟
☐ 五分熟
☐ 十分熟
☐ 全熟

🎧 **Track 105**

sick [sɪk]

形 有病的、患病的、想吐的、厭倦的

片 be sick of ……受夠

英英 not physically or mentally well; feeling nauseous and needing to vomit

例 You are so **sick**.
你有病。

☐ 三分熟
☐ 五分熟
☐ 七分熟
☐ 全熟

---

side [saɪd]

名 邊、旁邊、側面

形 旁邊的、側面的

同 ill 生病的

英英 the position to the left or right of something, place, or central point

例 You will see the store on your left **side**.
你會在左邊看到那家店。

☐ 三分熟
☐ 五分熟
☐ 七分熟
☐ 全熟

---

sight [saɪt]

名 視力、情景、景象

英英 having the ability or power of seeing

例 You need to have an eye **sight** test.
你需要檢查視力了。

☐ 三分熟
☐ 五分熟
☐ 七分熟
☐ 全熟

---

sil·ly [`sɪlɪ]

形 傻的、愚蠢的

同 foolish 愚蠢的

英英 showing a lack of common sense or judgment; foolish

例 **Silly** you.
你這小傻瓜。

☐ 三分熟
☐ 五分熟
☐ 七分熟
☐ 全熟

---

sil·ver [`sɪlvɚ]

名 銀

形 銀色的

英英 a grayish-white metallic chemical element used in making jewelry, utensils, etc.; a shiny grey-white color or appearance like that of silver

例 The spoon is made of **silver**.
這湯匙是銀做成的。

☐ 三分熟
☐ 五分熟
☐ 七分熟
☐ 全熟

---

sim·ple [`sɪmpl̩]

形 簡單的、簡易的

反 complex 複雜的

英英 easily understood or done; not difficult; plain and uncomplicated

例 The question is **simple**.
這問題很簡單。

☐ 三分熟
☐ 五分熟
☐ 七分熟
☐ 全熟

---

since [sɪns]

副 從……以來

介 自從

連 從……以來、因為、既然

英英 from a particular time in the past to the present time

例 I have been in love with you **since** the first sight.
從看到你的第一眼，我就愛上你了。

☐ 三分熟
☐ 五分熟
☐ 七分熟
☐ 全熟

---

sing [sɪŋ]

動 唱

英英 make musical sounds with the voice, usually with words set to a tune

例 Let's **sing** a song.
我們唱歌吧。

☐ 三分熟
☐ 五分熟
☐ 七分熟
☐ 全熟

S

sing·er [ˈsɪŋɚ]

名 歌唱家、歌手、
唱歌的人

英英 one who sings; especially, one whose profession is
to sing

例 She is the greatest **singer**.
她是最偉大的歌手。

☐ 三分熟
☐ 五分熟
☐ 七分熟
☐ 全熟

---

sir [sɝ]

名 先生
反 madam 小姐

英英 a formal and polite way of speaking to a man

例 Welcome, **sir**.
歡迎光臨，先生。

☐ 三分熟
☐ 五分熟
☐ 七分熟
☐ 全熟

---

sis·ter [ˈsɪstɚ]

名 姐妹、姐、妹
反 brother 兄弟

英英 a woman or girl with the same parents as her
siblings

例 My **sister** is growing fat.
我妹妹越來越胖了。

☐ 三分熟
☐ 五分熟
☐ 七分熟
☐ 全熟

---

sit [sɪt]

動 坐
反 stand 站

英英 be or cause to be in a position in which one's lower
body is resting on a surface, keeping the upper
body in a vertical position

例 The dog **sits** down.
那隻狗坐下來了。

☐ 三分熟
☐ 五分熟
☐ 七分熟
☐ 全熟

---

six [sɪks]

名 六

英英 one more than fivez

例 The dog has **six** babies.
這隻狗有六個小孩。

☐ 三分熟
☐ 五分熟
☐ 七分熟
☐ 全熟

---

six·teen [sɪksˈtin]

名 十六

英英 one more than fifteen and one less than seventeen

例 My son is **sixteen** years old, and I want to
give him a surprise party.
我的兒子 16 歲了，我想給他一個驚喜派對。

☐ 三分熟
☐ 五分熟
☐ 七分熟
☐ 全熟

---

six·ty [ˈsɪkstɪ]

名 六十

英英 ten more than fifty and ten less than seventy

例 The bag costs me **sixty** dollars.
這包包花了我六十塊。

☐ 三分熟
☐ 五分熟
☐ 七分熟
☐ 全熟

---

size [saɪz]

名 大小、尺寸

英英 the overall dimensions, size, or extent of something

例 The **size** of the shirt is too big.
這件襯衫的尺寸太大了。

☐ 三分熟
☐ 五分熟
☐ 七分熟
☐ 全熟

---

skill [skɪl]

名 技能
同 capability 技能

英英 the ability to do something well after extensive
practice; expertise or dexterity

例 Your basketball **skill** is good enough.
你籃球技巧已經夠好了。

☐ 三分熟
☐ 五分熟
☐ 七分熟
☐ 全熟

skin [skɪn]

名 皮、皮膚

英英 the natural outer layer of tissue forming the covering of the human body or animal

例 Your **skin** is too dark.
你的皮膚太黑了。

☐ 三分熟
☐ 五分熟
☐ 七分熟
☐ 全熟

---

sky [skaɪ]

名 天、天空

英英 the region above the earth in which clouds, the sun, moon, stars, etc. can be seen

例 The **sky** is gray.
天空很灰。

☐ 三分熟
☐ 五分熟
☐ 七分熟
☐ 全熟

---

sleep [slip]

動 睡
名 睡眠、睡眠期
反 wake 醒來

英英 a regularly recurring condition of body in which the mind and body are inactive

例 Go to **sleep** now.
現在立刻去睡覺。

☐ 三分熟
☐ 五分熟
☐ 七分熟
☐ 全熟

---

slow [slo]

形 慢的、緩慢的
副 慢
動 （使）慢下來
反 fast 快的

英英 doing, moving or capable of moving without much speed; to cause to move with less speed

例 The car is too **slow**.
這車太慢了。

☐ 三分熟
☐ 五分熟
☐ 七分熟
☐ 全熟

---

small [smɔl]

形 小的、少的
名 小東西
反 large 大的

英英 of less than normal in size or amount in comparison to something of a usual size; the small part of a thing

例 The house is too **small**.
這房子太小了。

☐ 三分熟
☐ 五分熟
☐ 七分熟
☐ 全熟

---

smart [smɑrt]

形 聰明的
同 intelligent 聰明的

英英 clean, tidy, stylish, bright and fresh in appearance; intelligent; the ability to think cleverly in difficult situations

例 The dog is very **smart**.
這隻狗很聰明。

☐ 三分熟
☐ 五分熟
☐ 七分熟
☐ 全熟

---

smell [smɛl]

動 嗅、聞到
名 氣味、香味
同 scent 氣味、香味

英英 to obtain the scent of; the faculty of perceiving when odors are present by using your nose

例 What is the dog **smelling**?
這隻狗在聞什麼？

☐ 三分熟
☐ 五分熟
☐ 七分熟
☐ 全熟

S

smile [smaɪl]

動 微笑
名 微笑
反 frown 皺眉

英英 when one's facial features are formed into a pleased, friendly, or amused expression, with the corners of the mouth turned up

例 I love the way you **smile**.
我喜歡你微笑的樣子。

☐ 三分熟
☐ 五分熟
☐ 七分熟
☐ 全熟

smoke [smok]

名 煙、煙塵
動 抽菸
同 fume 煙、氣

英英 a visible suspension of gas and small pieces of carbon or other particles in the air, produced when something is burned; to inhale and puff out the smoke of tobacco

例 Don't **smoke** here.
這邊不可以抽菸。

☐ 三分熟
☐ 五分熟
☐ 七分熟
☐ 全熟

snake [snek]

名 蛇

英英 a predatory reptile with a long slender, cylindrical limbless body, many kinds of which have a poisonous bite

例 I am afraid of **snake**.
我怕蛇。

☐ 三分熟
☐ 五分熟
☐ 七分熟
☐ 全熟

snow [sno]

名 雪
動 下雪

英英 atmospheric water vapor frozen into ice crystals and falling in light white flakes falling onto the ground forming a white layer; to fall in frozen crystals

例 It never **snows** in Taiwan.
臺灣從來不會下雪。

☐ 三分熟
☐ 五分熟
☐ 七分熟
☐ 全熟

so [so]

副 這樣、如此地
連 所以

英英 very, extremely, or to such a degree

例 **So**, what do you want to do now?
所以，你想做什麼？

☐ 三分熟
☐ 五分熟
☐ 七分熟
☐ 全熟

soap [sop]

名 肥皂

英英 substance used for washing the body, usually with a pleasant smell, and produces bubbles when used with water

例 I need a **soap** to take a bath.
我需要一塊肥皂洗澡。

☐ 三分熟
☐ 五分熟
☐ 七分熟
☐ 全熟

so·da [`sodə]

名 汽水、蘇打

英英 pop drink

例 I drink **soda** when I eat pizza.
我吃披薩的時候配汽水。

☐ 三分熟
☐ 五分熟
☐ 七分熟
☐ 全熟

🎧 **Track 109**

so·fa [ˈsofə]

名 沙發
同 couch 沙發

英英 a long seat with a back and arms that is soft and which many people can sit on at once

例 He lies on the **sofa** every weekend.
他每個週末都賴在沙發上。

☐ 三分熟
☐ 五分熟
☐ 七分熟
☐ 全熟

---

soft [sɔft]

形 軟的、柔和的
反 hard 硬的

英英 not hard or firm; easy to mould, cut, compress, or fold; not rough or coarse in texture

例 The girl's lips are **soft**.
那女孩的嘴唇很軟。

☐ 三分熟
☐ 五分熟
☐ 七分熟
☐ 全熟

---

soil [sɔɪl]

名 土壤
動 弄髒、弄汙
同 dirt 泥、土

英英 the material on the surface of the ground in which plants grow, typically consisting of organic remains, clay, and rock particles; to make dirty

例 The **soil** is good for growing plant.
這邊的土壤很適合種植。

☐ 三分熟
☐ 五分熟
☐ 七分熟
☐ 全熟

---

some [sʌm]

形 一些的、若干的
代 若干、一些
同 certain 某些、某幾個

英英 an unknown amount or number of something; a part of something

例 Give me **some** water.
給我一點水。

☐ 三分熟
☐ 五分熟
☐ 七分熟
☐ 全熟

---

some·one
[ˈsʌmˌwʌn]

代 一個人、某一個人
同 somebody 某一個人

英英 to refer to a single person in which you do not know who they are or when it is not important who they are, nor their name

例 **Someone** told me not to leave.
有人告訴我不要走。

☐ 三分熟
☐ 五分熟
☐ 七分熟
☐ 全熟

---

some·thing
[ˈsʌmθɪŋ]

代 某物、某事

英英 an unclear or unknown object, situation, quality or action

例 I have **something** for you.
我有個東西要給你。

☐ 三分熟
☐ 五分熟
☐ 七分熟
☐ 全熟

---

some·times
[ˈsʌmˌtaɪmz]

副 有時

英英 on some occasions but not always or often

例 I **sometimes** think about you.
我有時會想到你。

☐ 三分熟
☐ 五分熟
☐ 七分熟
☐ 全熟

---

son [sʌn]

名 兒子
反 daughter 女兒

英英 a male child born to you

例 My **son** is doing his homework.
我兒子正在寫作業。

☐ 三分熟
☐ 五分熟
☐ 七分熟
☐ 全熟

song [sɔŋ]

名 歌曲

英英 a poem or other words that go with music

例 This is my favorite **song**.
這是我最喜歡的歌。

☐ 三分熟
☐ 五分熟
☐ 七分熟
☐ 全熟

---

soon [sun]

副 很快地、不久
同 shortly 不久

英英 in or after a short period of time

例 He will dump you **soon**.
他很快就會甩了你。

☐ 三分熟
☐ 五分熟
☐ 七分熟
☐ 全熟

---

sorry [ˋsɔrɪ]

形 難過的、惋惜的、
抱歉的
反 glad 開心的

英英 feeling distress or pity about something wrong that you did through sympathy with someone else's misfortune

例 I feel **sorry** for you.
我替你感到難過。

☐ 三分熟
☐ 五分熟
☐ 七分熟
☐ 全熟

---

soul [sol]

名 靈魂、心靈
反 body 身體

英英 the part of a person which is not their body, the spiritual element of a person, regarded as immortal

例 You have a pure **soul**.
你有個純潔的靈魂。

☐ 三分熟
☐ 五分熟
☐ 七分熟
☐ 全熟

---

sound [saʊnd]

名 聲音、聲響
動 發出聲音、聽起來像
同 voice 聲音

英英 vibrations which are heard or that can be heard; to make a noise or sound

例 The **sound** is strange.
這聲音好奇怪。

☐ 三分熟
☐ 五分熟
☐ 七分熟
☐ 全熟

---

soup [sup]

名 湯
同 broth 湯

英英 a hot liquid dish made by boiling meat, fish, or vegetables in stock or water

例 My mom prepares chicken **soup** for me.
我媽幫我準備了雞湯。

☐ 三分熟
☐ 五分熟
☐ 七分熟
☐ 全熟

---

sour [ˋsaʊr]

形 酸的
動 變酸
名 酸的東西

英英 having a sharp, tart, or unpleasant taste like lemon or vinegar

例 The milk is **sour**.
牛奶酸了。

☐ 三分熟
☐ 五分熟
☐ 七分熟
☐ 全熟

---

south [saʊθ]

名 南、南方
形 南的、南方的
副 向南方、在南方
反 north 北方

英英 the direction on the right when facing the rising sun; lying in the direction of the point of the compass opposite the north

例 I am going to the **south**.
我要去南方。

☐ 三分熟
☐ 五分熟
☐ 七分熟
☐ 全熟

🎧 Track 111

space [spes]

名 空間、太空
動 隔開、分隔

英英 an empty ground or area available for use; a free or unoccupied area or expanse; to arrange with open places between

例 I need some more **space**.
我需要多一點空間。

□ 三分熟
□ 五分熟
□ 七分熟
□ 全熟

speak [spik]

動 說話、講話
同 talk 講話

英英 to say something using your voice; talk to in order to advise, pass on information, etc.

例 Do you **speak** English?
你說英文嗎？

□ 三分熟
□ 五分熟
□ 七分熟
□ 全熟

spe·cial [ˈspɛʃəl]

形 專門的、特別的
反 usual 平常的

英英 better, greater, more important, or otherwise different from what is usual

例 Is there anything **special**?
這邊有什麼特別的嗎？

□ 三分熟
□ 五分熟
□ 七分熟
□ 全熟

speech [spitʃ]

名 言談、說話
片 give a speech 做一場演講

英英 the expression of thoughts and feelings by talking, or an example of someone talking

例 The **speech** is touching.
這場演講很感人。

□ 三分熟
□ 五分熟
□ 七分熟
□ 全熟

spell [spɛl]

動 用字母拼、拼寫

英英 write down or tell someone the letters that form (a word) in correct sequence

例 How do you **spell** this word?
你怎麼拼這個字？

□ 三分熟
□ 五分熟
□ 七分熟
□ 全熟

spend [spɛnd]

動 花費、付錢
同 consume 花費

英英 pay out (money) in buying goods or hiring of services

例 I **spent** an hour doing my homework.
我花了一小時寫功課。

□ 三分熟
□ 五分熟
□ 七分熟
□ 全熟

spoon [spun]

名 湯匙、調羹

英英 an instrument consisting of a small, shallow bowl-like shape on a long handle, used for eating, stirring, and serving food

例 I eat the soup with **spoon**.
我用湯匙喝湯。

□ 三分熟
□ 五分熟
□ 七分熟
□ 全熟

sport [sport]

名 運動
同 exercise 運動

英英 an activity involving physical skill and exertion in which an individual or team competes against another or others

例 Basketball is my favorite **sport**.
籃球是我最愛的運動。

□ 三分熟
□ 五分熟
□ 七分熟
□ 全熟

spring [sprɪŋ]

名 跳躍、彈回、春天
動 跳、躍、彈跳
同 jump 跳

英英 the season after winter and before summer; to move rapidly upwards or forwards in a sudden motion

例 **Spring** is coming.
春天要來了。

☐ 三分熟
☐ 五分熟
☐ 七分熟
☐ 全熟

S

stair [stɛr]

名 樓梯

英英 each step in a set of fixed steps

例 Go up the **stairs**.
上樓。

☐ 三分熟
☐ 五分熟
☐ 七分熟
☐ 全熟

stand [stænd]

動 站起、立起
名 立場、觀點
反 sit 坐
片 stand with 結合、聯合、團結

英英 to be in or rise to a vertical position, supported by one's feet; position on an issue

例 **Stand** up, please.
請站起來。

☐ 三分熟
☐ 五分熟
☐ 七分熟
☐ 全熟

star [stɑr]

名 星、恆星
形 著名的、卓越的
動 扮演主角

英英 a ball of burning gases that is seen as a small point of light in the sky; distinguished; to appear as the principal actor in a play

例 There are many **stars** in the sky.
天空上有很多星星。

☐ 三分熟
☐ 五分熟
☐ 七分熟
☐ 全熟

start [stɑrt]

名 開始、起點
動 開始、著手
同 begin 開始

英英 to begin doing something; to do, be, happen, or engage in

例 We will **start** in a minute.
我們即將開始。

☐ 三分熟
☐ 五分熟
☐ 七分熟
☐ 全熟

state [stet]

名 狀態、狀況、情形；州
動 陳述、説明、闡明
同 declare 聲明、表示

英英 the condition that something or someone is in a particular time; to tell

例 What does this book **state**?
這本書闡述什麼？

☐ 三分熟
☐ 五分熟
☐ 七分熟
☐ 全熟

state·ment [ˋstetmənt]

名 陳述、聲明、宣佈

英英 a definite or clear expression of something in speech or writing; something that someone says or writes officially

例 The **statement** is illogical.
這聲明不合邏輯。

☐ 三分熟
☐ 五分熟
☐ 七分熟
☐ 全熟

sta·tion [ˋsteʃən]

名 車站

英英 a place where passenger trains stop on a railway line, with platforms and buildings for passengers to board and debark

例 My dad drives me to the **station**.
我爸載我去車站。

☐ 三分熟
☐ 五分熟
☐ 七分熟
☐ 全熟

stay [ste]

名 逗留、停留
動 停留
同 remain 留下

英英 to continue to stay in the same place

例 I will **stay** in Taipei.
我將要逗留在臺北。

☐ 三分熟
☐ 五分熟
☐ 七分熟
☐ 全熟

step [stɛp]

名 腳步、步驟
動 踏
同 pace 步

英英 the movement made in raising and setting down the foot; an act of lifting and setting down a foot or alternating feet, as in walking

例 Watch your **step**.
小心你的步伐。

☐ 三分熟
☐ 五分熟
☐ 七分熟
☐ 全熟

still [stɪl]

形 無聲的、不動的
副 仍然

英英 remain without moving; (of air or water) undisturbed by wind, sound, or current

例 The water is **still**.
水是不動的。

☐ 三分熟
☐ 五分熟
☐ 七分熟
☐ 全熟

stone [ston]

名 石、石頭
同 rock 石頭

英英 hard, solid non-metallic mineral of which rock is made

例 The house is built with **stones**.
這房子是石頭建成的。

☐ 三分熟
☐ 五分熟
☐ 七分熟
☐ 全熟

stop [stɑp]

名 停止
動 停止、結束
同 halt 停止

英英 to halt or bring to an end; prevent something from happening

例 **Stop** shouting.
停止大叫。

☐ 三分熟
☐ 五分熟
☐ 七分熟
☐ 全熟

sto·ry [ˋstorɪ]

名 故事
同 tale 故事

英英 a description of imaginary or real people and events told for entertainment

例 The **story** is interesting.
這故事很有趣。

☐ 三分熟
☐ 五分熟
☐ 七分熟
☐ 全熟

strange [strendʒ]

形 陌生的、奇怪的、
　 不熟悉的
反 familiar 熟悉的

英英 surprising because it is unusual; not previously visited, seen, or encountered

例 The man is very **strange**.
這男人很奇怪。

☐ 三分熟
☐ 五分熟
☐ 七分熟
☐ 全熟

street [strit]

名 街、街道

英英 a public road in a city, town, or village that has houses and buildings on it

例 The store is on the **street**.
這家店在這條街上。

☐ 三分熟
☐ 五分熟
☐ 七分熟
☐ 全熟

strong [strɔŋ]

形 強壯的、強健的
副 健壯地
反 weak 虛弱的

英英 physically powerful; showing ability to exert great force

例 The black man is very **strong**.
這黑人好強壯。

□ 三分熟
□ 五分熟
□ 七分熟
□ 全熟

stu·dent [ˋstjudn̩t]

名 學生
反 teacher 老師

英英 a person studying at a school, university or other place of higher education

例 I have never been a good **student**.
我從來都不是好學生。

□ 三分熟
□ 五分熟
□ 七分熟
□ 全熟

stud·y [ˋstʌdɪ]

名 學習
動 學習、研究

英英 the devotion of time and attention to acquiring knowledge and learning of a subject, usually in a school

例 The teacher asks us to **study** hard.
老師要我們認真讀書。

□ 三分熟
□ 五分熟
□ 七分熟
□ 全熟

stu·pid [ˋstjupɪd]

形 愚蠢的、笨的
反 wise 聰明的

英英 lacking intelligence or common sense, silly

例 My friends are **stupid**.
我朋友很愚蠢。

□ 三分熟
□ 五分熟
□ 七分熟
□ 全熟

such [sʌtʃ]

形 這樣的、如此的
代 這樣的人或物

英英 of a certain or similar type

例 I can't stand **such** an idiot.
我無法忍受這樣一個白癡。

□ 三分熟
□ 五分熟
□ 七分熟
□ 全熟

sug·ar [ˋʃʊgɚ]

名 糖
反 salt 鹽

英英 a sweet crystalline substance coming especially from sugar cane and sugar beet used as a seasoning and sweetener in foods

例 Add some **sugar** into the tea.
加點糖到茶裡面。

□ 三分熟
□ 五分熟
□ 七分熟
□ 全熟

sum·mer [ˋsʌmɚ]

名 夏天、夏季

英英 the season after spring and before autumn, when the weather is warmest

例 It's very hot in **summer**.
夏天很熱。

□ 三分熟
□ 五分熟
□ 七分熟
□ 全熟

sun [sʌn]

名 太陽、日
動 曬

英英 the star that shines bright during the day providing light and heat for earth, in which the earth orbits; to expose to the sun's rays

例 The **sun** will rise tomorrow.
明天太陽還是一樣升起。

□ 三分熟
□ 五分熟
□ 七分熟
□ 全熟

S

Sun·day/Sun.

[ˋsʌnde]

名 星期日

英英 the day of the week before Monday and following Saturday

例 He comes every **Sunday**.
他每週日都會來。

□ 三分熟
□ 五分熟
□ 七分熟
□ 全熟

---

su·per [ˋsupɚ]

形 很棒的、超級的

英英 excellent, very good

例 That's **super** cool!
這超級酷的！

□ 三分熟
□ 五分熟
□ 七分熟
□ 全熟

---

sup·per [ˋsʌpɚ]

名 晚餐、晚飯
反 breakfast 早餐

英英 a meal in the evening that is usually light or informal

例 I am preparing the **supper**.
我正在準備晚餐。

□ 三分熟
□ 五分熟
□ 七分熟
□ 全熟

---

sure [ʃʊr]

形 一定的、確信的
副 確定
反 doubtful 懷疑的

英英 certain; without a doubt

例 Are you **sure**?
你確定嗎？

□ 三分熟
□ 五分熟
□ 七分熟
□ 全熟

---

sur·prise

[sɚˋpraɪz]

名 驚喜、詫異
動 使驚喜、使詫異
同 amaze 使大為驚奇

英英 an unexpected incident causing a feeling of mild astonishment or shock; to strike with wonder

例 My friend gave me a **surprise**.
我朋友給了我一個驚喜。

□ 三分熟
□ 五分熟
□ 七分熟
□ 全熟

---

sweet [swit]

形 甜的、甜味的、窩心
名 糖果

英英 having a pleasant taste characteristic associated with sugar or honey; not salty, sour, or bitter; candy

例 It's so **sweet** of you.
你真窩心。

□ 三分熟
□ 五分熟
□ 七分熟
□ 全熟

---

swim [swɪm]

動 游、游泳
名 游泳

英英 propel oneself through a body of water by bodily movement; be immersed in or covered with liquid

例 The best sport in summer is **swimming**.
夏天最好的運動就是游泳。

□ 三分熟
□ 五分熟
□ 七分熟
□ 全熟

T

ta·ble [ˈtebḷ]
名 桌子
同 desk 桌子

英英 a piece of furniture consisting of four legs and a flat top used for eating, writing, or working at

例 Don't sit on the **table**.
不要坐在桌子上。

☐ 三分熟
☐ 五分熟
☐ 七分熟
☐ 全熟

tail [tel]
名 尾巴、尾部
動 尾隨、追蹤
反 head 率領

英英 the long and narrow part of an animal that sticks at the back, especially when extended beyond the rest of the body; to follow close behind

例 The dog is chasing its **tail**.
這隻狗在追著牠的尾巴。

☐ 三分熟
☐ 五分熟
☐ 七分熟
☐ 全熟

take [tek]
動 抓住、拾起、量出、吸引

英英 to take hold of something with one's hands; reach for and hold

例 **Take** a chance.
抓住機會。

☐ 三分熟
☐ 五分熟
☐ 七分熟
☐ 全熟

tale [tel]
名 故事
同 story 故事
片 fairy tale 童話

英英 a narrative or story, especially one that is imaginary

例 I used to love fairy **tale**.
我曾經喜歡童話。

☐ 三分熟
☐ 五分熟
☐ 七分熟
☐ 全熟

talk [tɔk]
名 談話、聊天
動 說話、對人講話
同 converse 談話

英英 say things to someone in order to give information or express ideas or feelings

例 I am **talking** to my sister.
我正在跟我妹講話。

☐ 三分熟
☐ 五分熟
☐ 七分熟
☐ 全熟

tall [tɔl]
形 高的
反 short 矮的

英英 of great or more height when compared to that of average height

例 He is not **tall** enough.
他不夠高。

☐ 三分熟
☐ 五分熟
☐ 七分熟
☐ 全熟

taste [test]
名 味覺
動 品嘗、辨味

英英 the sensation of flavor perceived in the mouth when in contact with food or substances; to test the flavor of

例 How does it **taste**?
這吃起來如何？

☐ 三分熟
☐ 五分熟
☐ 七分熟
☐ 全熟

🎧 Track 117

**tax·i·cab/tax·i/
cab** [ˈtæksɪˌkæb]/
[ˈtæksɪ]/[kæb]

名 計程車

英英 a motor vehicle licensed to transport passengers for payment of a fare based on each trip or distance

例 I will go to the party by **taxi**.
我會搭計程車去派對。

☐ 三分熟
☐ 五分熟
☐ 七分熟
☐ 全熟

---

tea [ti]

名 茶水、茶

英英 a hot drink made by pouring hot boiling water on the dried, crushed leaves of the tea plant

例 Do you need some **tea**?
你要喝茶嗎？

☐ 三分熟
☐ 五分熟
☐ 七分熟
☐ 全熟

---

teach [titʃ]

動 教、教書、教導

英英 to give lessons, or instruct in how to do something, especially in a school or as part of a recognized program

例 I **teach** English in high school.
我在高中教英文。

☐ 三分熟
☐ 五分熟
☐ 七分熟
☐ 全熟

---

teach·er [ˈtitʃɚ]

名 教師、老師

英英 a person who teaches in a school or college

例 The **teacher** is young.
這老師好年輕喔。

☐ 三分熟
☐ 五分熟
☐ 七分熟
☐ 全熟

---

tell [tɛl]

動 告訴、說明、分辨
同 inform 告知

英英 to say something to someone usually to communicate information; instruct to do something

例 He **told** me the truth.
他告訴我實話。

☐ 三分熟
☐ 五分熟
☐ 七分熟
☐ 全熟

---

ten [tɛn]

名 十

英英 one more than nine, and one less than eleven

例 I read **ten** books in a month.
我一個月閱讀十本書。

☐ 三分熟
☐ 五分熟
☐ 七分熟
☐ 全熟

---

than [ðæn]

連 比
介 與……比較

英英 used to join two parts to compare something or someone

例 Taipei is prettier **than** any other cities in the world.
臺北比世界上任何一個城市漂亮。

☐ 三分熟
☐ 五分熟
☐ 七分熟
☐ 全熟

---

thank [θæŋk]

動 感謝、謝謝
名 表示感激
同 appreciate 感謝

英英 express gratitude towards someone

例 **Thank** you very much.
非常謝謝你。

☐ 三分熟
☐ 五分熟
☐ 七分熟
☐ 全熟

that [ðæt] 形 那、那個 副 那麼、那樣	英英 to refer to a person, object, idea, etc. of which is separated from the speaker by space or time 例 **That** is a good question. 這是個好問題。	☐三分熟 ☐五分熟 ☐七分熟 ☐全熟
the [ðə] 冠 用於知道的人或物之 前、指特定的人或物	英英 to refer to things or people when a listener or reader has previous knowledge of particular things or people are being referred to 例 **The** girl is cute. 這女孩很可愛。	☐三分熟 ☐五分熟 ☐七分熟 ☐全熟
their(s) [ðɛr(z)] 代 他們的（東西）、 她們的（東西）、 它們的（東西）	英英 of or belonging to them not including the speaker 例 **Their** school is far. 他們學校很遠。	☐三分熟 ☐五分熟 ☐七分熟 ☐全熟
them [ðɛm] 代 他們	英英 used after a verb or preposition to refer to a group of people, animals, or things previously mentioned 例 Give it to **them**. 把這拿給他們。	☐三分熟 ☐五分熟 ☐七分熟 ☐全熟
then [ðɛn] 副 當時、那時、然後	英英 (at) a certain time (in the past or in the future) 例 **Then**, what did you do? 那你做了什麼？	☐三分熟 ☐五分熟 ☐七分熟 ☐全熟
there [ðɛr] 副 在那兒、往那兒 反 here 在這兒	英英 (to, at or in) a certain place 例 What's over **there**? 那兒有什麼？	☐三分熟 ☐五分熟 ☐七分熟 ☐全熟
these [ðiz] 代 這些、這些的 （this 的複數） 反 those 那些	英英 the pronoun plural of this 例 **These** are the best choices. 這些都是最好的選項。	☐三分熟 ☐五分熟 ☐七分熟 ☐全熟
they [ðe] 代 他們	英英 the subject of a verb to refer to people, animals or things already mentioned or, in a more general sense 例 **They** don't have money. 他們沒有錢。	☐三分熟 ☐五分熟 ☐七分熟 ☐全熟

T

🎧 **Track 119**

thing [θɪŋ]

名 東西、物體
同 object 物體

英英 an unclear material or object; an unspecified object
例 That is the best **thing** in the world.
這是世界上最好的東西。

☐三分熟
☐五分熟
☐七分熟
☐全熟

think [θɪŋk]

動 想、思考
同 consider 考慮
片 think of 想到

英英 have a particular opinion, belief, or idea about someone or something
例 What do you **think**?
你覺得如何？

☐三分熟
☐五分熟
☐七分熟
☐全熟

third [θɝd]

名 第三
形 第三的

英英 constituting number three in a sequence; 3rd
例 I got the **third** prize.
我得到第三名。

☐三分熟
☐五分熟
☐七分熟
☐全熟

thir·teen [ˋθɝtin]

名 十三

英英 one more than twelve, one less than fourteen
例 He won the prize **thirteen** times.
他得獎十三次了。

☐三分熟
☐五分熟
☐七分熟
☐全熟

thir·ty [ˋθɝtɪ]

名 三十

英英 ten less than forty, and ten more than twenty
例 There are **thirty** students in the class.
這班上有三十個學生。

☐三分熟
☐五分熟
☐七分熟
☐全熟

this [ðɪs]

形 這、這個
代 這個
反 that 那個

英英 used for a person, object, etc. to show which one is referred to
例 **This** is what I want.
這是我想要的。

☐三分熟
☐五分熟
☐七分熟
☐全熟

those [ðoz]

代 那些、那些的
（that 的複數）

英英 pronoun plural of that
例 **Those** are the best books.
那些是最好的書。

☐三分熟
☐五分熟
☐七分熟
☐全熟

though [ðo]

副 但是、然而
連 雖然、儘管
同 nevertheless 雖然

英英 despite the fact that; although; however
例 **Though** he is poor, he is diligent.
他雖然很窮，但很勤奮。

☐三分熟
☐五分熟
☐七分熟
☐全熟

thought [θɔt]

名 思考、思維

英英 the noun form of think; an idea or opinion produced by thinking or occurring suddenly in one's mind
例 You have great **thoughts**.
你有很棒的思維。

☐三分熟
☐五分熟
☐七分熟
☐全熟

thou·sand

[ˈθaʊzn̩d]

名 一千、多數、成千

英英 a large number; the number from 1,000 to 9,999

例 It costs me a **thousand** dollars.
這花了我一千塊。

☐ 三分熟
☐ 五分熟
☐ 七分熟
☐ 全熟

---

three [θri]

名 三

英英 one more than two, and one less than four

例 I have **three** sons.
我有三個兒子。

☐ 三分熟
☐ 五分熟
☐ 七分熟
☐ 全熟

---

throw [θro]

動 投、擲、扔

英英 to make something move through the air by using a force from a rapid movement of the arm and hand

例 **Throw** the ball to me.
把球丟給我。

☐ 三分熟
☐ 五分熟
☐ 七分熟
☐ 全熟

Thurs·day/Thur./

Thurs. [ˈθɝzde]

名 星期四

英英 the day of the week before Friday and after Wednesday

例 I have PE class on **Thursday**.
我星期四有體育課。

☐ 三分熟
☐ 五分熟
☐ 七分熟
☐ 全熟

---

thus [ðʌs]

副 因此、所以
同 therefore 因此

英英 as a result or consequence of this; therefore

例 **Thus**, I disagree with him.
因此，我不同意他。

☐ 三分熟
☐ 五分熟
☐ 七分熟
☐ 全熟

---

tick·et [ˈtɪkɪt]

名 車票、入場券

英英 a piece of paper, voucher, or card giving the holder admission to a place or event or to travel on public transport

例 Buy the **ticket** here.
在這裡買票。

☐ 三分熟
☐ 五分熟
☐ 七分熟
☐ 全熟

---

tie [taɪ]

名 領帶、領結
動 打結

英英 attach or fasten to something with string, cord, etc.; form into a knot or bow; a thing that ties

例 I bought a **tie** for my dad.
我買條領帶給我爸爸。

☐ 三分熟
☐ 五分熟
☐ 七分熟
☐ 全熟

---

ti·ger [ˈtaɪgɚ]

名 老虎

英英 a large solitary and wild cat with a yellow-brown coat striped with black, native to the forests of Asia

例 I am afraid of **tigers**.
我怕老虎。

☐ 三分熟
☐ 五分熟
☐ 七分熟
☐ 全熟

---

time [taɪm]

名 時間

英英 the ongoing progress of existence and events in the past, present, and future, regarded as a whole

例 What **time** is it now?
現在幾點了？

☐ 三分熟
☐ 五分熟
☐ 七分熟
☐ 全熟

T

Track 121

---

ti·ny [ˈtaɪnɪ]

形 極小的
反 giant 巨大的

英英 very small or minute

例 The bug is very **tiny**.
這隻蟲很小。

☐三分熟
☐五分熟
☐七分熟
☐全熟

---

tire [taɪr]

動 使疲倦
名 輪胎

英英 a rubber covering, typically inflated or surrounding an inflated inner tube, placed round a wheel for soft contact with the road

例 We need to change the **tire**.
我們需要換輪胎了。

☐三分熟
☐五分熟
☐七分熟
☐全熟

---

to [tu]

介 到、向、往

英英 used before a verb to show that it is in the infinitive form; used after some verbs, especially when the action described in the infinitive will happen later

例 Go **to** the school.
走去學校。

☐三分熟
☐五分熟
☐七分熟
☐全熟

---

to·day [təˈde]

名 今天
副 在今天、本日
反 tomorrow 明天

英英 on or during the course of a present day

例 I need to finish my work **today**.
我今天要完成我的工作。

☐三分熟
☐五分熟
☐七分熟
☐全熟

---

to·geth·er

[təˈgɛðɚ]

副 在一起、緊密地
同 alone 單獨地

英英 with or in close proximity to another person or people

例 We sang a song **together**.
我們一起唱歌。

☐三分熟
☐五分熟
☐七分熟
☐全熟

---

to·mor·row

[təˈmɔro]

名 明天
副 在明天

英英 on the day after today

例 Where are you going **tomorrow**?
你明天要去哪裡？

☐三分熟
☐五分熟
☐七分熟
☐全熟

---

tone [ton]

名 風格、音調

英英 a musical or vocal sound with reference to its pitch, quality, and strength

例 The **tone** is strange.
這音調好奇怪。

☐三分熟
☐五分熟
☐七分熟
☐全熟

---

to·night [təˈnaɪt]

名 今天晚上
副 今晚

英英 on the present or approaching evening or night

例 Do you have time **tonight**?
你今晚有空嗎？

☐三分熟
☐五分熟
☐七分熟
☐全熟

too [tu]

副 也

英英 more than what is needed or wanted; more than enough, suitable, or required

例 I want to go to the zoo, **too**.
我也想去動物園。

☐ 三分熟
☐ 五分熟
☐ 七分熟
☐ 全熟

T

---

tool [tul]

名 工具、用具
同 device 設備、儀器

英英 a device or instrument used for a specific function

例 You need some **tools** to fix the car.
你需要工具修車。

☐ 三分熟
☐ 五分熟
☐ 七分熟
☐ 全熟

---

top [tɑp]

形 頂端的
名 頂端
動 勝過、高於
反 bottom 底部

英英 the highest, first, or uppermost layer, point, part, or surface; to excel or surpass

例 We are at the **top** of the mountain.
我們在山頂上。

☐ 三分熟
☐ 五分熟
☐ 七分熟
☐ 全熟

---

to·tal [ˋtotl]

形 全部的
名 總數、全部
動 總計
同 entire 全部

英英 adding the everything for the whole number or amount

例 What's the **total** amount?
總數是多少？

☐ 三分熟
☐ 五分熟
☐ 七分熟
☐ 全熟

---

touch [tʌtʃ]

名 接觸、碰、觸摸
同 contact 接觸

英英 come into or be in contact with; to put your hand on something, contact with skin

例 Don't **touch** me.
不要碰我。

☐ 三分熟
☐ 五分熟
☐ 七分熟
☐ 全熟

---

to·ward(s)
[təˋword(z)]

介 對……、向……、
對於……

英英 to go or be in the direction of; getting nearer to (a time or goal)

例 She walked **toward** me.
她走向我。

☐ 三分熟
☐ 五分熟
☐ 七分熟
☐ 全熟

---

town [taʊn]

名 城鎮、鎮

英英 a settlement larger than a village and generally smaller than a city, with defined boundaries and it's own local government

例 Let's go to the **town**.
去鎮上吧。

☐ 三分熟
☐ 五分熟
☐ 七分熟
☐ 全熟

---

toy [tɔɪ]

名 玩具

英英 an object for a person to play with, typically a model or miniature replica of something

例 This **toy** is too expensive.
這玩具太貴了。

☐ 三分熟
☐ 五分熟
☐ 七分熟
☐ 全熟

🎧 Track 123

train [tren]

名 火車
動 教育、訓練
同 educate 教育

英英 a series of railway carriages or wagons moved as a unit by a locomotive, steam engine, or by integral motors; to teach (a person or animal) a particular skill or type of behavior through practice and instruction on a regular basis

例 The **train** is coming.
火車進站中。

☐ 三分熟
☐ 五分熟
☐ 七分熟
☐ 全熟

tree [tri]

名 樹

英英 a woody plant with a thick, typically single stem or trunk growing to a considerable height with branches and leaves

例 The **tree** is tall.
這棵樹很高。

☐ 三分熟
☐ 五分熟
☐ 七分熟
☐ 全熟

trip [trɪp]

名 旅行
動 絆倒
同 journey 旅行
片 take a trip 旅行

英英 a journey or excursion; to fall or stumble by latching one's foot on something

例 Let's take a **trip** to the South.
去南部旅行吧。

☐ 三分熟
☐ 五分熟
☐ 七分熟
☐ 全熟

trou·ble [ˈtrʌbl̩]

名 憂慮、煩惱、麻煩的事、困難
動 使煩惱、折磨
同 disturb 使心神不寧

英英 difficulty or problems; effort or exertion; to distress

例 You are in **trouble**.
你有煩惱了。

☐ 三分熟
☐ 五分熟
☐ 七分熟
☐ 全熟

true [tru]

形 真的、對的
反 false 假的、錯的

英英 real or actual, often factual; accurate and exact accord of events

例 Can it be **true**?
這有可能是真的嗎？

☐ 三分熟
☐ 五分熟
☐ 七分熟
☐ 全熟

try [traɪ]

名 試驗、嘗試
動 嘗試
同 attempt 企圖、嘗試

英英 to attempt or make an effort in order to do something

例 Would you like to have a **try**?
你要試試看嗎？

☐ 三分熟
☐ 五分熟
☐ 七分熟
☐ 全熟

T-shirt [ˈtiʃɜt]

名 T 恤

英英 a short-sleeved garment for the upper body, having the shape of a T when spread out flat

例 She wears **T-shirt** all the time.
她總是穿 T 恤。

☐ 三分熟
☐ 五分熟
☐ 七分熟
☐ 全熟

Tues·day/Tue.
Tues./ [ˈtjuzde]
名 星期二

| 英英 he day of the week before Wednesday and after Monday
| 例 Today is **Tuesday**.
今天是星期二。

☐ 三分熟
☐ 五分熟
☐ 七分熟
☐ 全熟

tum·my [ˈtʌmɪ]
名 （口語）肚子

英英 a person's stomach or abdomen
例 He hit my **tummy**.
他打我的肚子。

☐ 三分熟
☐ 五分熟
☐ 七分熟
☐ 全熟

turn [tɜn]
名 旋轉、轉動
動 旋轉、轉動
同 rotate 旋轉
片 turn on 打開（燈）
turn off 關掉（燈）

英英 move in a circular direction in a whole circle or in a partial circle around an axis
例 **Turn** around.
轉一圈。

☐ 三分熟
☐ 五分熟
☐ 七分熟
☐ 全熟

twelve [twɛlv]
名 十二

英英 two more than ten and one less than thirteen
例 A dozen means **twelve**.
一打有十二個。

☐ 三分熟
☐ 五分熟
☐ 七分熟
☐ 全熟

twen·ty [ˈtwɛntɪ]
名 二十

英英 ten less than thirty and ten more than ten
例 She got married at **twenty**.
她二十歲結婚。

☐ 三分熟
☐ 五分熟
☐ 七分熟
☐ 全熟

twice [twaɪs]
副 兩次、兩倍

英英 two times more than the given amount; double in degree or quantity
例 Her boyfriend is **twice** older than she is.
她男朋友的年紀是她的兩倍大。

☐ 三分熟
☐ 五分熟
☐ 七分熟
☐ 全熟

two [tu]
名 二

英英 one less than three and one more than one
例 I don't have any girlfriend but you have **two**!
我沒有女朋友，但是你竟然有兩個！

☐ 三分熟
☐ 五分熟
☐ 七分熟
☐ 全熟

T

Uu

🎧 Track 125

---

un·cle [ˈʌŋk!]

名 叔叔、伯伯、舅舅、姑父、姨父

英英 the brother of a person's father or mother or the husband of a person's aunt

例 **Uncle** Tom is coming.
湯姆叔叔要來了。

☐ 三分熟 ☐ 五分熟 ☐ 七分熟 ☐ 全熟

---

un·der [ˈʌndɚ]

介 小於、少於、低於
副 在下、在下面、往下面
反 over 在……上方

英英 either extending, laying, or directly below

例 The ball is **under** the table.
球在桌子下。

☐ 三分熟 ☐ 五分熟 ☐ 七分熟 ☐ 全熟

---

un·der·stand

[ˌʌndɚˈstænd]

動 瞭解、明白
同 comprehend 理解

英英 to know the intended meaning of (words, a language, or a speaker)

例 Why can't you **understand**?
為什麼你總是不明白。

☐ 三分熟 ☐ 五分熟 ☐ 七分熟 ☐ 全熟

---

u·nit [ˈjunɪt]

名 單位、單元

英英 an individual thing, group, or person regarded a whole single and complete; each of the individual components making up a larger whole

例 We learn how to say goodbye in the first **unit**.
我們在第一課學會怎麼說再見。

☐ 三分熟 ☐ 五分熟 ☐ 七分熟 ☐ 全熟

---

un·til/till

[ənˈtɪl]/[tɪl]

連 直到……為止
介 直到……為止

英英 up to (the point in time or the situation mentioned)

例 Not **until** we lose do we understand how to cherish.
直到我們失去才懂得珍惜。

☐ 三分熟 ☐ 五分熟 ☐ 七分熟 ☐ 全熟

---

up [ʌp]

副 向上地
介 在高處、向（在）上面
反 down 向下地

英英 towards a higher position; towards an above value, number or level

例 We wake **up** at six.
我們六點起床。

☐ 三分熟 ☐ 五分熟 ☐ 七分熟 ☐ 全熟

---

up·stairs

[ˈʌpˌstɛrz]

副 往（在）樓上
形 樓上的
名 樓上

英英 on or to an upper or higher floor

例 Go **upstairs**.
上樓。

☐ 三分熟 ☐ 五分熟 ☐ 七分熟 ☐ 全熟

---

us [ʌs]
代 我們

英英 used by a speaker to refer to themselves and one or more others as the object of a verb or preposition

例 Tell **us** your problem.
告訴我們你的問題。

☐三分熟
☐五分熟
☐七分熟
☐全熟

---

use [juz]
動 使用、消耗
名 使用

英英 to take, hold, or deploy to achieve something; consume or expend the whole of

例 How to **use** the smart phone?
智慧手機要怎麼用？

☐三分熟
☐五分熟
☐七分熟
☐全熟

---

use·ful [ˈjusfəl]
形 有用的、有益的、有幫助的

英英 able to be used for a practical purpose or in several ways

例 These tips are **useful**.
這些技巧很有用。

☐三分熟
☐五分熟
☐七分熟
☐全熟

Vv

veg·e·ta·ble
[ˈvɛdʒətəbl]
名 蔬菜
反 meat 肉類

英英 a plant or part of a plant used as food and eaten

例 You should eat **vegetables** every day.
你每天都該吃蔬菜。

☐三分熟
☐五分熟
☐七分熟
☐全熟

---

ver·y [ˈvɛrɪ]
副 很、非常

英英 to emphasize something in a high degree

例 I am **very** angry.
我很生氣。

☐三分熟
☐五分熟
☐七分熟
☐全熟

---

view [vju]
名 看見、景觀
動 觀看、視察
同 sight 看見、景象
片 view point 觀點

英英 to have the ability to see something or to be seen from a particular position, or vantage point

例 The **view** is great.
景色非常棒。

☐三分熟
☐五分熟
☐七分熟
☐全熟

---

vis·it [ˈvɪzɪt]
動 訪問
名 訪問

英英 to go to see and spend time with (someone) socially or as a guest

例 I will pay you a **visit**.
我會去拜訪你。

☐三分熟
☐五分熟
☐七分熟
☐全熟

135

🎧 Track 127

voice [vɔɪs]

名 聲音、發言

英英 the sound produced in a person's throat and spoken through the mouth, as speech or song

例 Your **voice** is tender.
你的聲音好溫和。

☐ 三分熟
☐ 五分熟
☐ 七分熟
☐ 全熟

Ww

wait [wet]

動 等待
名 等待、等待的時間

英英 maintain where one is or delay action until a particular time, person, or event has occurred

例 **Wait** a minute.
等一下。

☐ 三分熟
☐ 五分熟
☐ 七分熟
☐ 全熟

walk [wɔk]

動 走、步行
名 步行、走、散步

英英 move at a regular and fairly slow pace by lifting and setting down each foot in front of the other

例 I will **walk** there.
我會走去那邊。

☐ 三分熟
☐ 五分熟
☐ 七分熟
☐ 全熟

wall [wɔl]

名 牆壁

英英 a continuous vertical brick or stone structure enclosure that divides an area of land

例 Put the shoes against the **wall**.
把鞋子靠牆壁放。

☐ 三分熟
☐ 五分熟
☐ 七分熟
☐ 全熟

want [wɑnt]

動 想要、要
名 需要
同 desire 想要

英英 have a desire to do or to possess something; wish for

例 I **want** to go.
我想要走了。

☐ 三分熟
☐ 五分熟
☐ 七分熟
☐ 全熟

war [wɔr]

名 戰爭
反 peace 和平

英英 a state of armed conflict between different nations, states, or armed groups for opposing ideals

例 The **war** is over.
戰爭結束了。

☐ 三分熟
☐ 五分熟
☐ 七分熟
☐ 全熟

warm [wɔrm]

形 暖和的、溫暖的
動 使暖和
片 warm up 暖身

英英 of or at a fairly or comfortable temperature between hot and cold; to make heated

例 It's getting **warm**.
天氣越來越溫暖了。

☐ 三分熟
☐ 五分熟
☐ 七分熟
☐ 全熟

wash [wɑʃ]

動 洗、洗滌
名 洗、沖洗
同 clean 弄乾淨

英英 clean with either cold or warm water and, typically, soap or detergent

例 **Wash** your hands before the meal.
飯前先洗手。

☐ 三分熟
☐ 五分熟
☐ 七分熟
☐ 全熟

---

waste [west]

動 浪費、濫用
名 浪費
形 廢棄的、無用的
反 save 節省

英英 use carelessly, extravagantly, or to no purpose

例 Don't **waste** your time.
不要浪費時間。

☐ 三分熟
☐ 五分熟
☐ 七分熟
☐ 全熟

---

watch [wɑtʃ]

動 注視、觀看、注意
名 手錶
反 ignore 忽略

英英 look at attentively for a prolonged period of time; keep under careful or protective observation; small instrument showing the time

例 I bought a **watch** for you.
我買了隻手錶給你。

☐ 三分熟
☐ 五分熟
☐ 七分熟
☐ 全熟

---

wa·ter [ˈwɔtɚ]

名 水
動 澆水、灑水

英英 the liquid in which the seas, lakes, rivers, and rain are composed of, and is the basis of the fluids of living organisms; to sprinkle with water

例 Drink some **water**.
喝點水吧。

☐ 三分熟
☐ 五分熟
☐ 七分熟
☐ 全熟

---

way [we]

名 路、道路

英英 a method, style, or manner of doing something; the distance in space or time between one point to another

例 It's the **way** to home.
這是回家的道路。

☐ 三分熟
☐ 五分熟
☐ 七分熟
☐ 全熟

---

we [wi]

代 我們

英英 when the speaker and at least one other person are considered together or as a group

例 **We** need some more woods.
我們需要更多木頭。

☐ 三分熟
☐ 五分熟
☐ 七分熟
☐ 全熟

---

weak [wik]

形 無力的、虛弱的
同 feeble 虛弱的

英英 lacking physical strength and energy; liable to break or give way easily under pressure

例 She's ill and **weak**.
她病得很嚴重，身體很虛弱。

☐ 三分熟
☐ 五分熟
☐ 七分熟
☐ 全熟

🎧 **Track 129**

wear [wɛr]
動 穿、戴、耐久

英英 to put clothing, decoration, or protection on one's body

例 What will you **wear** tomorrow?
你明天會穿什麼？

☐ 三分熟
☐ 五分熟
☐ 七分熟
☐ 全熟

---

weath·er [ˈwɛðɚ]
名 天氣

英英 the conditions of the atmosphere at a place and time as regards temperature, wind, rain, etc.

例 What't the **weather** today?
今天的天氣如何？

☐ 三分熟
☐ 五分熟
☐ 七分熟
☐ 全熟

---

wed·ding [ˈwɛdɪŋ]
名 婚禮、結婚
同 marriage 婚禮、結婚

英英 a marriage ceremony

例 It's my best friend's **wedding**.
這是我最好的朋友的婚禮。

☐ 三分熟
☐ 五分熟
☐ 七分熟
☐ 全熟

Wedne·sday/
Wed./Weds.
[ˈwɛnzde]
名 星期三

英英 the day of the week before Thursday and following Tuesday

例 I have a meeting on **Wednesday**.
我星期三要開會。

☐ 三分熟
☐ 五分熟
☐ 七分熟
☐ 全熟

---

week [wik]
名 星期、工作日

英英 a period of seven days; the period of seven days generally starting from and to midnight on Saturday night

例 There are 52 **weeks** in a year.
一年有 52 週。

☐ 三分熟
☐ 五分熟
☐ 七分熟
☐ 全熟

---

week·end
[ˈwikˌɛnd]
名 週末
（星期六和星期日）

英英 Saturday and Sunday, in which many people do not work

例 How will you spend your **weekend**?
你週末要怎麼度過？

☐ 三分熟
☐ 五分熟
☐ 七分熟
☐ 全熟

---

weigh [we]
動 稱重

英英 to discover how heavy (someone or something) is

例 The car **weighs** more than five hundred kilo.
這車子超過五百公斤重。

☐ 三分熟
☐ 五分熟
☐ 七分熟
☐ 全熟

---

weight [wet]
名 重、重量

英英 a body's relative mass or the quantity of matter held by it, giving rise to a downward force; heaviness

例 I don't know her **weight**.
我不知道她的體重。

☐ 三分熟
☐ 五分熟
☐ 七分熟
☐ 全熟

wel·come

[ˈwɛlkəm]

動 歡迎
名 親切的接待
形 受歡迎的
感 （親切的招呼）歡迎

英英 an instance, polite words, or manner of greeting someone

例 **Welcome** home.
歡迎回家。

☐ 三分熟
☐ 五分熟
☐ 七分熟
☐ 全熟

---

well [wɛl]

形 健康的
副 好、令人滿意地
反 badly 壞、拙劣地

英英 healthy; in a good way; to a high or satisfactory standard

例 She doesn't feel **well** today.
她今天不太舒服。

☐ 三分熟
☐ 五分熟
☐ 七分熟
☐ 全熟

---

west [wɛst]

名 西方
形 西部的、西方的
副 向西方
反 east 東方

英英 the direction towards the point of the horizon where the sun sets at the equinoxes, on the left-hand side of a person who is facing north

例 I will to go the **west**.
我要向西方走。

☐ 三分熟
☐ 五分熟
☐ 七分熟
☐ 全熟

---

what [hwɑt]

形 什麼
代 （疑問代詞）什麼

英英 used to ask for information about people or things

例 **What**'s this?
這是什麼？

☐ 三分熟
☐ 五分熟
☐ 七分熟
☐ 全熟

---

when [hwɛn]

副 什麼時候、何時
連 當……時
代 （關係代詞）那時

英英 used to ask for information about people or things in relation to time

例 **When** will you come?
你何時會來？

☐ 三分熟
☐ 五分熟
☐ 七分熟
☐ 全熟

---

where [hwɛr]

副 在哪裡
代 在哪裡
名 地點

英英 to, at or in what place

例 **Where** are you?
你在哪裡？

☐ 三分熟
☐ 五分熟
☐ 七分熟
☐ 全熟

---

wheth·er [ˈhwɛðɚ]

連 是否、無論如何
同 if 是否

英英 to discuss choice between to or more things; reporting questions and expressing doubts

例 Let me know **whether** you will come.
告訴我你會不會來。

☐ 三分熟
☐ 五分熟
☐ 七分熟
☐ 全熟

W

Track 131

---

which [hwɪtʃ]

形 哪一個
代 哪一個

英英 used in questions and structures in which there is a fixed or limited set of answers or possibilities what one or ones

例 **Which** do you like, coffee or tea?
咖啡跟茶，你喜歡哪一個？

☐ 三分熟
☐ 五分熟
☐ 七分熟
☐ 全熟

---

while [hwaɪl]

名 時間
連 當……的時候、
　　另一方面

英英 a period of time during the time that, or occurring at the same time as

例 The bell rang **while** I was taking a shower.
當我在洗澡的時候，門鈴響了。

☐ 三分熟
☐ 五分熟
☐ 七分熟
☐ 全熟

---

white [hwaɪt]

形 白色的
名 白色
反 black 黑色

英英 of the color of milk or fresh snow, due to the reflection of the complete visible rays of light

例 The cat is **white**.
那隻貓是白色的。

☐ 三分熟
☐ 五分熟
☐ 七分熟
☐ 全熟

---

who [hu]

代 誰

英英 used especially in questions as the subject or object of a verb, when asking which person or people, or when asking what someone's name is

例 **Who** cares?
誰在乎？

☐ 三分熟
☐ 五分熟
☐ 七分熟
☐ 全熟

---

whole [hol]

形 全部的、整個的
名 全體、整體
反 partial 部分的

英英 complete, broken, or not divided; a total

例 It would be a **whole** new world.
這裡將會變成新的世界。

☐ 三分熟
☐ 五分熟
☐ 七分熟
☐ 全熟

---

whom [hum]

代 誰

英英 used instead of "who" as the object of a verb or preposition

例 **Whom** do you love?
你愛誰？

☐ 三分熟
☐ 五分熟
☐ 七分熟
☐ 全熟

---

whose [huz]

代 誰的

英英 used especially in questions when asking about which person owns or is responsible for something

例 **Whose** car is larger?
誰的車比較大？

☐ 三分熟
☐ 五分熟
☐ 七分熟
☐ 全熟

---

why [hwaɪ]

副 為什麼

英英 for what reason

例 **Why** are you late?
你為什麼遲到？

☐ 三分熟
☐ 五分熟
☐ 七分熟
☐ 全熟

---

wide [waɪd]

形 寬廣的
副 寬廣地
同 broad 寬的、闊的

英英 measuring a long distance of great or more than average with

例 The space is **wide**.
空間很寬廣。

□ 三分熟
□ 五分熟
□ 七分熟
□ 全熟

---

wife [waɪf]

名 妻子
反 husband 丈夫

英英 a married woman considered in relation to her husband

例 Do you want to be my **wife**?
你要當我老婆嗎？

□ 三分熟
□ 五分熟
□ 七分熟
□ 全熟

---

will [wɪl]

名 意志、意志力
助動 將、會

英英 mental power by which a person can direct his thoughts and actions; talk about what is may possibly happen in the future, the mental power used to control and direct your thoughts and actions

例 I **will** go.
我將要走了。

□ 三分熟
□ 五分熟
□ 七分熟
□ 全熟

---

win [wɪn]

動 獲勝、贏
反 lose 輸

英英 be successful or victorious in (a contest or conflict)

例 I **won** the game.
我贏了這場比賽。

□ 三分熟
□ 五分熟
□ 七分熟
□ 全熟

---

wind [wɪnd]

名 風
同 breeze 微風

英英 the natural movement of the air, especially in the form of a current blowing from a particular direction

例 Everything will go with the **wind**.
一切都會隨風而逝。

□ 三分熟
□ 五分熟
□ 七分熟
□ 全熟

---

win·dow [ˈwɪndo]

名 窗戶

英英 an opening in a wall or roof of a building or vehicle, fitted with glass in a frame to allow in light or air and people to see out

例 Open the **window**, please.
請打開窗戶。

□ 三分熟
□ 五分熟
□ 七分熟
□ 全熟

---

wine [waɪn]

名 葡萄酒

英英 an alcoholic drink made from fermented grapes

例 I love to drink **wine**.
我喜歡喝葡萄酒。

□ 三分熟
□ 五分熟
□ 七分熟
□ 全熟

---

win·ter [ˈwɪntɚ]

名 冬季
反 summer 夏天

英英 the coldest season of the year, after autumn and before spring

例 The **winter** in Taiwan is short.
臺灣的冬天很短。

□ 三分熟
□ 五分熟
□ 七分熟
□ 全熟

🎧 Track 133

wish [wɪʃ]

動 願望、希望
名 願望、希望

英英 desire something that cannot, probably, or be impossible to happen

例 I **wish** you were there.
我好希望你在這裡。

☐ 三分熟
☐ 五分熟
☐ 七分熟
☐ 全熟

with [wɪð]

介 具有、帶有、
　　和……一起、用
反 without 沒有

英英 in the company or presence of a person or thing

例 The girl **with** big eyes is pretty.
那大眼女孩很可愛。

☐ 三分熟
☐ 五分熟
☐ 七分熟
☐ 全熟

wom·an [ˈwʊmən]

名 成年女人、婦女
反 man 成年男人

英英 an adult human female

例 The **woman** is nice to me.
那女人對我很好。

☐ 三分熟
☐ 五分熟
☐ 七分熟
☐ 全熟

wood(s) [wʊd(z)]

名 木材、樹林

英英 a hard material which forms the branches and trunks of trees and which can be used as a building material

例 The table is made of **wood**.
這桌子是木頭做的。

☐ 三分熟
☐ 五分熟
☐ 七分熟
☐ 全熟

word [wɝd]

名 字、單字、話

英英 a group of letters or sounds in language which has meaning and can be either spoken or written

例 The **word** is too difficult for children.
這個字對小孩來說太難了。

☐ 三分熟
☐ 五分熟
☐ 七分熟
☐ 全熟

work [wɝk]

名 工作、勞動
動 操作、工作、做
同 labor 工作、勞動

英英 activity involving mental or exerting physical efforts done in order to achieve a result; to labor

例 I **work** hard every day.
我每天都很認真工作。

☐ 三分熟
☐ 五分熟
☐ 七分熟
☐ 全熟

work·er [ˈwɝkɚ]

名 工作者、工人

英英 a person who works; a person who achieves a specified thing or task

例 The **workers** are angry.
工人們很生氣。

☐ 三分熟
☐ 五分熟
☐ 七分熟
☐ 全熟

world [wɝld]

名 地球、世界

英英 the earth with all its countries and people

例 I believe the **world** is getting better.
我相信世界變得更好了。

☐ 三分熟
☐ 五分熟
☐ 七分熟
☐ 全熟

worm [wɝm]

名 蚯蚓或其他類似的小蟲
動 蠕行
同 crawl 蠕行

英英 a small creature, an earthworm or other creeping or burrowing invertebrate animal lacking limbs and having a long slender soft body; move by wriggling

例 The worm is **good** for plants.
蚯蚓對植物是益蟲。

□ 三分熟
□ 五分熟
□ 七分熟
□ 全熟

---

wor·ry [ˋwɝɪ]

名 憂慮、擔心
動 煩惱、擔心、發愁

英英 feel or cause to feel anxious over actual, unpleasant things or difficulties that might happen

例 Don't **worry** about me.
不要替我擔心。

□ 三分熟
□ 五分熟
□ 七分熟
□ 全熟

---

worse [wɝs]

形 更壞的、更差的
副 更壞、更糟
名 更壞的事
反 better 更好的

英英 less good, satisfactory, or pleasing than something else that is bad

例 It's getting **worse**.
狀況變得更差了。

□ 三分熟
□ 五分熟
□ 七分熟
□ 全熟

---

worst [wɝst]

形 最壞的、最差的
副 最差地、最壞地
名 最壞的情況
　（結果、行為）
反 best 最好的

英英 most bad, severe, or serious; that which is most corrupt

例 You are always the **worst** example.
你總是做最差的示範。

□ 三分熟
□ 五分熟
□ 七分熟
□ 全熟

---

write [raɪt]

動 書寫、寫下、寫字

英英 mark (letters, words, or other symbols) on a surface, with a pen, pencil, or similar tool

例 She **wrote** an interesting story.
她寫了個有趣的故事。

□ 三分熟
□ 五分熟
□ 七分熟
□ 全熟

---

writ·er [ˋraɪtɚ]

名 作者、作家
同 author 作者

英英 a person who has written a particular text, or who writes books or articles as an occupation

例 The **writer** is famous.
這作家很有名。

□ 三分熟
□ 五分熟
□ 七分熟
□ 全熟

---

wrong [rɔŋ]

形 壞的、錯的
副 錯誤地、不適當地
名 錯誤、壞事
同 false 錯的

英英 incorrect or not true; mistaken or in error

例 What's **wrong** with you?
你怎麼了？

□ 三分熟
□ 五分熟
□ 七分熟
□ 全熟

W

yam/ sweet po·ta·to

[jæm]/[swit pə`teto]

名 山藥、甘薯

英英 the root of a tropical plant which is cooked as a vegetable

例 I like to eat fried **yam**.
我喜歡吃炸地瓜。

☐ 三分熟
☐ 五分熟
☐ 七分熟
☐ 全熟

---

year [jɪr]

名 年、年歲

英英 the time it takes the earth to make one revolution around the sun

例 I haven't seen you for **years**.
好幾年沒有看到你了。

☐ 三分熟
☐ 五分熟
☐ 七分熟
☐ 全熟

---

yel·low [`jɛlo]

形 黃色的
名 黃色

英英 of the color between green and orange, as of egg yolks or ripe lemons

例 The **yellow** dress is cheap.
那件黃色裙子好便宜喔。

☐ 三分熟
☐ 五分熟
☐ 七分熟
☐ 全熟

---

yes/yeah

[jɛs]/[jɛə]

副 是的
名 是、好

英英 used to express confirmation, willingness, or agreement

例 **Yes**, I will marry you.
是的，我會跟你結婚。

☐ 三分熟
☐ 五分熟
☐ 七分熟
☐ 全熟

---

yes·ter·day

[`jɛstɚde]

名 昨天、昨日

英英 on the day before today

例 **Yesterday**, I was very tired.
昨天我很累。

☐ 三分熟
☐ 五分熟
☐ 七分熟
☐ 全熟

---

yet [jɛt]

副 直到此時、還（沒）
連 但是、而又
反 already 已經

英英 still; until the present time

例 I haven't got the mail **yet**.
我還沒收到信。

☐ 三分熟
☐ 五分熟
☐ 七分熟
☐ 全熟

---

you [ju]

代 你、你們

英英 used to refer to the person or people being spoken or written to

例 Are **you** a student?
你是學生嗎？

☐ 三分熟
☐ 五分熟
☐ 七分熟
☐ 全熟

young [jʌŋ]

形 年輕的、年幼的
名 青年
反 old 老的

英英 having lived or existed for only a short time; not old; youth

例 Keep a **young** heart.
常保持一顆年輕的心。

☐三分熟
☐五分熟
☐七分熟
☐全熟

---

your(s) [jʊr(z)]

形 你的（東西）、
你們的（東西）

英英 used to show that something belongs to or is connected with the person or group of people being spoken or written to

例 Is that **yours**?
這是你的嗎？

☐三分熟
☐五分熟
☐七分熟
☐全熟

---

yuck·y [jʌkɪ]

形 令人厭惡的、
令人不快的

英英 used to express strong distaste, unpleasantness, or disgust

例 The food is **yucky**.
這食物好噁心。

☐三分熟
☐五分熟
☐七分熟
☐全熟

---

yum·my [ˋjʌmɪ]

形 舒適的、愉快的、
美味的

英英 tasting extremely good, delicious

例 The cake is **yummy**.
這塊蛋糕好好吃。

☐三分熟
☐五分熟
☐七分熟
☐全熟

Zz

ze·ro [ˋzɪro]

名 零

英英 the figure 0; nought

例 I got **zero** on the exam.
這次考試我考了零分。

☐三分熟
☐五分熟
☐七分熟
☐全熟

---

zoo [zu]

名 動物園

英英 an establishment in which wild animals are kept for study, conservation, or put on display to the public

例 My children love to go to the **zoo**.
我的小孩很喜歡去動物園。

☐三分熟
☐五分熟
☐七分熟
☐全熟

LEVEL 2 音檔雲端連結

因各家手機系統不同，若無法直接掃描，
仍可以至以下電腦雲端連結下載收聽。
（https://tinyurl.com/4kbfvfjp）

LEVEL 2

初級基礎
英文能力

邁向
2200單字

Aa

🎧 Track 137

a·bil·i·ty [əˋbɪlətɪ]

名 能力
同 capacity 能力

英英 the power or capacity to do something
例 Due to his excellent **ability**, he makes tons of money.
因為他有傑出的能力，他賺了大把的鈔票。

☐ 三分熟
☐ 五分熟
☐ 七分熟
☐ 全熟

---

a·broad [əˋbrɔd]

副 在國外、到國外
同 overseas 在國外
片 go abroad 出國

英英 in or to a foreign country or countries
例 I will study **abroad**.
我要出國唸書。

☐ 三分熟
☐ 五分熟
☐ 七分熟
☐ 全熟

---

ab·sence

[ˋæbsn̩s]

名 缺席、缺乏
反 presence 出席

英英 the state of being away from a place or event
例 Your **absence** annoys us.
你的缺席讓我們很困擾。

☐ 三分熟
☐ 五分熟
☐ 七分熟
☐ 全熟

---

ab·sent [ˋæbsn̩t]

形 缺席的

英英 not present in an occasion
例 Is Sandy **absent** again?
珊蒂又缺席了嗎？

☐ 三分熟
☐ 五分熟
☐ 七分熟
☐ 全熟

---

ac·cept [əkˋsɛpt]

動 接受
反 refuse 拒絕

英英 to agree to receive something offered or proposed
例 Did you **accept** his idea?
你接受他的想法了嗎？

☐ 三分熟
☐ 五分熟
☐ 七分熟
☐ 全熟

---

ac·tive [ˋæktɪv]

形 活躍的
同 dynamic 充滿活力的

英英 moving or tending to move about vigorously
例 He is quite **active** in school.
他在學校很活躍。

☐ 三分熟
☐ 五分熟
☐ 七分熟
☐ 全熟

---

ad·dition [əˋdɪʃən]

名 加、加法
同 supplement 增補
片 in addition to
除了……

英英 the action or process of adding
例 In **addition** to milk, I love juice.
除了牛奶，我還喜歡果汁。

☐ 三分熟
☐ 五分熟
☐ 七分熟
☐ 全熟

ad·vance

[əd`væns]

名 前進
動 使前進
同 progress 前進

英英 to move forwards or to make progress

例 You are **advancing**.
你正在前進。

☐ 三分熟
☐ 五分熟
☐ 七分熟
☐ 全熟

A

---

af·fair [ə`fɛr]

名 事件
同 matter 事件

英英 an event or a situation that is being dealt with

例 Do you know about his **affair**?
你知道他的事情嗎？

☐ 三分熟
☐ 五分熟
☐ 七分熟
☐ 全熟

---

aid [ed]

名 援助
動 援助

英英 to give someone help or support

例 Someone **aided** me last night.
昨晚有人援助了我。

☐ 三分熟
☐ 五分熟
☐ 七分熟
☐ 全熟

---

aim [em]

名 瞄準、目標
動 企圖、瞄準
同 target 目標

英英 point a weapon or camera at a target; intend to do something

例 What's the **aim** of this paper?
這篇論文的目標是什麼？

☐ 三分熟
☐ 五分熟
☐ 七分熟
☐ 全熟

---

air·craft [`ɛr͵kræft]

名 飛機、飛行器
同 jet 噴射飛機

英英 any vehicle, which is able to fly

例 He loves **aircraft** so much that he wants to be a pilot.
他喜歡飛機喜歡到想當飛行員。

☐ 三分熟
☐ 五分熟
☐ 七分熟
☐ 全熟

---

air·line [`ɛr͵laɪn]

名 （飛機）航線、
　 航空公司

英英 an organization which is providing a regular passenger air service

例 Which **airline** are you going to choose for your vacation?
你這趟旅程要選哪家航空公司？

☐ 三分熟
☐ 五分熟
☐ 七分熟
☐ 全熟

---

a·larm [ə`lɑrm]

名 恐懼、警報器
動 使驚慌

英英 a device which is giving a warning of danger; to make someone anxious or frightened

例 The **alarm** is ringing. What's the matter?
警報器在響，發生什麼事了？

☐ 三分熟
☐ 五分熟
☐ 七分熟
☐ 全熟

---

al·bum [`ælbəm]

名 相簿、專輯

英英 a blank book for the insertion of photographs, stamps, or other items forming a collection

例 There are lots of old photos in the **album**.
這本相簿裡面有很多舊照片。

☐ 三分熟
☐ 五分熟
☐ 七分熟
☐ 全熟

Track 139

a·like [ə`laɪk]

形 相似的、相同的
副 相似地、相同地
反 different 不一樣的

英英 very similar

例 My sister and I are **alike**.
我妹妹跟我長得很像。

□ 三分熟
□ 五分熟
□ 七分熟
□ 全熟

a·live [ə`laɪv]

形 活的
反 dead 死的

英英 living; not dead

例 Is the man still **alive**?
這男人還活著嗎？

□ 三分熟
□ 五分熟
□ 七分熟
□ 全熟

al·mond [`ɑmənd]

名 杏仁、杏樹

英英 the oval edible nut-like kernel of the almond tree

例 **Almonds** are good for health.
杏仁對身體很好。

□ 三分熟
□ 五分熟
□ 七分熟
□ 全熟

a·loud [ə`laʊd]

副 高聲地、大聲地

英英 not silently; very loudly

例 Please read it **aloud**.
請大聲唸出來。

□ 三分熟
□ 五分熟
□ 七分熟
□ 全熟

al·pha·bet

[`ælfə‚bɛt]

名 字母、字母表

英英 an ordered set of letters or symbols used for writing a language

例 A is the first **alphabet** in English.
A 是英文字母中的第一個。

□ 三分熟
□ 五分熟
□ 七分熟
□ 全熟

al·though [ɔl`ðo]

連 雖然、縱然
同 though 雖然

英英 in spite of the fact that; but

例 **Although** she is fat, she is pretty.
雖然她很胖，但她很美。

□ 三分熟
□ 五分熟
□ 七分熟
□ 全熟

al·to·geth·er

[‚ɔltə`gɛðɚ]

副 完全地、總共
反 partly 部分地

英英 completely; in total

例 We said no **altogether**.
我們完全否認。

□ 三分熟
□ 五分熟
□ 七分熟
□ 全熟

a·mount [ə`maʊnt]

名 總數、合計
動 總計
同 sum 總計

英英 the total number, size or value of something; come to be a total when added the numbers together

例 What's the **amount** of the goods?
貨物合計多少？

□ 三分熟
□ 五分熟
□ 七分熟
□ 全熟

an·cient [`enʃənt]

形 古老的、古代的
同 antique 古老的

英英 belonging to or originating in the very distant past

例 The **ancient** people lived in a cave.
古老的人們住在山洞中。

□ 三分熟
□ 五分熟
□ 七分熟
□ 全熟

A

an·kle [ˈæŋkl̩]

名 腳踝

英英 the joint connecting the foot with the leg

例 I hurt my **ankle** so badly that I can't walk.
我腳踝傷得太重了，不能走路。

☐ 三分熟
☐ 五分熟
☐ 七分熟
☐ 全熟

an·y·bod·y/
an·y·one
[ˈɛnɪˌbɑdɪ]/[ˈɛnɪˌwʌn]

代 任何人

英英 any person

例 **Anyone** can help me?
誰可以幫我嗎？

☐ 三分熟
☐ 五分熟
☐ 七分熟
☐ 全熟

an·y·how
[ˈɛnɪˌhaʊ]

副 隨便、無論如何
同 however 無論如何

英英 anyway

例 I will tell you **anyhow**.
無論如何我都要告訴你。

☐ 三分熟
☐ 五分熟
☐ 七分熟
☐ 全熟

an·y·time
[ˈɛnɪˌtaɪm]

副 任何時候
同 whenever 無論何時

英英 at a time which is not or does not need to be decided or agreed

例 Call me **anytime**.
任何時候打給我吧。

☐ 三分熟
☐ 五分熟
☐ 七分熟
☐ 全熟

an·y·way [ˈɛnɪˌwe]

副 無論如何

英英 in any manner, anyhow

例 **Anyway**, I don't care about him.
無論如何，我不在乎他。

☐ 三分熟
☐ 五分熟
☐ 七分熟
☐ 全熟

an·y·where/
an·y·place
[ˈɛnɪˌhwɛr]/[ˈɛnɪˌples]

副 任何地方

英英 in or to any place

例 I will find you **anywhere**.
我要去任何地方找你。

☐ 三分熟
☐ 五分熟
☐ 七分熟
☐ 全熟

ap·art·ment
[əˈpɑrtmənt]

名 公寓
同 flat 公寓

英英 a flat; a room or suite of rooms forming one residence

例 I live in an **apartment** in Taipei.
我住在臺北的一間公寓。

☐ 三分熟
☐ 五分熟
☐ 七分熟
☐ 全熟

🎧 **Track 141**

---

ap·pear·ance

[ə`pɪrəns]

名 出現、露面
同 look 外表

英英 the way that someone or something looks

例 The **appearance** of the ghost is scary.
鬼魅的出現很可怕。

☐ 三分熟
☐ 五分熟
☐ 七分熟
☐ 全熟

---

ap·pe·tite

[`æpə͵taɪt]

名 食欲、胃口

英英 a physical desire to satisfy a bodily need, especially for food

例 The illness destroys my **appetite**.
生病讓我沒有食欲。

☐ 三分熟
☐ 五分熟
☐ 七分熟
☐ 全熟

---

ap·ply [ə`plaɪ]

動 請求、應用
同 request 請求

英英 to request or seek assistance or help

例 I am **applying** for this position.
我正在申請這職位。

☐ 三分熟
☐ 五分熟
☐ 七分熟
☐ 全熟

---

a·pron [`eprən]

名 圍裙
同 flap 圍裙

英英 a protective piece covering in the front of one's clothes and tied at the back

例 Wear an **apron** when cooking.
煮菜時要圍圍裙。

☐ 三分熟
☐ 五分熟
☐ 七分熟
☐ 全熟

---

ar·gue [`ɑrgju]

動 爭辯、辯論

英英 to put reasons against something; to debate

例 Don't **argue** about that.
別再為此事爭辯了。

☐ 三分熟
☐ 五分熟
☐ 七分熟
☐ 全熟

---

ar·gu·ment

[`ɑrgjəmənt]

名 爭論、議論
同 dispute 爭論

英英 the act of disagreeing or discussion using a reason

例 The **argument** of this essay is clear.
這篇文章的議論很清楚。

☐ 三分熟
☐ 五分熟
☐ 七分熟
☐ 全熟

---

arm [ɑrm]

名 手臂
動 武裝、備戰

英英 each of the two upper limbs of the human body from the shoulder to the hand; to supply with weapons

例 The baseball player's **arm** is strong.
這位棒球員的手臂很壯。

☐ 三分熟
☐ 五分熟
☐ 七分熟
☐ 全熟

---

arm·chair

[`ɑrm͵tʃɛr]

名 扶椅

英英 a large chair with side supports for the sitter's arms

例 My grandmother needs an **armchair** to rest.
我祖母要一張扶椅休息。

☐ 三分熟
☐ 五分熟
☐ 七分熟
☐ 全熟

A

ar·range [əˋrendʒ]

動 安排、籌備

英英	to organize or plan something
例	My mother always **arranges** everything for me. 我媽媽總是幫我安排好所有事情。

☐ 三分熟
☐ 五分熟
☐ 七分熟
☐ 全熟

---

ar·range·ment

[əˋrendʒmənt]

名 布置、準備
反 disturb 擾亂

英英	the result of arranging things in an ordered way
例	The **arrangement** of this party is perfect. 這派對的布置很完美。

☐ 三分熟
☐ 五分熟
☐ 七分熟
☐ 全熟

---

ar·rest [əˋrɛst]

動 逮捕、拘捕
名 阻止、扣留
反 release 釋放

英英	to seize by legal authority and take into custody; to stop or check
例	The police **arrest** the criminal. 警方逮捕嫌犯。

☐ 三分熟
☐ 五分熟
☐ 七分熟
☐ 全熟

---

ar·rive [əˋraɪv]

動 到達、來臨
反 leave 離開

英英	to reach a destination
例	We are **arriving** in Amsterdam. 我們正抵達阿姆斯特丹。

☐ 三分熟
☐ 五分熟
☐ 七分熟
☐ 全熟

---

ar·row [ˋæro]

名 箭
同 quarrel 箭

英英	a long stick with a sharp pointed head, designed to be shot from a bow
例	The warrior needs some **arrows**. 那些戰士需要一些箭。

☐ 三分熟
☐ 五分熟
☐ 七分熟
☐ 全熟

---

ar·ti·cle/es·say

[ˋɑrtɪkl]/[ˋɛse]

名 文章、論文

英英	a piece of writing in a newspaper or magazine
例	The **article** influences many people. 這篇文章影響很多人。

☐ 三分熟
☐ 五分熟
☐ 七分熟
☐ 全熟

---

art·ist [ˋɑrtɪst]

名 藝術家、大師

英英	a person who paints, draws or makes sculptures
例	He is not only a poet but an **artist**. 他不只是個詩人還是個藝術家。

☐ 三分熟
☐ 五分熟
☐ 七分熟
☐ 全熟

---

a·sleep [əˋslip]

形 睡著的
反 awake 醒著的

英英	sleeping or not awake
例	The boy falls **asleep**. 那男孩睡著了。

☐ 三分熟
☐ 五分熟
☐ 七分熟
☐ 全熟

🎧 **Track 143**

as·sis·tant
[ə`sɪstənt]

名 助手、助理
同 aid 助手

英英 a person who ranks below a senior person

例 My **assistant** will help you.
我的助手會幫你們。

□ 三分熟
□ 五分熟
□ 七分熟
□ 全熟

---

at·tack [ə`tæk]

動 攻擊
名 攻擊
同 assault 攻擊

英英 to try to hurt or defeat violently

例 The terrorist usually **attacks** the tourist spot.
恐怖分子總是攻擊知名觀光景點。

□ 三分熟
□ 五分熟
□ 七分熟
□ 全熟

---

at·tend [ə`tɛnd]

動 出席

英英 go to an event, place, etc.; to present

例 Will you **attend** the meeting?
你會出席會議嗎？

□ 三分熟
□ 五分熟
□ 七分熟
□ 全熟

---

at·ten·tion
[ə`tɛnʃən]

名 注意、專心
同 concern 注意

英英 the mental faculty of considering or taking notice

例 The film drew my **attention**.
這影片抓住我的注意力。

□ 三分熟
□ 五分熟
□ 七分熟
□ 全熟

---

a·void [ə`vɔɪd]

動 避開、避免
反 face 面對

英英 to keep from happening; to prevent something from happening

例 You should **avoid** the mistakes.
你應該要避免這些錯誤。

□ 三分熟
□ 五分熟
□ 七分熟
□ 全熟

Bb

ba·by·sit [`bebɪˏsɪt]

動 （臨時）照顧嬰孩

英英 to look after someone's child or children while their parents are out

例 Could you **babysit** my children?
你可以幫我照顧孩子嗎？

□ 三分熟
□ 五分熟
□ 七分熟
□ 全熟

---

ba·by·sit·ter
[`bebɪsɪtɚ]

名 保姆

英英 someone who takes care of your baby or child while you are out, usually by coming to your home

例 The teacher feels herself more like a **babysitter**.
那老師覺得自己更像保姆。

□ 三分熟
□ 五分熟
□ 七分熟
□ 全熟

B

back·ward
['bækwəd]

形 向後方的、面對後方的
反 forward 向前方的

英英 towards the direction that is opposite to the one in which you're moving

例 The living condition of the old man goes **backward**.
那老人的生活狀況向後退步了。

☐ 三分熟
☐ 五分熟
☐ 七分熟
☐ 全熟

back·wards
['bækwədz]

副 向後地
反 forwards 向前方地

英英 in the direction that opposite to the one is facing

例 The soldier can't go **backwards**.
士兵不可以往後走。

☐ 三分熟
☐ 五分熟
☐ 七分熟
☐ 全熟

bake [bek]

動 烘、烤
同 toast 烘、烤

英英 to cook food by dry heat in an oven

例 I will **bake** the cake for your birthday.
你生日的時候我會烤蛋糕給你。

☐ 三分熟
☐ 五分熟
☐ 七分熟
☐ 全熟

bak·er·y ['bekərɪ]

名 麵包坊、麵包店

英英 a place where makes and sells bread and cakes

例 Let's buy some bread in the **bakery**.
去麵包店買一點麵包吧。

☐ 三分熟
☐ 五分熟
☐ 七分熟
☐ 全熟

bal·co·ny
['bælkənɪ]

名 陽臺
同 porch 陽臺

英英 an enclosed platform on the outside of a building, with access from an upper-floor window or door

例 You can see the view from the **balcony**.
你可以從陽臺看到這景色。

☐ 三分熟
☐ 五分熟
☐ 七分熟
☐ 全熟

bam·boo [bæm'bu]

名 竹子

英英 a tall giant tropical grass with hollow woody stems

例 The table is made of **bamboo**.
這張桌子是由竹子所做成的。

☐ 三分熟
☐ 五分熟
☐ 七分熟
☐ 全熟

bank·er ['bæŋkə]

名 銀行家

英英 a person who runs or owns a bank

例 To be a **banker**, you must know more about finance.
要當一名銀行家，你必須要懂財務。

☐ 三分熟
☐ 五分熟
☐ 七分熟
☐ 全熟

bar·be·cue/
BBQ ['bɑrbɪkju]

名 烤肉
同 roast 烤肉

英英 an outdoor meal at which food is grilled on a rack over a charcoal fire

例 We usually have a **barbecue** on Moon Festival.
我們中秋節通常會烤肉。

☐ 三分熟
☐ 五分熟
☐ 七分熟
☐ 全熟

🎧 **Track 145**

bark [bɑrk]

動 （狗）吠叫
名 吠聲
同 roar 吼叫（獅子）

英英 to give a bark; the loud noise that is made by a dog or other animals

例 I am scared by the dog's **bark**.
我被狗叫聲嚇到了。

☐ 三分熟
☐ 五分熟
☐ 七分熟
☐ 全熟

---

base·ment [`besmənt]

名 地下室、地窖
同 cellar 地窖

英英 a room or floor partly or entirely below ground level

例 I put it in the **basement**.
我把它放在地下室。

☐ 三分熟
☐ 五分熟
☐ 七分熟
☐ 全熟

---

basics [`besɪks]

名 基礎、原理
反 trivial 瑣碎的

英英 the simplest and most important facts, ideas or things

例 It is a **basic** question.
這是很基礎的問題。

☐ 三分熟
☐ 五分熟
☐ 七分熟
☐ 全熟

---

ba·sis [`besɪs]

名 根據、基礎
同 bottom 底部
名詞複數 bases

英英 the foundation of a theory or facts

例 The **basis** of my theory is from this paper.
我理論的根據是這篇論文。

☐ 三分熟
☐ 五分熟
☐ 七分熟
☐ 全熟

---

bat·tle [`bætl̩]

名 戰役
動 作戰
同 combat 戰鬥

英英 a sustained fight between armed forces; to fight for something

例 Many people died in the **battle**.
很多人死於這場戰役。

☐ 三分熟
☐ 五分熟
☐ 七分熟
☐ 全熟

---

bead [bid]

名 珠子、串珠
動 穿成一串
同 pearl 珠子

英英 a small piece of glass, stone, etc., threaded in a string through holes to make a necklace; to thread the beads together

例 The kids **beaded** a bracelet for their mother.
那些孩子們串手鍊給媽媽。

☐ 三分熟
☐ 五分熟
☐ 七分熟
☐ 全熟

---

bean [bin]

名 豆子、沒有價值的東西
同 straw 沒有價值的東西

英英 an edible seed growing in long pods, eaten as a vegetable

例 Tofu is made from soy **bean**.
豆腐是由黃豆製成的。

☐ 三分熟
☐ 五分熟
☐ 七分熟
☐ 全熟

bear [bɛr]

名 熊
動 忍受
同 endure 忍受

英英 a large, heavy mammal with thick fur and a very short tail; to tolerate or endure something

例 I can't **bear** your misbehavior.
我無法忍受你錯誤的行為。

☐ 三分熟
☐ 五分熟
☐ 七分熟
☐ 全熟

beard [bɪrd]

名 鬍子

英英 a growth of hair on the chin and lower cheeks of a man's face

例 The man with **beard** is mysterious.
那有鬍子的男人好神祕。

☐ 三分熟
☐ 五分熟
☐ 七分熟
☐ 全熟

bed·room

[ˋbɛdˌrum]

名 臥房

英英 a room for people to sleep in

例 Where is your **bedroom**?
你的房間在哪裡？

☐ 三分熟
☐ 五分熟
☐ 七分熟
☐ 全熟

beef [bif]

名 牛肉

英英 the flesh of a cow, bull, or ox, used as food

例 He loves to eat **beef**.
他喜歡吃牛肉。

☐ 三分熟
☐ 五分熟
☐ 七分熟
☐ 全熟

beep [bip]

名 警笛聲
動 發出嘟嘟聲

英英 a short, high-pitched sound made by electronic equipment or a vehicle horn; to make a sound of beep

例 The **beep** annoyed me.
那警笛聲讓我很緊張。

☐ 三分熟
☐ 五分熟
☐ 七分熟
☐ 全熟

beer [bɪr]

名 啤酒
同 bitter 苦

英英 an alcoholic drink made from grain

例 The **beer** in German is famous.
德國啤酒很有名。

☐ 三分熟
☐ 五分熟
☐ 七分熟
☐ 全熟

bee·tle [ˋbitl̩]

名 甲蟲
動 急走

英英 an insect with the forewings modified into hard wing cases; to walk very quickly

例 I am afraid of **beetles**.
我很怕甲蟲。

☐ 三分熟
☐ 五分熟
☐ 七分熟
☐ 全熟

beg [bɛg]

動 乞討、懇求
同 appeal 懇求

英英 to ask for something, especially food or money

例 I **beg** your pardon.
我乞求你的原諒。

☐ 三分熟
☐ 五分熟
☐ 七分熟
☐ 全熟

🎧 **Track 147**

---

be·gin·ner

[bɪˋgɪnɚ]

名 初學者
同 freshman 新手

英英 a person who is starting to learn something for first time

例 Don't blame him. He is just a **beginner**.
不要太苛責他。他只是個初學者。

☐ 三分熟
☐ 五分熟
☐ 七分熟
☐ 全熟

---

be·lief [bɪˋlif]

名 相信、信念
同 faith 信念

英英 a feeling that something is true, especially one without proof

例 It is my **belief** that what goes around comes around.
善有善報是我的信念。

☐ 三分熟
☐ 五分熟
☐ 七分熟
☐ 全熟

---

be·liev·a·ble

[bɪˋlivəbl̩]

形 可信任的
同 credible 可信的

英英 something can be believed because it seems real or true

例 Is it **believable** that he will pass the exam?
他將通過考試，可以信任嗎？

☐ 三分熟
☐ 五分熟
☐ 七分熟
☐ 全熟

---

belt [bɛlt]

名 皮帶
動 圍繞
同 strap 皮帶

英英 a strip of leather or other material worn round the waist to support clothes or to carry weapons; to fasten with a belt

例 The **belt** will make you in trend.
這條皮帶會讓你更有型。

☐ 三分熟
☐ 五分熟
☐ 七分熟
☐ 全熟

---

bench [bɛntʃ]

名 長凳
同 settle 長椅

英英 a long seat for more than one person to sit on

例 She sat on the **bench** in the park whole day long.
他整天都坐在公園的長凳上。

☐ 三分熟
☐ 五分熟
☐ 七分熟
☐ 全熟

---

bend [bɛnd]

動 使彎曲
名 彎曲
反 stretch 伸直

英英 to give or have a curved or angled shape or form

例 I **bend** the ruler.
我把尺弄彎了。

☐ 三分熟
☐ 五分熟
☐ 七分熟
☐ 全熟

---

be·sides [bɪˋsaɪdz]

介 除了……之外
副 並且
同 otherwise 除此之外

英英 in addition to; apart from

例 **Besides**, I like oranges.
此外，我還喜歡柳橙。

☐ 三分熟
☐ 五分熟
☐ 七分熟
☐ 全熟

---

bet [bɛt]

動 下賭注
名 打賭
同 gamble 打賭

英英 to risk money on a gamble; the act of gambling
例 I **bet** you will win.
我賭你會贏。

☐ 三分熟
☐ 五分熟
☐ 七分熟
☐ 全熟

be·yond [bɪˋjɑnd]

介 在遠處、超過
副 此外
反 within 不超過

英英 at or to the further side of something; further
例 There is a river **beyond** the hill.
在山丘之後有條小溪。

☐ 三分熟
☐ 五分熟
☐ 七分熟
☐ 全熟

bill [bɪl]

名 帳單
同 check 帳單

英英 a printed or written paper which states the money is owed for goods or services
例 Who will pay for the **bill**?
誰要付帳？

☐ 三分熟
☐ 五分熟
☐ 七分熟
☐ 全熟

bind [baɪnd]

動 綁、包紮
反 release 鬆開

英英 tie or fasten tightly togethe
例 The nurse **binds** the wound.
護士包紮傷口。

☐ 三分熟
☐ 五分熟
☐ 七分熟
☐ 全熟

bit·ter [ˋbɪtɚ]

形 苦的、嚴厲的
反 sweet 甜的

英英 having a sharp, pungent taste or smell; not sweet
例 It's **bitter** to grow up.
長大是很苦澀的。

☐ 三分熟
☐ 五分熟
☐ 七分熟
☐ 全熟

black·board

[ˋblækˏbord]

名 黑板

英英 a large board with a dark surface for writing on with chalk
例 The teacher writes down the words on the **blackboard**.
老師在黑板上寫下字。

☐ 三分熟
☐ 五分熟
☐ 七分熟
☐ 全熟

blank [blæŋk]

形 空白的
名 空白
同 empty 空的

英英 not marked or decorated; being very bare or plain
例 I need a **blank** paper.
我需要一張白紙。

☐ 三分熟
☐ 五分熟
☐ 七分熟
☐ 全熟

blind [blaɪnd]

形 瞎的
片 love is blind
愛情是盲目的

英英 lacking the power of sight; unable to see
例 The **blind** can play the piano well.
那個瞎掉的男人很會彈鋼琴。

☐ 三分熟
☐ 五分熟
☐ 七分熟
☐ 全熟

B

blood·y [ˈblʌdɪ]

形 流血的

英英 covered with or composed of blood

例 The wound is **bloody**.
這傷口在流血。

☐ 三分熟
☐ 五分熟
☐ 七分熟
☐ 全熟

---

board [bord]

名 板、佈告欄
同 wood 木板

英英 a long, thin, flat piece of wood which is used in building

例 We use the **board** to make the door.
我們用木板做門。

☐ 三分熟
☐ 五分熟
☐ 七分熟
☐ 全熟

---

boil [bɔɪl]

動 （水）沸騰、使發怒
名 煮
同 rage 發怒

英英 to reach the temperature at which a liquid starts to turn into gas

例 **Boil** the water before you drink it.
在喝水之前先把水煮沸。

☐ 三分熟
☐ 五分熟
☐ 七分熟
☐ 全熟

---

bomb [bɑm]

名 炸彈
動 轟炸

英英 a container of explosive or incendiary material, designed to damage buildings or kill people; to explode a bomb

例 The **bomb** is threatening everyone.
炸彈威脅大家的安全。

☐ 三分熟
☐ 五分熟
☐ 七分熟
☐ 全熟

---

bon·y [ˈbonɪ]

形 多骨的、骨瘦如柴的
同 skinny 骨瘦如柴的

英英 of, like, or containing bones

例 The cat is **bony**.
這隻貓瘦骨如柴。

☐ 三分熟
☐ 五分熟
☐ 七分熟
☐ 全熟

---

book·case

[ˈbʊkˌkes]

名 書櫃、書架

英英 an open cabinet containing shelves on which to keep books

例 My **bookcase** has been full.
我的書櫃是滿的。

☐ 三分熟
☐ 五分熟
☐ 七分熟
☐ 全熟

---

bor·row [ˈbɑro]

動 借來、採用
反 loan 借出

英英 to take and use something belonging to someone else with the intention of returning it

例 I **borrow** the car from my brother.
我跟我哥哥借車。

☐ 三分熟
☐ 五分熟
☐ 七分熟
☐ 全熟

---

boss [bɔs]

名 老闆、主人
動 指揮、監督
同 manager 負責人、
　　經理

英英 a person who is in charge of shop or organization; to be in charge of something

例 My **boss** assigned me this project.
老闆指定我完成這項計畫。

☐ 三分熟
☐ 五分熟
☐ 七分熟
☐ 全熟

both·er [ˈbɑðɚ]

動 打擾
同 annoy 打擾

英英 to take the trouble to do; to disturb

例 Don't **bother** me. I am busy now.
我現在很忙，不要打擾我。

☐ 三分熟
☐ 五分熟
☐ 七分熟
☐ 全熟

B

bot·tle [ˈbɑtl̩]

名 瓶
動 用瓶裝
同 container 容器

英英 a container with a narrow neck, which is used for storing liquids; to place something in bottles

例 I drank a **bottle** of water every day.
我每天喝一瓶水。

☐ 三分熟
☐ 五分熟
☐ 七分熟
☐ 全熟

bow [baʊ]

名 彎腰、鞠躬
動 向下彎

英英 to bend your head or upper body (in greeting or respect)

例 In Japan, it's common to greet people by a **bow**.
在日本，人們很常鞠躬問候他人。

☐ 三分熟
☐ 五分熟
☐ 七分熟
☐ 全熟

bowl·ing [ˈbolɪŋ]

名 保齡球

英英 the game of bowls

例 We love playing **bowling** in the weekend.
我們喜歡週末打保齡球。

☐ 三分熟
☐ 五分熟
☐ 七分熟
☐ 全熟

brain [bren]

名 腦、智力
同 intelligence 智力
片 brainwash 洗腦

英英 an organ of soft nervous tissue contained in the skull, which control thought, memory and feeling

例 **Brain** is important to do this job.
做這份工作，智力很重要。

☐ 三分熟
☐ 五分熟
☐ 七分熟
☐ 全熟

branch [bræntʃ]

名 枝狀物、分店、分公司
動 分支
反 trunk 樹幹

英英 a part of a tree which grows out from the trunk; a chain store or company; divide something into parts

例 There are many **branches** of our company around the world.
我們公司的分店遍及全世界。

☐ 三分熟
☐ 五分熟
☐ 七分熟
☐ 全熟

brand [brænd]

名 品牌
動 打烙印
同 mark 做記號

英英 a type of product manufactured by a company under a particular name; to mark something with a branding iron

例 She always buys the shoes with this **brand**.
她總是買這牌子的鞋子。

☐ 三分熟
☐ 五分熟
☐ 七分熟
☐ 全熟

brick [brɪk]

名 磚頭、磚塊

英英 a small rectangular block of fired or sun-dried clay, used in building

例 We build the house with **bricks**.
我們用磚頭蓋房子。

☐ 三分熟
☐ 五分熟
☐ 七分熟
☐ 全熟

🎧 Track 151

brief [brif]

形 短暫的
名 摘要、短文
反 long 長的
片 in brief 簡而言之

英英 lasting a short time; a summary of the facts

例 I will make a **brief** introduction.
我將會做個簡短的介紹。

□ 三分熟
□ 五分熟
□ 七分熟
□ 全熟

---

broad [brɔd]

形 寬闊的
反 narrow 窄的

英英 very wide

例 The space of this house is **broad**.
這房間的空間很寬廣。

□ 三分熟
□ 五分熟
□ 七分熟
□ 全熟

---

broad·cast

[`brɔd،kæst]

動 廣播、播出
名 廣播節目
同 announce 播報

英英 to tell many people by radio; a radio show or program

例 **Broadcast** is important for my grandma to know the news.
廣播對我奶奶來說是得知新聞的重要管道。

□ 三分熟
□ 五分熟
□ 七分熟
□ 全熟

---

brunch [brʌntʃ]

名 早午餐

英英 a late morning meal eaten between breakfast time and lunch time

例 My wife made a **brunch** for me this morning.
我太太今天早上做了早午餐給我。

□ 三分熟
□ 五分熟
□ 七分熟
□ 全熟

---

brush [brʌʃ]

名 刷子
動 刷、擦掉
同 wipe 擦去

英英 an object with a handle and a block of bristles, hair, or wire, which is used for cleaning or painting; to clean with a brush

例 **Brush** your teeth.
去刷牙。

□ 三分熟
□ 五分熟
□ 七分熟
□ 全熟

---

bun/roll

[bʌn]/[rol]

名 小圓麵包、麵包卷
同 roll 麵包卷

英英 a small cake or a small loaf of bread

例 Would you like to have some **bun** before the meal?
你需要餐前麵包嗎？

□ 三分熟
□ 五分熟
□ 七分熟
□ 全熟

---

bun·dle [`bʌnd!]

名 捆、包裹
同 package 包裹

英英 a collection of things or quantity of material tied up together

例 I need a **bundle** of rope.
我需要一捆的繩子。

□ 三分熟
□ 五分熟
□ 七分熟
□ 全熟

burn [bɝn]

動 燃燒
名 烙印
同 fire 燃燒

英英 to produce light; a type of injury that is caused by heat

例 What's **burning**?
什麼在燃燒？

☐ 三分熟
☐ 五分熟
☐ 七分熟
☐ 全熟

burst [bɝst]

動 破裂、爆炸
名 猝發、爆發
同 explode 爆炸

英英 to break suddenly and violently apart

例 I **burst** out laughing when I heard the joke.
當我聽到笑話時，我爆笑出來。

☐ 三分熟
☐ 五分熟
☐ 七分熟
☐ 全熟

busi·ness [ˈbɪznɪs]

名 商業、買賣
同 commerce 商業

英英 the activity of selling or buying goods or services

例 I studied a lot about **business** in my college.
我大學期間學了很多商業相關。

☐ 三分熟
☐ 五分熟
☐ 七分熟
☐ 全熟

but·ton [ˈbʌtn̩]

名 扣子
動 用扣子扣住
同 clasp 扣住

英英 a small disc or knob sewn on to an article of clothing to fasten it by being pushed through a buttonhole; to fasten with button

例 I am sewing the **button** of my coat.
我在縫大衣的扣子。

☐ 三分熟
☐ 五分熟
☐ 七分熟
☐ 全熟

Cc

cab·bage

[ˈkæbɪdʒ]

名 包心菜

英英 a vegetable with thick green or purple leaves surrounding a spherical heart

例 I don't like to eat **cabbage**.
我不喜歡吃包心菜。

☐ 三分熟
☐ 五分熟
☐ 七分熟
☐ 全熟

ca·ble [ˈkebl̩]

名 纜繩、電纜
同 wire 電線

英英 a thick rope of wire

例 I am looking for my **cable** to charge my phone.
我在找我的電線要幫手機充電。

☐ 三分熟
☐ 五分熟
☐ 七分熟
☐ 全熟

café/cafe [kəˈfe]

名 咖啡館

英英 a small restaurant selling light meals and drinks, such as sandwiches and coffee

例 I will meet her in the **café**.
我跟她約在咖啡廳。

☐ 三分熟
☐ 五分熟
☐ 七分熟
☐ 全熟

caf·e·te·ri·a

[ˌkæfəˋtɪrɪə]

名 自助餐館
同 restaurant 餐廳

英英 a restaurant which you need to serve yourself

例 I am going to the **cafeteria** for dinner.
我要去自助餐吃晚餐。

☐ 三分熟
☐ 五分熟
☐ 七分熟
☐ 全熟

---

cal·en·dar

[ˋkæləndɚ]

名 日曆

英英 a chart or series of pages showing the days, weeks, and months of a particular year

例 I have marked your birthday on my **calendar**.
我在我的日曆上記下你的生日了。

☐ 三分熟
☐ 五分熟
☐ 七分熟
☐ 全熟

---

calm [kɑm]

形 平靜的
名 平靜
動 使平靜
同 peaceful 平靜的

英英 not showing or feeling nervousness; to make someone peaceful

例 Stay **calm** so that you can make a decision.
保持冷靜才能做決定。

☐ 三分熟
☐ 五分熟
☐ 七分熟
☐ 全熟

---

can·cel [ˋkænsl]

動 取消
同 erase 清除

英英 decide that a planned event or thing will not take place

例 I will **cancel** our meeting.
我會取消我們的約會。

☐ 三分熟
☐ 五分熟
☐ 七分熟
☐ 全熟

---

can·cer [ˋkænsɚ]

名 癌、腫瘤

英英 a disease caused by an uncontrolled division of abnormal cells in a part of the body

例 My grandfather died of **cancer**.
我祖父死於癌症。

☐ 三分熟
☐ 五分熟
☐ 七分熟
☐ 全熟

---

can·dle [ˋkændl]

名 蠟燭、燭光
同 torch 光芒

英英 a stick or block of wax with a central wick which is lit to produce light when it burns

例 We lit the **candle** at night.
我們晚上點燃蠟燭。

☐ 三分熟
☐ 五分熟
☐ 七分熟
☐ 全熟

---

cap·tain [ˋkæptɪn]

名 船長、艦長
同 chief 首領、長官

英英 the person in command of a ship

例 The **captain** avoided the shipwreck.
船長避免了船難。

☐ 三分熟
☐ 五分熟
☐ 七分熟
☐ 全熟

---

car·pet [ˋkɑrpɪt]

名 地毯
動 鋪地毯
同 mat 地席

英英 a floor covering made from woven fabric; to cover with a carpet

例 In Taiwan, we don't always have a **carpet** in the house.
在臺灣，我們不太常會在家裡放地毯。

☐ 三分熟
☐ 五分熟
☐ 七分熟
☐ 全熟

car·rot [ˈkærət]

名 胡蘿蔔

英英 the tapering orange root of a plant which is eaten as a vegetable

例 We feed the rabit some **carrots**.
我們餵兔子吃紅蘿蔔。

□三分熟
□五分熟
□七分熟
□全熟

---

cart [kɑrt]

名 手拉車

英英 an open horse-drawn vehicle with two or four wheels, used for carrying things or passengers

例 Let's borrow a **cart** to move it.
我們借個手推車搬動它。

□三分熟
□五分熟
□七分熟
□全熟

---

car·toon [kɑrˈtun]

名 卡通

英英 a drawing executed in an exaggerated style for humorous effect

例 **Cartoon** was very important for many kids.
卡通對於很多小孩來說都是很重要的。

□三分熟
□五分熟
□七分熟
□全熟

---

cash [kæʃ]

名 現金
動 付現
同 currency 貨幣

英英 money in coins or notes; to pay by cash

例 Would you like to pay in **cash**?
你要付現嗎？

□三分熟
□五分熟
□七分熟
□全熟

---

cas·sette [kæˈsɛt]

名 卡帶、盒子

英英 a sealed plastic case containing audio tape, videotape or film for insertion into a recorder or camera

例 Many children nowadays have never seen **cassette**.
現在很多小孩都沒看過卡帶了。

□三分熟
□五分熟
□七分熟
□全熟

---

cast·le [ˈkæsl̩]

名 城堡
同 palace 皇宮

英英 a large strong building which is built in the past by a ruler or important person of high rank, to protect the people inside from attack

例 I like to visit **castles** in Europe.
我喜歡去歐洲參觀城堡。

□三分熟
□五分熟
□七分熟
□全熟

---

cave [kev]

名 洞穴
動 挖掘
同 hole 洞

英英 a large natural underground chamber; to dig something

例 There are many bats in the **cave**.
洞穴中有很多的蝙蝠。

□三分熟
□五分熟
□七分熟
□全熟

---

ceil·ing [ˈsilɪŋ]

名 天花板
反 floor 地板

英英 the upper inside surface of a room'

例 There is a mosquito on the **ceiling**.
天花板上有一隻蚊子。

□三分熟
□五分熟
□七分熟
□全熟

🎧 **Track 155**

cell [sɛl]

名 細胞

英英 the smallest structural and functional unit of an organism, existing as independent units of life

例 The **cells** of her skin are hurt.
她皮膚細胞受到傷害。

☐ 三分熟
☐ 五分熟
☐ 七分熟
☐ 全熟

---

cen·tral [ˋsɛntrəl]

形 中央的

英英 in or near the center

例 I live near the **central** station.
我住在中央車站附近。

☐ 三分熟
☐ 五分熟
☐ 七分熟
☐ 全熟

---

cen·tu·ry

[ˋsɛntʃərɪ]

名 世紀

英英 one hundred years

例 Many things have changed in this **century**.
在這世紀中有很多東西都變了。

☐ 三分熟
☐ 五分熟
☐ 七分熟
☐ 全熟

---

ce·re·al [ˋsɪrɪəl]

名 穀類作物

英英 a grain used for food, for example wheat or maize

例 I eat **cereal** every morning.
我每天早上都吃麥片穀物。

☐ 三分熟
☐ 五分熟
☐ 七分熟
☐ 全熟

---

chalk [tʃɔk]

名 粉筆

英英 a piece of calcite, usually in the shape of a crayon, that is used to write on blackboards

例 The teacher writes down the word with a **chalk**.
那老師用粉筆寫下這個字。

☐ 三分熟
☐ 五分熟
☐ 七分熟
☐ 全熟

---

change [tʃendʒ]

動 改變、兌換
名 零錢、變化
同 coin 硬幣

英英 make something different or become different; a metal disc or piece used as money

例 Nothing lasts but **changes**.
只有改變是不會變的。

☐ 三分熟
☐ 五分熟
☐ 七分熟
☐ 全熟

---

char·ac·ter

[ˋkærɪktɚ]

名 個性、角色

英英 the qualities distinctive to an individual

例 She is my favorite **character** in the movie.
她是我在這部電影中最喜歡的角色。

☐ 三分熟
☐ 五分熟
☐ 七分熟
☐ 全熟

---

charge [tʃɑrdʒ]

動 索價、命令
名 費用、職責
同 rate 費用

英英 demand an amount as a price for a service or goods; a price asked

例 The **charge** is too high.
這要價太高了。

☐ 三分熟
☐ 五分熟
☐ 七分熟
☐ 全熟

cheap [tʃip]

形 低價的、易取得的
副 低價地
反 expensive 昂貴的

英英 low in price; being available very easily
例 The dress is **cheap**.
這件裙子很便宜。

☐ 三分熟
☐ 五分熟
☐ 七分熟
☐ 全熟

cheat [tʃit]

動 欺騙
名 詐欺、騙子
同 liar 騙子

英英 act dishonestly or unfairly in order to take an advantage of someone
例 Don't **cheat** on me.
不要欺騙我。

☐ 三分熟
☐ 五分熟
☐ 七分熟
☐ 全熟

chem·i·cal

[ˋkɛmɪkl̩]

形 化學的
名 化學

英英 relating to chemistry or chemicals
例 The **chemical** change is amazing!
這化學變化太神奇了！

☐ 三分熟
☐ 五分熟
☐ 七分熟
☐ 全熟

chess [tʃɛs]

名 西洋棋

英英 a board game for two players, the object of which is to put the opponent's king under a direct attack, leading to checkmate
例 I don't like to play **chess**.
我不喜歡下西洋棋。

☐ 三分熟
☐ 五分熟
☐ 七分熟
☐ 全熟

child·ish [ˋtʃaɪdɪʃ]

形 孩子氣的
同 naive 天真的

英英 silly and immature
例 You are too **childish** to understand the fact.
你太孩子氣了，無法理解這事情。

☐ 三分熟
☐ 五分熟
☐ 七分熟
☐ 全熟

child·like

[ˋtʃaɪldlaɪk]

形 純真的
反 mature 成熟的

英英 having the good qualities, such as innocence, associated with a child
例 Every bad guy used to be **childlike**.
所有的壞人都曾經純真過。

☐ 三分熟
☐ 五分熟
☐ 七分熟
☐ 全熟

chin [tʃin]

名 下巴

英英 the protruding part of the face below the mouth
例 He pointed the direction with his **chin**.
他用下巴指了方向。

☐ 三分熟
☐ 五分熟
☐ 七分熟
☐ 全熟

choc·o·late

[ˋtʃɔkəlɪt]

名 巧克力

英英 a food made from roasted and ground cacao seeds, typically sweetened and eaten as confectionery
例 **Chocolate** sells like hot cakes on Valentine's Day.
情人節的巧克力都賣得很好。

☐ 三分熟
☐ 五分熟
☐ 七分熟
☐ 全熟

C

Track 157

---

choice [tʃɔɪs]

名 選擇
形 精選的
同 selection 選擇

英英 an act of choosing; of very good quality

例 What's your **choice**?
你的選擇是什麼？

☐ 三分熟
☐ 五分熟
☐ 七分熟
☐ 全熟

---

choose [tʃuz]

動 選擇
同 select 選擇

英英 pick out as being the best of two or more alternatives

例 **Choose** one color.
選一個顏色。

☐ 三分熟
☐ 五分熟
☐ 七分熟
☐ 全熟

---

chop·stick(s)

[ˈtʃɑpˌstɪk(s)]

名 筷子

英英 each of a pair of small, thin sticks held in one hand and used while eating

例 We eat with **chopsticks**.
我們用筷子吃飯。

☐ 三分熟
☐ 五分熟
☐ 七分熟
☐ 全熟

---

cir·cle [ˈsɝkl]

名 圓形
動 圍繞
同 round 環繞

英英 a round plane figure whose boundary consists of points equidistant from the center; to be situated all the way around

例 Draw a **circle** first.
先畫一個圓形。

☐ 三分熟
☐ 五分熟
☐ 七分熟
☐ 全熟

---

cit·i·zen [ˈsɪtəzn̩]

名 公民、居民
同 inhabitant 居民

英英 someone who is a member of a particular nation or town

例 The **citizens** have the right to vote.
公民擁有投票權。

☐ 三分熟
☐ 五分熟
☐ 七分熟
☐ 全熟

---

claim [klem]

動 主張、聲稱
名 要求、權利
同 right 權利

英英 state as being the case, without being able to give proof; to request something

例 He **claimed** that he has done nothing wrong.
他聲稱沒有犯任何錯。

☐ 三分熟
☐ 五分熟
☐ 七分熟
☐ 全熟

---

clap [klæp]

動 鼓（掌）、拍擊
名 拍擊聲

英英 strike the palms of one's hands together repeatedly; a sound of clap

例 Everyone **claps** their hands to welcome the movie star.
大家鼓掌歡迎電影明星。

☐ 三分熟
☐ 五分熟
☐ 七分熟
☐ 全熟

---

clas·sic [ˈklæsɪk]

形 古典的
名 經典作品
同 ancient 古代的

英英 judged over a period of time to be of the highest quality; a work of art which is very valuable or with high quality

例 I prefer **classics**.
我喜歡閱讀經典作品。

☐ 三分熟
☐ 五分熟
☐ 七分熟
☐ 全熟

---

claw [klɔ]

名 爪
動 抓
同 grip 抓、緊握

英英 a curved, pointed nail on the end of the foot in birds, lizards, and some mammals; to scratch with the claws

例 The eagle is waving its **claw**.
那隻老鷹在揮舞他的爪子。

☐ 三分熟
☐ 五分熟
☐ 七分熟
☐ 全熟

---

clay [kle]

名 黏土
同 mud 土

英英 a sticky substance that can be molded when wet and baked to make bricks and pottery

例 I made a cup with **clay**.
我用黏土做了個杯子。

☐ 三分熟
☐ 五分熟
☐ 七分熟
☐ 全熟

---

clean·er [klinɚ]

名 清潔工、清潔劑
同 detergent 清潔劑

英英 a person or thing that cleans

例 The **cleaner** will have lots of things to do.
清潔工有很多事情要做了。

☐ 三分熟
☐ 五分熟
☐ 七分熟
☐ 全熟

---

clerk [klɝk]

名 職員

英英 a person who works in an office or bank to keep records or accounts and to undertake other routine administrative duties

例 The **clerk** helped me to find the goods.
那店員幫我找到貨品

☐ 三分熟
☐ 五分熟
☐ 七分熟
☐ 全熟

---

clev·er [ˋklɛvɚ]

形 聰明的、伶俐的
反 stupid 愚蠢的

英英 skilled at doing something

例 The boy is **clever**.
那男孩很聰明。

☐ 三分熟
☐ 五分熟
☐ 七分熟
☐ 全熟

---

cli·mate [ˋklaɪmɪt]

名 氣候
同 weather 天氣

英英 the general weather conditions prevailing in an area over a long period

例 The **climate** in Taiwan is hot and humid.
臺灣的氣候溫暖又潮濕。

☐ 三分熟
☐ 五分熟
☐ 七分熟
☐ 全熟

---

clos·et [ˋklɑzɪt]

名 櫥櫃
同 cabinet 櫥櫃

英英 a tall cupboard or wardrobe

例 My **closet** is full of dress.
我整個櫥櫃都是洋裝。

☐ 三分熟
☐ 五分熟
☐ 七分熟
☐ 全熟

---

cloth [klɔθ]

名 布料
同 textile 紡織品

英英 woven, knitted, or felted fabric made from a soft fiber such as wool or cotton

例 I love the color of the **cloth**.
我喜歡這款布料的顏色。

☐ 三分熟
☐ 五分熟
☐ 七分熟
☐ 全熟

---

clothe [kloð]

動 穿衣、給……穿衣

英英 provide with clothes

例 Let's **clothe** our baby!
我們幫小寶寶穿上衣服吧！

☐ 三分熟
☐ 五分熟
☐ 七分熟
☐ 全熟

C

Track 159

clothes [kloz]

名 衣服
同 clothing 衣服

英英 items which is worn to cover the body

例 I went to the department store to buy some **clothes**.
我去百貨公司買衣服。

☐ 三分熟
☐ 五分熟
☐ 七分熟
☐ 全熟

cloth·ing [ˈkloðɪŋ]

名 衣服
同 clothes 衣服

英英 clothes collectively

例 The **clothing** of my sister is always perfect.
我姐姐的衣服總是很完美。

☐ 三分熟
☐ 五分熟
☐ 七分熟
☐ 全熟

cloud·y [ˈklaʊdɪ]

形 烏雲密佈的、多雲的
反 bright 晴朗的

英英 with a lot of clouds

例 It's **cloudy** tonight.
今晚烏雲密佈。

☐ 三分熟
☐ 五分熟
☐ 七分熟
☐ 全熟

clown [klaʊn]

名 小丑、丑角
動 扮丑角
同 comic 滑稽人物

英英 a comic entertainer who is wearing a traditional costume and exaggerated make-up; to act like a clown

例 Who knows the sadness of a **clown**?
誰知道小丑的哀傷？

☐ 三分熟
☐ 五分熟
☐ 七分熟
☐ 全熟

club [klʌb]

名 俱樂部、社團
同 association 協會、社團

英英 an association dedicated to a particular interest or activity

例 We went to the night **club** every night.
我們每天去夜店。

☐ 三分熟
☐ 五分熟
☐ 七分熟
☐ 全熟

coach [kotʃ]

名 教練、顧問
動 訓練
同 counselor 顧問、參事

英英 a tutor who gives private teaching to somebody; to train or give a training

例 The **coach** of Spur is the best.
馬刺隊有最好的教練。

☐ 三分熟
☐ 五分熟
☐ 七分熟
☐ 全熟

coal [kol]

名 煤
同 fuel 燃料

英英 a hot fragment of wood that is left from a fire

例 China needs lots of **coal**.
中國需要大量的煤炭。

☐ 三分熟
☐ 五分熟
☐ 七分熟
☐ 全熟

cock [kɑk]

名 公雞
同 rooster 公雞

英英 a male chicken

例 You can't make a **cock** lay eggs.
你沒辦法讓公雞孵蛋。

☐ 三分熟
☐ 五分熟
☐ 七分熟
☐ 全熟

cock·roach/ roach
[ˈkɑkˌrotʃ]/[rotʃ]

名 蟑螂

英英 a beetle-like insect with long antennae and leg

例 I am afraid of **cockroachs**.
我很怕蟑螂。

☐ 三分熟
☐ 五分熟
☐ 七分熟
☐ 全熟

coin [kɔɪn]

名 硬幣
動 鑄造
同 money 錢幣

英英 a flat disc or piece of metal with an official stamp, used as money; to make coins

例 Give me some **coins**.
給我一些銅板。

☐ 三分熟
☐ 五分熟
☐ 七分熟
☐ 全熟

col·lect [kəˈlɛkt]

動 收集
同 gather 收集

英英 to bring things or gather things together

例 We are **collecting** stamps.
我們正在收集郵票。

☐ 三分熟
☐ 五分熟
☐ 七分熟
☐ 全熟

col·or·ful [ˈkʌləfəl]

形 富有色彩的

英英 having many or varied colors

例 She has a **colorful** life.
她有精彩的人生。

☐ 三分熟
☐ 五分熟
☐ 七分熟
☐ 全熟

comb [kom]

名 梳子
動 梳、刷
同 brush 梳子、刷

英英 an article with a row of narrow teeth, used for arranging the hair; to arrange hair with a tool

例 I am **combing** my hair.
我正在梳頭。

☐ 三分熟
☐ 五分熟
☐ 七分熟
☐ 全熟

com·fort·a·ble
[ˈkʌmfətəbl̩]

形 舒服的
同 content 滿意的

英英 providing or enjoying physical comfort

例 The sofa is so **comfortable** that I don't want to get up from it.
這沙發好舒服，我都不想要起來了。

☐ 三分熟
☐ 五分熟
☐ 七分熟
☐ 全熟

com·pa·ny
[ˈkʌmpənɪ]

名 公司、同伴
同 enterprise 公司

英英 a commercial business

例 Do you work in this **company**?
你在這家公司工作嗎？

☐ 三分熟
☐ 五分熟
☐ 七分熟
☐ 全熟

comp·are
[kəmˈpɛr]

動 比較
同 contrast 對比

英英 to estimate, measure, or note the similarity or dissimilarity between things

例 I am **comparing** the price to decide what to buy.
我在比價再決定要買什麼。

☐ 三分熟
☐ 五分熟
☐ 七分熟
☐ 全熟

🎧 **Track 161**

com·plain
[kəm`plen]

動 抱怨
同 grumble 抱怨

英英 express dissatisfaction or annoyance
例 He **complains** about his job all the time.
他總是抱怨他的工作。

☐ 三分熟
☐ 五分熟
☐ 七分熟
☐ 全熟

com·plete
[kəm`plit]

形 完整的
動 完成
同 conclude 結束

英英 having appropriate parts; entire; to finish something
例 Make a **complete** sentence.
造一個完整的句子。

☐ 三分熟
☐ 五分熟
☐ 七分熟
☐ 全熟

com·put·er
[kəm`pjutə]

名 電腦

英英 an electronic device which is used to store and process information in accordance with a predetermined set of instruction
例 Who can repair my **computer**?
誰可以幫我修電腦？

☐ 三分熟
☐ 五分熟
☐ 七分熟
☐ 全熟

con·firm [kən`fɝm]

動 證實
同 establish 證實

英英 establish the truth or correctness of something or someone
例 The star **confirmed** the rumor.
那位明星證實了謠言。

☐ 三分熟
☐ 五分熟
☐ 七分熟
☐ 全熟

con·flict
[`kɑnflɪkt]/[kən`flɪkt]

名 衝突、爭鬥
動 衝突
同 clash 衝突

英英 a serious disagreement or argument
例 There was a **conflict** between them.
他們之間有衝突。

☐ 三分熟
☐ 五分熟
☐ 七分熟
☐ 全熟

Con·fu·cius
[kən`fjuʃəs]

名 孔子

英英 Chinese philosopher whose ideas and sayings were collected after his death then became the basis of a philosophical doctrine known a Confucianism
例 **Confucius** is said to be the best teacher.
孔子被稱為是最好的老師了。

☐ 三分熟
☐ 五分熟
☐ 七分熟
☐ 全熟

con·grat·u·la·tions
[kənˌgrætʃəˋleʃənz]

名 祝賀、恭喜
同 blessing 祝福

英英 praise or good wishes on a special occasion
例 Are you getting married? **Congratulations**!
你要結婚啦？真是恭喜！

☐ 三分熟
☐ 五分熟
☐ 七分熟
☐ 全熟

C

con·sid·er
[kənˋsɪdɚ]

動 仔細考慮、把……視為
同 deliberate 仔細考慮

英英 think carefully about

例 I have never **considered** about that.
我從沒想過這個。

☐ 三分熟
☐ 五分熟
☐ 七分熟
☐ 全熟

con·tact
[ˋkɑntækt]/[kənˋtækt]

名 接觸、親近
動 接觸
同 approach 接近

英英 the state or condition of physical touching; to keep in touch with someone

例 Don't **contact** the patient.
不要接觸這名病患。

☐ 三分熟
☐ 五分熟
☐ 七分熟
☐ 全熟

con·tain [kənˋten]

動 包含、含有
反 exclude 不包括

英英 have or hold within

例 The price **contains** the tax.
這報價含有稅額。

☐ 三分熟
☐ 五分熟
☐ 七分熟
☐ 全熟

con·trol [kənˋtrol]

名 管理、控制
動 支配、控制
同 command 控制、指揮

英英 the power to influence people's behavior or manner; have command of

例 The dog is out of **control**.
這隻狗失控了。

☐ 三分熟
☐ 五分熟
☐ 七分熟
☐ 全熟

con·trol·ler
[kənˋtrolɚ]

名 管理員
同 administrator 管理人

英英 a person who controls something, or someone who is responsible for what a particular organization does

例 I am looking for the **controller**.
我正在找管理員。

☐ 三分熟
☐ 五分熟
☐ 七分熟
☐ 全熟

con·ve·nient
[kənˋvinjənt]

形 方便的、合宜的
同 suitable 適當的

英英 fitting in well with a person's needs, activities, and plans

例 It is more **convenient** in Taipei.
臺北很方便。

☐ 三分熟
☐ 五分熟
☐ 七分熟
☐ 全熟

con·ver·sa·tion
[kɑnvɚˋseʃən]

名 交談、談話
同 dialogue 交談

英英 an informal spoken exchange of news and ideas between two or more people

例 We had a pleasant **conversation**
我們有個愉快的對話。

☐ 三分熟
☐ 五分熟
☐ 七分熟
☐ 全熟

🎧 **Track 163**

cook·er [kʊkɚ]

名 炊具

英英 an object for cooking food, typically including an oven, hob, and grill

例 I bought some **cookers** to cook.
我買了些廚具。

☐ 三分熟
☐ 五分熟
☐ 七分熟
☐ 全熟

---

cop·y/Xe·rox/ xe·rox

[ˈkɑpɪ]/[ˈzɪrɑks]

名 拷貝
同 imitate 仿製

英英 a thing which is made to be similar or identical to another

例 Give me a **copy** of your passport.
給我一份你的護照影本。

☐ 三分熟
☐ 五分熟
☐ 七分熟
☐ 全熟

---

cor·ner [ˈkɔrnɚ]

名 角落
同 angle 角

英英 a place or angle where two or more sides or edges meet

例 The poor girl is sitting in the **corner**.
那可憐的小女孩坐在角落。

☐ 三分熟
☐ 五分熟
☐ 七分熟
☐ 全熟

---

cost·ly [ˈkɔstlɪ]

形 價格高的
同 expensive 昂貴的

英英 very expensive

例 The dress is so **costly** that I can't afford it.
這洋裝太貴我無法負擔。

☐ 三分熟
☐ 五分熟
☐ 七分熟
☐ 全熟

---

cot·ton [ˈkɑtn̩]

名 棉花

英英 a soft white fibrous substance which surrounds the seeds of a tropical and subtropical plant, used to make cloth or thread for sewing

例 The clothes is made of **cotton**.
這件衣服是棉花製成。

☐ 三分熟
☐ 五分熟
☐ 七分熟
☐ 全熟

---

cough [kɔf]

動 咳出
名 咳嗽

英英 expel air from the lungs with a sudden sharp sound

例 I kept **coughing** because I was seriously sick.
我一直咳嗽，因為我生了重病。

☐ 三分熟
☐ 五分熟
☐ 七分熟
☐ 全熟

---

coun·try·side

[ˈkʌntrɪˌsaɪd]

名 鄉間

英英 the land and scenery of a rural area

例 I was in the **countryside** last weekend.
上週末我人在鄉下。

☐ 三分熟
☐ 五分熟
☐ 七分熟
☐ 全熟

---

coun·ty [ˈkaʊntɪ]

名 郡、縣

英英 a region created by territorial division for the purpose of local government

例 In which **county** do you live?
你住在哪個縣？

☐ 三分熟
☐ 五分熟
☐ 七分熟
☐ 全熟

C

---

cou·ple [ˈkʌpl̩]

名 配偶、一對
動 結合

英英 two individuals of the same kind considered together; to connect or combine with something

例 You are a **couple** made in heaven.
你們真是天造地設的一對啊！

☐ 三分熟
☐ 五分熟
☐ 七分熟
☐ 全熟

---

cour·age [ˈkɝɪdʒ]

名 勇氣
反 fear 恐懼

英英 the ability to do something that frightens one

例 I don't have the **courage** to say "I love you" to her.
我沒有勇氣跟她說我愛她。

☐ 三分熟
☐ 五分熟
☐ 七分熟
☐ 全熟

---

court [kort]

名 法院

英英 an assembly that conducts judicial business

例 I will see you in the **court**.
我們法院見。

☐ 三分熟
☐ 五分熟
☐ 七分熟
☐ 全熟

---

cou·sin [ˈkʌzn̩]

名 堂（表）兄弟姊妹

英英 a child of one's uncle or aunt

例 The movie star is your **cousin**.
那電影明星是你的表哥。

☐ 三分熟
☐ 五分熟
☐ 七分熟
☐ 全熟

---

crab [kræb]

名 蟹

英英 a sea animal, with a broad shell and five pairs of legs, the first of which are modified as pincers

例 I saw many **crabs** near the river.
我在河邊看到很多螃蟹。

☐ 三分熟
☐ 五分熟
☐ 七分熟
☐ 全熟

---

crane [kren]

名 起重機、鶴

英英 a tall machine which is used for moving heavy objects by suspending them from a projecting arm

例 Only **cranes** can help you to move the car.
只有起重機可以幫你移動這臺車。

☐ 三分熟
☐ 五分熟
☐ 七分熟
☐ 全熟

---

cray·on [ˈkreən]

名 蠟筆

英英 stick of colored chalk or wax, used for drawing

例 The kids draw a picture with a **crayon**.
孩子們用蠟筆作畫。

☐ 三分熟
☐ 五分熟
☐ 七分熟
☐ 全熟

---

cra·zy [ˈkrezɪ]

形 發狂的、瘋癲的
同 mad 發狂的

英英 insane or unbalanced, especially in an aggressive way

例 I am **crazy** about her!
我發狂的迷戀她。

☐ 三分熟
☐ 五分熟
☐ 七分熟
☐ 全熟

---

cream [krim]

名 乳酪、乳製品

英英 the thick white or pale yellow fatty liquid which rises to the top when milk is left to stand

例 We need some more **cream** to make the cake.
我們需要一些乳酪才能做蛋糕。

☐ 三分熟
☐ 五分熟
☐ 七分熟
☐ 全熟

🎧 Track 165

cre·ate [krɪˋet]

動 創造
同 design 設計

英英 bring into existence

例 Who **creates** human beings?
誰創造了人類？

☐ 三分熟
☐ 五分熟
☐ 七分熟
☐ 全熟

---

crime [kraɪm]

名 罪、犯罪行為
同 sin 罪

英英 an offence against an individual or the state which is punishable by law

例 Is your **crime** forgivable?
你的犯行是可以原諒的嗎？

☐ 三分熟
☐ 五分熟
☐ 七分熟
☐ 全熟

---

cri·sis [ˋkraɪsɪs]

名 危機
同 emergency 緊急關頭
名詞複數 crises

英英 a time of danger or difficulty

例 Due to the help of my family, I can go through the **crisis**.
多虧了我家人的幫忙，我度過了這個危機。

☐ 三分熟
☐ 五分熟
☐ 七分熟
☐ 全熟

---

crop [krɑp]

名 農作物
同 growth 產物

英英 a plant, especially

例 Many people in China make a living by **crops**.
許多中國人靠農作物維生。

☐ 三分熟
☐ 五分熟
☐ 七分熟
☐ 全熟

---

cross [krɔs]

名 十字形、交叉
動 使交叉、橫過、反對
同 oppose 反對

英英 a mark, object, or figure formed by two short intersecting lines or pieces; to go to the other side of

例 What does a **cross** mean?
十字架的意思是什麼？

☐ 三分熟
☐ 五分熟
☐ 七分熟
☐ 全熟

---

crow [kro]

名 烏鴉
動 啼叫

英英 a large perching bird with mostly glossy black plumage, a heavy bill, and a raucous voice; to make a large sound

例 There are many **crows** in Japan.
日本有很多的烏鴉。

☐ 三分熟
☐ 五分熟
☐ 七分熟
☐ 全熟

---

crowd [kraʊd]

名 人群、群眾
動 擁擠
同 group 群眾

英英 a large number of people gathered together; (people) fill in a space completely

例 A **crowd** of girls rush to the hunk.
一群女孩衝向那個小鮮肉。

☐ 三分熟
☐ 五分熟
☐ 七分熟
☐ 全熟

---

cru·el [ˋkruəl]

形 殘忍的、無情的
同 mean 殘忍的

英英 disregarding or suffering of others; causing pain or suffering

例 Time is the **cruelest** killer.
時間是最殘忍的殺手。

☐ 三分熟
☐ 五分熟
☐ 七分熟
☐ 全熟

D

cul·ture [ˈkʌltʃɚ]

名 文化

英英 the arts and other style of human intellectual achievement regarded collectively

例 What can stand for Taiwanese **culture**?
什麼可以代表臺灣文化？

☐ 三分熟
☐ 五分熟
☐ 七分熟
☐ 全熟

---

cure [kjʊr]

動 治療
名 治療
同 heal 治療

英英 relieve someone of the symptoms of a disease or condition

例 The pain can never be **cured**.
這種傷害永遠無法被治癒的。

☐ 三分熟
☐ 五分熟
☐ 七分熟
☐ 全熟

---

cu·ri·ous [ˈkjʊrɪəs]

形 求知的、好奇的

英英 eager to know or learn something new

例 Are you **curious** about the field of biology?
你對生物這領域感到好奇嗎？

☐ 三分熟
☐ 五分熟
☐ 七分熟
☐ 全熟

---

cur·tain/drape

[ˈkɝtn̩]/[drep]

名 窗簾
動 掩蔽

英英 a piece of material suspended at the top to form a screen, which is hung at a window in pairs or between the stage; to provide a cover

例 I need a **curtain** so that others can't see through my house.
我需要窗簾，這樣人家就不會看透我的房子了。

☐ 三分熟
☐ 五分熟
☐ 七分熟
☐ 全熟

---

cus·tom [ˈkʌstəm]

名 習俗、習慣
同 tradition 習俗、傳統

英英 a traditional way of behaving or doing something that is specific to a particular society, place, or time

例 I am not familiar with Korean **custom**.
我對韓國習俗不熟悉。

☐ 三分熟
☐ 五分熟
☐ 七分熟
☐ 全熟

---

cus·tom·er

[ˈkʌstəmɚ]

名 顧客、客戶
同 client 客戶

英英 a person who buys goods or services from a shop or business

例 Put your **customers** first.
顧客至上。

☐ 三分熟
☐ 五分熟
☐ 七分熟
☐ 全熟

Dd

dai·ly [ˈdelɪ]

形 每日的
名 日報

英英 done, happening, or produced every day; a newspaper published every day

例 My **daily** routine is boring.
我每日的行程很無聊。

☐ 三分熟
☐ 五分熟
☐ 七分熟
☐ 全熟

🎧 **Track 167**

dam·age
[ˈdæmɪdʒ]

名 損害、損失
動 毀損

英英 physical harm reducing the value or usefulness of something; to destroy something

例 My car was **damaged** in the car accident.
我的車在車禍中嚴重損毀。

☐ 三分熟
☐ 五分熟
☐ 七分熟
☐ 全熟

dan·ger·ous
[ˈdendʒərəs]

形 危險的
反 secure 安全的

英英 likely to cause harm or danger

例 It's **dangerous** to love somebody too much.
愛太深是很危險的。

☐ 三分熟
☐ 五分熟
☐ 七分熟
☐ 全熟

da·ta [ˈdetə]

名 資料、事實、材料
同 information 資料

英英 facts and statistics used for reference or analysis use

例 Could you please analyze the **data** for me?
你可以為我分析資料嗎？

☐ 三分熟
☐ 五分熟
☐ 七分熟
☐ 全熟

dawn [dɔn]

名 黎明、破曉
動 開始出現、頓悟
反 dusk 黃昏

英英 the first appearance of light in the sky in the morning; start to show up

例 We woke up at **dawn** this morning.
我們今天天一亮就起床了。

☐ 三分熟
☐ 五分熟
☐ 七分熟
☐ 全熟

deaf [dɛf]

形 耳聾

英英 without ability of hearing

例 She's **deaf** so she can't hear you.
她耳聾了，所以聽不到你說話。

☐ 三分熟
☐ 五分熟
☐ 七分熟
☐ 全熟

de·bate [dɪˈbet]

名 討論、辯論
動 討論、辯論
同 discuss 討論

英英 a formal discussion in a public meeting , in which opposing arguments are presented

例 The need of the construction of the MRT in this city is **debatable**.
在這城市建造捷運的重要性是可以討論的。

☐ 三分熟
☐ 五分熟
☐ 七分熟
☐ 全熟

debt [dɛt]

名 債、欠款
同 obligation 債、欠款
片 in debt 負債

英英 a sum of money owed; the state of owing money

例 You will be in **debt** if you don't pay your credit card bill.
如果你不付卡單，你會負債累累。

☐ 三分熟
☐ 五分熟
☐ 七分熟
☐ 全熟

de·ci·sion
[dɪˈsɪʒən]

名 決定、決斷力
同 determination 決定

英英 a conclusion or resolution reached after consideration

例 It is hard to make such a **decision**.
要做這種決定很難。

☐ 三分熟
☐ 五分熟
☐ 七分熟
☐ 全熟

D

dec·o·rate

[ˈdɛkəˌret]

動 裝飾、布置
同 beautify 裝飾

英英 to make more attractive by well-arranged

例 We are **decorating** our house for Christmas.
我們正在為了耶誕節布置我們的房子。

☐ 三分熟
☐ 五分熟
☐ 七分熟
☐ 全熟

de·gree [dɪˈgri]

名 學位、程度
同 extent 程度

英英 the amount, level, or extent to which something happens

例 When will you get your master **degree**?
你何時才能拿到碩士學位？

☐ 三分熟
☐ 五分熟
☐ 七分熟
☐ 全熟

de·lay [dɪˈle]

動 延緩
名 耽擱

英英 make late or slow

例 Don't **delay** our goods.
不要耽擱我們的貨品。

☐ 三分熟
☐ 五分熟
☐ 七分熟
☐ 全熟

de·li·cious

[dɪˈlɪʃəs]

形 美味的
同 yummy 美味的

英英 describing something tastes very good

例 The food in this restaurant is **delicious**.
這家餐廳的食物很美味。

☐ 三分熟
☐ 五分熟
☐ 七分熟
☐ 全熟

de·liv·er [dɪˈlɪvɚ]

動 傳送、遞送
同 transfer 傳送

英英 to bring and hand over something to someone

例 The postman **delivers** the package in the morning.
郵差在早上送來這個包裹的。

☐ 三分熟
☐ 五分熟
☐ 七分熟
☐ 全熟

den·tist [ˈdɛntɪst]

名 牙醫、牙科醫生

英英 a person who is qualified to treat the diseases and conditions that affect the teeth

例 I had a toothache so I went to see a **dentist**.
我牙齒痛所以去看牙醫了。

☐ 三分熟
☐ 五分熟
☐ 七分熟
☐ 全熟

de·ny [dɪˈnaɪ]

動 否認、拒絕
同 reject 拒絕

英英 to refuse to admit the truth

例 I **deny** that I love him.
我否認我喜歡他。

☐ 三分熟
☐ 五分熟
☐ 七分熟
☐ 全熟

de·part·ment

[dɪˈpɑrtmənt]

名 部門、處、局、系所
同 section 部門

英英 a division of a large organization or building, dealing with a specific area of activity

例 We are in Chinese **department**.
我們在中文系。

☐ 三分熟
☐ 五分熟
☐ 七分熟
☐ 全熟

🎧 **Track 169**

---

de·pend [dɪˋpɛnd]

動 依賴、依靠
同 rely 依賴
片 depend on
　　視……而定

| 英英 to rely on something or somebody |
| 例 She is timid, so she is very **dependent** on her brother.
她膽子小，所以很依賴哥哥。 |

☐ 三分熟
☐ 五分熟
☐ 七分熟
☐ 全熟

---

depth [dɛpθ]

名 深度、深淵
同 gravity 深遠

| 英英 the distance from the top to down, from the surface to inwards, or from front to back |
| 例 Do you know the **depth** of the lake?
你知道湖深多少嗎？ |

☐ 三分熟
☐ 五分熟
☐ 七分熟
☐ 全熟

---

de·scribe

[dɪˋskraɪb]

動 敘述、描述
同 define 解釋

| 英英 give a detailed expression in words of |
| 例 Can you **describe** what you saw?
你可以描述一下你看到什麼嗎？ |

☐ 三分熟
☐ 五分熟
☐ 七分熟
☐ 全熟

---

de·sert

[ˋdɛzɚt]/[dɪˋzɝt]

名 沙漠、荒地
動 拋棄、丟開
形 荒蕪的
反 fertile 肥沃的

| 英英 leave without help or support; a waterless, desolate land with little or no vegetation and covered with sand; to throw away or abandon |
| 例 Have you ever been to a **desert**?
你去過沙漠嗎？ |

☐ 三分熟
☐ 五分熟
☐ 七分熟
☐ 全熟

---

de·sign [dɪˋzaɪn]

名 設計
動 設計
同 sketch 設計、構思

| 英英 a plan or drawing produced to show the look of something before it is built or made |
| 例 Who **designed** this great building?
誰設計了這麼偉大的一座建築？ |

☐ 三分熟
☐ 五分熟
☐ 七分熟
☐ 全熟

---

de·sire [dɪˋzaɪr]

名 渴望、期望
同 fancy 渴望

| 英英 a strong feeling of wanting to have something or wishing for something to occur |
| 例 I have a **desire** to see you.
我渴望見到你。 |

☐ 三分熟
☐ 五分熟
☐ 七分熟
☐ 全熟

---

des·sert [dɪˋzɝt]

名 餐後點心、甜點

| 英英 the sweet course eaten at the end of a meal |
| 例 Do you want to order some **dessert**?
你想要點甜點嗎？ |

☐ 三分熟
☐ 五分熟
☐ 七分熟
☐ 全熟

de·tect [dɪˋtɛkt]

動 查出、探出、發現
同 discover 發現

英英 to discover the presence or existence of

例 Do you **detect** something wrong?
你察覺出有什麼異樣了嗎？

☐ 三分熟
☐ 五分熟
☐ 七分熟
☐ 全熟

---

de·vel·op

[dɪˋvɛləp]

動 發展、開發

英英 to become or make larger or more advanced

例 The village is **developing** fast now.
這個小村莊正在快速發展。

☐ 三分熟
☐ 五分熟
☐ 七分熟
☐ 全熟

---

de·vel·op·ment

[dɪˋvɛləpmənt]

名 發展、開發

英英 the action of developing or the state of being developed

例 The **development** of the country causes lots of pollution.
這國家的發展造成大量的污染。

☐ 三分熟
☐ 五分熟
☐ 七分熟
☐ 全熟

---

dew [dju]

名 露水、露

英英 small drops of water that form when atmospheric vapor condenses on cool surfaces at night

例 The **dew** makes my helmet wet.
露水讓我的安全帽都濕了。

☐ 三分熟
☐ 五分熟
☐ 七分熟
☐ 全熟

---

di·al [ˋdaɪəl]

名 刻度盤
動 撥（電話）
同 call 打電話

英英 a disc marked to show the time on a clock or to indicate a reading or measurement by means of a pointer; to make a phone call

例 I will **dial** my daughter.
我會打電話給我女兒。

☐ 三分熟
☐ 五分熟
☐ 七分熟
☐ 全熟

---

dia·mond

[ˋdaɪmənd]

名 鑽石

英英 very hard native crystaline carbon valued as a gem

例 The girl loves **diamonds**.
那女孩很愛鑽石。

☐ 三分熟
☐ 五分熟
☐ 七分熟
☐ 全熟

---

di·a·ry [ˋdaɪərɪ]

名 日誌、日記本
同 journal 日誌
片 keep a diary 寫日記

英英 a book in which a person keeps a daily record of things

例 I keep a **diary** every day.
我每天寫日記。

☐ 三分熟
☐ 五分熟
☐ 七分熟
☐ 全熟

---

dic·tion·ar·y

[ˋdɪkʃənˌɛrɪ]

名 字典、辭典

英英 a book that lists the words of a language and gives their meaning

例 I learned this word when flipping over the **dictionary**.
當我隨手翻這本字典時，學到了這個字彙。

☐ 三分熟
☐ 五分熟
☐ 七分熟
☐ 全熟

🎧 **Track 171**

dif·fer·ence

[ˈdɪfərəns]

名 差異、差別
反 similarity 相似處

英英 the state or condition of being dissimilar

例 What's the **difference** between human beings and other animals?
人類和其他動物的差別是什麼？

☐ 三分熟
☐ 五分熟
☐ 七分熟
☐ 全熟

dif·fi·cul·ty

[ˈdɪfəˌkʌltɪ]

名 困難
反 ease 簡單

英英 the state or condition of being difficult

例 She told her teacher the **difficulty** she had.
她告訴老師她遇到的困難。

☐ 三分熟
☐ 五分熟
☐ 七分熟
☐ 全熟

di·no·saur

[ˈdaɪnəˌsɔr]

名 恐龍

英英 an extinct reptile of the Mesozoic era

例 What caused the extinction of **dinosaurs**?
是什麼讓恐龍絕跡的？

☐ 三分熟
☐ 五分熟
☐ 七分熟
☐ 全熟

di·rec·tion

[dəˈrɛkʃən]

名 指導、方向
同 way 方向

英英 a way along which someone or something moves

例 Could anyone tell us the **direction** to our hotel?
有人可以告訴我們去飯店的方向嗎？

☐ 三分熟
☐ 五分熟
☐ 七分熟
☐ 全熟

di·rec·tor

[dəˈrɛktə]

名 指揮者、導演

英英 a person who is in charge of a department, organization, or event

例 The movie is directed by the greatest **director** in this country.
這部電影是由這國家最棒的導演所導的。

☐ 三分熟
☐ 五分熟
☐ 七分熟
☐ 全熟

dis·agree

[ˌdɪsəˈgri]

動 不符合、不同意
反 agree 同意

英英 have a different opinion; not agree with someone

例 Does anybody **disagree** with the professor?
有人不同意教授嗎？

☐ 三分熟
☐ 五分熟
☐ 七分熟
☐ 全熟

dis·agree·ment

[ˌdɪsəˈgrimənt]

名 意見不合、不同意
反 agreement 同意

英英 an argument or a situation in which people have different opinion

例 He shows his **disagreement** in this essay.
在他這篇文章中顯示出他的不認同。

☐ 三分熟
☐ 五分熟
☐ 七分熟
☐ 全熟

D

dis·ap·pear
[ˌdɪsəˋpɪr]

動 消失、不見
同 appear 出現

英英 cease to be visible

例 The strange sound **disappears**.
奇怪的聲音消失了。

☐ 三分熟
☐ 五分熟
☐ 七分熟
☐ 全熟

dis·cuss [dɪˋskʌs]

動 討論、商議
同 consult 商議
片 disscuss about 討論

英英 talk about so as to reach a decision

例 We **discussed** about this issue many times in college.
當我們在大學時，討論過這個議題很多次。

☐ 三分熟
☐ 五分熟
☐ 七分熟
☐ 全熟

dis·cus·sion
[dɪˋskʌʃən]

名 討論、商議
同 consultation 商議

英英 the action or process of discussing something

例 We always learned a lot in the **discussion**.
我們總是在討論中學到很多。

☐ 三分熟
☐ 五分熟
☐ 七分熟
☐ 全熟

dis·hon·est
[dɪsˋɑnɪst]

形 不誠實的
反 honest 誠實的

英英 not honest, trustworthy, or sincere

例 The teacher is angry because the students are **dishonest**.
這老師很生氣，因為學生不誠實。

☐ 三分熟
☐ 五分熟
☐ 七分熟
☐ 全熟

dis·play [dɪˋsple]

動 展出
名 展示、展覽
同 show 展示

英英 put on show in a noticeable and attractive way; to show something in a noticeable way

例 The china **displayed** in the museum is unique.
這博物館展出的瓷器很獨特。

☐ 三分熟
☐ 五分熟
☐ 七分熟
☐ 全熟

dis·tance
[ˋdɪstəns]

名 距離
同 length 距離、長度

英英 the length of the space between two points or two things

例 The **distance** between the subway and the hotel is acceptable.
從地鐵到旅館的距離是可以接受的。

☐ 三分熟
☐ 五分熟
☐ 七分熟
☐ 全熟

dis·tant [ˋdɪstənt]

形 疏遠的、有距離的

英英 far away in space or time

例 She is **distant** to others.
她對人群是有距離的。

☐ 三分熟
☐ 五分熟
☐ 十分熟
☐ 全熟

🎧 Track 173

di·vide [dəˋvaɪd]

動 分開
同 separate 分開

英英 to separate into parts

例 Could you **divide** the pizza into eight pieces?
你可以將披薩分成八塊嗎？

☐ 三分熟
☐ 五分熟
☐ 七分熟
☐ 全熟

---

di·vi·sion [dəˋvɪʒən]

名 分割、除去

英英 the action or process of dividing two things

例 The teacher's **division** of the cake is not fair for the kids.
這老師分割蛋糕的方式對孩子來說不太公平。

☐ 三分熟
☐ 五分熟
☐ 七分熟
☐ 全熟

---

diz·zy [ˋdɪzɪ]

形 暈眩的、被弄糊塗的

英英 having a sensation of spinning around and losing one's balance

例 I feel **dizzy** today.
我今天覺得暈眩。

☐ 三分熟
☐ 五分熟
☐ 七分熟
☐ 全熟

---

dol·phin [ˋdɑlfɪn]

名 海豚

英英 a small gregarious toothed whale with a beak-like snout and a curved fin on the back

例 I saw many **dolphins** on the ferry.
我在渡輪上看到很多海豚。

☐ 三分熟
☐ 五分熟
☐ 七分熟
☐ 全熟

---

don·key [ˋdɑŋkɪ]

名 驢子、傻瓜
同 mule 驢，騾子

英英 a domesticated hoofed mammal of the horse family with long ears

例 The farmer bought a **donkey**.
那個農夫買了一頭驢。

☐ 三分熟
☐ 五分熟
☐ 七分熟
☐ 全熟

---

dot [dɑt]

名 圓點
動 以點表示

英英 a small round spot; to mark with a dot

例 The skirt with **dots** is lovely.
那有圓點的裙子很可愛。

☐ 三分熟
☐ 五分熟
☐ 七分熟
☐ 全熟

---

dou·ble [ˋdʌbḷ]

形 雙倍的
副 加倍地、雙倍地
名 二倍
動 加倍
反 single 單一的

英英 consisting of two equal or similar parts or things; to become double

例 I love the burger with **double** cheese.
我喜歡有雙層起司的漢堡。

☐ 三分熟
☐ 五分熟
☐ 七分熟
☐ 全熟

---

doubt [daʊt]

名 疑問
動 懷疑
反 believe 相信

英英 a feeling of uncertainty; to question the truth of something

例 Dare you **doubt** what she told you?
你敢懷疑她說的話嗎？

☐ 三分熟
☐ 五分熟
☐ 七分熟
☐ 全熟

dough·nut

[ˋdoˏnʌt]

名 油炸圈餅、甜甜圈

英英 a small fried cake or ring of sweetened dough

例 I bought a **doughnut** for snack.
我買了甜甜圈當點心。

☐ 三分熟
☐ 五分熟
☐ 七分熟
☐ 全熟

---

down·town

[ˋdaʊnˋtaʊn]

副 鬧區的
名 鬧區、商業區

英英 in the central area of a city; a business or busy area in a city.

例 We went to the **downtown** every weekend.
我們每週都去鬧區。

☐ 三分熟
☐ 五分熟
☐ 七分熟
☐ 全熟

Dr. [ˋdɑktɚ]

名 醫生、博士
同 doctor 醫生

英英 a person who is qualified to practice medicine or operation

例 **Dr.** Lee encourages us to exercise more.
李醫生鼓勵我們多運動。

☐ 三分熟
☐ 五分熟
☐ 七分熟
☐ 全熟

---

drag [dræg]

動 拖曳
同 pull 拖、拉

英英 to pull along forcefully or roughly

例 The workers **dragged** the machine.
工人們拖曳這臺機器。

☐ 三分熟
☐ 五分熟
☐ 七分熟
☐ 全熟

---

drag·on [ˋdrægən]

名 龍

英英 a mythical monster like a giant reptile, typically able to breathe out fire

例 In Chinese culture, **dragon** is a symbol of the empire.
在中國文化中，龍是皇帝的象徵。

☐ 三分熟
☐ 五分熟
☐ 七分熟
☐ 全熟

---

drag·on·fly

[ˋdrægənˏflaɪ]

名 蜻蜓

英英 a fast-flying long-bodied insect with two pairs of large transparent wings

例 I used to chase **dragonflies** when I was little.
我小時候常常追著蜻蜓跑。

☐ 三分熟
☐ 五分熟
☐ 七分熟
☐ 全熟

---

dra·ma [ˋdræmə]

名 劇本、戲劇
同 theater 戲劇

英英 a play or an exciting series of events

例 Do you love the **dramas** of Shakespeare?
你喜歡莎翁戲劇嗎？

☐ 三分熟
☐ 五分熟
☐ 七分熟
☐ 全熟

---

draw·er [ˋdrɔɚ]

名 抽屜、製圖員

英英 a lidless storage compartment made to slide horizontally in and out of a desk or chest

例 There is a lot of money in the **drawer**.
抽屜裡面有很多錢。

☐ 三分熟
☐ 五分熟
☐ 十分熟
☐ 全熟

🎧 **Track 175**

draw·ing [ˈdrɔɪŋ]

名 繪圖
同 illustration 圖表

英英 a picture or diagram made with a pencil, pen, or crayon rather than paint

例 The **drawing** of the kids is cute.
那些孩子們的繪圖很可愛。

☐ 三分熟
☐ 五分熟
☐ 七分熟
☐ 全熟

dress [drɛs]

名 洋裝
動 穿衣服
同 clothe 穿衣服

英英 put on one's clothes; a piece of clothing designed for women or girls which cover the body from the half top to legs

例 I bought some pretty **dresses** for my girlfriend.
我買了漂亮的裙子給我女朋友。

☐ 三分熟
☐ 五分熟
☐ 七分熟
☐ 全熟

drop [drɑp]

動 （使）滴下、滴

英英 fall or cause to fall on the ground

例 The books **dropped** in the earthquake.
地震時書掉下來了。

☐ 三分熟
☐ 五分熟
☐ 七分熟
☐ 全熟

drug [drʌg]

名 藥、藥物
同 medicine 藥
片 take drug 吸毒

英英 a medicine which has a marked effect when taken into the body

例 He took **drug**!
他吸毒！

☐ 三分熟
☐ 五分熟
☐ 七分熟
☐ 全熟

drug·store [ˈdrʌɡˌstor]

名 藥房
同 pharmacy 藥房

英英 a store which sells medicine or make-up, etc.

例 I went to the **drugstore** to buy some medicine for my headache.
我去藥房買了頭痛藥。

☐ 三分熟
☐ 五分熟
☐ 七分熟
☐ 全熟

drum [drʌm]

名 鼓

英英 an instrument with a skin stretched across a rounded frame, sounded by being struck with sticks or the hands

例 The kids love playing **drums**.
這些孩子們喜歡打鼓。

☐ 三分熟
☐ 五分熟
☐ 七分熟
☐ 全熟

dry·er [draɪɚ]

名 烘乾機、吹風機

英英 a machine which is used for drying something, especially the hair

例 There is no **dryer** in the hotel!
這家飯店內沒有吹風機！

☐ 三分熟
☐ 五分熟
☐ 七分熟
☐ 全熟

dull [dʌl]

形 遲鈍的、單調的
同 flat 單調的

英英 lacking interest or excitement; lacking brightness or sheen

例 The knife is too **dull** to cut the watermelon.
這刀子太鈍了，沒辦法切西瓜。

☐ 三分熟
☐ 五分熟
☐ 七分熟
☐ 全熟

E

dumb [dʌm]

形 啞的、笨的
反 smart 聰明的

英英 unable to speak; lacking the power of speech; temporarily unable or unwilling to speak

例 Why doesn't he answer me? Is he **dumb**?
他怎麼都不回答我？他是啞巴嗎？

☐三分熟
☐五分熟
☐七分熟
☐全熟

---

dump·ling
[ˋdʌmplɪŋ]

名 麵團、餃子

英英 a small savory ball of dough boiled in water or in a stew

例 We eat boiled **dumplings** on Chinese New Year Eve.
我們在除夕的時候吃水餃。

☐三分熟
☐五分熟
☐七分熟
☐全熟

---

du·ty [ˋdjutɪ]

名 責任、義務
同 responsibility 責任

英英 a moral or legal obligation

例 It is my **duty** to help people like you.
幫助你們這些人是我的責任。

☐三分熟
☐五分熟
☐七分熟
☐全熟

Ee

earn [ɝn]

動 賺取、得到
同 obtain 得到

英英 to get money in return for labor or services

例 It is not polite to ask people how much they **earn**.
問人家賺多少是不太禮貌的。

☐三分熟
☐五分熟
☐七分熟
☐全熟

---

earth·quake
[ˋɝθ͵kwek]

名 地震
同 tremor 地震

英英 a sudden hard shaking of the ground as a result of movements within the earth's crust

例 Many people died in the **earthquake**.
許多人在地震中喪生。

☐三分熟
☐五分熟
☐七分熟
☐全熟

---

east·ern [ˋistɚn]

形 東方的、東方人
反 western 西方的

英英 directed towards the east or facing the east

例 The **eastern** are mysterious for the western.
對於西方人來說，東方人是很神祕的。

☐三分熟
☐五分熟
☐七分熟
☐全熟

---

ed·u·ca·tion
[͵ɛdʒəˋkeʃən]

名 教育
同 instruction 教育

英英 the process of educating or being educated

例 **Education** is important for the development of a country.
教育對於一個國家的發展來說是很重要的。

☐三分熟
☐五分熟
☐七分熟
☐全熟

🎧 **Track 177**

ef·fect [əˈfɛkt]

名 影響、效果
動 引起、招致
同 produce 引起

英英 a change which is a result of an action or other event; to cause something to happen

例 What's the **effect** of this medicine?
這藥品的效果如何？

☐ 三分熟
☐ 五分熟
☐ 七分熟
☐ 全熟

---

ef·fec·tive

[əˈfɛktɪv]

形 有效的
反 vain 無效的

英英 producing a desired or pleasant result

例 The communication is not **effective** enough.
這溝通不夠有效。

☐ 三分熟
☐ 五分熟
☐ 七分熟
☐ 全熟

---

ef·fort [ˈɛfət]

名 努力
同 attempt 努力嘗試

英英 a vigorous or determined attempt; physical or mental effort

例 She made an **effort** but she still failed.
她努力過了，但還是失敗了。

☐ 三分熟
☐ 五分熟
☐ 七分熟
☐ 全熟

---

el·der [ˈɛldə]

形 年長的
名 長輩
反 junior 晚輩

英英 a person of greater age than oneself; of a greater age

例 I yield my seat to the **elder**.
我把座位讓給年長者。

☐ 三分熟
☐ 五分熟
☐ 七分熟
☐ 全熟

---

e·lect [ɪˈlɛkt]

動 挑選、選舉
形 挑選的
同 select 挑選

英英 choose someone to hold public office or another position by voting; to choose someone or something

例 He was **elected** as the president.
他被選為總統。

☐ 三分熟
☐ 五分熟
☐ 七分熟
☐ 全熟

---

el·e·ment

[ˈɛləmənt]

名 基本要素
同 component 構成要素

英英 a basic part or unit

例 What's the most important **element** of composing a song?
創作歌曲最重要的基本要素是什麼？

☐ 三分熟
☐ 五分熟
☐ 七分熟
☐ 全熟

---

el·e·va·tor

[ˈɛləˌvetə]

名 升降機、電梯
同 escalator 電扶梯

英英 a machine consisting of an endless belt with scoops attached, used for carrying people or goods up and down

例 I took the **elevator** to the second floor.
我搭電梯到二樓。

☐ 三分熟
☐ 五分熟
☐ 七分熟
☐ 全熟

e·mot·ion

[ɪ`moʃən]

名 情感
同 feeling 情感

英英 a strong feeling, such as joy or anger

例 Men tend to hide their **emotions**.
男人傾向隱藏他們的情感。

□三分熟
□五分熟
□七分熟
□全熟

en·cour·age

[ɪn`kɝɪdʒ]

動 鼓勵
同 inspire 激勵

英英 to give support or confidence to someone

例 The teacher **encouraged** the students to discuss.
這老師鼓勵學生多討論。

□三分熟
□五分熟
□七分熟
□全熟

en·cour·age·ment

[ɪn`kɝɪdʒmənt]

名 鼓勵
同 incentive 鼓勵

英英 when someone talks or behaves in a way that gives you confidence or support to do something

例 The **encouragement** of parents is important.
父母的鼓勵是很重要的。

□三分熟
□五分熟
□七分熟
□全熟

end·ing [`ɛndɪŋ]

名 結局、結束
同 terminal 終點

英英 an end or final part

例 Unlike comedy, the **ending** of life is not always positive.
不同於喜劇，生命的結局不一定是好的。

□三分熟
□五分熟
□七分熟
□全熟

en·e·my [`ɛnəmɪ]

名 敵人
同 opponent 敵手

英英 a person who is actively opposed someone or something

例 The USA is regarded as the **enemy** in the Middle East.
在中東，美國被視為是敵人。

□三分熟
□五分熟
□七分熟
□全熟

en·er·gy [`ɛnɚdʒɪ]

名 能量、精力
同 strength 力量

英英 the strength which is required for sustained activity

例 You gave me **energy** to keep working.
你給我能量讓我繼續工作。

□三分熟
□五分熟
□七分熟
□全熟

en·joy [ɪn`dʒɔɪ]

動 享受、欣賞
同 appreciate 欣賞

英英 to enjoy oneself have a good time

例 I **enjoy** seeing a movie alone.
我喜歡獨自看電影。

□三分熟
□五分熟
□七分熟
□全熟

en·joy·ment

[ɪn`dʒɔɪmənt]

名 享受、愉快
同 pleasure 愉快

英英 when you enjoy something

例 The **enjoyment** of being alone makes her single.
享受一個人的生活讓她至今單身。

□三分熟
□五分熟
□七分熟
□全熟

🎧 **Track 179**

---

en·tire [ɪnˋtaɪr]

形 全部的
反 partial 部分的

英英 with no part left out; whole

例 The **entire** crew welcome his coming.
所有的機組人員歡迎他的到來。

☐ 三分熟
☐ 五分熟
☐ 七分熟
☐ 全熟

---

en·trance

[ˋɛntrəns]

名 入口
同 exit 出口

英英 an opening that allows people to get into a place

例 Where is the **entrance** of the building?
這棟大樓的入口在哪裡？

☐ 三分熟
☐ 五分熟
☐ 七分熟
☐ 全熟

---

en·ve·lope

[ˋɛnvəˌlop]

名 信封

英英 a flat paper container with a sealable flap, used to enclose a letter or document

例 My parents gave me a red **envelope** on Chinese New Year Eve.
我爸媽在除夕的時候給我紅包。

☐ 三分熟
☐ 五分熟
☐ 七分熟
☐ 全熟

---

en·vi·ron·ment

[ɪnˋvaɪrənmənt]

名 環境

英英 the surroundings in which people, animals or plants lives

例 I don't want my children to be born in such a terrible **environment**.
我不想要我的孩子生在這麼糟糕的環境。

☐ 三分熟
☐ 五分熟
☐ 七分熟
☐ 全熟

---

e·ras·er [ɪˋresɚ]

名 橡皮擦

英英 a piece of rubber which is used to erase or wipe out something written

例 May I borrow an **eraser**?
我可以借一個橡皮擦嗎？

☐ 三分熟
☐ 五分熟
☐ 七分熟
☐ 全熟

---

er·ror [ˋɛrɚ]

名 錯誤
同 mistake 錯誤

英英 a mistake

例 It was an accidental **error**.
這是意外的錯誤。

☐ 三分熟
☐ 五分熟
☐ 七分熟
☐ 全熟

---

es·pe·cial·ly

[əˋspɛʃəlɪ]

副 特別地
反 mostly 一般地

英英 in particular; very much

例 The elder, **especially** men, suffer from this disease.
年長者，特別是男性，會得到這種疾病。

☐ 三分熟
☐ 五分熟
☐ 七分熟
☐ 全熟

---

e·vent [ɪˋvɛnt]

名 事件
同 episode 事件

英英 a thing that happens, takes place or occurs

例 The 228 **event** is widely discussed in recent years.
228 事件在近年廣泛的被討論著。

☐ 三分熟
☐ 五分熟
☐ 七分熟
☐ 全熟

E

ex·act [ɪgˋzækt]

形 正確的
同 precise 準確的

英英 accurate; correct

例 Tell me an **exact** number of the people joining the party.
告訴我正確要參加派對的人數。

□三分熟
□五分熟
□七分熟
□全熟

ex·cel·lent [ˋɛksḷənt]

形 最好的
同 admirable 極好的

英英 extremely good; outstanding

例 The students are **excellent**.
這些學生都很優秀。

□三分熟
□五分熟
□七分熟
□全熟

ex·cite [ɪkˋsaɪt]

動 刺激、鼓舞
反 calm 使鎮定

英英 cause strong feelings of enthusiasm

例 The news **excited** many people.
這新聞鼓舞了很多人。

□三分熟
□五分熟
□七分熟
□全熟

ex·cite·ment [ɪkˋsaɪtmənt]

名 興奮、激動
同 turmoil 騷動

英英 a feeling of being excited, or an exciting event

例 The sudden **excitement** made them drink a lot.
一時的興奮，讓他們喝了很多。

□三分熟
□五分熟
□七分熟
□全熟

ex·cuse [ɪkˋskjuz]

名 藉口
動 原諒
反 blame 責備

英英 a reason that you give to explain the mistake you made; to forgive a person

例 Don't give me any **excuse**.
不要給我任何的藉口。

□三分熟
□五分熟
□七分熟
□全熟

ex·er·cise [ˋɛksɚͺsaɪz]

名 練習
動 運動
同 practice 練習

英英 activity requiring physical effort to make you keep health and fitness

例 I want to do some more **exercise**.
我想要做更多的運動。

□三分熟
□五分熟
□七分熟
□全熟

ex·ist [ɪgˋzɪst]

動 存在
同 be 存在

英英 have objective reality or being

例 Do you believe that God **exists**?
你相信神的存在嗎？

□三分熟
□五分熟
□七分熟
□全熟

ex·pect [ɪkˋspɛkt]

動 期望
同 suppose 期望

英英 regard someone as likely to do or achieve something

例 I didn't **expect** to meet you here.
我沒期望在這裡遇到你。

□二分熟
□五分熟
□七分熟
□全熟

Track 181

---

ex·pen·sive
[ɪk`spɛnsɪv]

形 昂貴的
反 cheap 便宜的

英英 costing a lot of money

例 The apartment in Taipei is too **expensive** for the young people.
臺北的公寓對年輕人來說還是太貴了。

☐ 三分熟
☐ 五分熟
☐ 七分熟
☐ 全熟

---

ex·pe·ri·ence
[ɪk`spɪrɪəns]

名 經驗
動 體驗
同 occurrence 經歷、事件

英英 the process of having knowledge or skill from doing something

例 She has lots of **experience** in it.
對於這種事情她很有經驗。

☐ 三分熟
☐ 五分熟
☐ 七分熟
☐ 全熟

---

ex·pert [`ɛkspɝt]

形 熟練的
名 專家
反 amateur 業餘、外行

英英 a person who is very knowledgeable about or skilful in a particular field; very good or skilled

例 He's a financial **expert**.
他是金融專家。

☐ 三分熟
☐ 五分熟
☐ 七分熟
☐ 全熟

---

ex·plain [ɪk`splen]

動 解釋

英英 to make things clear by giving a detailed description

例 Can I **explain**?
我可以解釋嗎？

☐ 三分熟
☐ 五分熟
☐ 七分熟
☐ 全熟

---

ex·press [ɪk`sprɛs]

動 表達、說明
同 indicate 表明

英英 to present a thought or feeling in words or by gestures and conduct

例 I don't know how to **express** my appreciation.
我不知如何表達我的謝意。

☐ 三分熟
☐ 五分熟
☐ 七分熟
☐ 全熟

---

ex·tra [`ɛkstrə]

形 額外的
副 特別地
同 additional 額外的

英英 added to something or an amount or number

例 The **extra** charge is not reasonable.
額外的收費是不合理的。

☐ 三分熟
☐ 五分熟
☐ 七分熟
☐ 全熟

---

eye·brow/brow
[`aɪˌbraʊ]/[braʊ]

名 眉毛

英英 the strip of hair growing above a person's eye socket

例 Her **eyebrows** are very dark.
她的眉毛很深。

☐ 三分熟
☐ 五分熟
☐ 七分熟
☐ 全熟

Ff

F

fail [fel] 動 失敗、不及格 反 achieve 實現、達到	英英 be unsuccessful 例 He **failed** many times before he succeeded. 在他成功之前失敗了很多次。	□三分熟 □五分熟 □七分熟 □全熟
fail·ure [ˈfeljɚ] 名 失敗、失策 同 success 成功	英英 an unsuccessful thing 例 His **failure** is not surprising. 他的失敗並不意外。	□三分熟 □五分熟 □七分熟 □全熟
fair [fɛr] 形 公平的、合理的 副 光明正大地 同 just 公正的	英英 in a stuitable or legal manner 例 It is not **fair**! 這不公平！	□三分熟 □五分熟 □七分熟 □全熟
fa·mous [ˈfeməs] 形 有名的、出名的	英英 being known by many people 例 Taiwan is **famous** for food. 臺灣以食物出名。	□三分熟 □五分熟 □七分熟 □全熟
fault [fɔlt] 名 責任、過失 動 犯錯 同 error 過失	英英 a mistake; to make mistakes 例 It is not my **fault**. 這不是我的過失。	□三分熟 □五分熟 □七分熟 □全熟
fa·vor [ˈfevɚ] 名 喜好 動 贊成 動 give a favor 幫忙	英英 a kind, friendly or obliging act that is freely granted 例 The professor didn't read my essay with **favor**. 那位教授不喜好我的文章。	□三分熟 □五分熟 □七分熟 □全熟
fa·vor·ite [ˈfevɚrɪt] 形 最喜歡的 同 precious 珍愛的	英英 preferred to all others of the same kind 例 My **favorite** color is red. 我最喜歡的顏色是紅色。	□三分熟 □五分熟 □七分熟 □全熟
fear·ful [ˈfɪrfəl] 形 可怕的、嚇人的 同 afraid 害怕的	英英 showing or causing fear 例 The story is **fearful** for kids. 對小孩米說，這故事太可怕了。	□三分熟 □五分熟 □七分熟 □全熟

fee [fi]

名 費用
同 fare 費用

英英 a payment made in exchange for advices or services

例 The **fee** is too high.
這費用太高了。

☐ 三分熟
☐ 五分熟
☐ 七分熟
☐ 全熟

---

fe·male [ˋfimel]

形 女性的
名 女性
同 feminine 女性的

英英 relating to or characteristic of female

例 The book is not friendly to **female** readers.
這本書對女性讀者不太友善。

☐ 三分熟
☐ 五分熟
☐ 七分熟
☐ 全熟

---

fence [fɛns]

名 籬笆、圍牆
動 防衛、防護

英英 a barrier enclosing an area, typically consisting of posts connected by wire or wood; to protect with a fence

例 The wolf jumped through the **fence** and ate the chicken.
狼越過籬笆還吃了雞。

☐ 三分熟
☐ 五分熟
☐ 七分熟
☐ 全熟

---

fes·ti·val [ˋfɛstɪvl̩]

名 節日
同 holiday 節日

英英 a day or period of celebration, typically for religious events

例 We eat rice dumplings on Dragon Boat **Festival**.
我們在端午節吃粽子。

☐ 三分熟
☐ 五分熟
☐ 七分熟
☐ 全熟

---

fe·ver [ˋfivɚ]

名 發燒、熱、入迷

英英 a higher body temperature, usually accompanied by shivering, headache, and in severe instances, delirium

例 I didn't come because I had a **fever** yesterday.
我昨天發燒了所以沒來。

☐ 三分熟
☐ 五分熟
☐ 七分熟
☐ 全熟

---

field [fild]

名 田野、領域

英英 an area of open land, in which planted with crops or pastures

例 What is your academic **field**?
你研究領域是什麼？

☐ 三分熟
☐ 五分熟
☐ 七分熟
☐ 全熟

---

fight·er [ˋfaɪtɚ]

名 戰士

英英 a fast military aircraft designed for attacking other aircraft

例 She is called **fighter**.
她被稱為是戰士。

☐ 三分熟
☐ 五分熟
☐ 七分熟
☐ 全熟

fig·ure [ˈfɪgjɚ]

名 人影、畫像、數字
動 演算
同 symbol 數位、符號

英英 a number or numerical symbol

例 There was a **figure** at the corner.
在轉角處有個人影。

☐ 三分熟
☐ 五分熟
☐ 七分熟
☐ 全熟

F

film [fɪlm]

名 電影、膠捲
同 cinema 電影

英英 a thin flexible strip of plastic or other material coated with light-sensitive emulsion for exposure in a camera

例 The **film** is interesting.
這部電影很有趣。

☐ 三分熟
☐ 五分熟
☐ 七分熟
☐ 全熟

fire·man/ fire·wom·an

[ˈfaɪrmən]/[ˈfaɪrwʊmən]

名 消防員／女消防員

英英 a male / female firefighter

例 The **firemen** saved the family's life.
消防員救了這家人的性命。

☐ 三分熟
☐ 五分熟
☐ 七分熟
☐ 全熟

firm [fɝm]

形 堅固的
副 牢固地
名 公司
同 enterprise 公司

英英 having a hard surface or structure

例 The castle is **firm**.
這座城很堅固。

☐ 三分熟
☐ 五分熟
☐ 七分熟
☐ 全熟

fish·er·man

[ˈfɪʃɚmən]

名 漁夫

英英 a person who catches fish for a living

例 The **fisherman** caught lots of fish.
這漁夫捕了很多的魚。

☐ 三分熟
☐ 五分熟
☐ 七分熟
☐ 全熟

fit [fɪt]

形 適合的
動 適合
名 適合
同 suit 適合

英英 of a suitable quality, standard to meet the required purpose

例 It doesn't **fit** me well.
這不太適合我。

☐ 三分熟
☐ 五分熟
☐ 七分熟
☐ 全熟

fix [fɪks]

動 使穩固、修理
同 repair 修理

英英 to attach or position securely; to repair or restore

例 Could you please **fix** my car?
你可以幫我修車嗎？

☐ 三分熟
☐ 五分熟
☐ 七分熟
☐ 全熟

🎧**Track 185**

---

flag [flæg]

名 旗、旗幟
同 banner 旗、橫幅

英英 a piece of cloth which is raised on or attached to a pole and used as an emblem or marker

例 Do you know the colors of the national **flag** of the USA?
你知道美國國旗的顏色嗎？

☐三分熟
☐五分熟
☐七分熟
☐全熟

---

flash [flæʃ]

動 閃亮
名 一瞬間
同 flame 照亮

英英 to shine or cause to shine with a bright; a very short time

例 No **flash** is allowed in the museum.
在博物館內不可以用閃光燈。

☐三分熟
☐五分熟
☐七分熟
☐全熟

---

flash·light/

flash [ˈflæʃˌlaɪt]/[flæʃ]

名 手電筒、閃光
同 lantern 燈籠

英英 an electric torch with a strong beam

例 We go to the cave with **flashlights**.
我們拿著手電筒進山洞。

☐三分熟
☐五分熟
☐七分熟
☐全熟

---

flat [flæt]

名 平的東西、公寓
形 平坦的

英英 having a level and even surface; a set of rooms in a building for living

例 We moved to the **flat** in Taipei.
我們搬到在臺北的一間公寓。

☐三分熟
☐五分熟
☐七分熟
☐全熟

---

flight [flaɪt]

名 飛行

英英 the action or process of flying

例 Wish you a safe **flight**.
祝你搭機平安。

☐三分熟
☐五分熟
☐七分熟
☐全熟

---

flood [flʌd]

名 洪水、水災
動 淹沒
反 drought 旱災

英英 an overflow of a large amount of water over dry land; to cover with water in a flood

例 There is a **flood** almost every summer here.
這裡幾乎每年夏天都會淹水。

☐三分熟
☐五分熟
☐七分熟
☐全熟

---

flour [flaʊr]

名 麵粉
動 撒粉於

英英 a powder obtained by grain, which is used to make bread, cakes, and pastry

例 We need **flour** to make a cake.
我們需要麵粉做蛋糕。

☐三分熟
☐五分熟
☐七分熟
☐全熟

---

flow [flo]

動 流出、流動
名 流程、流量
同 stream 流動

英英 to move steadily and continuously in a current or stream; the process of flowing

例 The milk **flew** out of the bottle.
牛奶流出瓶子了。

☐三分熟
☐五分熟
☐七分熟
☐全熟

flu [flu]

名 流行性感冒
片 catch the flu
得到流感

英英 influenza or any similar, milder infection

例 My son tend to catch the **flu** easily.
我的兒子很容易得到流行性感冒。

□三分熟
□五分熟
□七分熟
□全熟

---

flute [flut]

名 橫笛、用笛吹奏

英英 to speak in a melodious way; a musical wind instrument consisting of a tube with a series of finger holes or keys

例 I have learned to play the **flute** since I was ten.
我從十歲就開始學吹橫笛。

□三分熟
□五分熟
□七分熟
□全熟

---

fo·cus [ˈfokəs]

名 焦點、焦距
動 使集中在焦點、集中
同 concentrate 集中

英英 the center of activity or something; to pay attention to a particular thing

例 Don't **focus** too much on the appearance.
不要把焦點放在外表。

□三分熟
□五分熟
□七分熟
□全熟

---

fog·gy [ˈfɑgɪ]

形 多霧的、朦朧的

英英 full of fog

例 London is always **foggy**.
倫敦總是多霧的。

□三分熟
□五分熟
□七分熟
□全熟

---

fol·low·ing [ˈfɑloɪŋ]

名 下一個
形 接著的
同 next 下一個

英英 coming after

例 The **following** questions will be discussed next week.
接下來的問題會在下週討論。

□三分熟
□五分熟
□七分熟
□全熟

---

fool [ful]

名 傻子
動 愚弄、欺騙
同 trick 戲弄

英英 a person who acts in a silly way; to make fun of someone

例 Love is not time's **fool**.
愛非時間的弄臣。

□三分熟
□五分熟
□七分熟
□全熟

---

fool·ish [ˈfulɪʃ]

形 愚笨的、愚蠢的
反 wise 聰明的

英英 being silly or unwise

例 You might feel him **foolish**, but actually he is very wise.
你可能會覺得他很愚蠢，但事實上他是非常有智慧的。

□三分熟
□五分熟
□七分熟
□全熟

🎧 Track 187

foot·ball [ˋfʊtˏbɔl]

名 足球、橄欖球

英英 the team game involving kicking a ball

例 He teaches kids to play **football**.
他教孩子們踢足球。

☐ 三分熟
☐ 五分熟
☐ 七分熟
☐ 全熟

---

for·eign·er
[ˋfɔrɪnɚ]

名 外國人

英英 a person from a foreign country

例 Many **foreigners** don't like the smell of stinky tofu.
很多外國人不喜歡臭豆腐的味道。

☐ 三分熟
☐ 五分熟
☐ 七分熟
☐ 全熟

---

for·give [fɚˋgɪv]

動 原諒、寬恕
反 punish 處罰

英英 to stop feeling angry or resentful towards someone for a mistake

例 It is not so easy to **forgive** and forget.
既往不咎不是那麼容易的。

☐ 三分熟
☐ 五分熟
☐ 七分熟
☐ 全熟

---

form [fɔrm]

名 形式、表格
動 形成
同 construct 構成

英英 a way in which something exists or appears; to develop or make into a certain form

例 Do you know how to write an essay in MLA **form**?
你知道要如何用 MLA 的格式寫論文嗎？

☐ 三分熟
☐ 五分熟
☐ 七分熟
☐ 全熟

---

for·mal [ˋfɔrml̩]

形 正式的、有禮的

英英 officially recognized; in a polite way

例 We don't usually say that in **formal** English.
在正式的英文中，我們通常不會這樣說。

☐ 三分熟
☐ 五分熟
☐ 七分熟
☐ 全熟

---

for·mer [ˋfɔrmɚ]

形 以前的、先前的
反 present 現在的

英英 having been previously

例 His success is the result of the contribution of the **former**.
他的成功是前人努力的結果。

☐ 三分熟
☐ 五分熟
☐ 七分熟
☐ 全熟

---

for·ward [ˋfɔrwɚd]

形 向前的
名 前鋒
動 發送
同 send 發送

英英 toward or tending to the front; an attacking player in sports; to send something to someone

例 I am looking **forward** to seeing you.
我很期待見到你。

☐ 三分熟
☐ 五分熟
☐ 七分熟
☐ 全熟

---

for·wards
[ˋfɔrwɚdz]

副 今後、將來、向前

英英 in the direction that one is facing

例 Go **forwards** and you will see a convenient store.
直走後，你就會看到便利商店。

☐ 三分熟
☐ 五分熟
☐ 七分熟
☐ 全熟

fox [fɑks]

名 狐狸、狡猾的人

英英 an animal of the dog family which is with a pointed muzzle, bushy tail, and a reddish coat

例 A **fox** is considered smart in many cultures.
在許多文化中都把狐狸視為是聰明的。

☐ 三分熟
☐ 五分熟
☐ 七分熟
☐ 全熟

frank [fræŋk]

形 率直的、坦白的
同 sincere 真誠的

英英 honest and direct; telling the truth

例 I like her because she's **frank**.
我很喜歡她，因為她很率直。

☐ 三分熟
☐ 五分熟
☐ 七分熟
☐ 全熟

free·dom [ˈfridəm]

名 自由、解放、解脫
同 liberty 自由

英英 the power or right to act, speak, or think freely

例 People need to have the **freedom** to say whatever they want.
人們需要有言論自由。

☐ 三分熟
☐ 五分熟
☐ 七分熟
☐ 全熟

free·zer [ˈfrizɚ]

名 冰庫、冷凍庫
同 refrigerator 冰箱

英英 a refrigerated container, operated by electricity, which is used for preserving food at very low temperatures

例 There is no **freezer** in the hostel.
這間青年旅館沒有冰箱。

☐ 三分熟
☐ 五分熟
☐ 七分熟
☐ 全熟

friend·ly [ˈfrɛndlɪ]

形 友善的、親切的
同 kind 親切的

英英 kind and pleasant

例 The environment is **friendly** to children.
這環境對孩子是很有善的。

☐ 三分熟
☐ 五分熟
☐ 七分熟
☐ 全熟

fright [fraɪt]

名 驚駭、恐怖、驚嚇
同 panic 驚恐

英英 a sudden intense feeling of fear or shock

例 The **fright** in her childhood made her timid.
童年的驚嚇讓她很膽小。

☐ 三分熟
☐ 五分熟
☐ 七分熟
☐ 全熟

fright·en [ˈfraɪtn̩]

動 震驚、使害怕
同 scare 使恐懼

英英 cause to be afraid or scared

例 I was **frightened** by the news.
我被這新聞嚇到了。

☐ 三分熟
☐ 五分熟
☐ 七分熟
☐ 全熟

func·tion [ˈfʌŋkʃən]

名 功能、作用

英英 an activity that is natural to or the purpose of a person or thing

例 What's the **function** of the machine?
這臺機器的功能是什麼？

☐ 三分熟
☐ 五分熟
☐ 七分熟
☐ 全熟

F

Track 189

fur·ther [ˈfɝðɚ]

副 更進一步地
形 較遠的
動 助長

英英 over a greater expanse of space or time; to help the progress

例 Could you tell me **further** about that?
你可以更進一步的跟我說明嗎？

☐ 三分熟
☐ 五分熟
☐ 七分熟
☐ 全熟

fu·ture [ˈfjutʃɚ]

名 未來、將來
反 past 過往

英英 time that will come after the present

例 What's your **future** plan?
你未來的計畫是什麼？

☐ 三分熟
☐ 五分熟
☐ 七分熟
☐ 全熟

Gg

gain [ɡen]

動 得到、獲得
名 得到、獲得
同 obtain 得到

英英 to obtain or secure

例 I **gained** lots of weight at Christmas.
我在耶誕節多了好幾公斤。

☐ 三分熟
☐ 五分熟
☐ 七分熟
☐ 全熟

ga·rage [ɡəˈrɑdʒ]

名 車庫

英英 a building for parking a motor vehicle or vehicles next to the houses

例 I bought a house with a **garage**.
我買了間有車庫的房子。

☐ 三分熟
☐ 五分熟
☐ 七分熟
☐ 全熟

gar·bage

[ˈɡɑrbɪdʒ]

名 垃圾

英英 domestic rubbish or waste

例 The **garbage** smells terrible.
這垃圾聞起來很可怕。

☐ 三分熟
☐ 五分熟
☐ 七分熟
☐ 全熟

gar·den·er

[ˈɡɑrdn̩ɚ]

名 園丁、花匠

英英 someone who grows plants in a garden, growing plants

例 The **gardener** makes the garden perfect.
這園丁讓花園很完美。

☐ 三分熟
☐ 五分熟
☐ 七分熟
☐ 全熟

gate [ɡet]

名 門、閘門

英英 a hinged barrier which is used to close an opening in a wall, fence, or hedge

例 Where is the **gate**?
大門在哪裡啊？

☐ 三分熟
☐ 五分熟
☐ 七分熟
☐ 全熟

gath·er [ˈɡæðɚ]

動 集合、聚集
同 collect 收集

英英 come or bring together

例 I **gathered** the apples.
我在撿蘋果。

☐ 三分熟
☐ 五分熟
☐ 七分熟
☐ 全熟

gen·er·al

[ˋdʒɛnərəl]

名 將領、將軍
形 普遍的、一般的

英英 chief or principal; a commander of an army, or an army officer ranking above lieutenant general; not special or specialized

例 The **general's** decision caused the cruel war.

這將軍的決定造成了這場殘酷的戰爭。

□三分熟
□五分熟
□七分熟
□全熟

gen·er·ous

[ˋdʒɛnərəs]

形 慷慨的、大方的、寬厚的
反 harsh 嚴厲的

英英 freely giving more than is expected

例 The girl who gives me food is very **generous**.

這個給我食物的女孩很大方。

□三分熟
□五分熟
□七分熟
□全熟

gen·tle [ˋdʒɛnt!]

形 溫和的、上流的
同 soft 柔和的

英英 mild or kind; not rough or violent

例 The man is so **gentle** that many women are into him.

那男人很溫柔，很多女人都為他瘋狂。

□三分熟
□五分熟
□七分熟
□全熟

gen·tle·man

[ˋdʒɛnt!mən]

名 紳士、家世好的男人

英英 a courteous or honorable man

例 Ladies and **gentlemen**, please pay attention.

各位先生女士，請注意。

□三分熟
□五分熟
□七分熟
□全熟

ge·og·ra·phy

[dʒiˋɑgrəfɪ]

名 地理（學）

英英 the study of the physical features of the earth and of human activity

例 He is good at **geography**.

他的地理很好。

□三分熟
□五分熟
□七分熟
□全熟

gi·ant [ˋdʒaɪənt]

名 巨人
形 巨大的、龐大的
同 huge 巨大的

英英 an imaginary or mythical being of human but extremely tall and strong; very large

例 The trees in the rainforest are **giant**.

熱帶雨林的樹很高大。

□三分熟
□五分熟
□七分熟
□全熟

gi·raffe [dʒəˋræf]

名 長頸鹿

英英 large mammal with a very long neck and forelegs, the tallest living animal

例 I saw **giraffes** in the zoo.

我在動物園看過長頸鹿。

□三分熟
□五分熟
□七分熟
□全熟

Track 191

glove(s) [glʌv(z)]

名 手套

英英 a covering for the hand having separate parts for each finger and the thumb

例 I gave him a pair of **gloves** as a Christmas gift.
我送他一副手套當作聖誕禮物。

- 三分熟
- 五分熟
- 七分熟
- 全熟

glue [glu]

名 膠水、黏膠

動 黏、固著

英英 a substance used for sticking objects or materials together; to fasten with glue

例 I **glued** the stamp on the envelope.
我把郵票黏在信封上。

- 三分熟
- 五分熟
- 七分熟
- 全熟

goal [gɔl]

名 目標、終點

同 destination 終點

英英 an aim or desired result

例 My **goal** is winning the first prize.
我的目標是得到第一名。

- 三分熟
- 五分熟
- 七分熟
- 全熟

goat [got]

名 山羊

英英 a hardy domesticated mammal that has back ward-curving horns and a beard

例 How can the **goat** stand on the rock?
這隻山羊是如何站在這塊巨岩上？

- 三分熟
- 五分熟
- 七分熟
- 全熟

gold·en [ˋgoldn̩]

形 金色的、黃金的

英英 made of or resembling gold

例 His **golden** hair is charming.
他金色的頭髮很迷人。

- 三分熟
- 五分熟
- 七分熟
- 全熟

golf [gɔlf]

名 高爾夫球

動 打高爾夫球

英英 a game played on an outdoor course, the aim of which is to strike a small, hard ball with a club into a series of small holes with the fewest possible strokes; to play golf

例 Would you like to play **golf** with me?
你可以陪我打高爾夫球嗎？

- 三分熟
- 五分熟
- 七分熟
- 全熟

gov·ern [ˋgʌvɚn]

動 統治、治理

同 regulate 管理

英英 conduct the policy and affairs of a nation, organization, or people

例 How did the king **govern** the kingdom?
這國王如何統治這個國家的？

- 三分熟
- 五分熟
- 七分熟
- 全熟

gov·ern·ment
[ˋgʌvɚnmənt]

名 政府

同 administration 政府

英英 the governing body of a state

例 The whole world is watching the next step of the **government**.
全世界都在關注這個政府的下一步會採取什麼措施。

- 三分熟
- 五分熟
- 七分熟
- 全熟

grade [gred]

名 年級、等級

英英 a specified level of rank or quality

例 My son is at the first **grade** now.
我的兒子現在一年級。

三分熟 / 五分熟 / 七分熟 / 全熟

grape [grep]

名 葡萄、葡萄樹

英英 a green, purple, or black berry growing in clusters on a vine, eaten as fruit and used in making wine

例 I want to eat **grapes**.
我想要吃葡萄。

三分熟 / 五分熟 / 七分熟 / 全熟

grass·y [ˈgræsɪ]

形 多草的

英英 covered with or resembling grass

例 The farm is **grassy**.
這塊地很多草。

三分熟 / 五分熟 / 七分熟 / 全熟

greed·y [ˈgridɪ]

形 貪婪的

英英 having or showing greed

例 The poor kids are not **greedy**. They just want to survive.
這些貧窮的小孩不是貪婪，他們只是想要活下來。

三分熟 / 五分熟 / 七分熟 / 全熟

greet [grit]

動 迎接、問候

同 hail 招呼

英英 give a word or sign of welcome when meeting

例 We **greeted** the teacher this morning.
我們今天早上有跟老師打招呼。

三分熟 / 五分熟 / 七分熟 / 全熟

growth [groθ]

名 成長、發育

同 progress 進步

英英 the process of growing

例 The **growth** of children makes parents satisfied.
孩子的成長讓家長很滿意。

三分熟 / 五分熟 / 七分熟 / 全熟

guard [gɑrd]

名 警衛

動 防護、守衛

英英 to watch over in order to protect or control; a person whose job is to watch over a door or building

例 The **guard** stopped us.
警衛攔住了我們。

三分熟 / 五分熟 / 七分熟 / 全熟

gua·va [ˈgwɑvə]

名 芭樂

英英 tropical American fruit with pink juicy flesh

例 The richness of vitamn C in a **guava** makes me eat it more.
芭樂富含維他命 C，這讓我想多吃一點芭樂。

三分熟 / 五分熟 / 七分熟 / 全熟

gui·tar [gɪˈtɑr]

名 吉他

英英 a stringed musical instrument with six or twelve strings, played by plucking or strumming with the fingers

例 The boy playing the **guitar** attracts many girls.
那位彈著吉他的男孩吸引了很多女孩。

三分熟 / 五分熟 / 七分熟 / 全熟

🎧 Track 193

guy [gaɪ]

名 傢伙

英英 a man; people of either sex

例 The **guy** is not polite to me.
那傢伙對我很不禮貌。

☐ 三分熟
☐ 五分熟
☐ 七分熟
☐ 全熟

Hh

hab·it [ˈhæbɪt]

名 習慣

英英 a regular tendency or practice

例 Getting up early becomes my **habit**.
早起已經變成我的習慣了。

☐ 三分熟
☐ 五分熟
☐ 七分熟
☐ 全熟

hall [hɔl]

名 廳、堂

英英 the room or space just inside the front entrance of a house

例 I will meet you in the **hall**.
我們在大廳碰面。

☐ 三分熟
☐ 五分熟
☐ 七分熟
☐ 全熟

ham·burg·er/ burg·er

[ˈhæmbɝɡɚ]/[ˈbɝɡɚ]

名 漢堡

英英 a small flat cake of minced beef, fried or grilled and typically served in a bread roll

例 I ate lots of **hamburgers** in the USA.
我在美國吃了很多的漢堡。

☐ 三分熟
☐ 五分熟
☐ 七分熟
☐ 全熟

ham·mer [ˈhæmɚ]

名 鐵錘
動 錘打

英英 tool containing a heavy metal head mounted at the end of a handle, used for driving in nails; to hit with a hammer

例 I use a **hammer** and nails to fix the table.
我用鐵錘還有釘子修這張桌子。

☐ 三分熟
☐ 五分熟
☐ 七分熟
☐ 全熟

hand·ker·chief

[ˈhæŋkɚtʃɪf]

名 手帕

英英 square of cotton or other material for wiping one's nose

例 The lady wiped her tears with a **handkerchief**.
那位女士用手帕擦拭淚水。

☐ 三分熟
☐ 五分熟
☐ 七分熟
☐ 全熟

han·dle [ˈhændl]

名 把手
動 觸、手執、管理、對付
同 manage 管理

英英 to feel with the hands; to manage something

例 Could you **handle** the problem by yourself?
你可以獨自處理這問題嗎？

☐ 三分熟
☐ 五分熟
☐ 七分熟
☐ 全熟

H

hand·some

[ˈhænsəm]

形 英俊的
同 attractive 吸引人的

英英 very good-looking
例 The singer is very **handsome**!
這歌手好帥喔！

☐ 三分熟
☐ 五分熟
☐ 七分熟
☐ 全熟

hang [hæŋ]

動 吊、掛
同 suspend 吊、掛
片 hang out 閒逛

英英 to fix something at the top with the lower part not attached
例 I am **hanging** the clothes.
我正在把衣服掛上。

☐ 三分熟
☐ 五分熟
☐ 七分熟
☐ 全熟

hard·ly [ˈhɑrdlɪ]

副 勉強地、僅僅
同 barely 僅僅

英英 scarcely; barely
例 **Hardly** can I hear you.
我幾乎不能聽到你說話。

☐ 三分熟
☐ 五分熟
☐ 七分熟
☐ 全熟

hate·ful [ˈhetfəl]

形 可恨的、很討厭的
同 hostile 不友善的

英英 arousing or deserving of hatred
例 Cockroache is **hateful**.
蟑螂很討人厭。

☐ 三分熟
☐ 五分熟
☐ 七分熟
☐ 全熟

heal·thy [ˈhɛlθɪ]

形 健康的

英英 having good health
例 Live a **healthy** life.
過著健康的生活。

☐ 三分熟
☐ 五分熟
☐ 七分熟
☐ 全熟

heat·er [ˈhitɚ]

名 加熱器

英英 a device for heating something
例 We need a **heater** in winter.
我們在冬天會需要一個加熱器。

☐ 三分熟
☐ 五分熟
☐ 七分熟
☐ 全熟

height [haɪt]

名 高度

英英 the measurement of someone or something from head to foot
例 The **height** of the basketball player is unbelievable.
這籃球員的身高讓人難以置信。

☐ 三分熟
☐ 五分熟
☐ 七分熟
☐ 全熟

help·ful [ˈhɛlpfəl]

形 有用的
同 usetul 有用的

英英 very useful
例 The book is quite **helpful** for a starter like you.
這本書對於你這種初學者來說很有幫助。

☐ 三分熟
☐ 五分熟
☐ 七分熟
☐ 全熟

🎧 **Track 195**

hen [hɛn]

名 母雞

英英 a female bird, especially of a domestic fowl

例 The **hen** is laying eggs.
這隻母雞正在孵蛋。

☐ 三分熟
☐ 五分熟
☐ 七分熟
☐ 全熟

---

he·ro/her·o·ine

[ˈhɪro]/[ˈhɛroˏɪn]

名 英雄、勇士／女傑、
女英雄

英英 a person, who is admired for their courage or outstanding

例 The **hero** saved our life!
這位英雄救了我們的性命！

☐ 三分熟
☐ 五分熟
☐ 七分熟
☐ 全熟

---

hide [haɪd]

動 隱藏
同 conceal 隱藏

英英 put or keep out of sight

例 You can't **hide** the truth forever.
你不可能永遠隱藏著真相。

☐ 三分熟
☐ 五分熟
☐ 七分熟
☐ 全熟

---

high·way [ˈhaɪˏwe]

名 公路、大路
同 road 路

英英 a main or public road

例 You can't ride on the **highway**.
你不可以騎上高速公路。

☐ 三分熟
☐ 五分熟
☐ 七分熟
☐ 全熟

---

hip [hɪp]

名 臀部、屁股

英英 the part of the body at the buttocks

例 Her **hips** are sexy.
她的臀部很性感。

☐ 三分熟
☐ 五分熟
☐ 七分熟
☐ 全熟

**hip·po·pot·a·mus/
hip·po**

[ˏhɪpəˈpɑtəməs]/[ˈhɪpo]

名 河馬

英英 a large African mammal with a thick skin and massive jaws, living partly on land and partly in water

例 There are many **hippopotamuses** around the river.
這條河附近有很多的河馬。

☐ 三分熟
☐ 五分熟
☐ 七分熟
☐ 全熟

---

hire [haɪr]

動 雇用、租用
名 雇用、租金
同 employ 雇用

英英 obtain the temporary use of something in return for payment

例 My mother **hired** a babysitter when I was little.
我小時候我媽媽有雇用一名保母。

☐ 三分熟
☐ 五分熟
☐ 七分熟
☐ 全熟

---

hob·by [ˈhɑbɪ]

名 興趣、嗜好
同 pastime 娛樂

英英 an activity followed regularly for pleasure

例 What's your **hobby**?
你的興趣是什麼？

☐ 三分熟
☐ 五分熟
☐ 七分熟
☐ 全熟

hold·er [`holdɚ]

名 持有者、所有人

英英 someone who officially owns something

例 He's the **holder** of the house.
他是房子的持有者。

☐ 三分熟
☐ 五分熟
☐ 七分熟
☐ 全熟

---

home·sick [`homˌsɪk]

形 想家的、思鄉的

英英 feeling upset because one is missing one's home

例 I was **homesick** when I was in the USA.
我在美國的時候很想家。

☐ 三分熟
☐ 五分熟
☐ 七分熟
☐ 全熟

---

hon·est [`ɑnɪst]

形 誠實的、耿直的
同 truthful 誠實的

英英 truthful and sincere

例 As an **honest** child, you should have told me that you took the money.
既然你是個誠實的小孩，你應該要告訴我你拿走了錢。

☐ 三分熟
☐ 五分熟
☐ 七分熟
☐ 全熟

---

hon·ey [`hʌnɪ]

名 蜂蜜、花蜜

英英 a sweet, sticky yellowish-brown fluid made by bees from flower nectar

例 I add some **honey** into the milk tea.
我在奶茶裡面加了一點蜂蜜。

☐ 三分熟
☐ 五分熟
☐ 七分熟
☐ 全熟

---

hop [hɑp]

動 跳過、單腳跳
名 單腳跳、跳舞
同 jump 跳

英英 move by jumping on one foot

例 The children run and **hop** in the yard.
孩子們在院子裡面跑跳。

☐ 三分熟
☐ 五分熟
☐ 七分熟
☐ 全熟

---

hos·pi·tal [`hɑspɪtl̩]

名 醫院
同 clinic 診所

英英 an institution providing medical and surgical treatment and nursing care for people who is sick or injured

例 The patient was sent to the **hospital**.
這名病患被送到醫院了。

☐ 三分熟
☐ 五分熟
☐ 七分熟
☐ 全熟

---

host/host·ess [host]/[`hostɪs]

名 主人、女主人

英英 a person who receives or entertains guests

例 The host and the **hostess** welcome us warmly.
主人跟女主人很歡迎我們。

☐ 三分熟
☐ 五分熟
☐ 七分熟
☐ 全熟

---

ho·tel [ho`tɛl]

名 旅館
同 hostel 青年旅舍

英英 an establishment providing accommodation and meals for travelers and tourists

例 Which **hotel** will you stay on this weekend?
你這週末將會待在哪個旅館？

☐ 三分熟
☐ 五分熟
☐ 七分熟
☐ 全熟

🎧 Track 197

how·ev·er

[haʊˋɛvɚ]

副 無論如何
連 然而

英英 in whatever way

例 She wants to lose some weight. **However**, she eats lots of junk food every day.
她想要減肥，但是她每天還是吃很多垃圾食物。

☐ 三分熟
☐ 五分熟
☐ 七分熟
☐ 全熟

hum [hʌm]

名 嗡嗡聲
動 作嗡嗡聲

英英 make a low, steady continuous sound like that of a bee; the sound of hum

例 Can you hear the **hum**?
你聽得到嗡嗡聲嗎？

☐ 三分熟
☐ 五分熟
☐ 七分熟
☐ 全熟

hum·ble [ˋhʌmbl̩]

形 身份卑微的、謙虛的
同 modest 謙虛的

英英 having or showing modesty

例 The professor is **humble**.
這位教授很謙虛。

☐ 三分熟
☐ 五分熟
☐ 七分熟
☐ 全熟

hu·mid [ˋhjumɪd]

形 潮濕的
同 moist 潮濕的

英英 marked by a high level of water vapor in the atmosphere

例 The climate in Taiwan is hot and **humid**.
臺灣的氣候溫暖又潮濕。

☐ 三分熟
☐ 五分熟
☐ 七分熟
☐ 全熟

hu·mor [ˋhjumɚ]

名 詼諧、幽默
同 comedy 喜劇

英英 the quality of being amusing or comic

例 You don't have any sense of **humor**.
你沒有任何的幽默感。

☐ 三分熟
☐ 五分熟
☐ 七分熟
☐ 全熟

hun·ger [ˋhʌngɚ]

名 餓、饑餓

英英 a feeling of discomfort or weakness caused by a lack of food

例 **Hunger** can make people different.
饑餓可以讓人不一樣。

☐ 三分熟
☐ 五分熟
☐ 七分熟
☐ 全熟

hunt [hʌnt]

動 獵取
名 打獵
同 chase 追捕

英英 pursue and kill a wild animal for sport or food

例 He **hunted** a rabbit.
他獵到一頭兔子。

☐ 三分熟
☐ 五分熟
☐ 七分熟
☐ 全熟

hunt·er [ˋhʌntɚ]

名 獵人

英英 a person or animal that hunts

例 The **hunter** went into the forest with confidence.
那位獵人很有信心地走向森林。

☐ 三分熟
☐ 五分熟
☐ 七分熟
☐ 全熟

hur·ry [ˈhɝɪ]

動 （使）趕緊
名 倉促
同 rush 倉促

英英 to move or act very quickly

例 Please **hurry** up.
請加快腳步。

☐ 三分熟
☐ 五分熟
☐ 七分熟
☐ 全熟

Ii

ig·nore [ɪgˈnor]

動 忽視、不理睬
同 neglect 忽視

英英 to disregard intentionally

例 The government **ignores** the need of people.
政府忽略人民的需求。

☐ 三分熟
☐ 五分熟
☐ 七分熟
☐ 全熟

ill [ɪl]

名 疾病、壞事
形 生病的
副 壞地
同 sick 生病的

英英 not in full health; unwell

例 She's not here because she's **ill** today.
她生病了，所以沒來。

☐ 三分熟
☐ 五分熟
☐ 七分熟
☐ 全熟

i·mag·ine

[ɪˈmædʒɪn]

動 想像、設想
同 suppose 設想

英英 form a mental image or concept of

例 Can you **imagine** that she's getting married?
你可以想像她要結婚了嗎？

☐ 三分熟
☐ 五分熟
☐ 七分熟
☐ 全熟

im·por·tance

[ɪmˈpɔrtn̩s]

名 重要性

英英 of great significance or value

例 Do you know the **importance** of health?
你知道健康的重要性嗎？

☐ 三分熟
☐ 五分熟
☐ 七分熟
☐ 全熟

im·prove [ɪmˈpruv]

動 改善、促進

英英 make something better or become better

例 How do you **improve** your English?
你怎麼改善你的英文的？

☐ 三分熟
☐ 五分熟
☐ 七分熟
☐ 全熟

im·prove·ment

[ɪmˈpruvmənt]

名 改善

英英 a state of improving or being improved

例 The **improvement** of this department is seeable.
這個部門的進步是可見的。

☐ 三分熟
☐ 五分熟
☐ 七分熟
☐ 全熟

🎧 **Track 199**

---

in·clude [ɪnˋklud]

動 包含、包括、含有
同 contain 包含

英英 contain as part of a whole

例 I love everything about you, **including** your defects.
我愛你的一切，包含你的缺陷。

□ 三分熟
□ 五分熟
□ 七分熟
□ 全熟

---

in·come [ˋɪnˌkʌm]

名 所得、收入
同 earnings 收入

英英 money received from work or through investments

例 How do you manage your **income**?
你如何規畫你的收入？

□ 三分熟
□ 五分熟
□ 七分熟
□ 全熟

---

in·crease

[ˋɪnkris]/[ɪnˋkris]

名 增加
動 增加
反 reduce 減少

英英 make or become greater in size, amount or degree

例 Do you want to **increase** your income?
你想要增加收入嗎？

□ 三分熟
□ 五分熟
□ 七分熟
□ 全熟

---

in·de·pen·dence

[ˌɪndɪˋpɛndəns]

名 自立、獨立

英英 the fact or state of being independent

例 The announcement of the **independence** of the nation stunned the whole world.
這國家宣告獨立震驚全球。

□ 三分熟
□ 五分熟
□ 七分熟
□ 全熟

---

in·de·pend·ent

[ˌɪndɪˋpɛndənt]

形 獨立的

英英 free from outside control or influence

例 The woman is very **independent**. She can do everything by herself.
這女人非常的獨立，她什麼都可以自己來。

□ 三分熟
□ 五分熟
□ 七分熟
□ 全熟

---

in·di·cate

[ˋɪndəˌket]

動 指出、指示
同 imply 暗示

英英 point out; show

例 Could you **indicate** your own problem?
你可以指出你自己的問題嗎？

□ 三分熟
□ 五分熟
□ 七分熟
□ 全熟

---

in·dus·try

[ˋɪndəstrɪ]

名 工業

英英 economic activity concerned with the processing of raw materials and manufacture of goods in factories

例 The **industry** causes lots of air pollution.
工業造成很多的空氣污染。

□ 三分熟
□ 五分熟
□ 七分熟
□ 全熟

---

in·flu·ence

[`ɪnflʊəns]

名 影響
動 影響

英英 the power or ability to affect someone's beliefs or actions

例 My mother **influences** me a lot.
我媽媽對我的影響很大。

□三分熟
□五分熟
□七分熟
□全熟

---

ink [ɪŋk]

名 墨水、墨汁
動 塗上墨水

英英 a colored fluid used for writing, drawing, or printing; to write or mark with ink

例 I can't write without **ink**.
沒有墨水我沒辦法寫字。

□三分熟
□五分熟
□七分熟
□全熟

---

in·sect [`ɪnsɛkt]

名 昆蟲
同 bug 蟲子

英英 a small invertebrate animal with a head, thorax, and abdomen, six legs, and usually one or two pairs of wings

例 There are lots of **insects** in the forest.
在森林裡面有很多的昆蟲。

□三分熟
□五分熟
□七分熟
□全熟

---

in·sist [ɪn`sɪst]

動 堅持、強調
片 insist on 堅持

英英 to state forcefully, without accepting refusal or contradiction

例 My mother **insists** on the importance of education.
我媽媽堅持教育的重要性。

□三分熟
□五分熟
□七分熟
□全熟

---

in·stance

[`ɪnsɪstəns]

名 實例
動 舉證
同 example 例子

英英 an example or single occurrence of something; to mention as an example

例 I love many kinds of fruits. For **instance**, apples, bananas and oranges.
我喜歡水果，舉例來說，蘋果、香蕉跟柳丁。

□三分熟
□五分熟
□七分熟
□全熟

---

in·stant [`ɪnsɪstənt]

形 立即的、瞬間的
名 立即
同 immediate 立即的

英英 immediate; urgent

例 Thank you for your **instant** help.
感謝你及時相助。

□三分熟
□五分熟
□七分熟
□全熟

---

in·stru·ment

[`ɪnstrəmənt]

名 樂器、器具

英英 a device for producing musical sounds

例 I learned to play many kinds of **instruments** when I was little.
我小時候學過很多種樂器。

□三分熟
□五分熟
□七分熟
□全熟

🎧**Track 201**

in·ter·nat·ion·al

[ˌɪntɚˋnæʃənḷ]

形 國際的
同 universal 全世界的

英英 existing or occurring between nations

例 The equipment in the **international** airport is perfect.
這座國際機場的設備是一流的。

☐ 三分熟
☐ 五分熟
☐ 七分熟
☐ 全熟

in·ter·view

[ˋɪntɚˌvju]

名 面談
動 面談、會面

英英 an occasion on which a journalist or broadcaster to ask questions to a person of public interest

例 I am going to have an **interview** this afternoon.
我今天下午有一場面試。

☐ 三分熟
☐ 五分熟
☐ 七分熟
☐ 全熟

in·tro·duce

[ˌɪntrəˋdjus]

動 介紹、引進

英英 to bring into use or operation for the first time

例 May I **introduce** our product to you?
我可以向你介紹我們的產品嗎？

☐ 三分熟
☐ 五分熟
☐ 七分熟
☐ 全熟

in·vent [ɪnˋvɛnt]

動 發明、創造

英英 create or design a new device

例 Do you know who **invented** computers?
你知道是誰發明了電腦嗎？

☐ 三分熟
☐ 五分熟
☐ 七分熟
☐ 全熟

in·vi·ta·tion

[ˌɪnvəˋteʃən]

名 請帖、邀請

英英 a written or verbal request inviting someone to go somewhere or to do something

例 Thank you for your **invitation**.
感謝你的邀請。

☐ 三分熟
☐ 五分熟
☐ 七分熟
☐ 全熟

in·vite [ɪnˋvaɪt]

動 邀請、招待

英英 ask in a friendly or formal way to go somewhere or to do something

例 Do you want to **invite** her to your party?
你想要邀請她來你的派對嗎？

☐ 三分熟
☐ 五分熟
☐ 七分熟
☐ 全熟

is·land [ˋaɪlənd]

名 島、安全島

英英 a piece of land surrounded by water

例 Bali is a lovely **island**.
峇里島是一座美麗的小島。

☐ 三分熟
☐ 五分熟
☐ 七分熟
☐ 全熟

i·tem [ˋaɪtəm]

名 項目、條款、專案
同 segment 專案

英英 an individual article

例 Some **items** on the list are not reasonable.
這列表上面有些專案不太合理。

☐ 三分熟
☐ 五分熟
☐ 七分熟
☐ 全熟

jack·et [ˈdʒækɪt]

名 夾克
同 coat 外套

英英 a short coat, usually with sleeves

例 I bought a **jacket** for the coming winter.
我為即將到來的冬天買了件夾克。

☐ 三分熟
☐ 五分熟
☐ 七分熟
☐ 全熟

jam [dʒæm]

動 阻塞
名 果醬
片 traffic jam 塞車

英英 to squeeze or pack something tightly into a container; a conserve and spread made from fruit and sugar

例 I was late because of the traffic **jam**.
因為塞車，我遲到了。

☐ 三分熟
☐ 五分熟
☐ 七分熟
☐ 全熟

jazz [dʒæz]

名 爵士樂

英英 a type of music of black American origin characterized by improvisation and a regular rhythm

例 I love **jazz** music in the 1920s.
我喜歡二〇年代的爵士樂。

☐ 三分熟
☐ 五分熟
☐ 七分熟
☐ 全熟

jeans [dʒinz]

名 牛仔褲
同 pants 褲子

英英 strong blue cotton cloth which are worn informally

例 The girl in blue **jeans** is my sister.
穿著藍色牛仔褲的那個女孩是我妹妹。

☐ 三分熟
☐ 五分熟
☐ 七分熟
☐ 全熟

jeep [dʒip]

名 吉普車

英英 a small, motor vehicle with four-wheel drive

例 Have you ever been in a **jeep**?
你曾經搭過吉普車嗎？

☐ 三分熟
☐ 五分熟
☐ 七分熟
☐ 全熟

jog [dʒɑg]

動 慢跑

英英 to run at a steady pace, especially for exercise

例 I go **jogging** every afternoon.
我每天下午都會去慢跑。

☐ 三分熟
☐ 五分熟
☐ 七分熟
☐ 全熟

joint [dʒɔɪnt]

名 接合處
形 共同的

英英 a point at which two parts are joined; shared and held by two or more people

例 The **joint** of the door is fragile.
這門的接合處很脆弱。

☐ 三分熟
☐ 五分熟
☐ 七分熟
☐ 全熟

judge [dʒʌdʒ]

名 法官，裁判
動 裁決
同 umpire 裁判

英英 a public officer appointed to decide cases in a law court; to make an opinion about something or someone

例 Do you believe the justice a **judge** will bring?
你相信法官帶來的正義嗎？

☐ 三分熟
☐ 五分熟
☐ 七分熟
☐ 全熟

🎧 Track 203

**judge·ment/
judg·ment**

[ˈdʒʌdʒmənt]

名 判斷力

英英 the ability to make considered decisions or opinions

例 Don't put a **judgement** on someone easily.
不要輕易的判定一個人。

☐ 三分熟
☐ 五分熟
☐ 七分熟
☐ 全熟

---

juic·y [ˈdʒusɪ]

形 多汁的

英英 describes a fruit or vegetable full of juice

例 The fruit in Thailand is **juicy**.
泰國的水果很多汁。

☐ 三分熟
☐ 五分熟
☐ 七分熟
☐ 全熟

Kk

ketch·up [ˈkɛtʃəp]

名 番茄醬

英英 a spicy sauce made from tomatoes and vinegar

例 I prefer to eat French fries with **ketchup**.
我喜歡吃薯條配番茄醬。

☐ 三分熟
☐ 五分熟
☐ 七分熟
☐ 全熟

---

kin·der·gar·ten

[ˈkɪndɚˌgartn̩]

名 幼稚園

英英 a nursery school for young children

例 My kids are in this **kindergarten**.
我的小孩在這家幼稚園。

☐ 三分熟
☐ 五分熟
☐ 七分熟
☐ 全熟

---

king·dom

[ˈkɪŋdəm]

名 王國

英英 a country or state ruled by a king or queen

例 In the **kingdom** of love, no one is smart.
在愛情的國度裡，沒有人是聰明的。

☐ 三分熟
☐ 五分熟
☐ 七分熟
☐ 全熟

---

knock [nɑk]

動 敲、擊
名 敲打聲
同 hit 打擊

英英 strike a surface noisily for attracting attention; the sound of knocking

例 **Knock** the door and enter.
敲門入內。

☐ 三分熟
☐ 五分熟
☐ 七分熟
☐ 全熟

---

knowl·edge

[ˈnɑlɪdʒ]

名 知識
同 scholarship 學問

英英 information and skills acquired through experience or education

例 I don't have any **knowledge** in investment.
我沒有任何投資理財的知識。

☐ 三分熟
☐ 五分熟
☐ 七分熟
☐ 全熟

---

ko·a·la [kəˈɑlə]

名 無尾熊

英英 a bear-like tree-dwelling Australian animal that has thick grey fur and feeds on eucalyptus leaves

例 There are lots of **koalas** in Australia.
在澳洲有很多的無尾熊。

☐ 三分熟
☐ 五分熟
☐ 七分熟
☐ 全熟

la·dy·bug/ la·dy·bird

[ˈledɪˌbʌg]/[ˈledɪˌbɝd]

名 瓢蟲

英英 a small red or yellow beetle with a domed back, typically with black spots

例 We used to see lots of **ladybugs** in this farm.
我們曾經在這塊農田中看到很多瓢蟲。

☐三分熟
☐五分熟
☐七分熟
☐全熟

lane [len]

名 小路、巷
同 path 小路

英英 a narrow road

例 I saw a poor dog in this **lane** last night.
我昨天晚上在這條小路上看到一隻可憐的小狗。

☐三分熟
☐五分熟
☐七分熟
☐全熟

lan·guage

[ˈlæŋgwɪdʒ]

名 語言

英英 the method of human communication, either spoken or written, containing the use of words in a structured and conventional way

例 She can speak many **languages**.
她會說很多種語言。

☐三分熟
☐五分熟
☐七分熟
☐全熟

lan·tern [ˈlæntɚn]

名 燈籠
同 lamp 燈

英英 a lamp with a transparent case protecting the flame or electric bulb

例 In ancient China, people use **lanterns** at night.
在古中國，人們晚上都是用燈籠的。

☐三分熟
☐五分熟
☐七分熟
☐全熟

lap [læp]

名 膝部
動 舐、輕拍

英英 the flat area between the waist and knees of a seated person; to lick something

例 I sat down and I put my bag on my **laps**.
我坐下，然後把包包放在我的膝上。

☐三分熟
☐五分熟
☐七分熟
☐全熟

lat·est [ˈletɪst]

形 最後的

英英 the most recent or newest

例 It is the **latest** album of Jolin.
這是喬琳最新的專輯。

☐三分熟
☐五分熟
☐七分熟
☐全熟

law·yer [ˈlɔjɚ]

名 律師

英英 a person whose job is to practice or study law

例 The **lawyer** is persuasive.
這律師的話很能讓人信服。

☐三分熟
☐五分熟
☐七分熟
☐全熟

lead·er·ship

[ˈlidɚʃɪp]

名 領導力
同 guidance 領導

英英 the ability of being a leader or the qualities a good leader should have

例 The **leadership** of the leader is doubtful.
這領導者的領導能力是讓人質疑的。

☐三分熟
☐五分熟
☐七分熟
☐全熟

Track 205

le·gal [ˈligl̩]

形 合法的
同 lawful 合法的

英英 of, based on, or required by the law

例 It is not **legal** to drink in the public in the town.
在這個鎮上，公然飲酒是不合法的。

☐ 三分熟
☐ 五分熟
☐ 七分熟
☐ 全熟

---

lem·on [ˈlɛmən]

名 檸檬

英英 a pale yellow oval citrus fruit with thick skin and fragrant, acidic juice

例 I add some **lemon** in the drink.
我在飲料中加了點檸檬。

☐ 三分熟
☐ 五分熟
☐ 七分熟
☐ 全熟

---

lem·on·ade

[ˌlɛmənˈed]

名 檸檬水

英英 a sweetened drink made from lemon juice

例 May I have some **lemonade**?
可以給我一點檸檬水嗎？

☐ 三分熟
☐ 五分熟
☐ 七分熟
☐ 全熟

---

lend [lɛnd]

動 借出
反 borrow 借來
片 lend some money to 借錢給……

英英 allow someone to use something under an agreement to pay it back later

例 I **lent** some money to Doris.
我借了一點錢給朵莉絲。

☐ 三分熟
☐ 五分熟
☐ 七分熟
☐ 全熟

---

length [lɛŋkθ]

名 長度

英英 the measurement or extent of something from end to end

例 What's the **length** of the table?
這桌子的長度如何呢？

☐ 三分熟
☐ 五分熟
☐ 七分熟
☐ 全熟

---

leop·ard [ˈlɛpəd]

名 豹

英英 a large solitary cat that has a fawn or brown coat with black spots, found in the forests of Africa and southern Asia

例 A **leopard** can run very fast.
豹可以跑很快。

☐ 三分熟
☐ 五分熟
☐ 七分熟
☐ 全熟

---

let·tuce [ˈlɛtɪs]

名 萵苣

英英 a plant with edible leaves that are usually eaten in salads

例 I made a sandwitch with **lettuce**.
我用點萵苣做了三明治。

☐ 三分熟
☐ 五分熟
☐ 七分熟
☐ 全熟

---

li·bra·ry [ˈlaɪˌbrɛrɪ]

名 圖書館

英英 a building or room containing a collection of books for use by the public or the members of an institution

例 I studied in the **library**.
我去圖書館讀書。

☐ 三分熟
☐ 五分熟
☐ 七分熟
☐ 全熟

L

lick [lɪk]
名／動 舔食、舔

英英 pass the tongue over something, typically for tasting

例 The boy **licked** the lollipop.
那小男孩舔了一口棒棒糖。

□ 三分熟
□ 五分熟
□ 七分熟
□ 全熟

lid [lɪd]
名 蓋子

英英 a removable or hinged cover for the top of a container

例 Mom put a **lid** on the pot.
媽媽用蓋子蓋在鍋子上。

□ 三分熟
□ 五分熟
□ 七分熟
□ 全熟

light·ning [ˈlaɪtnɪŋ]
名 閃電

英英 a bright flash in the sky which produced by a high-voltage electricity discharge between a cloud and the ground

例 The dog is afraid of **lightning**.
這隻狗會怕閃電。

□ 三分熟
□ 五分熟
□ 七分熟
□ 全熟

lim·it [ˈlɪmɪt]
名 限度、極限
動 限制
同 extreme 極限

英英 the furthest extent of one's endurance; to set a limit to

例 What's the **limit** of your budget?
你預算的上限是多少？

□ 三分熟
□ 五分熟
□ 七分熟
□ 全熟

link [lɪŋk]
名 關聯
動 連結
同 connect 連結

英英 a relationship or connection between someone or something; to make or form a link with somethin

例 What's the **link** between your points?
你所提的要點有什麼關聯？

□ 三分熟
□ 五分熟
□ 七分熟
□ 全熟

liq·uid [ˈlɪkwɪd]
名 液體

英英 a substance with a consistency like that of water or oil

例 Coke is a kind of black **liquid**.
可樂是一種黑色的液體。

□ 三分熟
□ 五分熟
□ 七分熟
□ 全熟

lis·ten·er [ˈlɪsn̩ɚ]
名 聽眾、聽者

英英 a person who listens

例 The **listeners** are confused by your speech!
聽眾被你的演講給搞糊塗了！

□ 三分熟
□ 五分熟
□ 七分熟
□ 全熟

loaf [lof]
名 一塊
名詞複數 loaves

英英 a quantity of bread that is shaped and baked in one piece

例 I bought a **loaf** of bread for my breakfast.
我買了一條麵包當早餐。

□ 三分熟
□ 五分熟
□ 七分熟
□ 全熟

Track 207

lo·cal [ˈlokḷ]

形 當地的
名 當地居民
同 regional 地區的

英英 relating to a particular area; a person who is living in a particular area

例 The **local** weather is good today.
當地氣候很好。

☐ 三分熟
☐ 五分熟
☐ 七分熟
☐ 全熟

---

lo·cate [ˈloket]

動 設置、居住

英英 be situated or living in a particular place

例 The house is **located** in the jungle.
這房子設置在叢林裡面。

☐ 三分熟
☐ 五分熟
☐ 七分熟
☐ 全熟

---

lock [lɑk]

名 鎖
動 鎖上

英英 a mechanism for keeping a door or container closed, typically operated by a key; to keep a door closed with a lock

例 Could you **lock** the door, please?
你可以把門鎖上嗎？

☐ 三分熟
☐ 五分熟
☐ 七分熟
☐ 全熟

---

log [lɔg]

名 圓木
動 伐木、把……記入航海日誌
同 wood 木頭

英英 a part of the trunk or a large branch of a tree that has been cut off; to cut logs

例 We need some **logs** to make a table.
我們需要一些圓木做桌子。

☐ 三分熟
☐ 五分熟
☐ 七分熟
☐ 全熟

---

lone [lon]

形 孤單的

英英 having no companions; solitary

例 The **lone** puppy is poor.
那隻孤單的小狗狗好可憐喔。

☐ 三分熟
☐ 五分熟
☐ 七分熟
☐ 全熟

---

lone·ly [ˈlonlɪ]

形 孤單的、寂寞的
同 solitary 寂寞的

英英 being sad because one has no friends or company

例 Sometimes, I feel **lonely**.
有時候我覺得很孤單。

☐ 三分熟
☐ 五分熟
☐ 七分熟
☐ 全熟

---

lose [luz]

動 遺失、失去、輸
同 fail 失敗、失去

英英 become unable to find

例 I **lost** my wallet!
我遺失了錢包！

☐ 三分熟
☐ 五分熟
☐ 七分熟
☐ 全熟

---

los·er [ˈluzɚ]

名 失敗者、輸家

英英 a person who is defeated in a competition or unsuccessful

例 You are such a **loser**.
你真的是輸家。

☐ 三分熟
☐ 五分熟
☐ 七分熟
☐ 全熟

M

loss [lɔs]

名 損失

英英 the state of no longer having something

例 The **loss** of her mother made her sorrowful.
失去母親讓她悲痛欲絕。

☐ 三分熟
☐ 五分熟
☐ 七分熟
☐ 全熟

---

love·ly [ˈlʌvlɪ]

形 美麗的、可愛的

英英 extremely beautiful; very pleasant

例 Who wants to hurt such a **lovely** girl like her?
誰會想要傷害像她這麼可愛的女孩呢？

☐ 三分熟
☐ 五分熟
☐ 七分熟
☐ 全熟

---

lov·er [ˈlʌvɚ]

名 愛人

英英 a person who is defeated in a competition or unsuccessful

例 You are my first and last **lover**.
你是我第一個也是最後一個愛人了。

☐ 三分熟
☐ 五分熟
☐ 七分熟
☐ 全熟

---

low·er [ˈloɚ]

動 降低

英英 to reduce something; cause to move downward

例 Could you **lower** the volumn?
你可以降低音量嗎？

☐ 三分熟
☐ 五分熟
☐ 七分熟
☐ 全熟

---

luck [lʌk]

名 幸運
同 fortune 幸運

英英 good things that happen to you by chance

例 I wish you good **luck**.
祝你幸運。

☐ 三分熟
☐ 五分熟
☐ 七分熟
☐ 全熟

Mm

mag·a·zine
[ˌmæɡəˈzin]

名 雜誌

英英 a type of large thin book with a paper cover that you can buy every week or month, containing articles, photographs, etc.

例 The **magazine** I am reading talks about health.
我正在看的雜誌講的是健康議題。

☐ 三分熟
☐ 五分熟
☐ 七分熟
☐ 全熟

---

ma·gic [ˈmædʒɪk]

名 魔術
形 魔術的

英英 the power of apparently influencing events by using mysterious or supernatural forces

例 The **magic** attracted many people's attention.
魔術吸引了許多人的注意力。

☐ 三分熟
☐ 五分熟
☐ 七分熟
☐ 全熟

---

ma·gi·cian
[məˈdʒɪʃən]

名 魔術師

英英 a person who can do magic tricks

例 The **magician** is amazing.
這位魔術師真的太厲害了。

☐ 三分熟
☐ 五分熟
☐ 七分熟
☐ 全熟

main [men]

形 主要的
名 要點
同 principal 主要的

英英 being the largest or most important than others of the same type; the importance

例 What's the **main** idea of this article?
這篇文章的主旨是什麼？

☐ 三分熟
☐ 五分熟
☐ 七分熟
☐ 全熟

---

main·tain

[men`ten]

動 維持
同 keep 維持

英英 cause or enable a condition or state of affairs to continue

例 How do you **maintain** such good figure?
你怎麼維持好身材的？

☐ 三分熟
☐ 五分熟
☐ 七分熟
☐ 全熟

---

male [mel]

形 男性的
名 男性
反 female 女性的

英英 belonging to the sex that does not give birth to babies or connected with this sex

例 **Male** peacocks are more beautiful than female ones.
雄孔雀比雌孔雀漂亮。

☐ 三分熟
☐ 五分熟
☐ 七分熟
☐ 全熟

---

man·da·rin

[`mændərɪn]

名 國語、中文

英英 the standard literary and official form of Chinese

例 Can anyone speak **Mandarin** Chinese?
有人會說中文嗎？

☐ 三分熟
☐ 五分熟
☐ 七分熟
☐ 全熟

---

man·go [`mæŋgo]

名 芒果

英英 a oval tropical fruit with smooth yellow or red skin, soft orange flesh and a large stone inside

例 The **mangos** in Thailand are sweeter than that of Taiwan.
泰國的芒果比臺灣的甜。

☐ 三分熟
☐ 五分熟
☐ 七分熟
☐ 全熟

---

man·ner [`mænɚ]

名 方法、禮貌
同 form 方法

英英 the way that something is done or happens

例 Please mind your **manner**.
請注意你的禮貌。

☐ 三分熟
☐ 五分熟
☐ 七分熟
☐ 全熟

---

mark [mɑrk]

動 標記
名 記號
同 sign 記號

英英 use a symbol to give information; a symbol used as a mark

例 Don't forget to **mark** your girlfriend's birthday on the calendar.
別忘了把你女友的生日標記在日曆上。

☐ 三分熟
☐ 五分熟
☐ 七分熟
☐ 全熟

---

mar·riage

[`mærɪdʒ]

名 婚姻

英英 the legal relationship between a husband and wife

例 Gay **marriage** is legalized in most western countries.
同性婚姻在西方大部分的國家是合法的。

☐ 三分熟
☐ 五分熟
☐ 七分熟
☐ 全熟

mask [mæsk]

名 面具
動 遮蓋

英英 a covering for all or part of the face, used for protection or hygiene; to cover with a mask

例 In Taiwan, people wear a **mask** when they are sick.
在臺灣，人們感冒的時候都會戴口罩。

☐ 三分熟
☐ 五分熟
☐ 七分熟
☐ 全熟

---

mass [mæs]

名 大量、數量
同 quantity 數量

英英 a large amount of something that does not have a definite shape or form

例 Her betrayal is widely discussed by the **mass** media.
她的背叛被媒體廣泛的討論著。

☐ 三分熟
☐ 五分熟
☐ 七分熟
☐ 全熟

---

mat [mæt]

名 墊子、席子
同 rug 毯子

英英 a small piece of carpet or strong material that is used to cover part of a floor

例 I put a **mat** at the bathroom.
我在廁所放了一個墊子。

☐ 三分熟
☐ 五分熟
☐ 七分熟
☐ 全熟

---

match [mætʃ]

名 火柴、比賽
動 相配

英英 a contest in which people or teams compete against each other; a short wooden stick covered with a special chemical at one end, which used to make a fire; to be equal to

例 Have you ever heard "The Little **Match** Girl" ?
你聽過《賣火柴的小女孩》嗎？

☐ 三分熟
☐ 五分熟
☐ 七分熟
☐ 全熟

---

mate [met]

名 配偶
動 配對
片 soul mate 靈魂伴侶

英英 an animal's sexual partner; come together for brceding

例 I feel she's my soul **mate** in spite of our difference.
儘管我們有許多相異處，我依舊覺得她是我的靈魂伴侶。

☐ 三分熟
☐ 五分熟
☐ 七分熟
☐ 全熟

---

ma·te·ri·al
[məˈtɪrɪəl]

名 物質
同 composition 物質

英英 a substance that things can be made from

例 They are rich in their **material** life, but poor in their spiritual life.
他們物質生活上很富有，但是精神生活上卻很貧瘠。

☐ 三分熟
☐ 五分熟
☐ 七分熟
☐ 全熟

---

meal [mil]

名 一餐、餐

英英 an occasion when people sit down to have food

例 How many calories do you consume in a **meal**?
你一餐攝取多少卡路里？

☐ 三分熟
☐ 五分熟
☐ 七分熟
☐ 全熟

M

221

🎧 Track 211

mean·ing [ˋminɪŋ]

名 意義
同 implication 含意

英英 the thing or idea that a sound or word, sign represents

例 What's the **meaning** of life?
生命的意義是什麼？

☐ 三分熟
☐ 五分熟
☐ 七分熟
☐ 全熟

means [minz]

名 方法

英英 an agent or method for achieving a result

例 He wants to make money by any **means**.
他不管任何方法都要賺錢。

☐ 三分熟
☐ 五分熟
☐ 七分熟
☐ 全熟

mea·sur·a·ble
[ˋmɛʒərəbḷ]

形 可測量的

英英 that can be measured

例 The distance between these stars is not **measurable**.
這些恆星間的距離不是可以測量的。

☐ 三分熟
☐ 五分熟
☐ 七分熟
☐ 全熟

mea·sure [ˋmɛʒɚ]

動 測量

英英 determine the size, amount, or degree of something by comparison with a standard unit

例 Could you **measure** the length of the tree?
你可以量這棵樹的高度嗎？

☐ 三分熟
☐ 五分熟
☐ 七分熟
☐ 全熟

mea·sur·ement
[ˋmɛʒɚmənt]

名 測量
同 estimate 估計

英英 the act or the process of finding the size, quantity or degree of something

例 The **measurement** of Ancient Egypt is unbelievable.
古埃及人的測量讓人難以置信。

☐ 三分熟
☐ 五分熟
☐ 七分熟
☐ 全熟

med·i·cine
[ˋmɛdəsṇ]

名 醫學、藥物
同 drug 藥物

英英 the science or practice of the treatment and prevention of disease

例 I need to take **medicine** after meals.
我需要在餐後服藥。

☐ 三分熟
☐ 五分熟
☐ 七分熟
☐ 全熟

meet·ing [ˋmitɪŋ]

名 會議

英英 an gathering of people for a discussion or other purpose

例 I have a **meeting** in the afternoon.
我在午後有一場會議。

☐ 三分熟
☐ 五分熟
☐ 七分熟
☐ 全熟

mel·o·dy [ˋmɛlədɪ]

名 旋律
同 tune 旋律

英英 a tune; a sequence of notes that is musically satisfying

例 The **melody** of the song is beautiful.
這首歌的旋律很美。

☐ 三分熟
☐ 五分熟
☐ 七分熟
☐ 全熟

mel·on [ˈmɛlən]

名 瓜、甜瓜

英英 a large round fruit with sweet flesh and many seeds

例 I love to eat **melons** in the summer.
我喜歡在夏天吃瓜類。

☐ 三分熟
☐ 五分熟
☐ 七分熟
☐ 全熟

M

---

mem·ber

[ˈmɛmbɚ]

名 成員

英英 a person, an animal or a plant that belongs to a particular group

例 The **members** of the reading club love this novel.
讀書會的成員都很喜歡這本書。

☐ 三分熟
☐ 五分熟
☐ 七分熟
☐ 全熟

---

mem·o·ry

[ˈmɛmərɪ]

名 記憶、回憶

英英 the faculty by which the mind stores and remembers information

例 It's hard to get along with **memory**.
跟回憶共處很難。

☐ 三分熟
☐ 五分熟
☐ 七分熟
☐ 全熟

---

me·nu [ˈmɛnju]

名 菜單

英英 a list of the food that is available at a restaurant

例 Please give me a **menu**.
請給我菜單。

☐ 三分熟
☐ 五分熟
☐ 七分熟
☐ 全熟

---

mes·sage

[ˈmɛsɪdʒ]

名 訊息

英英 a verbal or written communication or information

例 Since he is not in, would you like to leave a **message** for him?
既然他不在，您要不要留個訊息給他？

☐ 三分熟
☐ 五分熟
☐ 七分熟
☐ 全熟

---

met·al [ˈmɛtl̩]

名 金屬
形 金屬的

英英 a type of solid mineral substance that is usually hard and shiny and that heat and electricity can travel through

例 The **metal** table is heavy.
這個金屬的桌子很重。

☐ 三分熟
☐ 五分熟
☐ 七分熟
☐ 全熟

---

me·ter [ˈmitɚ]

名 公尺

英英 in names of measuring instruments

例 The child is taller than one **meter**.
這孩子已經不只一米高了。

☐ 三分熟
☐ 五分熟
☐ 七分熟
☐ 全熟

---

meth·od [ˈmɛθəd]

名 方法
同 style 方式

英英 a particular way of doing something

例 Which teaching **method** will you apply?
你將採取哪一種的教學方法？

☐ 三分熟
☐ 五分熟
☐ 七分熟
☐ 全熟

🎧 **Track 213**

mil·i·tar·y

[ˋmɪləˌtɛrɪ]

形 軍事的
名 軍事
同 army 軍隊

英英 connected with soldiers or the armed forces

例 **Military** service is required in this country.
在這個國家，當兵是必要的。

☐ 三分熟
☐ 五分熟
☐ 七分熟
☐ 全熟

---

mil·lion [ˋmɪljən]

名 百萬

英英 1,000,000; a very large amount

例 He won a **million** dollars by lottery.
他藉由樂透贏得百萬元。

☐ 三分熟
☐ 五分熟
☐ 七分熟
☐ 全熟

---

mine [maɪn]

名 礦、礦坑
代 我的東西

英英 a deep hole under the ground where minerals are dug; things that I own

例 The bag is not **mine**.
這不是我的包包。

☐ 三分熟
☐ 五分熟
☐ 七分熟
☐ 全熟

---

mi·nus [ˋmaɪnəs]

介 減、減去
形 減的
名 負數
反 plus 加的

英英 with the subtraction of; a negative value

例 Two **minus** one equals one.
二減一等於一。

☐ 三分熟
☐ 五分熟
☐ 七分熟
☐ 全熟

---

mir·ror [ˋmɪrɚ]

名 鏡子
動 反映

英英 a piece of special flat glass that reflects images, so that someone can see themselves on it; to show a reflection

例 What do you see in a **mirror**?
你在鏡子裡面看到什麼？

☐ 三分熟
☐ 五分熟
☐ 七分熟
☐ 全熟

---

mix [mɪks]

動 混合
名 混合物
同 combine 結合

英英 to combine two or more things together, usually in a way that means they cannot easily be separated; a mixture

例 I **mix** mango juice with orange juice.
我把芒果汁跟柳橙汁混在一起。

☐ 三分熟
☐ 五分熟
☐ 七分熟
☐ 全熟

---

mod·el [ˋmɑdl̩]

名 模型、模特兒
動 模仿

英英 a three-dimensional representation of a person or thing, typically on a smaller scale; use as an example for something else

例 The **model** is too thin.
這個模特兒太瘦了。

☐ 三分熟
☐ 五分熟
☐ 七分熟
☐ 全熟

M

mo·dern [ˈmɑdən]

形 現代的
反 ancient 古代的

英英 of the present time or recent time

例 **Modern** people always forget that family and health are the most important things.
現代人總是會忘記家庭跟健康才是最重要的。

☐ 三分熟
☐ 五分熟
☐ 七分熟
☐ 全熟

mon·ster

[ˈmɑnstɚ]

名 怪物

英英 a large, ugly, and frightening imaginary creature

例 The boy became a **monster** after drinking the liquid.
喝完這種溶液後，男孩變成了怪獸。

☐ 三分熟
☐ 五分熟
☐ 七分熟
☐ 全熟

mos·qui·to

[məˈskito]

名 蚊子

英英 a small fly, some kinds of which transmit parasitic diseases through the bite of the bloodsucking female

例 There are lots of **mosquitos** in the forest.
森林中有很多的蚊子。

☐ 三分熟
☐ 五分熟
☐ 七分熟
☐ 全熟

moth [mɔθ]

名 蛾、蛀蟲

英英 a flying insect with a long thin body and four large wings

例 It is said that **moths** always fly to the fire.
聽說飛蛾會撲火。

☐ 三分熟
☐ 五分熟
☐ 七分熟
☐ 全熟

mo·tion [ˈmoʃən]

名 運動、動作
同 movement 運動

英英 the act or process of moving or the way something moves

例 The old man is in slow **motion**.
這老人的動作很慢。

☐ 三分熟
☐ 五分熟
☐ 七分熟
☐ 全熟

mo·tor·cy·cle

[ˈmotɚˌsaɪkḷ]

名 摩托車

英英 a two-wheeled vehicle that is powered by a motor

例 I can't ride a **motorcycle**.
我不會騎摩托車。

☐ 三分熟
☐ 五分熟
☐ 七分熟
☐ 全熟

mov·a·ble

[ˈmuvəbḷ]

形 可移動的
同 mobile 移動式的

英英 able to be moved from one place or position to another

例 The closet is not **movable**.
這櫥櫃不是可移動的。

☐ 三分熟
☐ 五分熟
☐ 七分熟
☐ 全熟

🎧 **Track 215**

MRT/
mass rapid transit
/sub·way/
un·der·ground/
me·tro

[mæsˋræpɪdˋtrænsɪt]/

[ˋsʌbˏwe]/[ˋʌndɚˏgraund]/

[ˋmɛtro]

名 地下道、地下鐵

英英 a tunnel under a road for use by pedestrians

例 I go to work by **MRT**.
我搭捷運去上班。

☐ 三分熟 ☐ 五分熟 ☐ 七分熟 ☐ 全熟

---

mule [mjul]

名 騾

英英 the offspring of a male donkey and a female horse, typically sterile

例 The farmer rode a **mule** to town.
這農夫騎著騾子進城。

☐ 三分熟 ☐ 五分熟 ☐ 七分熟 ☐ 全熟

---

mul·ti·ply

[ˋmʌltəplaɪ]

動 增加、繁殖、相乘

英英 to add a number to itself a particular number of times

例 Three **multiplied** by two equals six.
三乘二等於六。

☐ 三分熟 ☐ 五分熟 ☐ 七分熟 ☐ 全熟

---

mu·se·um

[mjuˋziəm]

名 博物館

英英 a building in which objects of artistic, cultural, historical or scientific interest are kept and shown to the public

例 I went to many **museums** in Paris.
我去過巴黎很多間博物館。

☐ 三分熟 ☐ 五分熟 ☐ 七分熟 ☐ 全熟

---

mu·si·cian

[mjuˋzɪʃn]

名 音樂家

英英 a person who plays a musical instrument

例 Mozart is my favorite **musician**.
莫札特是我最喜歡的音樂家。

☐ 三分熟 ☐ 五分熟 ☐ 七分熟 ☐ 全熟

Nn

---

nail [nel]

名 指甲、釘子
動 敲

英英 a thin hard metal covering the outer tip of the fingers or toes; to knock with a nail or nails

例 I am cutting my **nails**.
我正在剪指甲。

☐ 三分熟 ☐ 五分熟 ☐ 七分熟 ☐ 全熟

---

na·ked [ˋnekɪd]

形 裸露的、赤裸的

英英 without wearing clothes

例 The woman is almost **naked**!
這女人幾乎是全裸的！

☐ 三分熟
☐ 五分熟
☐ 七分熟
☐ 全熟

napkin [ˋnæpkɪn]

名 餐巾紙

英英 piece of fabric or paper used at meals for keeping your clothes clean and cleaning your lips and fingers

例 He used a **napkin** to wipe his shirt.
他用一張餐巾紙去擦拭他的衣服。

☐ 三分熟
☐ 五分熟
☐ 七分熟
☐ 全熟

nar·row [ˋnæro]

形 窄的、狹長的
動 變窄
同 tight 緊的

英英 of small width in comparison to length; to become or make narrow

例 I can't put the sofa into the **narrow** room.
我無法將沙發放入這狹窄的房間。

☐ 三分熟
☐ 五分熟
☐ 七分熟
☐ 全熟

na·tion·al [ˋnæʃənl̩]

形 國家的

英英 connected with a particular country; shared by a whole country

例 Moon Festival is a **national** holiday.
中秋節是國定假日。

☐ 三分熟
☐ 五分熟
☐ 七分熟
☐ 全熟

nat·u·ral [ˋnætʃərəl]

形 天然生成的

英英 existing in or derived from nature; not made by humankind

例 She's a **natural** beauty.
她是天生的美女。

☐ 三分熟
☐ 五分熟
☐ 七分熟
☐ 全熟

naugh·ty [ˋnɔtɪ]

形 不服從的、淘氣的

英英 disobedient; badly behaved.

例 My son is **naughty** in kindergarten.
我兒子在幼稚園很頑皮。

☐ 三分熟
☐ 五分熟
☐ 七分熟
☐ 全熟

near·by [ˋnɪrˋbaɪ]

形 短距離內的
副 不遠地
同 around 附近

英英 near in position; not far away

例 The convenient store is **nearby**.
便利商店就在不遠處。

☐ 三分熟
☐ 五分熟
☐ 七分熟
☐ 全熟

near·ly [ˋnɪrlɪ]

副 幾乎
同 almost 幾乎

英英 very close to; almost

例 **Nearly** can I see you without my glasses.
沒有眼鏡，我幾乎看不到你。

☐ 三分熟
☐ 五分熟
☐ 七分熟
☐ 全熟

N

🎧 **Track 217**

neat [nit]

形 整潔的
反 dirty 髒的

英英 very tidy or well arranged

例 The house is **neat**.
這間房子很整潔。

☐ 三分熟
☐ 五分熟
☐ 七分熟
☐ 全熟

---

nec·es·sa·ry
[ˋnɛsəͺsɛrɪ]

形 必要的、不可缺少的

英英 that is needed for a purpose or a reason

例 Exams are **necessary** evil.
考試是必要之惡。

☐ 三分熟
☐ 五分熟
☐ 七分熟
☐ 全熟

---

neck·lace
[ˋnɛklɪs]

名 項圈、項鍊

英英 an ornamental chain or string of jewels worn round the neck

例 I bought a **necklace** for my girlfriend.
我買條項鍊給我女朋友。

☐ 三分熟
☐ 五分熟
☐ 七分熟
☐ 全熟

---

nee·dle [ˋnidl̩]

名 針、縫衣針
動 用針縫

英英 a small thin piece of steel which is used for sewing, with a point at one end and a hole for the thread at the other; to sew with a needle

例 I am doing **needle** work.
我正在縫衣服。

☐ 三分熟
☐ 五分熟
☐ 七分熟
☐ 全熟

---

neg·a·tive
[ˋnɛgətɪv]

形 否定的、消極的
名 反駁、否認、陰性

英英 denying or implying something; denial or refusal

例 He always gives people **negative** answers.
他總是給人消極的答案。

☐ 三分熟
☐ 五分熟
☐ 七分熟
☐ 全熟

---

neigh·bor [ˋnebɚ]

動 靠近於……
名 鄰居

英英 a person living next door to or very near to another; to get close to something

例 I don't like my **neighbor**.
我不喜歡我的鄰居。

☐ 三分熟
☐ 五分熟
☐ 七分熟
☐ 全熟

---

nei·ther [ˋniðɚ]

副 兩者都不
代 也非、也不
連 兩者都不
反 both 兩者都

英英 not one nor the other of two things or people

例 **Neither** Amy nor Linda is my cup of tea.
艾咪跟玲妲都不是我的菜。

☐ 三分熟
☐ 五分熟
☐ 七分熟
☐ 全熟

---

neph·ew [ˋnɛfju]

名 侄子、外甥

英英 a son of one's brother or sister, or of one's brother-in-law or sister-in-law

例 My **nephew** is one year old.
我侄子一歲了。

☐ 三分熟
☐ 五分熟
☐ 七分熟
☐ 全熟

nest [nɛst]

名 鳥巢
動 築巢

英英 the place in which the eggs of other animals are laid and hatched; to make a nest

例 I found a **nest** on the tree.
我在樹上發現了一個鳥巢。

☐ 三分熟
☐ 五分熟
☐ 七分熟
☐ 全熟

N

---

net [nɛt]

名 網
動 用網捕捉、結網

英英 a fabric of thread woven into meshes, and used for catching fish, birds, butterflies, etc; to catch with a net

例 I use a **net** to catch a butterfly.
我用網子抓蝴蝶。

☐ 三分熟
☐ 五分熟
☐ 七分熟
☐ 全熟

---

niece [nis]

名 侄女、外甥女

英英 a daughter of one's brother or sister, or of one's brother-in-law or sister-in-law

例 My sister just gave birth to my **niece**.
我姊姊剛生下我侄女。

☐ 三分熟
☐ 五分熟
☐ 七分熟
☐ 全熟

---

no·bod·y [ˈnoˌbɑdɪ]

代 無人
名 無名小卒

英英 a person who has no importance or influence; no person

例 He's just a **nobody**!
他不過就是個無名小卒。

☐ 三分熟
☐ 五分熟
☐ 七分熟
☐ 全熟

---

nod [nɑd]

動 點、彎曲
名 點頭

英英 to move your head down and up for showing agreement, approval or greeting

例 My boss **nodded** his head to show his agreement.
我老闆點頭贊成。

☐ 三分熟
☐ 五分熟
☐ 七分熟
☐ 全熟

---

none [nʌn]

代 沒有人

英英 not any; no one

例 **None** of us knows his name.
我們之中沒有人知道他的名字。

☐ 三分熟
☐ 五分熟
☐ 七分熟
☐ 全熟

---

noo·dle [ˈnudl̩]

名 麵條

英英 a long thin strip of pasta which is eaten by Chinese and Italian people

例 I ate **noodles** this evening.
我今天晚上吃麵。

☐ 三分熟
☐ 五分熟
☐ 七分熟
☐ 全熟

---

north·ern [ˈnɔrðən]

形 北方的

英英 situated in the north or facing north

例 His lover comes from **northern** China.
他的情人來自中國北方。

☐ 三分熟
☐ 五分熟
☐ 七分熟
☐ 全熟

🎧 Track 219

note·book

[ˋnotˏbʊk]

名 筆記本

英英 a small book for writing notes in

例 I kept all my notes in the same **notebook**.
我把我的筆記全都記在同一本筆記本上了。

□ 三分熟
□ 五分熟
□ 七分熟
□ 全熟

nov·el [ˋnɑvḷ]

形 新穎的、新奇的
名 長篇小說
同 original 新穎的

英英 a long story in a book, in which the characters and events are usually imaginary; very new and original

例 I love to read **novels**.
我喜歡讀小說。

□ 三分熟
□ 五分熟
□ 七分熟
□ 全熟

nut [nʌt]

名 堅果、螺帽

英英 a fruit consisting of a hard or tough shell around an eatable core

例 They drank beer and ate **nuts**.
他們吃堅果配啤酒。

□ 三分熟
□ 五分熟
□ 七分熟
□ 全熟

Oo

o·bey [əˋbe]

動 遵行、服從
同 submit 服從

英英 to do what you are told or expected to do

例 I never **obey** the dominance.
我從不服從霸權。

□ 三分熟
□ 五分熟
□ 七分熟
□ 全熟

ob·ject

[ˋabdʒɪkt]/[əbˋdʒɛkt]

名 物體
動 抗議、反對
同 thing 物、東西
反 agree 同意

英英 a material thing that can be seen, touched and felt; to express disapproval

例 He **objected** to their proposal.
他反對他們的提議。

□ 三分熟
□ 五分熟
□ 七分熟
□ 全熟

oc·cur [əˋkɝ]

動 發生、存在、出現
同 happen 發生

英英 to happen or occur

例 It **occurs** to me what happened last week.
這讓我想起上週發生的事情。

□ 三分熟
□ 五分熟
□ 七分熟
□ 全熟

of·fer [ˋɔfɚ]

名 提供
動 建議、提供

英英 to say that you are willing to do something for somebody or provide something to someone

例 This would be the best **offer**.
這是最好的報價了。

□ 三分熟
□ 五分熟
□ 七分熟
□ 全熟

of·fi·cial [əˋfɪʃəl]

形 官方的、法定的
名 官員、公務員
同 authorize 公認

英英 relating to an authority of responsibilities; a person who is having official duties

例 It is unseen in **official** rules.
這不在官方的條規中。

☐三分熟 ☐五分熟 ☐七分熟 ☐全熟

o·mit [oˋmɪt]

動 遺漏、省略、忽略
同 neglect 忽略

英英 not to include something or somebody because you have forgotten it or them

例 You must have **omitted** something.
你一定有遺漏什麼。

☐三分熟 ☐五分熟 ☐七分熟 ☐全熟

on·ion [ˋʌnjən]

名 洋蔥

英英 a vegetable, which has a pungent taste and smell and composed of several concentric layers

例 You need some **onions** to make pasta.
你需要洋蔥做義大利麵。

☐三分熟 ☐五分熟 ☐七分熟 ☐全熟

op·er·ate [ˋɑpəˏret]

動 運轉、操作

英英 to work in a particular way

例 Do you know how to **operate** the machinie?
你知道如何操作這臺機器嗎？

☐三分熟 ☐五分熟 ☐七分熟 ☐全熟

o·pin·ion [əˋpɪnjən]

名 觀點、意見
同 view 觀點

英英 a view or judgment about something

例 In my **opinion**, this proposal is perfect.
就我的觀點來說，這提議很完美。

☐三分熟 ☐五分熟 ☐七分熟 ☐全熟

or·di·nar·y [ˋɔrdnˏɛrɪ]

形 普通的
同 usual 平常的

英英 not unusual or different in any way

例 Do you know the life of **ordinary** people?
你知道普通人的生活是怎樣的嗎？

☐三分熟 ☐五分熟 ☐七分熟 ☐全熟

or·gan [ˋɔrgən]

名 器官

英英 body part of an animal or plant adapted for a particular function, such as the heart or kidneys

例 Some of his **organs** are problematic.
他有些器官有點問題。

☐三分熟 ☐五分熟 ☐七分熟 ☐全熟

or·gan·i·za·tion [ˏɔrgənəˋzeʃən]

名 組織、機構
同 institution 機構

英英 a group of people who form a business or club together in order to achieve the same aim

例 Everyone in the **organization** is selfish.
這機構的每個人都很自私。

☐三分熟 ☐五分熟 ☐七分熟 ☐全熟

🎧 **Track 221**

or·gan·ize
[ˋɔrgənˌaɪz]

動 組織、系統化

英英 to arrange for something to happen

例 I need to **organize** the system.
我想要系統化這組織。

☐ 三分熟
☐ 五分熟
☐ 七分熟
☐ 全熟

ov·en [ˋʌvən]

名 爐子、烤箱
同 stove 爐子

英英 an enclosed cooker with a door, in which food is cooked or heated

例 I put the turkey into the **oven**.
我把火雞放到烤箱裡面了。

☐ 三分熟
☐ 五分熟
☐ 七分熟
☐ 全熟

o·ver·pass
[ˌovəˋpæs]

名 天橋、高架橋

英英 a structure which carries one road over the top of another one

例 I am on the **overpass**.
我在天橋上。

☐ 三分熟
☐ 五分熟
☐ 七分熟
☐ 全熟

over·seas
[ˌovəˋsiz]

形 國外的、在國外的
副 在海外、在國外
同 abroad 在國外

英英 relating to a foreign country

例 I will be an **overseas** student.
我將要變成海外學生。

☐ 三分熟
☐ 五分熟
☐ 七分熟
☐ 全熟

owl [aʊl]

名 貓頭鷹

英英 a gray bird that kills other creatures for food with large round eyes, that hunts at night

例 There are some **owls** on the tree.
樹上有幾隻貓頭鷹。

☐ 三分熟
☐ 五分熟
☐ 七分熟
☐ 全熟

own·er [ˋonə]

名 物主、所有者
同 holder 持有者

英英 a person who owns something

例 The **owner** of the cattle doesn't want to sell this cattle.
這頭牛的主人不想賣這頭牛。

☐ 三分熟
☐ 五分熟
☐ 七分熟
☐ 全熟

ox [ɑks]

名 公牛
名詞複數 oxen

英英 a male cow

例 There are some **oxen** on the farm.
在農場上有幾頭公牛。

☐ 三分熟
☐ 五分熟
☐ 七分熟
☐ 全熟

Pp

P

pack [pæk]
名 一包
動 打包

英英 a cardboard or paper container and the items inside it; to place things into a bag or container

例 Could you please **pack** it for me?
請問你可以幫我打包嗎？

☐ 三分熟
☐ 五分熟
☐ 七分熟
☐ 全熟

pac·kage
[ˈpækɪdʒ]

名 包裹
動 包裝

英英 a box or bag in which things are wrapped or packed; to put into wrapping

例 I got a **package** this morning.
我今天早上收到一個包裹。

☐ 三分熟
☐ 五分熟
☐ 七分熟
☐ 全熟

pain [pen]
名 疼痛
動 傷害

英英 the feelings that you have in your body when you have been hurt

例 The **pain** of losing a child makes her crazy.
失去孩子的傷痛讓她瘋掉。

☐ 三分熟
☐ 五分熟
☐ 七分熟
☐ 全熟

pain·ful [ˈpenfəl]
形 痛苦的

英英 affected with pain or sorrow

例 The disease makes him **painful**.
疾病讓他很痛苦。

☐ 三分熟
☐ 五分熟
☐ 七分熟
☐ 全熟

paint·er [ˈpentɚ]
名 畫家

英英 an artist who paints pictures or draws

例 Da Vinci is also known as a **painter**.
達文西也被視為是一個畫家。

☐ 三分熟
☐ 五分熟
☐ 七分熟
☐ 全熟

paint·ing [ˈpentɪŋ]
名 繪畫

英英 a picture that has been painted

例 What's the value of the **painting**?
這幅畫的價值多少？

☐ 三分熟
☐ 五分熟
☐ 七分熟
☐ 全熟

pa·ja·mas
[pəˈdʒæməz]

名 睡衣
名詞複數 pajamas

英英 a suit of loose trousers and jacket for sleeping in

例 Why are you wearing **pajamas** at noon?
你怎麼會在中午穿著睡衣呢？

☐ 三分熟
☐ 五分熟
☐ 七分熟
☐ 全熟

palm [pɑm]
名 手掌

英英 the inner surface of the hand between the wrist and fingers

例 He put the nuts on his **palms**.
他把堅果放在他的手掌心。

☐ 三分熟
☐ 五分熟
☐ 七分熟
☐ 全熟

Track 223

pan [pæn]

名 平底鍋

英英 a metal container with a handle or handles, which is used for cooking food in

例 I used the **pan** to make this dish.
我用這個平底鍋做出這道菜的。

☐ 三分熟
☐ 五分熟
☐ 七分熟
☐ 全熟

---

pan·da [ˈpændə]

名 貓熊

英英 a large black and white bear-like animal , that lives in China and is very rare

例 **Pandas** are the most representative animal in China.
貓熊是中國最具代表性的動物。

☐ 三分熟
☐ 五分熟
☐ 七分熟
☐ 全熟

---

pa·pa·ya [pəˈpaɪə]

名 木瓜

英英 a tropical fruit like an elongated melon, with edible orange flesh and small black seeds

例 I prefer to drink **papaya** smoothie.
我比較想喝木瓜牛奶。

☐ 三分熟
☐ 五分熟
☐ 七分熟
☐ 全熟

---

par·don [ˈpɑrdn̩]

名 原諒
動 寬恕
同 forgive 原諒

英英 the action of forgiving somebody for something

例 **Pardon** me. Can you say that again?
對不起。 你能再說一遍嗎？

☐ 三分熟
☐ 五分熟
☐ 七分熟
☐ 全熟

---

par·rot [ˈpærət]

名 鸚鵡

英英 a mainly tropical bird with brightly colored plumage and a strong down-curved hooked bill

例 The **parrot** can speak many languages!
這隻鸚鵡會說很多語言！

☐ 三分熟
☐ 五分熟
☐ 七分熟
☐ 全熟

---

par·tic·u·lar
[pɚˈtɪkjələ]

形 特別的
同 special 特別的

英英 used to emphasize that you are referring to one individual person, thing or type of thing and not others

例 Some **particular** students may have this kind of question.
有些特別的學生會有這種問題。

☐ 三分熟
☐ 五分熟
☐ 七分熟
☐ 全熟

---

part·ner [ˈpɑrtnɚ]

名 夥伴

英英 a person who takes part in an undertaking with another or others, especially in a business with shared risks and profits

例 He is the best **partner** I have ever had.
他是我最好的夥伴。

☐ 三分熟
☐ 五分熟
☐ 七分熟
☐ 全熟

pas·sen·ger

[ˈpæsn̩dʒɚ]

名 旅客

英英 a person who is travelling in a vehicle, ship, or aircraft other than the driver, pilot, or crew

例 All the **passengers** are boarding.
所有旅客都在登機。

□ 三分熟
□ 五分熟
□ 七分熟
□ 全熟

---

paste [pest]

名 漿糊
動 黏貼
同 glue 黏著劑、膠水

英英 a soft wet mixture, usually made of a powder and a liquid; to stick with paste

例 I am **pasting** the stamps on the envelope.
我正在把郵票黏到信封上。

□ 三分熟
□ 五分熟
□ 七分熟
□ 全熟

---

pat [pæt]

動 輕拍
名 拍
同 tap 輕拍

英英 to touch someone or something gently several times with your hand

例 The father is **patting** his daughter.
這位父親輕拍他的女兒。

□ 三分熟
□ 五分熟
□ 七分熟
□ 全熟

---

path [pæθ]

名 路徑
同 route 路程

英英 a way or track laid down for walking

例 She found a beautiful flower on the **path**.
她在這條路徑上發現一朵漂亮的小花。

□ 三分熟
□ 五分熟
□ 七分熟
□ 全熟

---

pa·tient [ˈpeʃənt]

形 忍耐的
名 病人

英英 able to wait for a long time or accept annoying behaviors or difficulties without becoming angry; someone who is sick or ill

例 The doctor is very **patient**.
這位醫生很有耐心。

□ 三分熟
□ 五分熟
□ 七分熟
□ 全熟

---

pat·tern [ˈpætərn]

名 模型、圖樣
動 仿照

英英 a regular or discernible form or order in which a series of things occur; to use something as a sample

例 I love the **pattern** on the clothes.
我喜歡這件衣服的圖樣。

□ 三分熟
□ 五分熟
□ 七分熟
□ 全熟

---

peace [pis]

名 和平
反 war 戰爭

英英 a situation or a period of time in which there is no war or violence in a country or an area

例 World **peace** is the only wish of her.
世界和平是她唯一的願望。

□ 三分熟
□ 五分熟
□ 七分熟
□ 全熟

---

peace·ful [ˈpisfəl]

形 和平的
同 quiet 平靜的

英英 free from disturbance; calm

例 The country is very **peaceful**.
這國家很和平。

□ 三分熟
□ 五分熟
□ 七分熟
□ 全熟

🎧 **Track 225**

peach [pitʃ]

名 桃子

英英 a round fruit with soft red and yellow skin, flesh and a stone inside

例 I ate a **peach** after dinner.
我在晚餐過後吃了顆桃子。

☐ 三分熟
☐ 五分熟
☐ 七分熟
☐ 全熟

---

pea·nut [ˈpiˌnʌt]

名 花生

英英 a nut that grows underground in a thin shell

例 Mice love **peanuts**.
老鼠喜歡花生。

☐ 三分熟
☐ 五分熟
☐ 七分熟
☐ 全熟

---

pear [pɛr]

名 梨子

英英 a yellowish-green or brownish-green fruit, narrow at the stalk and wider towards the tip

例 We bought some **pears** in the supermarket.
我們在超市買了些梨子。

☐ 三分熟
☐ 五分熟
☐ 七分熟
☐ 全熟

---

pen·guin [ˈpɛngwɪn]

名 企鵝

英英 a black and white seabird that lives in the Antarctic

例 **Penguins** live in antarctic continent.
企鵝住在南極大陸。

☐ 三分熟
☐ 五分熟
☐ 七分熟
☐ 全熟

---

pep·per [ˈpɛpɚ]

名 胡椒

英英 a hot-tasting powder made from peppercorns, used for adding flavor in food

例 I added some **pepper** into the soup.
我在湯裡面加了一些胡椒。

☐ 三分熟
☐ 五分熟
☐ 七分熟
☐ 全熟

---

per [pɚ]

介 每、經由
同 through 經由

英英 used to express the cost or amount of something for each person

例 The candy costs me 1 dollar **per** gram.
這些糖果每一克要花我一塊錢。

☐ 三分熟
☐ 五分熟
☐ 七分熟
☐ 全熟

---

per·fect [ˈpɝfɪkt]

形 完美的
同 ideal 完美的、理想的

英英 having all the required qualities or characteristics

例 My girlfriend is almost **perfect**.
我女友幾乎是完美的。

☐ 三分熟
☐ 五分熟
☐ 七分熟
☐ 全熟

---

pe·ri·od [ˈpɪrɪəd]

名 期間、時代
同 era 時代
片 in a period 生理期

英英 a particular length of time

例 In this **period**, human beings lived in the cave.
在這時期，人類住在洞穴中。

☐ 三分熟
☐ 五分熟
☐ 七分熟
☐ 全熟

per·son·al [ˈpɝsn̩l]

形 個人的
同 private 私人的

英英 your own; not belonging to anyone else

例 May I ask you a **personal** question?
我可以問你一個私人的問題嗎？

☐ 三分熟
☐ 五分熟
☐ 七分熟
☐ 全熟

P

pho·to·graph/ pho·to

[ˈfotəˌɡræf]/[ˈfoto]

名 照片
動 照相

英英 a picture made with a camera, in which an image is focused on to film and then made visible; to take pictures

例 May I take a **photo** of you?
我可以為你拍張照嗎？

☐ 三分熟
☐ 五分熟
☐ 七分熟
☐ 全熟

pho·tog·ra·pher

[fəˈtɑɡrəfə]

名 攝影師

英英 a person whose job is to take photographs

例 The **photographer** took a photo in the mountains.
這位攝影師在山上攝影。

☐ 三分熟
☐ 五分熟
☐ 七分熟
☐ 全熟

phrase [frez]

名 片語
動 表意

英英 a group of words without a finite verb; to express with words

例 People use lots of **phrases** in a conversation.
人們在對話中會用很多的片語。

☐ 三分熟
☐ 五分熟
☐ 七分熟
☐ 全熟

pick [pɪk]

動 摘、選擇
名 選擇
片 pick up 撿起來

英英 to remove a flower or fruit from where it is growing; to make a choice

例 Please **pick** up the pen for me.
請幫我拿起筆來。

☐ 三分熟
☐ 五分熟
☐ 七分熟
☐ 全熟

pic·nic [ˈpɪknɪk]

名 野餐
動 去野餐
片 go picnic 去野餐

英英 an outdoor activity that you take a meal with you to eat in an informal way; to have an outdoor activity that you take a meal with you to eat in an informal way

例 If it rains tomorrow, we will cancel the **picnic**.
如果明天下雨，我們將會取消野餐。

☐ 三分熟
☐ 五分熟
☐ 七分熟
☐ 全熟

pi·geon [ˈpɪdʒən]

名 鴿子
同 dove 鴿子

英英 a fat grey and white bird with short legs

例 People used to use **pigeons** to send letters.
人們曾經用鴿子在送信。

☐ 三分熟
☐ 五分熟
☐ 七分熟
☐ 全熟

pile [paɪl]

名 堆
動 堆積
同 heap 堆積

英英 a heap of things laid or lying one on top of another

例 There is a **pile** of woods.
這邊有一堆木頭。

☐ 三分熟
☐ 五分熟
☐ 七分熟
☐ 全熟

🎧 **Track 227**

pil·low [ˋpɪlo]

名 枕頭
動 以……為枕
同 cushion 靠墊

英英 a square or rectangular piece of fabric filled with soft material, used to rest your head on in bed; to sleep with putting your head on a pillow

例 You need a good **pillow** so that you can sleep well.
你需要一個好的枕頭才能睡得好。

☐ 三分熟
☐ 五分熟
☐ 七分熟
☐ 全熟

---

pin [pɪn]

名 針
動 釘住
同 clip 夾住

英英 thin piece of metal with a sharp point at one end and a round head at the other

例 I used a **pin** to fix the clothes.
我用針固定衣服。

☐ 三分熟
☐ 五分熟
☐ 七分熟
☐ 全熟

---

pine·ap·ple

[ˋpaɪnˏæpḷ]

名 鳳梨

英英 a tropical fruit with thick rough skin, sweet yellow flesh with a lot of juice

例 I want to eat **pineapple** cake.
我要吃鳳梨酥。

☐ 三分熟
☐ 五分熟
☐ 七分熟
☐ 全熟

---

ping-pong/ ta·ble ten·nis

[ˋpɪŋˏpɑŋ]/[ˋtebḷˋtɛnɪs]

名 乒乓球

英英 a game resembling tennis but played on a table with paddles and a light hollow ball

例 I learn to play **ping-pong** in the PE class.
我在體育課學會打乒乓球。

☐ 三分熟
☐ 五分熟
☐ 七分熟
☐ 全熟

---

pink [pɪŋk]

形 粉紅的
名 粉紅色

英英 of a color intermediate between red and white

例 The girl in **pink** is my sister.
那穿著粉紅色衣服的女孩是我妹妹。

☐ 三分熟
☐ 五分熟
☐ 七分熟
☐ 全熟

---

pipe [paɪp]

名 管子
動 以管傳送
同 tube 管子

英英 a tube through which liquids and gases can flow; to deliver something with a pipe

例 The man pour some water into the bottle with a **pipe**.
這男人用管子把水倒入瓶子中。

☐ 三分熟
☐ 五分熟
☐ 七分熟
☐ 全熟

---

pitch [pɪtʃ]

動 投擲、間距
同 throw 投、擲

英英 to throw somebody or something forcefully; the distance between two or more things

例 I **pitch** a hundred balls every day.
我每天投一百顆球。

☐ 三分熟
☐ 五分熟
☐ 七分熟
☐ 全熟

piz·za [ˋpitsə]

名 披薩

英英 a dish of Italian origin, consisting of a flat, round base of dough baked with a topping of tomatoes, cheese, and other ingredients

例 I can't eat a **pizza** because I am on a diet.
我不能吃披薩，因為我正在減肥。

□三分熟
□五分熟
□七分熟
□全熟

---

plain [plen]

形 平坦的
名 平原

英英 very even; not rough; a flat grassland

例 The rain in Spain is mostly on the **plain**.
西班牙的雨，大部分都下在平原。

□三分熟
□五分熟
□七分熟
□全熟

---

plan·et [ˋplænɪt]

名 行星

英英 a celestial body moving in an elliptical orbit round a star

例 It is the **planet** where the Little Prince comes from.
這是小王子來自的星球。

□三分熟
□五分熟
□七分熟
□全熟

---

plate [plet]

名 盤子
同 dish 盤子

英英 a flat, usually round, dish that you put food on

例 The **plate** is filled with delicious food.
這盤子裝滿了好吃的食物。

□三分熟
□五分熟
□七分熟
□全熟

---

plat·form [ˋplætˌfɔrm]

名 平臺、月臺
同 stage 平臺

英英 the flat area beside the track at a train station where you get on or off the train

例 I am waiting for the train on **platform** 3.
我在三號月臺等火車。

□三分熟
□五分熟
□七分熟
□全熟

---

play·ful [ˋplefəl]

形 愛玩的

英英 fond of games and amusement

例 "I am just kidding," said he, with a **playful** smile.
「我只是開玩笑的。」他帶著一抹玩弄的微笑說著。

□三分熟
□五分熟
□七分熟
□全熟

---

pleas·ant [ˋplɛznt]

形 愉快的

英英 enjoyable and pleasing

例 Wish you a **pleasant** day.
祝你有愉快的一天。

□三分熟
□五分熟
□七分熟
□全熟

---

pleas·ure [ˋplɛʒɚ]

名 愉悅
反 misery 悲慘

英英 a state of feeling or being happy

例 I can get lots of **pleasure** when I achieve this goal.
當我達到這個目標時，我可以得到許多的愉悅感。

□三分熟
□五分熟
□七分熟
□全熟

P

🎧 Track 229

plus [plʌs]

介 加
名 加號
形 加的
同 additional 附加的

英英 with the addition of

例 One **plus** one equals two.
一加一等於二。

☐ 三分熟
☐ 五分熟
☐ 七分熟
☐ 全熟

---

po·em [`poɪm]

名 詩

英英 a literary composition in verse, typically concerned with the expression of feelings or imaginative description

例 I read lots of **poems** in the literature class.
我在文學課讀到很多的詩。

☐ 三分熟
☐ 五分熟
☐ 七分熟
☐ 全熟

---

po·et [`poɪt]

名 詩人

英英 a person who writes poems

例 Shakespeare is more like a **poet** than a dramatist in many Asian countries.
在亞洲許多國家，莎士比亞比較像是詩人而非戲劇家。

☐ 三分熟
☐ 五分熟
☐ 七分熟
☐ 全熟

---

poi·son [`pɔɪzn̩]

名 毒藥
動 下毒

英英 a substance that causes death or harm if it is swallowed into the body; to make harm with poison

例 The **poisoned** apple makes Snow White die.
毒蘋果讓白雪公主死掉了。

☐ 三分熟
☐ 五分熟
☐ 七分熟
☐ 全熟

---

pol·i·cy [`pɑləsɪ]

名 政策

英英 a course or principle of action adopted or proposed by an organization or individual

例 The **policy** of this party wins him lots of votes.
這政黨的政策讓他贏得許多選票。

☐ 三分熟
☐ 五分熟
☐ 七分熟
☐ 全熟

---

po·lite [pə`laɪt]

形 有禮貌的

英英 having or showing good manners and respect for the feelings of others

例 People like the **polite** boy.
大家都喜歡這有禮貌的男孩。

☐ 三分熟
☐ 五分熟
☐ 七分熟
☐ 全熟

---

pop·u·lar
[`pɑpjələ]

形 流行的

英英 liked or enjoyed by a large number of people

例 The song is **popular** in Taiwan.
這首歌在臺灣很流行。

☐ 三分熟
☐ 五分熟
☐ 七分熟
☐ 全熟

---

pop·u·la·tion
[ˌpɑpjə`leʃən]

名 人口

英英 all the inhabitants of a place

例 China is a country with a great amount of **population**.
中國是個有大量人口的國家。

☐ 三分熟
☐ 五分熟
☐ 七分熟
☐ 全熟

P

pork [pork]

名 豬肉

英英 meat from a pig that has not been cured

例 I made this dish with **pork**.
我這道菜是用豬肉做的。

---

port [port]

名 港口
同 harbor 海港

英英 a town or city with a harbor; to hold a gun

例 I went to the **port** to take a ferry.
我去港口搭渡輪。

---

pose [poz]

動 擺出
名 姿勢
同 posture 姿勢

英英 to sit or stand in a particular position in order to be painted, drawn or photographed; to display something

例 The **pose** in the picture is weird.
這張照片的姿勢好奇怪喔。

---

pos·i·tive

[`pazətɪv]

形 確信的、積極的、正的
同 certain 確信的

英英 feeling confident and hopeful

例 Give me a **positive** answer.
給我一個正面的答案。

---

pos·si·bil·i·ty

[ˌpasə`bɪlətɪ]

名 可能性

英英 the state or fact of being possible

例 Is there any **possibility** for her to marry him?
她有跟他結婚的可能性嗎？

---

post [post]

名 郵件
動 郵寄、公佈、快速地

英英 the official system which is used for sending and delivering letters, packages, etc.; to send letters or packages by postal system

例 I will **post** it on Facebook.
我會公佈在臉書上。

---

post·card

[`post͵kard]

名 明信片

英英 a card for sending a message by post without an envelope

例 I just got a **postcard** from the States.
我收到一張從美國來的明信片。

---

pot [pat]

名 鍋、壺
同 vessel 器皿

英英 a deep round, metal container which is used for cooking things in

例 The water in the **pot** is boiling.
這壺子裡的水滾了。

🎧**Track 231**

---

po·ta·to [pəˋteto]

名 馬鈴薯

英英 a starchy plant tuber which is cooked and eaten as a vegetable

例 French fries are made of **potatoes**.
薯條是馬鈴薯做成的。

☐ 三分熟
☐ 五分熟
☐ 七分熟
☐ 全熟

---

pound [paʊnd]

名 磅、英磅
動 重擊

英英 the unit of money in Britain, worth 100 pence; to hit forcefully

例 I get three **pounds** in this week!
我這禮拜胖了三英磅。

☐ 三分熟
☐ 五分熟
☐ 七分熟
☐ 全熟

---

pow·er·ful

[ˋpaʊəfəl]

形 有力的

英英 being able to control and influence people and events

例 The man is **powerful**.
這男人很有力。

☐ 三分熟
☐ 五分熟
☐ 七分熟
☐ 全熟

---

praise [prez]

動 稱讚
名 榮耀
同 compliment 稱讚

英英 express warm approval of or admiration for; the express of approval

例 The principal **praised** the student for his diligence.
校長讚揚這位學生的勤奮。

☐ 三分熟
☐ 五分熟
☐ 七分熟
☐ 全熟

---

pray [pre]

動 祈禱
同 beg 祈求

英英 to speak to God, especially to give thanks or ask for help

例 I will **pray** for you.
我會為你祈禱。

☐ 三分熟
☐ 五分熟
☐ 七分熟
☐ 全熟

---

pre·fer [prɪˋfɝ]

動 偏愛、較喜歡
同 favor 偏愛

英英 like someone or something better than another or others

例 I **prefer** the pink one.
我偏愛粉紅色的。

☐ 三分熟
☐ 五分熟
☐ 七分熟
☐ 全熟

---

pres·ence

[ˋprɛzn̩s]

名 出席
同 attendance 出席

英英 the state of being in a particular place

例 His **presence** surprised the teacher.
他的出席讓老師很意外。

☐ 三分熟
☐ 五分熟
☐ 七分熟
☐ 全熟

---

pres·ent

[ˋprɛzn̩t]/[prɪˋzɛnt]

形 目前的
名 片刻、禮物
動 呈現
同 gift 禮物

英英 the period of time which is happening now; a gift; to appear formally before others.

例 Today is the best **present**.
今天就是最好的當下。（把握時光。）

☐ 三分熟
☐ 五分熟
☐ 七分熟
☐ 全熟

---

pres·i·dent

[ˋprɛzədənt]

名 總統

英英 the leader of a republic or a nation

例 The **president** is guilty.
這總統是有罪的。

☐ 三分熟
☐ 五分熟
☐ 七分熟
☐ 全熟

P

---

press [prɛs]

名 印刷機、新聞界
動 壓下、強迫
同 force 強迫
片 press conference
記者會

英英 the journalists and photographers who work for newspapers and magazines; to apply pressure to something

例 You can open the door by **pressing** the button.
你按下這個鈕就可以開門。

☐ 三分熟
☐ 五分熟
☐ 七分熟
☐ 全熟

---

pride [praɪd]

名 自豪
動 使自豪

英英 a feeling of pleasure or satisfaction when you have done something well; to make pride

例 His **pride** makes him fail.
他的自傲讓他失敗了。

☐ 三分熟
☐ 五分熟
☐ 七分熟
☐ 全熟

---

prince [prɪns]

名 王子

英英 the son or grandson of the king or queen

例 I feel he's my **Prince** Charming.
我覺得他是我的白馬王子。

☐ 三分熟
☐ 五分熟
☐ 七分熟
☐ 全熟

---

prin·cess

[ˋprɪnsɪs]

名 公主

英英 the daughter or granddaughter of the king or queen

例 She considers herself a **princess**.
她以為自己是公主。

☐ 三分熟
☐ 五分熟
☐ 七分熟
☐ 全熟

---

prin·ci·pal

[ˋprɪnsəpl̩]

形 首要的
名 校長、首長

英英 most important; the head of a school

例 I think betrayal is the **principal** reason of their divorce.
我覺得背叛是他們離婚的主要原因。

☐ 三分熟
☐ 五分熟
☐ 七分熟
☐ 全熟

---

prin·ci·ple

[ˋprɪnsəpl̩]

名 原則
同 standard 規範

英英 a law, a rule or a theory that something is based on

例 The **principles** make her uncomfortable.
這些規則讓她很不舒服。

☐ 三分熟
☐ 五分熟
☐ 七分熟
☐ 全熟

---

print·er [ˋprɪntɚ]

名 印刷工、印表機

英英 a person whose job is commercial printing

例 My **printer** doesn't work.
我的印表機壞掉了。

☐ 三分熟
☐ 五分熟
☐ 七分熟
☐ 全熟

🎧 **Track 233**

pris·on [ˋprɪzn̩]

名 監獄
同 jail 監獄
片 in prison 坐牢

英英 a building where people are kept as a punishment for a crime they have committed

例 The school is like a **prison** for her.
對她來説，學校就像是監獄一樣。

☐ 三分熟
☐ 五分熟
☐ 七分熟
☐ 全熟

pris·on·er

[ˋprɪzn̩ɚ]

名 囚犯

英英 a person who is kept in prison as a punishment because of a crime they have committed

例 Give the **prisoner** a chance.
給這些囚犯一點機會。

☐ 三分熟
☐ 五分熟
☐ 七分熟
☐ 全熟

pri·vate [ˋpraɪvɪt]

形 私密的

英英 for or belonging to one particular person or group only

例 She denied to answer any question about her **private** life.
她拒絕回答任何關於她私人生活的問題。

☐ 三分熟
☐ 五分熟
☐ 七分熟
☐ 全熟

prize [praɪz]

名 獎品
動 獎賞、撬開
同 reward 獎品

英英 an award that is given to a person who wins a competition or race; to give an award

例 I won the first **prize**.
我贏得頭獎。

☐ 三分熟
☐ 五分熟
☐ 七分熟
☐ 全熟

pro·duce

[prəˋdjus]/[ˋprɑdjus]

動 生產
名 產品
同 make 生產

英英 make, manufacture, or create; goods that are made

例 These shoes are **produced** in Vietnam.
這些鞋子是越南生產的。

☐ 三分熟
☐ 五分熟
☐ 七分熟
☐ 全熟

pro·duc·er

[prəˋdjusɚ]

名 製造者

英英 a person, a company or a country that grows or makes food, goods or materials

例 The **producer** of the computer denied their fault.
這電腦的製造者否認他們的錯誤。

☐ 三分熟
☐ 五分熟
☐ 七分熟
☐ 全熟

pro·gress

[ˋprɑgrɛs]/[prəˋgrɛs]

名 進展
動 進行
同 proceed 進行

英英 the process of improving or developing; to move towards a destination

例 His **progress** amazed the teacher.
他的進展讓老師大吃一驚。

☐ 三分熟
☐ 五分熟
☐ 七分熟
☐ 全熟

proj·ect
[ˋprɑdʒɛkt]/[prəˋdʒɛkt]

名 計畫
動 推出、投射

英英 an enterprise carefully planned to achieve a particular aim; throw or cause to move forward

例 My boss is interested in the **project**.
我的老闆對這個計畫充滿興趣。

☐ 三分熟
☐ 五分熟
☐ 七分熟
☐ 全熟

prom·ise [ˋprɑmɪs]
名 諾言
動 約定
同 swear 承諾

英英 a statement that tells somebody that you will do or not do something; to make a promise

例 I **promise** I will always love you.
我承諾會永遠愛你。

☐ 三分熟
☐ 五分熟
☐ 七分熟
☐ 全熟

pro·nounce
[prəˋnaʊns]

動 發音

英英 make the sound of a word or words

例 How do you **pronounce** this word?
你怎麼唸這個字？

☐ 三分熟
☐ 五分熟
☐ 七分熟
☐ 全熟

pro·pose [prəˋpoz]
動 提議、求婚
同 offer 提議

英英 to suggest a plan or an idea for people to think about and decide

例 Many people in the country **propose** to legalize gay marriage.
這國家有很多人提議將同性婚姻合法化。

☐ 三分熟
☐ 五分熟
☐ 七分熟
☐ 全熟

pro·tect [prəˋtɛkt]
動 保護

英英 keep safe from harm or injury

例 Parents shouldn't **protect** their children too much.
父母不應該太保護小孩。

☐ 三分熟
☐ 五分熟
☐ 七分熟
☐ 全熟

proud [praʊd]
形 驕傲的
同 arrogant 傲慢的

英英 feeling pleased and satisfied about something that you own or have achieved

例 You are too **proud**.
你太驕傲了。

☐ 三分熟
☐ 五分熟
☐ 七分熟
☐ 全熟

pro·vide [prəˋvaɪd]
動 提供
同 supply 提供
片 provide with 提供……

英英 make available for use; to supply

例 The school **provides** him with scholarship.
這學校提供他獎學金。

☐ 三分熟
☐ 五分熟
☐ 七分熟
☐ 全熟

pud·ding [ˋpʊdɪŋ]
名 布丁

英英 a sweet dish eaten at the end of a meal

例 I ate a **pudding** in the afternoon.
我下午吃了個布丁。

☐ 三分熟
☐ 五分熟
☐ 七分熟
☐ 全熟

🎧 **Track 235**

pump [pʌmp]

名 抽水機
動 抽水、汲取

英英 a mechanical device using suction or pressure to raise or move liquids, compress gases, or force air into inflatable objects; to raise or move water

例 This is the first **pump** in the village.
這是村子裡第一個抽水機。

☐ 三分熟
☐ 五分熟
☐ 七分熟
☐ 全熟

pump·kin [ˈpʌmpkɪn]

名 南瓜

英英 a large round vegetable with thick orange skin

例 We make a **pumpkin** lantern on Halloween.
我們在萬聖節做南瓜燈。

☐ 三分熟
☐ 五分熟
☐ 七分熟
☐ 全熟

pun·ish [ˈpʌnɪʃ]

動 處罰

英英 impose a penalty on someone for an offence

例 The teacher **punishes** the naughty students.
老師懲罰不乖的學生。

☐ 三分熟
☐ 五分熟
☐ 七分熟
☐ 全熟

pun·ish·ment [ˈpʌnɪʃmənt]

名 處罰

英英 an act or a way of punishing someone

例 The **punishment** of the school is too strict for a five-year-old child.
這學校的處罰對於一個五歲大的小孩來説太嚴格了。

☐ 三分熟
☐ 五分熟
☐ 七分熟
☐ 全熟

pu·pil [ˈpjupl]

名 學生、瞳孔
同 student 學生

英英 a person who is taught by another, especially a school child

例 I have been a **pupil** of the goldsmith for a decade.
我當這金匠的學生已經有十年了。

☐ 三分熟
☐ 五分熟
☐ 七分熟
☐ 全熟

pup·pet [ˈpʌpɪt]

名 木偶、傀儡
同 doll 玩偶

英英 a model of a person or an animal that can be made to move by people using strings

例 I love to collect **puppets**.
我喜歡搜集木偶。

☐ 三分熟
☐ 五分熟
☐ 七分熟
☐ 全熟

pup·py [ˈpʌpɪ]

名 小狗

英英 a young dog

例 She saw a lovely **puppy** on the street.
她在路上看到一隻可愛的小狗。

☐ 三分熟
☐ 五分熟
☐ 七分熟
☐ 全熟

purse [pɝs]

名 錢包
同 wallet 錢包

英英 a small bag for carrying money

例 Where is my **purse**?
我的錢包在哪裡？

☐ 三分熟
☐ 五分熟
☐ 七分熟
☐ 全熟

puz·zle [ˈpʌzl̩]

名 難題、謎
動 迷惑
同 mystery 謎

英英 a game that you have to think about carefully in order to give an answer of it; to make something difficult to understand

例 Can you solve the **puzzle**?
你可以解開這難題嗎？

☐ 三分熟
☐ 五分熟
☐ 七分熟
☐ 全熟

Q

Qq

qual·i·ty [ˈkwɑlətɪ]

名 品質

英英 the standard of something when it is compared to other things like it

例 The **quality** of the goods is not good enough.
這商品的品質不夠好。

☐ 三分熟
☐ 五分熟
☐ 七分熟
☐ 全熟

quan·ti·ty

[ˈkwɑntətɪ]

名 數量

英英 an exact amount or number

例 Tell me the **quantity** of your goods.
告訴我你的商品數量。

☐ 三分熟
☐ 五分熟
☐ 七分熟
☐ 全熟

quar·ter [ˈkwɔrtɚ]

名 四分之一
動 分為四等分

英英 one of four equal parts of something; to divide something into four parts

例 Give me a **quarter** of the cake.
給我四分之一塊蛋糕。

☐ 三分熟
☐ 五分熟
☐ 七分熟
☐ 全熟

quit [kwɪt]

動 離去、解除

英英 to leave, resign from a job, or stop

例 I **quitted** my job.
我離職了。

☐ 三分熟
☐ 五分熟
☐ 七分熟
☐ 全熟

quiz [kwɪz]

名 測驗
動 對……進行測驗
同 test 測驗
名詞複數 quizzes

英英 a competition or game in which people answer questions to test their knowledge; to test someone or something

例 I am preparing for the **quiz** tomorrow.
我正在準備明天的測驗。

☐ 三分熟
☐ 五分熟
☐ 七分熟
☐ 全熟

Rr

🔊 Track 237

rab·bit [ˈræbɪt]

名 兔子

英英 a small animal with long ears, soft fur and a short tail

例 The **rabbit** is as big as a cat.
這隻兔子跟貓一樣大。

☐ 三分熟
☐ 五分熟
☐ 七分熟
☐ 全熟

---

rain·y [ˈrenɪ]

形 多雨的

英英 having a lot of rain

例 It's a **rainy** day.
這是一個多雨的日子。

☐ 三分熟
☐ 五分熟
☐ 七分熟
☐ 全熟

---

range [rendʒ]

名 範圍
動 排列
同 limit 範圍

英英 the amount, number or size of something between an upper and a lower limit; to arrange in a row

例 The **range** of her academic study is wide.
她研究範圍很廣。

☐ 三分熟
☐ 五分熟
☐ 七分熟
☐ 全熟

---

rap·id [ˈræpɪd]

形 迅速的
同 quick 迅速的

英英 happening very quickly or at great speed

例 The **rapid** act of his saved her life.
他迅速的動作救了她一命。

☐ 三分熟
☐ 五分熟
☐ 七分熟
☐ 全熟

---

rare [rɛr]

形 稀有的

英英 not seen or happening very often

例 It's **rare** to see a panda here.
在這邊，貓熊是很稀有的。

☐ 三分熟
☐ 五分熟
☐ 七分熟
☐ 全熟

---

rath·er [ˈræðɚ]

副 寧願
片 would rather 寧可

英英 indicating someone's preference in a particular matter

例 I would **rather** die.
我寧死不屈。

☐ 三分熟
☐ 五分熟
☐ 七分熟
☐ 全熟

---

real·i·ty [rɪˈælətɪ]

名 真實
同 truth 真實

英英 the true situation and the problems that exactly exist in life

例 The **reality** is cruel.
事實是很殘酷的。

☐ 三分熟
☐ 五分熟
☐ 七分熟
☐ 全熟

---

real·ize [ˈriəˌlaɪz]

動 實現、瞭解

英英 to understand clearly or become fully aware of something

例 She works hard to **realize** her dream.
她很努力實現夢想。

☐ 三分熟
☐ 五分熟
☐ 七分熟
☐ 全熟

R

re·cent [ˈrisn̩t]
形 最近的

英英 that happened or began only a short time ago
例 ETF has been popular in **recent** years.
近幾年 ETF 很流行。

☐ 三分熟 ☐ 五分熟 ☐ 七分熟 ☐ 全熟

re·cord
[ˈrɛkɚd]/[rɪˈkɔrd]
名 記錄、唱片
動 記錄

英英 a piece of information forming something that has occurred, been said, etc.; to make a record of something
例 He broke the **record** in this competition.
他在這場比賽中打破紀錄了。

☐ 三分熟 ☐ 五分熟 ☐ 七分熟 ☐ 全熟

rec·tan·gle
[ˈrɛktæŋgl̩]
名 長方形

英英 a flat shape with four straight sides, two of which are longer than the other two, and four angles of 90°
例 The shape of the building is not **rectangle**.
這棟建築不是長方形的。

☐ 三分熟 ☐ 五分熟 ☐ 七分熟 ☐ 全熟

re·frig·er·a·tor/fridge/ice·box
[rɪˈfrɪdʒɚˌretɚ]/[frɪdʒ]/[ˈaɪsˌbaks]
名 冰箱

英英 an equipment which is artificially kept cool and used to store food and drink in the kitchen
例 I put the milk into the **refrigerator**.
我把牛奶放入冰箱之中。

☐ 三分熟 ☐ 五分熟 ☐ 七分熟 ☐ 全熟

re·fuse [rɪˈfjuz]
動 拒絕
同 reject 拒絕

英英 to say that you will not do what somebody has asked you to do
例 I **refuse** to forgive her.
我拒絕原諒她。

☐ 三分熟 ☐ 五分熟 ☐ 七分熟 ☐ 全熟

re·gard [rɪˈgard]
動 注視、認為
名 注視
同 judge 認為

英英 to think of in a particular way
例 I **regard** her as my best friend.
我將她視為我最好的朋友。

☐ 三分熟 ☐ 五分熟 ☐ 七分熟 ☐ 全熟

re·gion [ˈridʒən]
名 區域
同 zone 區域

英英 a large area of land, usually without exact limits or borders
例 The **region** is not ruled by the king.
這區域不受國王的統轄。

☐ 三分熟 ☐ 五分熟 ☐ 七分熟 ☐ 全熟

Track 239

reg·u·lar [ˋrɛgjələ]

形 平常的、定期的、規律的

同 usual 平常的

英英 happening or doing something often

例 I know its **regular** schedule.
我知道它平常的時刻表。

☐ 三分熟
☐ 五分熟
☐ 七分熟
☐ 全熟

---

re·ject [rɪˋdʒɛkt]

動 拒絕

英英 to refuse to consider or disagree to

例 I **reject** to help him.
我拒絕幫助他。

☐ 三分熟
☐ 五分熟
☐ 七分熟
☐ 全熟

---

re·la·tion [rɪˋleʃən]

名 關係

英英 the way in which two people or groups behave towards each other

例 Parents and children **relation** is important for the development of a child.
親子關係對於孩子的發展來說很重要。

☐ 三分熟
☐ 五分熟
☐ 七分熟
☐ 全熟

---

re·la·tion·ship

[rɪˋleʃənʃɪp]

名 關係

英英 the way in which two or more people or things are connected, or the state of being connected

例 I can't believe that he's in a **relationship** with the super star!
我不敢相信他竟然跟那大明星交往！

☐ 三分熟
☐ 五分熟
☐ 七分熟
☐ 全熟

---

re·peat [rɪˋpit]

動 重複

名 重複

英英 to say or write something again and again

例 Please **repeat** after me.
請跟我重複一次。

☐ 三分熟
☐ 五分熟
☐ 七分熟
☐ 全熟

---

re·ply [rɪˋplaɪ]

動 回答、答覆

同 respond 回答

英英 to say or write something in response to something else that has been said or written

例 He didn't **reply** my question.
他並沒有回答我的問題。

☐ 三分熟
☐ 五分熟
☐ 七分熟
☐ 全熟

---

re·port·er

[rɪˋportə]

名 記者

同 journalist 記者

英英 a person who collects and reports news for newspapers, magazine or television

例 **Reporters** have to go to work even when typhoon comes.
就算在颱風天，記者還是要上班。

☐ 三分熟
☐ 五分熟
☐ 七分熟
☐ 全熟

---

re·quire [rɪˋkwaɪr]

動 需要

同 need 需要

英英 to need something or someone

例 Being patient is **required** to get this job.
這份工作很需要耐心。

☐ 三分熟
☐ 五分熟
☐ 七分熟
☐ 全熟

re·quire·ment

[rɪ`kwaɪrmənt]

名 需要

英英 something required or needed

例 A **requirement** of a child can be more than you think.
一個孩子的需求可能比你想像中還多。

☐ 三分熟
☐ 五分熟
☐ 七分熟
☐ 全熟

---

re·spect [rɪ`spɛkt]

名 尊重
動 尊重、尊敬
同 adore 尊敬

英英 feeling of admiration for someone or something because of their good qualities or achievements

例 I **respect** the teacher.
我很尊敬我的老師。

☐ 三分熟
☐ 五分熟
☐ 七分熟
☐ 全熟

---

re·spon·si·ble

[rɪ`spɑnsəbḷ]

形 負責任的

英英 having an obligation to do something

例 She is **responsible** for her job.
她對她的工作很負責任。

☐ 三分熟
☐ 五分熟
☐ 七分熟
☐ 全熟

---

res·tau·rant

[`rɛstərənt]

名 餐廳

英英 a place where you can buy and have a meal

例 I'll see you in the **restaurant**!
我們餐廳見喔！

☐ 三分熟
☐ 五分熟
☐ 七分熟
☐ 全熟

---

rest·room

[`rɛstrum]

名 洗手間、廁所

英英 room with a toilet in a public place, such as a department store or restaurant

例 I need to go to the **restroom** now.
我現在要去一下洗手間。

☐ 三分熟
☐ 五分熟
☐ 七分熟
☐ 全熟

---

re·sult [rɪ`zʌlt]

名 結果
動 導致
同 consequence 結果

英英 a consequence or outcome (of something); to make a consequence

例 The **result** is not satisfying.
這結果不是讓人很滿意。

☐ 三分熟
☐ 五分熟
☐ 七分熟
☐ 全熟

---

re·view [rɪ`vju]

名 複習
動 回顧、檢查
同 recall 回憶

英英 an examination of something with the intention; to view again

例 We will **review** the lesson in the next class.
下堂課我們會複習這一課。

☐ 三分熟
☐ 五分熟
☐ 七分熟
☐ 全熟

---

rich·es [`rɪtʃɪz]

名 財產
同 wealth 財產

英英 material wealth or valuable objects

例 Having a well-paid job is not the only way to **riches**.
坐擁高薪不只是通往財富唯一的道路。

☐ 三分熟
☐ 五分熟
☐ 十分熟
☐ 全熟

R

🎧 Track 241

rock [rɑk]

動 搖動

名 岩石

英英 to move your body forwards and backwards in a regular way; the hard solid stone that forms part of the surface of the earth and some other planet

例 I took a picture on the **rock**.
我在這顆巨岩上拍照。

☐三分熟
☐五分熟
☐七分熟
☐全熟

---

rock·y [ˋrɑkɪ]

形 岩石的、搖擺的

英英 consisting or formed of rock

例 The roads in the countryside of Vietnam are always **rocky**.
越南鄉下的路總是很多岩石。

☐三分熟
☐五分熟
☐七分熟
☐全熟

---

role [rol]

名 角色

英英 the position that somebody has or is expected to have in an event, in society or in a relation

例 My mother plays an important **role** in my life.
我的母親在我人生中扮演很重要的角色。

☐三分熟
☐五分熟
☐七分熟
☐全熟

---

roy·al [ˋrɔɪəl]

形 皇家的

同 noble 貴族的

英英 connected with or belonging to the king or queen

例 The **royal** guards are standing around here.
皇家護衛站在這附近。

☐三分熟
☐五分熟
☐七分熟
☐全熟

---

rude [rud]

形 野蠻的、粗魯的

英英 very impolite or ill-mannered

例 Don't be **rude** to your teacher.
不可以對你的老師那麼粗魯。

☐三分熟
☐五分熟
☐七分熟
☐全熟

---

rul·er [ˋrulɚ]

名 統治者

同 sovereign 統治者

英英 a person who rules or governs a country or an organization

例 He is the **ruler** of the kingdom.
他是這國度的統治者。

☐三分熟
☐五分熟
☐七分熟
☐全熟

---

run·ner [ˋrʌnɚ]

名 跑者

英英 a person or an animal that runs, especially in a race

例 Who is the fastest **runner** in the world?
誰是當今世界上最快的跑者？

☐三分熟
☐五分熟
☐七分熟
☐全熟

---

rush [rʌʃ]

動 突擊

名 急忙、突進

片 in a rush 匆忙

英英 to move or act with urgent haste; to be hurry

例 He **rushed** to the classroom to have an exam.
他急忙衝進去教室考試。

☐三分熟
☐五分熟
☐七分熟
☐全熟

Ss

safe·ty [ˈseftɪ]

名 安全
同 security 安全

英英 the condition of being safe; preventing injury or damage
例 **Safety** is the first priority.
安全第一。

☐ 三分熟
☐ 五分熟
☐ 七分熟
☐ 全熟

---

sail·or [ˈselɚ]

名 船員、海員

英英 a person who works on a ship as a member of the crew
例 A **sailor** can't be seasick.
船員不可以暈船。

☐ 三分熟
☐ 五分熟
☐ 七分熟
☐ 全熟

---

sal·ad [ˈsæləd]

名 生菜食品、沙拉

英英 a dish of raw vegetables
例 I ate **salad** as my dinner.
我晚餐吃沙拉。

☐ 三分熟
☐ 五分熟
☐ 七分熟
☐ 全熟

---

salt·y [ˈsɔltɪ]

形 鹹的

英英 containing or tasting of salt
例 The dish is too **salty**.
這道菜太鹹了。

☐ 三分熟
☐ 五分熟
☐ 七分熟
☐ 全熟

---

sam·ple [ˈsæmpl̩]

名 樣本

英英 a number of people or things taken from a larger group and used in tests to provide information about the group
例 Give me a **sample**.
給我一個樣本。

☐ 三分熟
☐ 五分熟
☐ 七分熟
☐ 全熟

---

sand·wich [ˈsændwɪtʃ]

名 三明治

英英 two slices of bread, often spread with butter and a layer of meat, cheese, etc. between them
例 I ate a **sandwich** in the morning.
我早上吃了一個三明治。

☐ 三分熟
☐ 五分熟
☐ 七分熟
☐ 全熟

---

sat·is·fy [ˈsætɪsˌfaɪ]

動 使滿足
同 please 使滿意

英英 meet the expectations, needs, or desires of
例 I will do everything to **satisfy** my wife
我將盡一切努力令我老婆滿意。

☐ 三分熟
☐ 五分熟
☐ 七分熟
☐ 全熟

---

sauce [sɔs]

名 調味醬
動 加調味醬於……

英英 a thick liquid that is eaten with food for adding flavour to it; to add sauce into something
例 The **sauce** makes the dish successful.
這調味料讓這道菜很成功。

☐ 三分熟
☐ 五分熟
☐ 七分熟
☐ 全熟

🎧 Track 243

sci·ence [ˈsɑɪəns]

名 科學

英英 the study of the intellectual and practical activity encompassing the systematic structure and behaviour of the physical and natural world through observation and experiment

例 I am not good at **science**.
我的自然科學不太好。

☐ 三分熟
☐ 五分熟
☐ 七分熟
☐ 全熟

---

sci·en·tist

[ˈsaɪəntɪst]

名 科學家

英英 a person who studies about natural sciences

例 The **scientist** invented one of the greatest inventions in the world.
這科學家發明了世界上最偉大的發明。

☐ 三分熟
☐ 五分熟
☐ 七分熟
☐ 全熟

---

scis·sors [ˈsɪzəz]

名 剪刀
名詞複數 scissors

英英 an object for cutting paper or fabric, that has two sharp blades with handles, joined together in the middle

例 I need **scissors** to cut the paper.
我需要剪刀剪紙。

☐ 三分熟
☐ 五分熟
☐ 七分熟
☐ 全熟

---

score [skor]

名 分數
動 得分、評分

英英 the number of points, goals, etc. scored by each player or team in a game or competition; to get a score

例 I want to get a good **score**.
我想要考高分。

☐ 三分熟
☐ 五分熟
☐ 七分熟
☐ 全熟

---

screen [skrin]

名 螢幕

英英 an upright partition used to divide a room and give shelter

例 My mom looked at the **screen** of my cell phone.
我媽媽看了一下我手機螢幕。

☐ 三分熟
☐ 五分熟
☐ 七分熟
☐ 全熟

---

search [sɜtʃ]

動 搜索、搜尋
名 調查、檢索
同 seek 尋找

英英 an attempt to find somebody or something carefully; to look for carefully something

例 I am **searching** for the answer.
我正在找答案。

☐ 三分熟
☐ 五分熟
☐ 七分熟
☐ 全熟

---

se·cret [ˈsikrɪt]

名 祕密

英英 kept hidden from others

例 I won't tell you the **secret**.
我不會告訴你這祕密。

☐ 三分熟
☐ 五分熟
☐ 七分熟
☐ 全熟

sec·re·ta·ry
[ˈsɛkrəˌtɛrɪ]

名 祕書

英英 a person who works in an office, working for another person, dealing with letters and telephone calls, typing and arranging meetings with people, etc.

例 It is said that the boss has an affair with the **secretary**.
聽說老闆跟祕書有婚外情。

☐ 三分熟
☐ 五分熟
☐ 七分熟
☐ 全熟

sec·tion [ˈsɛkʃən]

名 部分

英英 any of the divided parts

例 In this **section**, we will talk about new-born babies.
在這部分，我們將會討論新生嬰兒。

☐ 三分熟
☐ 五分熟
☐ 七分熟
☐ 全熟

se·lect [səˈlɛkt]

動 挑選
同 pick 挑選

英英 carefully choose as being the best or most suitable

例 We will **select** the best student to represent for our class.
我們將會選出最優秀的學生代表我們班。

☐ 三分熟
☐ 五分熟
☐ 七分熟
☐ 全熟

se·lec·tion
[səˈlɛkʃən]

名 選擇、選定

英英 the process of choosing somebody or something carefully from a group

例 Most students in the class disagree with the **selection** of the teacher.
大部分學生都不同意那老師的選擇。

☐ 三分熟
☐ 五分熟
☐ 七分熟
☐ 全熟

se·mes·ter
[səˈmɛstɚ]

名 半學年、一學期

英英 one of the two periods that the school or college year is divided into

例 In this **semester**, we will have three exams.
在這學期，我們會有三個段考。

☐ 三分熟
☐ 五分熟
☐ 七分熟
☐ 全熟

sep·a·rate
[ˈsɛpəˌret]

形 分開的
動 分開

英英 forming a unit by itself; not joined to something else

例 The twin brothers were **separated** when they were little.
這對雙胞胎兄弟從小就被分開了。

☐ 三分熟
☐ 五分熟
☐ 七分熟
☐ 全熟

se·ri·ous [ˈsɪrɪəs]

形 嚴肅的

英英 bad or dangerous

例 He asked me a **serious** question.
他問了我一個嚴肅的問題。

☐ 三分熟
☐ 五分熟
☐ 七分熟
☐ 全熟

S

Track 245

ser·vant [ˋsɝvənt]
名 僕人、傭人

英英 a person who works in another person's house, and do the houseworks for them

例 The millionaire mistreated his **servant**.
這位富豪虐待他的僕人。

☐ 三分熟 ☐ 五分熟 ☐ 七分熟 ☐ 全熟

set·tle [ˋsɛtl]
動 安排、解決
片 settle down 安定

英英 to put an end to an argument or a disagreement; to solve something

例 After we **settled** down, I started to look for a job.
在我們安排妥當後，我開始找一個工作。

☐ 三分熟 ☐ 五分熟 ☐ 七分熟 ☐ 全熟

set·tle·ment [ˋsɛtlmənt]
名 解決、安排

英英 an official agreement that ends an argument between two people or groups

例 The **settlement** makes me relaxed.
這安排讓我鬆了口氣。

☐ 三分熟 ☐ 五分熟 ☐ 七分熟 ☐ 全熟

share [ʃɛr]
名 份、佔有
動 共用
片 share with 分享

英英 to have or use something at the same time as somebody else; a part of something

例 I don't want to **share** the cake with my sister.
我不想要跟我妹妹分享這塊蛋糕。

☐ 三分熟 ☐ 五分熟 ☐ 七分熟 ☐ 全熟

shelf [ʃɛlf]
名 棚架、架子

英英 a flat board, made of wood, metal or glass, which is fixed to the wall or forming part of a cupboard or bookcase

例 Give me the book on the **shelf**.
請給我架子上的書。

☐ 三分熟 ☐ 五分熟 ☐ 七分熟 ☐ 全熟

shell [ʃɛl]
名 貝殼
動 剝

英英 the hard outer part of eggs, nuts, some seeds and some animals; to remove the shell

例 I collect many **shells** on the beach.
我在沙灘上撿到很多貝殼。

☐ 三分熟 ☐ 五分熟 ☐ 七分熟 ☐ 全熟

shock [ʃɑk]
名 衝擊
動 震撼、震驚
同 frighten 驚恐

英英 an unpleasant feeling as a result of something bad happening; cause to feel shocked

例 I was **shocked** by the movie.
我被這部電影嚇到了。

☐ 三分熟 ☐ 五分熟 ☐ 七分熟 ☐ 全熟

shoot [ʃut]
動 射傷、射擊
名 射擊、嫩芽

英英 to fire something or someone with a weapon, such as a gun

例 The **soldier** was shot.
這名士兵被射傷。

☐ 三分熟 ☐ 五分熟 ☐ 七分熟 ☐ 全熟

S

shorts [ʃɔrts]
名 短褲

英英 short trousers or pants that end above or at the knee, worn when playing sports in hot weather

例 I wear blue **shorts**.
我穿著藍色的短褲。

☐ 三分熟
☐ 五分熟
☐ 七分熟
☐ 全熟

---

show·er [ˈʃaʊɚ]
名 陣雨、淋浴
動 淋浴、澆水

英英 a brief and usually light fall of rain or snow; wash oneself in a shower

例 I took a **shower** after I came home.
我回家後沖了個澡。

☐ 三分熟
☐ 五分熟
☐ 七分熟
☐ 全熟

---

shrimp [ʃrɪmp]
名 蝦子

英英 a small shellfish that can be eaten, like a prawn but smaller

例 I made some soup with **shrimps** in it.
我煮了一些湯，裡面有蝦子。

☐ 三分熟
☐ 五分熟
☐ 七分熟
☐ 全熟

---

side·walk
[ˈsaɪdˌwɔk]
名 人行道
同 pavement 人行道

英英 a pavement

例 I saw him on the **sidewalk**.
我在人行道上看到他。

☐ 三分熟
☐ 五分熟
☐ 七分熟
☐ 全熟

---

sign [saɪn]
名 記號、標誌
動 簽署

英英 a symbol showing that something exists, is happening or may happen in the future; write someone's name on something

例 Please **sign** here.
請在這裡簽名。

☐ 三分熟
☐ 五分熟
☐ 七分熟
☐ 全熟

---

si·lence [ˈsaɪləns]
名 沉默
動 使……靜下來

英英 complete absence of sound; to make someone quiet

例 The **silence** made me embarrassed.
這一陣沉默讓我很尷尬。

☐ 三分熟
☐ 五分熟
☐ 七分熟
☐ 全熟

---

si·lent [ˈsaɪlənt]
形 沉默的

英英 of a person , not speaking

例 He is a **silent** person.
他是一個沉默寡言的人。

☐ 三分熟
☐ 五分熟
☐ 七分熟
☐ 全熟

---

silk [sɪlk]
名 絲、綢

英英 a fine, soft lustrous fibre produced by silkworms

例 The clothes are made of **silk**.
這件衣服是絲綢做的。

☐ 三分熟
☐ 五分熟
☐ 七分熟
☐ 全熟

🎧 Track 247

sim·i·lar [ˈsɪmələ]

形 相似的、類似的
同 alike 相似的

英英 like somebody or something but not exactly the same

例 These bags are **similar**.
這些包包都很相似。

☐ 三分熟
☐ 五分熟
☐ 七分熟
☐ 全熟

sim·ply [ˈsɪmplɪ]

副 簡單地、樸實地、僅僅

英英 used to emphasize how easy something is

例 I will **simply** tell you the summary of the story.
我只會簡單地跟你說故事的大綱。

☐ 三分熟
☐ 五分熟
☐ 七分熟
☐ 全熟

sin·gle [ˈsɪŋg!]

形 單一的
名 單一

英英 the only one

例 I have been **single** for years after she dumped me.
在她甩了我以後，我單身了很多年。

☐ 三分熟
☐ 五分熟
☐ 七分熟
☐ 全熟

sink [sɪŋk]

動 沉沒、沉
名 水槽

英英 to go down below the surface in the water or liquid; a water basin

例 I burst out crying when seeing the Titanic **sinking**.
當我看到鐵達尼號沉下去的時候我哭了出來。

☐ 三分熟
☐ 五分熟
☐ 七分熟
☐ 全熟

skill·ful/skilled

[ˈskɪlfəl]/[skɪld]

形 熟練的、靈巧的

英英 having or showing skill

例 He is **skillful** in fixing the car.
他很熟練的修車。

☐ 三分熟
☐ 五分熟
☐ 七分熟
☐ 全熟

skin·ny [ˈskɪnɪ]

形 皮包骨的

英英 very thin, especially in a way that you find unpleasant or ugly

例 The girl is **skinny**.
這女孩瘦的只剩皮包骨。

☐ 三分熟
☐ 五分熟
☐ 七分熟
☐ 全熟

skirt [skɝt]

名 裙子

英英 woman's outer garment fastened around the waist and hanging down around the legs

例 I love to wear this pretty **skirt**.
我喜歡穿這件漂亮的裙子。

☐ 三分熟
☐ 五分熟
☐ 七分熟
☐ 全熟

sleep·y [ˈslipɪ]

形 想睡的、睏的

英英 needing sleep

例 I am **sleepy** in the class.
我上課的時候很想睡。

☐ 三分熟
☐ 五分熟
☐ 七分熟
☐ 全熟

slen·der [ˋslɛndɚ]

形 苗條的
同 slim 苗條的

英英 gracefully thin

例 She wants to be **slender**.
她很想要變苗條。

☐ 三分熟
☐ 五分熟
☐ 七分熟
☐ 全熟

S

---

slide [slaɪd]

動 滑動
名 滑梯、投影片

英英 to move easily over a smooth or wet surface; a structure with a smooth surface for kids to slide down

例 A cat is lying on the **slide**.
溜滑梯上躺著一隻貓。

☐ 三分熟
☐ 五分熟
☐ 七分熟
☐ 全熟

---

slim [slɪm]

形 苗條的
動 變細

英英 gracefully thin or slenderly built; to become or make thin

例 I am jealous of her **slim** waist.
我很忌妒她苗條的腰。

☐ 三分熟
☐ 五分熟
☐ 七分熟
☐ 全熟

---

slip [slɪp]

動 滑倒

英英 to slide a short distance accidentally so that you almost fall

例 I **slipped** in the bathroom.
我在浴室滑倒了。

☐ 三分熟
☐ 五分熟
☐ 七分熟
☐ 全熟

---

slip·per(s)

[ˋslɪpɚ(z)]

名 拖鞋

英英 a comfortable slip-on shoe that is worn indoors

例 I put my **slippers** at the door.
我在門口放了我的拖鞋。

☐ 三分熟
☐ 五分熟
☐ 七分熟
☐ 全熟

---

snack [snæk]

名 小吃、點心
動 吃點心

英英 a small meal between formal meals, usually eaten in a hurry; to have a small meal between formal meals

例 I ate some **snack** in the afternoon.
我在午後吃了點小吃。

☐ 三分熟
☐ 五分熟
☐ 七分熟
☐ 全熟

---

snail [snel]

名 蝸牛

英英 a slow-moving mollusc with a spiral shell into which the whole body can be withdrawn

例 There are some **snails** on the leaf.
葉子上有幾隻蝸牛。

☐ 三分熟
☐ 五分熟
☐ 七分熟
☐ 全熟

---

snow·y [snoɪ]

形 多雪的、積雪的

英英 covered with snow

例 The mountain is always **snowy**.
這座山總是積雪。

☐ 三分熟
☐ 五分熟
☐ 七分熟
☐ 全熟

🎧 **Track 249**

---

soc·cer [ˋsɑkɚ]

名 足球

英英 a form of football played with a round ball which may not be handled during play, the object being to score goals by kicking or heading the ball into the opponents' goal

例 I love to play **soccer**.
我喜歡踢足球。

□三分熟
□五分熟
□七分熟
□全熟

---

so·cial [ˋsoʃəl]

形 社會的

英英 connected with society

例 Bullying is a **social** problem.
霸凌是社會的問題。

□三分熟
□五分熟
□七分熟
□全熟

---

so·ci·e·ty

[səˋsaɪətɪ]

名 社會
同 community 社區、社會

英英 a group of people living together in a more or less ordered community

例 The **society** pays little attention on this issue.
這社會不太注意這個議題。

□三分熟
□五分熟
□七分熟
□全熟

---

sock(s) [sɑk(s)]

名 短襪

英英 a piece of clothing that is worn over the foot, ankle and lower part of the leg

例 The **socks** smell terrible.
這些襪子很難聞。

□三分熟
□五分熟
□七分熟
□全熟

---

sol·dier [ˋsoldʒɚ]

名 軍人

英英 a member of an army, especially one who is not an officer

例 Being a **soldier** is honorable in this country.
在這國家，當軍人是很光榮的事情。

□三分熟
□五分熟
□七分熟
□全熟

---

so·lu·tion

[səˋluʃən]

名 溶解、解決、解釋
同 explanation 解釋

英英 a means of solving a problem

例 Tell me your **solution**.
告訴我你的解決方法。

□三分熟
□五分熟
□七分熟
□全熟

---

solve [sɑlv]

動 解決

英英 to find a way of dealing with a problem or difficult situation

例 I don't know how to **solve** this problem.
我不知道如何解決這問題。

□三分熟
□五分熟
□七分熟
□全熟

S

some·bod·y

[ˈsʌmˌbɑdɪ]

代 某人、有人
名 重要人物
同 someone 某人

英英 someone; important person

例 **Somebody** must help her.
一定要有人幫她。

☐ 三分熟
☐ 五分熟
☐ 七分熟
☐ 全熟

some·where

[ˈsʌmˌhwɛr]

副 在某處

英英 in, at or to some place that you do not know

例 I must have put my wallet **somewhere** in the room.
我一定是把錢包放在這房間的某處。

☐ 三分熟
☐ 五分熟
☐ 七分熟
☐ 全熟

sort [sɔrt]

名 種
動 一致、調和

英英 a category of people or things with a common feature or features; to arrange systematically in groups

例 What **sort** of books attracts teenagers?
哪一種書可以吸引青少年？

☐ 三分熟
☐ 五分熟
☐ 七分熟
☐ 全熟

source [sors]

名 來源、水源地
同 origin 起源

英英 a place or person that you get something from

例 What's the **source** of this article?
這篇文章來源是什麼？

☐ 三分熟
☐ 五分熟
☐ 七分熟
☐ 全熟

south·ern

[ˈsʌðən]

形 南方的

英英 situated in or facing the south.

例 I am going to **southern** America this year.
我今年要去南美洲。

☐ 三分熟
☐ 五分熟
☐ 七分熟
☐ 全熟

soy·bean/
soy·a/soy

[ˈsɔɪˌbin]/[ˈsɔɪə]/[sɔɪ]

名 大豆、黃豆

英英 a plant of the pea family which produces an edible bean that is high in protein

例 Tofu is made of **soybean**.
豆腐是黃豆做的。

☐ 三分熟
☐ 五分熟
☐ 七分熟
☐ 全熟

speak·er [ˈspikə]

名 演說者

英英 a person who gives a speech

例 The **speaker** touched me.
這演講者感動我的心。

☐ 三分熟
☐ 五分熟
☐ 七分熟
☐ 全熟

speed [spid]

名 速度、急速
動 加速
同 haste 急速

英英 the rate at which someone or something moves or operates, moving quickly; to move more quickly

例 The ambulance rushed to the hospital at high **speed**.
這輛救護車以高速衝到醫院。

☐ 三分熟
☐ 五分熟
☐ 七分熟
☐ 全熟

261

🎧 **Track 251**

spell·ing [ˈspɛlɪŋ]

名 拼讀、拼法

英英 the act of forming words correctly from individual letters

例 How do you **spell** this word?
你怎麼拼這個字的？

☐ 三分熟
☐ 五分熟
☐ 七分熟
☐ 全熟

spi·der [ˈspaɪdɚ]

名 蜘蛛

英英 a small ugly creature with eight thin legs

例 My sister is afraid of **spiders**.
我姐姐很怕蜘蛛。

☐ 三分熟
☐ 五分熟
☐ 七分熟
☐ 全熟

spin·ach [ˈspɪnɪtʃ]

名 菠菜

英英 a plant with large dark green leaves which are eaten as a vegetable

例 I don't like to eat **spinach**.
我不喜歡吃菠菜。

☐ 三分熟
☐ 五分熟
☐ 七分熟
☐ 全熟

spir·it [ˈspɪrɪt]

名 精神
同 soul 精神、靈魂

英英 the part of a person that includes their mind, feelings and character

例 Art can purify our **spirit**.
藝術可以淨化人心。

☐ 三分熟
☐ 五分熟
☐ 七分熟
☐ 全熟

spot [spɑt]

動 弄髒、認出
名 點
同 stain 弄髒

英英 a small round mark differing in color from the surface around it; to make something unclean

例 I **spotted** the shirt when I ate pasta.
當我在吃義大利麵的時候弄髒了我的襯衫。

☐ 三分熟
☐ 五分熟
☐ 七分熟
☐ 全熟

spread [sprɛd]

動 展開、傳佈
名 寬度、桌布
同 extend 擴展

英英 to open something that has been folded so that it covers a larger area than before; the width or extent

例 The news was **spread** rapidly.
這新聞很快速的傳開了。

☐ 三分熟
☐ 五分熟
☐ 七分熟
☐ 全熟

spring [sprɪŋ]

動 彈開、突然提出
名 泉水、春天

英英 the season after winter and before summer; to move suddenly upwards or forwards

例 Japan is famous for its hot **spring**.
日本以溫泉聞名。

☐ 三分熟
☐ 五分熟
☐ 七分熟
☐ 全熟

square [skwɛr]

形 公正的、方正的
名 正方形、廣場

英英 fair or honest; a plane figure with four equal straight sides and four right angles

例 Did you see the **square** box?
你有看到那個方形的箱子嗎？

☐ 三分熟
☐ 五分熟
☐ 七分熟
☐ 全熟

S

squir·rel [ˋskwɝəl]

名 松鼠
名詞複數 squirrels

英英 a small animal with a long thick tail and red, grey or black fur

例 There are many **squirrels** in the park.
公園裡面有很多的松鼠。

☐三分熟
☐五分熟
☐七分熟
☐全熟

stage [stedʒ]

名 舞臺、階段
動 上演
片 on the stage 上演

英英 a point, period, or step in a process or development; to present a performance

例 The opera is on the **stage** now.
這齣歌劇正在上演。

☐三分熟
☐五分熟
☐七分熟
☐全熟

stamp [stæmp]

動 壓印
名 郵票、印章

英英 imporess with a device that leaves a mark.; a small piece of paper recording payment of postage

例 I am collecting **stamps**.
我正在集郵。

☐三分熟
☐五分熟
☐七分熟
☐全熟

stan·dard

[ˋstændɚd]

名 標準
形 標準的
同 model 標準

英英 a required or agreed level of quality; accpted as normal or average

例 It's a **standard** format.
這是一個標準的格式。

☐三分熟
☐五分熟
☐七分熟
☐全熟

steak [stek]

名 牛排

英英 a thick slice of good quality beef

例 I had a **steak** for dinner on my birthday.
我生日那天晚餐吃牛排。

☐三分熟
☐五分熟
☐七分熟
☐全熟

steal [stil]

動 偷、騙取

英英 illegally take something without permission and without intending to return it

例 The student **stole** his classmates' money.
這學生偷同學的錢。

☐三分熟
☐五分熟
☐七分熟
☐全熟

steam [stim]

名 蒸汽
動 蒸、使蒸發、
　以蒸汽開動

英英 the hot gas that water changes into when it boils; to produce with steam

例 I will **steam** the dumplings tonight.
我今天晚上會蒸這些餃子。

☐三分熟
☐五分熟
☐七分熟
☐全熟

steel [stil]

名 鋼、鋼鐵

英英 a hard, strong grey or bluish-grey alloy of iron with carbon, used as a structural material and in buidling things

例 I don't think it is a good time to invest in **steel**.
我不認為現在是投資鋼鐵的好時機。

☐三分熟
☐五分熟
☐七分熟
☐全熟

🎧 **Track 253**

stick [stɪk]

名 棍、棒
動 黏
同 attach 貼上

英英 a thin piece of wood that has been broken from a tree; to fixed something in a particular place

例 The children hit the dog with **sticks**.
這些小孩用棒子打這隻狗。

□三分熟
□五分熟
□七分熟
□全熟

---

stom·ach [ˈstʌmək]

名 胃
同 belly 胃

英英 the internal organ in which the first part of digestion occurs

例 I threw up due to problems with my **stomach**.
我吐了，因為我的胃有點問題。

□三分熟
□五分熟
□七分熟
□全熟

---

storm [stɔrm]

名 風暴
動 襲擊

英英 very bad weather with strong winds and rain, and often thunder and lightning; attach suddenly

例 The **storm** is coming.
暴風雨就要來臨了。

□三分熟
□五分熟
□七分熟
□全熟

---

stove [stov]

名 火爐、爐子
同 oven 爐子

英英 a piece of equipment that can burn various fuels and is used for heating rooms

例 He is standing near the **stove** in case the soup might be burned.
他站在爐子邊以防湯煮焦了。

□三分熟
□五分熟
□七分熟
□全熟

---

straight [stret]

形 筆直的、正直的

英英 extending uniformly in one direction only

例 The road is not **straight**.
這條路沒有很直。

□三分熟
□五分熟
□七分熟
□全熟

---

strang·er [ˈstrendʒɚ]

名 陌生人

英英 a person that you do not know

例 I always tell my kids not to talk to **strangers**.
我總是告訴我的小孩不要跟陌生人講話。

□三分熟
□五分熟
□七分熟
□全熟

---

straw [strɔ]

名 稻草

英英 stems of wheat or other grain plants that have been cut and dried

例 The kid was born on the **straw**.
那小孩是在稻草上誕生的。

□三分熟
□五分熟
□七分熟
□全熟

---

straw·ber·ry [ˈstrɔˌbɛrɪ]

名 草莓

英英 a sweet soft red fruit with a seed-studded surface

例 Have you ever tried **strawberry** cake?
你有吃過草莓蛋糕嗎？

□三分熟
□五分熟
□七分熟
□全熟

stream [strim]

名 小溪
動 流動

英英 a small narrow river; to move in a flow

例 I used to play near the **stream**.
我以前在小溪邊玩耍。

☐ 三分熟
☐ 五分熟
☐ 七分熟
☐ 全熟

stress [strɛs]

名 壓力
動 強調、著重
同 emphasis 強調

英英 pressure put on something that can make it lose its shape; to emphasize

例 She quitted her job because of the **stress**.
她因為壓力離職了。

☐ 三分熟
☐ 五分熟
☐ 七分熟
☐ 全熟

stretch [strɛtʃ]

動／名 伸展

英英 be able to be made longer or wider without tearing or breaking

例 I **stretched** my legs after the class.
下課後，我伸展我的雙腳。

☐ 三分熟
☐ 五分熟
☐ 七分熟
☐ 全熟

strict [strɪkt]

形 嚴格的
同 harsh 嚴厲的

英英 that must be obeyed exactly

例 The teachers in this school are **strict**.
這學校的老師都很嚴格。

☐ 三分熟
☐ 五分熟
☐ 七分熟
☐ 全熟

strike [straɪk]

動 打擊、達成（協定）
名 罷工
片 go on strike 罷工

英英 deliver a blow to something; refuse to work as a form of organized protest

例 The workers in this country go on **strike** very often.
這國家的工人很常罷工。

☐ 三分熟
☐ 五分熟
☐ 七分熟
☐ 全熟

string [strɪŋ]

名 弦、繩子、一串

英英 a material made of several threads twisted together, used to tie things together

例 I used a **string** to fix the box.
我用繩子固定箱子。

☐ 三分熟
☐ 五分熟
☐ 七分熟
☐ 全熟

strug·gle [ˈstrʌgl̩]

動 努力、奮鬥
名 掙扎、奮鬥

英英 to try very hard to do or achieve something when it is difficult

例 Even the children in this country need to **struggle** for life.
這國家連孩子都要為生活奮鬥。

☐ 三分熟
☐ 五分熟
☐ 七分熟
☐ 全熟

sub·ject [ˈsʌbdʒɪkt]

名 主題、科目
形 服從的、易受……的
同 topic 主題

英英 a person or thing that is being discussed, studied, or dealt with; under the control or authority of

例 What's the **subject** of this article?
這篇文章的主題是什麼？

☐ 三分熟
☐ 五分熟
☐ 十分熟
☐ 全熟

S

🎧 Track 255

sub·tract

[səbˋtrækt]

動 扣除、移走

英英 to take a number or an amount away from another number or amount

例 **Subtract** 1 from 5 and you have 4.
五減一得四。

☐ 三分熟
☐ 五分熟
☐ 七分熟
☐ 全熟

---

sub·way [ˋsʌbˏwe]

名 地下鐵

英英 a path that goes under a road, etc., which people can use to cross to the other side

例 I took the **subway** in Tokyo.
我在東京搭地下鐵。

☐ 三分熟
☐ 五分熟
☐ 七分熟
☐ 全熟

---

suc·ceed [səkˋsid]

動 成功

英英 achieve an aim or goal

例 Everyone wants to **succeed**.
大家都想要成功。

☐ 三分熟
☐ 五分熟
☐ 七分熟
☐ 全熟

---

suc·cess [səkˋsɛs]

名 成功

英英 the fact that you have achieved something you want and have been trying to do or get

例 **Success** means efforts.
成功意味著努力。

☐ 三分熟
☐ 五分熟
☐ 七分熟
☐ 全熟

---

suc·cess·ful

[səkˋsɛsfəl]

形 成功的

英英 achieving your aims or what was intended

例 She is a **successful** buesinese woman.
她是個成功的商業人士。

☐ 三分熟
☐ 五分熟
☐ 七分熟
☐ 全熟

---

sud·den [ˋsʌdn̩]

形 突然的
名 意外、突然
片 all of a sudden 突然間

英英 occurring or done quickly and unexpectedly; the unexpected event

例 All of a **sudden**, there was a thunder.
突然來一陣雷聲。

☐ 三分熟
☐ 五分熟
☐ 七分熟
☐ 全熟

---

suit [sut]

名 套
動 適合
同 fit 適合

英英 a set of clothes made of the same fabric, including a jacket and trousers, pants or a skirt; to be acceptable to

例 The dress **suits** you well.
這件洋裝很適合你。

☐ 三分熟
☐ 五分熟
☐ 七分熟
☐ 全熟

---

sun·ny [ˋsʌnɪ]

形 充滿陽光的
同 bright 晴朗的

英英 with a lot of light from the sun

例 On such a **sunny** day, I want to go to the mountains.
在這樣充滿陽光的一天，我想要去山上。

☐ 三分熟
☐ 五分熟
☐ 七分熟
☐ 全熟

su·per·mar·ket

[ˈsupɚˌmarkɪt]

名 超級市場

英英 a large self-service shop selling foods and household goods

例 Tissue paper is on sale in the **supermarket** now.
衛生紙在超級市場特價中。

☐ 三分熟
☐ 五分熟
☐ 七分熟
☐ 全熟

---

sup·ply [səˈplaɪ]

動 供給
名 供應品
同 furnish 供給

英英 to provide with something needed to someone; a stock available

例 **Supply** meets demand.
供需平衡了。

☐ 三分熟
☐ 五分熟
☐ 七分熟
☐ 全熟

---

sup·port [səˈport]

動 支持
名 支持者、支撐物
同 uphold 支持

英英 to help or encourage somebody or something by saying or showing that you agree with; a person that supports

例 My family **support** me.
我的家人支援我。

☐ 三分熟
☐ 五分熟
☐ 七分熟
☐ 全熟

---

sur·face [ˈsɝfɪs]

名 表面
動 使形成表面
同 exterior 表面

英英 the outside layer of something; to make the outside layer for somethin

例 The **surface** of the moon is covered with rocks.
月球表面覆蓋著岩石。

☐ 三分熟
☐ 五分熟
☐ 七分熟
☐ 全熟

---

sur·vive [səˈvaɪv]

動 倖存、殘存

英英 continue to live or exist

例 They just want to **survive** in the war.
他們只是想要在戰爭中倖存。

☐ 三分熟
☐ 五分熟
☐ 七分熟
☐ 全熟

---

swal·low [ˈswɑlo]

名 燕子
動 吞咽

英英 cause or allow food, drink, etc. to pass down the throat; a swift-flying songbird with a forked tail, feeding on insects in flight

例 I **swallowed** all the food on the table when I was hungry.
當我饑餓的時候，我吞下整桌的食物。

☐ 三分熟
☐ 五分熟
☐ 七分熟
☐ 全熟

---

swan [swɑn]

名 天鵝

英英 a large graceful bird that is usually white and has a long thin neck, which is living on or near water

例 There are some **swans** on the lake.
湖上有幾隻天鵝。

☐ 三分熟
☐ 五分熟
☐ 七分熟
☐ 全熟

---

sweat·er [ˈswɛtɚ]

名 毛衣、厚運動衫

英英 a thick knitted woollen or cotton piece of clothing for the upper part of the body, with long sleeves

例 I wore a **sweater** under the jacket.
在夾克外套下，我穿了一件毛衣。

☐ 三分熟
☐ 五分熟
☐ 七分熟
☐ 全熟

S

🎧 **Track 257**

sweep [swip]

動 掃、打掃
名 掃除、掠過

英英 to clean an area by brushing away dirt or litter

例 You need to **sweep** the floor.
你要掃地。

☐ 三分熟
☐ 五分熟
☐ 七分熟
☐ 全熟

swing [swɪŋ]

動 搖動

英英 to move back and forth or from side to side as if suspended

例 The branches on the tree are **swinging**.
樹枝在搖動。

☐ 三分熟
☐ 五分熟
☐ 七分熟
☐ 全熟

sym·bol [ˈsɪmbḷ]

名 象徵、標誌
同 sign 標誌

英英 a person, an object, an event, etc. that represents some particular things

例 Do you know the **symbol** of Japan?
你知道日本的標誌是什麼嗎？

☐ 三分熟
☐ 五分熟
☐ 七分熟
☐ 全熟

Tt

tal·ent [ˈtælənt]

名 天分、天賦

英英 natural gifted skill

例 She doesn't have enough **talent** in art.
她在藝術上面沒有太多天賦。

☐ 三分熟
☐ 五分熟
☐ 七分熟
☐ 全熟

talk·a·tive

[ˈtɔkətɪv]

形 健談的
反 mute 沉默的

英英 liking to talk a lot

例 The salesman is quite **talkative**.
這位銷售員很健談。

☐ 三分熟
☐ 五分熟
☐ 七分熟
☐ 全熟

tan·ge·rine

[ˈtændʒəˌrin]

名 柑、桔

英英 a small citrus fruit with a loose skin

例 We usually eat lots of **tangerines** in autumn.
我們通常在秋天吃很多的橘子。

☐ 三分熟
☐ 五分熟
☐ 七分熟
☐ 全熟

tank [tæŋk]

名 水槽、坦克

英英 a large container for holding liquid or gas

例 The troop is equipped with many **tanks**.
這部隊備有很多坦克。

☐ 三分熟
☐ 五分熟
☐ 七分熟
☐ 全熟

tape [tep]

名 帶、卷尺、磁帶
動 用卷尺測量
同 record 磁帶、唱片

英英 a long narrow strip of magnetic material that is used for recording sounds, pictures or information; to measure with a tape

例 People don't use a **tape** to play music now.
現在人不會用錄音帶播放音樂了。

☐ 三分熟
☐ 五分熟
☐ 七分熟
☐ 全熟

T

tar·get [ˈtɑrgɪt]

名 目標、靶子
同 goal 目標

英英 a person, object, or place selected as the aim of an attack
例 What's your **target**?
你的目標是什麼？

☐ 三分熟
☐ 五分熟
☐ 七分熟
☐ 全熟

task [tæsk]

名 任務
同 work 任務

英英 a piece of work that someone has to do
例 The **task** is too difficult.
這任務太難了。

☐ 三分熟
☐ 五分熟
☐ 七分熟
☐ 全熟

tast·y [ˈtestɪ]

形 好吃的
同 delicious 好吃的

英英 describes something is very good to eat
例 The food in this restaurant is **tasty**.
這間餐廳的食物很好吃。

☐ 三分熟
☐ 五分熟
☐ 七分熟
☐ 全熟

team [tim]

名 隊
同 group 組、隊

英英 a group of players forming one side in a competitive game or sport
例 I am glad to work in this **team**.
我很榮幸可以在這團隊工作。

☐ 三分熟
☐ 五分熟
☐ 七分熟
☐ 全熟

tear [tɪr]/[tɛr]

名 眼淚
動 撕、撕破

英英 a drop of liquid that comes out of your eye when you cry; to slit something into piece
例 I burst into **tears** when getting the bad news.
當我聽到噩耗，忍不住流了眼淚。

☐ 三分熟
☐ 五分熟
☐ 七分熟
☐ 全熟

teen(s) [tin(z)]

名 十多歲

英英 relating to teenagers
例 **Teens** are troublesome for parents.
父母總為十多歲的孩子傷腦筋。

☐ 三分熟
☐ 五分熟
☐ 七分熟
☐ 全熟

teen·age [ˈtinˌedʒ]

形 十幾歲的

英英 denoting, relating to, or characteristic of a teenager or teenagers
例 Most **teenage** boys are interested in girls.
大部分十幾歲的男孩都會對女孩感到興趣。

☐ 三分熟
☐ 五分熟
☐ 七分熟
☐ 全熟

teen·ag·er

[ˈtinˌedʒɚ]

名 青少年

英英 a person who is between 13 and 19 years old
例 **Teenagers** are faced with lots of difficulties.
青少年正面臨許多的困難。

☐ 三分熟
☐ 五分熟
☐ 七分熟
☐ 全熟

tel·e·phone/phone

[ˈtɛləˌfon]/[fon]

名 電話
動 打電話

英英 a device for talking to somebody else over long distances, using wires or radio; a machine used for this
例 The **telephone** is ringing.
電話正在響。

☐ 三分熟
☐ 五分熟
☐ 七分熟
☐ 全熟

Track 259

tel·e·vi·sion/TV

[ˈtɛləˌvɪʒən]

名 電視

英英 a device for converting visual images and sound into electrical signals, transmitting them by radio or other means, and displaying them electronically on a screen

例 She watches **TV** every day.
她每天看電視。

☐ 三分熟
☐ 五分熟
☐ 七分熟
☐ 全熟

tem·ple [ˈtɛmpl̩]

名 寺院、神殿

英英 a building which is used for the worship of a god or gods

例 Many Japanese visit Longshan **temple**.
很多日本人會拜訪龍山寺。

☐ 三分熟
☐ 五分熟
☐ 七分熟
☐ 全熟

ten·nis [ˈtɛnɪs]

名 網球

英英 a game for two or four players, who use rackets to strike a ball over a net stretched across a court

例 Would you like to play **tennis** with me?
你想要跟我一起打網球嗎？

☐ 三分熟
☐ 五分熟
☐ 七分熟
☐ 全熟

tent [tɛnt]

名 帳篷

英英 a shelter made of a large sheet of canvas, that is supported by poles and ropes fixed to the ground, and usually is used especially for camping

例 You need to prepare a **tent** to go camping.
要去露營時，你需要準備一頂帳篷。

☐ 三分熟
☐ 五分熟
☐ 七分熟
☐ 全熟

term [tɝm]

名 條件、期限、術語
動 稱呼

英英 a word or phrase used as the name of something, especially one connected with a particular type of language; to call by a particular term

例 It is a special **term** for medicine.
這是藥學的一個專有名詞。

☐ 三分熟
☐ 五分熟
☐ 七分熟
☐ 全熟

ter·ri·ble [ˈtɛrəbl̩]

形 可怕的、駭人的
同 horrible 可怕的

英英 extremely bad or unpleasant

例 It is a **terrible** idea.
這是一個可怕的想法。

☐ 三分熟
☐ 五分熟
☐ 七分熟
☐ 全熟

ter·rif·ic [təˈrɪfɪk]

形 驚人的

英英 excellent; wonderful

例 She got a **terrific** job.
她得到一個驚人的工作。

☐ 三分熟
☐ 五分熟
☐ 七分熟
☐ 全熟

test [tɛst]

名 考試
動 試驗、檢驗

英英 a procedure intended to establish the quality or reliability of something; subject to test

例 We have a **test** tomorrow.
我們明天有一個考試。

☐ 三分熟
☐ 五分熟
☐ 七分熟
☐ 全熟

T

text·book

[ˈtɛkstˌbʊk]

名 教科書

英英 a book that teaches a particular subject and that is used by students of schools and colleges

例 Don't forget to bring your **textbook** tomorrow.
明天不要忘記帶你的課本來。

☐ 三分熟
☐ 五分熟
☐ 七分熟
☐ 全熟

---

the·a·ter [ˈθiətɚ]

名 戲院、劇場
反 stadium 劇場

英英 a building where theatrical performances or motion-picture shows can be presented

例 I go to the **theater** to watch the opera.
我們去戲院看歌劇。

☐ 三分熟
☐ 五分熟
☐ 七分熟
☐ 全熟

---

there·fore

[ˈðɛrˌfor]

副 因此、所以
同 hence 因此

英英 for that reason; consequently

例 I was tired. **Therefore**, I went to bed early last night.
我很累，因此我昨天很早就睡了。

☐ 三分熟
☐ 五分熟
☐ 七分熟
☐ 全熟

---

thick [θɪk]

形 厚的、密的

英英 having more depth or extent from one surface to its opposite than usual

例 The book is very **thick**.
這本書很厚。

☐ 三分熟
☐ 五分熟
☐ 七分熟
☐ 全熟

---

thief [θif]

名 小偷、盜賊
名詞複數 thieves

英英 a person who steals something from another person or place

例 There is a **thief** in this neighbor.
這鄰里有小偷。

☐ 三分熟
☐ 五分熟
☐ 七分熟
☐ 全熟

---

thin [θɪn]

形 薄的、稀疏的、瘦的
同 slender 薄的

英英 having little extent from one surface to its opposite

例 His hair is very **thin**..
他的頭髮非常稀疏。

☐ 三分熟
☐ 五分熟
☐ 七分熟
☐ 全熟

---

thirs·ty [ˈθɝstɪ]

形 口渴的

英英 feeling thirst

例 I'm very **thirsty**. Could you please give me some water?
我口很渴，可以給我一些水嗎？

☐ 三分熟
☐ 五分熟
☐ 七分熟
☐ 全熟

---

throat [θrot]

名 喉嚨
片 sore throat 喉嚨痛

英英 the tube in the neck that takes food and air into the body; the front part of the neck

例 I have a sore **throat**.
我喉嚨痛。

☐ 三分熟
☐ 五分熟
☐ 七分熟
☐ 全熟

🎧 Track 261

through [θru]

介 經過、通過
副 全部、到最後

英英 moving in one side and out of the other side

例 I walk **through** the hall every day.
我每天都會經過這個大廳。

☐ 三分熟
☐ 五分熟
☐ 七分熟
☐ 全熟

through·out

[θru`aʊt]

介 遍佈、遍及
副 徹頭徹尾

英英 in or into every part of something

例 **Throughout** the whole essay, I can't find your argument.
我徹頭徹尾地無法找到你這篇文章的論點。

☐ 三分熟
☐ 五分熟
☐ 七分熟
☐ 全熟

thumb [θʌm]

名 拇指
動 用拇指翻

英英 the short, thick first digit of the hand, set lower and apart from the other four and opposable to them; to touch or press with a thumb

例 I pressed the button with my **thumb**.
我用拇指按按鈕。

☐ 三分熟
☐ 五分熟
☐ 七分熟
☐ 全熟

thun·der [`θʌndɚ]

名 雷、打雷
動 打雷

英英 the loud noise that you hear after a flash of lightning in the sky; thunder sounds

例 I was afraid of **thunder**.
我以前很怕打雷。

☐ 三分熟
☐ 五分熟
☐ 七分熟
☐ 全熟

tip [tɪp]

名 小費、暗示
動 付小費

英英 a small amount of extra money that you give to somebody because you're given the service; to give a small amount of extra money to somebody

例 How much would you like to **tip** the waitress?
你打算付多少小費給這服務生？

☐ 三分熟
☐ 五分熟
☐ 七分熟
☐ 全熟

ti·tle [`taɪtl]

名 稱號、標題
動 加標題
同 headline 標題

英英 the name of a book, poem, piece article or piece of music, etc.; to add a title for a book or article, etc.

例 The **title** of the article attracts me to read it.
這篇文章的標題讓我想讀這篇文章。

☐ 三分熟
☐ 五分熟
☐ 七分熟
☐ 全熟

toast [tost]

名 土司麵包
動 烤、烤麵包

英英 sliced bread browned on both sides by exposure to radiant heat; to brown bread

例 I only eat **toast** for breakfast.
我只有早餐會吃吐司。

☐ 三分熟
☐ 五分熟
☐ 七分熟
☐ 全熟

toe [to]

名 腳趾

英英 one of the five small parts that stick out from the foot

例 Can you touch your **toe**?
你可以碰到你的腳趾嗎？

☐ 三分熟
☐ 五分熟
☐ 七分熟
☐ 全熟

T

---

tofu/bean curd
[`tofu]/[bin kɝd]

名 豆腐

英英 curd made from soya beans, usually used in Asian and vegetarian cookery

例 **Tofu** is popular in many Asian countries.
豆腐在很多亞洲國家都很受歡迎。

☐ 三分熟
☐ 五分熟
☐ 七分熟
☐ 全熟

---

toi·let [`tɔɪlɪt]

名 洗手間

英英 a room for washing and dressing yourself

例 Where is the **toilet**?
洗手間在哪裡？

☐ 三分熟
☐ 五分熟
☐ 七分熟
☐ 全熟

---

to·ma·to [tə`meto]

名 番茄

英英 a glossy red or yellow edible fruit, usually eaten as a vegetable or in salads

例 I need some **tomatoes** to make a sandwich.
我需要一些番茄做三明治。

☐ 三分熟
☐ 五分熟
☐ 七分熟
☐ 全熟

---

tongue [tʌŋ]

名 舌、舌頭

英英 the soft part in the mouth that moves around, used for tasting, swallowing, speaking

例 To pronounce the sound, you need to curl your **tongue**.
發這個音需要捲舌頭。

☐ 三分熟
☐ 五分熟
☐ 七分熟
☐ 全熟

---

tooth [tuθ]

名 牙齒、齒
名詞複數 teeth

英英 any of the hard white objects in the mouth used for biting and chewing food

例 The old man has no **tooth**.
這老人沒有牙齒了。

☐ 三分熟
☐ 五分熟
☐ 七分熟
☐ 全熟

---

top·ic [`tɑpɪk]

名 主題、談論
同 theme 主題

英英 a subject of a text or speech

例 The **topic** of today's class is morality.
今天課程的主題是道德。

☐ 三分熟
☐ 五分熟
☐ 七分熟
☐ 全熟

---

tour [tʊr]

名 旅行
動 遊覽
同 travel 旅行

英英 a journey made for pleasure during which several different towns or countries are visited; to visit

例 Is there any **tour** to the island?
有沒有行程是可以到這個島的？

☐ 三分熟
☐ 五分熟
☐ 七分熟
☐ 全熟

---

tow·el [taʊl]

名 毛巾

英英 a piece of thick cloth or paper which is used for drying

例 I bring a **towel** to gym.
我帶一條毛巾去健身房。

☐ 三分熟
☐ 五分熟
☐ 七分熟
☐ 全熟

🎧 **Track 263**

tow·er [ˈtaʊɚ]

名 塔
動 高聳

英英 a tall narrow building, especially of a church or castle; rise to reach a great height

例 Everyone visits Eiffel **Tower** when they come to Paris.
大家到巴黎都會造訪艾菲爾鐵塔。

☐ 三分熟
☐ 五分熟
☐ 七分熟
☐ 全熟

track [træk]

名 路線
動 追蹤

英英 a rough path or minor road; to follow the movements

例 The **track** of our journey is perfect.
我們旅途的路線很完美。

☐ 三分熟
☐ 五分熟
☐ 七分熟
☐ 全熟

trade [tred]

名 商業、貿易
動 交易

英英 the activity of buying and selling or of exchanging goods or services between people or countries; to buy and sell

例 Business **trade** is always difficult for me.
對我來說商務貿易一直都是很難的。

☐ 三分熟
☐ 五分熟
☐ 七分熟
☐ 全熟

tra·di·tion

[trəˈdɪʃən]

名 傳統
同 custom 習俗

英英 the transmission of customs or beliefs from generation to generation

例 In Taiwanese **tradition**, four is unlucky.
在臺灣的傳統，四是不吉祥的。

☐ 三分熟
☐ 五分熟
☐ 七分熟
☐ 全熟

tra·di·tion·al

[trəˈdɪʃənl]

形 傳統的

英英 being part of the beliefs, customs or way of life of a particular group of people, that have been kept for a long time

例 Many girls nowadays want to have a **traditional** wedding.
現代很多女生都想要有一場傳統的婚禮。

☐ 三分熟
☐ 五分熟
☐ 七分熟
☐ 全熟

traf·fic [ˈtræfɪk]

名 交通
片 traffic jam 交通壅塞

英英 vehicles moving on public roads

例 I am late because of the **traffic** jam.
因為交通壅塞，我遲到了。

☐ 三分熟
☐ 五分熟
☐ 七分熟
☐ 全熟

trap [træp]

名 圈套、陷阱
動 誘捕
同 snare 誘捕

英英 a piece of equipment which is set for catching animals; to set a piece of equipment for catching animals

例 A bear is in the **trap**.
有一隻熊掉入陷阱之中。

☐ 三分熟
☐ 五分熟
☐ 七分熟
☐ 全熟

trav·el [ˈtrævl̩]

動 旅行
名 旅行

英英 to go from one place to another, especially over a long distance

例 I want to **travel** to Paris.
我想要到巴黎去旅行。

☐ 三分熟
☐ 五分熟
☐ 七分熟
☐ 全熟

---

trea·sure [ˈtrɛʒɚ]

名 寶物、財寶
動 收藏、珍藏

英英 a quantity of precious metals, gems, or other valuable objects; to keep carefully

例 I **treasure** my girlfriend.
我很珍惜我的女朋友。

☐ 三分熟
☐ 五分熟
☐ 七分熟
☐ 全熟

---

treat [trit]

動 處理、對待

英英 to behave in a particular way towards somebody or something

例 Don't **treat** me like a child.
不要把我當成是小孩子。

☐ 三分熟
☐ 五分熟
☐ 七分熟
☐ 全熟

---

treat·ment
[ˈtritmənt]

名 款待

英英 the manner of treating someone or something

例 Thank you for the **treatment**.
謝謝你的款待。

☐ 三分熟
☐ 五分熟
☐ 七分熟
☐ 全熟

---

tri·al [ˈtraɪəl]

名 審問、試驗
同 experiment 實驗

英英 a formal examination of evidence in a court of law by a judge and often a jury, to decide if somebody accused of a crime is guilty or not

例 The **trial** made the student cry.
這審問讓這學生哭了出來。

☐ 三分熟
☐ 五分熟
☐ 七分熟
☐ 全熟

---

tri·an·gle
[ˈtraɪˌæŋgl̩]

名 三角形

英英 a flat shape with three straight sides and three angles; a thing in the shape of a triangle

例 The gift box is a **triangle**.
這禮物盒是三角形的。

☐ 三分熟
☐ 五分熟
☐ 七分熟
☐ 全熟

---

trick [trɪk]

名 詭計
動 欺騙、欺詐
片 trick or treat
不給糖就搗蛋

英英 something that you do for deceiving somebody or annoying somebody; to deceive someone

例 Don't **trick** on me.
不要騙我。

☐ 三分熟
☐ 五分熟
☐ 七分熟
☐ 全熟

---

trou·sers
[ˈtraʊzɚz]

名 褲、褲子
同 pants 褲子

英英 a piece of clothing that covers the body from the waist down and is divided into two parts to cover each leg separately

例 The **trousers** are too long for me.
這褲子對我來說太長了。

☐ 三分熟
☐ 五分熟
☐ 七分熟
☐ 全熟

🎧 **Track 265**

truck [trʌk]

名 卡車
同 van 貨車

英英 a large road vehicle, which is used for carrying things

例 She can drive a **truck**!
她會開卡車！

☐ 三分熟
☐ 五分熟
☐ 七分熟
☐ 全熟

---

trum·pet [ˈtrʌmpɪt]

名 喇叭、小號
動 吹喇叭

英英 a brass musical instrument made of a curved metal tube that you blow into, with three valves for changing the note; to play the trumpet

例 I am having a **trumpet** lesson.
我等一下有一堂小喇叭的課。

☐ 三分熟
☐ 五分熟
☐ 七分熟
☐ 全熟

---

trust [trʌst]

名 信任
動 信任
同 believe 相信

英英 the belief that someone or something is good or honest

例 Do you **trust** me?
你信任我嗎？

☐ 三分熟
☐ 五分熟
☐ 七分熟
☐ 全熟

---

truth [truθ]

名 真相、真理
同 reality 事實

英英 the quality or state of being true

例 It is an unacceptable **truth**.
這是一個無法接受的事實。

☐ 三分熟
☐ 五分熟
☐ 七分熟
☐ 全熟

---

tube [tjub]

名 管、管子
同 pipe 管子

英英 a long hollow pipe made of metal, plastic, rubber, etc., through which liquids or gases move from one place to another

例 Water flows through the **tube**.
水流經過這管子。

☐ 三分熟
☐ 五分熟
☐ 七分熟
☐ 全熟

---

tun·nel [ˈtʌn!]

名 隧道、地道

英英 a passage built underground

例 There is a **tunnel** between France and England.
在英法之間有一條海底隧道。

☐ 三分熟
☐ 五分熟
☐ 七分熟
☐ 全熟

---

tur·key [ˈtɜkɪ]

名 火雞

英英 a large bird native to North America, which is grown for its meat on farms

例 We eat **turkey** on Thanksgiving.
我們在感恩節吃火雞。

☐ 三分熟
☐ 五分熟
☐ 七分熟
☐ 全熟

---

tur·tle [ˈtɜt!]

名 龜、海龜

英英 a large reptile with a hard shell, which lives in the sea

例 I saw many **turtles** when I went diving.
當我潛水的時候看到很多海龜。

☐ 三分熟
☐ 五分熟
☐ 七分熟
☐ 全熟

type [taɪp]

名 類型
動 打字

英英 a group of people or things that share the same qualities or features; to write with a type writer or computer

例 He can **type** very fast.
他打字很快。

☐ 三分熟
☐ 五分熟
☐ 七分熟
☐ 全熟

---

ty·phoon [taɪˋfun]

名 颱風

英英 a tropical storm found in the West Pacific Ocean

例 A **typhoon**'s coming.
有個颱風要來了。

☐ 三分熟
☐ 五分熟
☐ 七分熟
☐ 全熟

Uu

U

ug·ly [ˋʌglɪ]

形 醜的、難看的

英英 unpleasant to look at

例 **Ugly** though she is, she is very kind.
雖然她很醜，但她很善良。

☐ 三分熟
☐ 五分熟
☐ 七分熟
☐ 全熟

---

um·brel·la

[ʌmˋbrɛlə]

名 雨傘

英英 a device consisting of a circular fabric canopy on a folding metal frame supported by a central rod, used as protection against rain

例 Don't forget to bring an **umbrella**.
別忘了帶一把傘出門。

☐ 三分熟
☐ 五分熟
☐ 七分熟
☐ 全熟

---

un·der·wear

[ˋʌndɚˏwɛr]

名 內衣

英英 clothes that you wear under other clothes and next to the skin

例 You should wear an **underwear** under the shirt.
你應該要在襯衫裡面穿一件內衣。

☐ 三分熟
☐ 五分熟
☐ 七分熟
☐ 全熟

---

u·ni·form

[ˋjunəˏfɔrm]

名 制服、校服、使一致
同 outfit 全套服裝

英英 the clothing worn by members of the same organization or school by children attending certain schools; to make the same

例 The **uniform** in this school is beautiful.
這學校的制服很漂亮。

☐ 三分熟
☐ 五分熟
☐ 七分熟
☐ 全熟

---

up·on [əˋpɑn]

介 在……上面

英英 used to show that something is above something else

例 The picture is put **upon** the table.
這照片放在桌子上。

☐ 三分熟
☐ 五分熟
☐ 七分熟
☐ 全熟

🎧 **Track 267**

up·per [`ʌpɚ]
副 在上位
同 superior 上級的

英英 situated above another part
例 She wants to be in the **upper** class.
她想要躋身上流社會。

☐ 三分熟
☐ 五分熟
☐ 七分熟
☐ 全熟

used [juzd]
形 用過的、二手的

英英 describes something that is used by someone, not new
例 The **used** book is much cheaper.
二手書便宜很多。

☐ 三分熟
☐ 五分熟
☐ 七分熟
☐ 全熟

used to [just tu]
副 習慣的

英英 used to say that something happened continuously or frequently during a period in the past
例 I am **used to** getting up early.
我習慣早起。

☐ 三分熟
☐ 五分熟
☐ 七分熟
☐ 全熟

us·er [`juzɚ]
名 使用者
同 consumer 消費者

英英 a person or thing that uses something
例 The **users** complain about the bugs in the game.
這使用者在抱怨遊戲中的錯誤。

☐ 三分熟
☐ 五分熟
☐ 七分熟
☐ 全熟

u·su·al [`juʒʊəl]
形 通常的、平常的
同 ordinary 平常的

英英 habitually occurring or done
例 A **usual** child doesn't say things like this.
平常的小孩不會說這樣的話。

☐ 三分熟
☐ 五分熟
☐ 七分熟
☐ 全熟

Vv

va·ca·tion
[ve`keʃən]
名 假期
動 度假
同 holiday 假期

英英 a holiday period between terms in universities and law courts or when an office is vacant; to take a holiday
例 What would you like to do in summer **vacation**?
你暑假想要做什麼？

☐ 三分熟
☐ 五分熟
☐ 七分熟
☐ 全熟

val·ley [`vælɪ]
名 溪谷、山谷

英英 a low area between hills or mountains
例 Many people prefer to live in the **valley**.
許多人都偏好住在溪谷處。

☐ 三分熟
☐ 五分熟
☐ 七分熟
☐ 全熟

val·ue [`vælju]
名 價值
動 重視、評價

英英 the regard that something is kept to deserve; importance or worth; to regard something is important
例 The **value** of the house is unmeasurable.
這屋子的價值是無法估計的。

☐ 三分熟
☐ 五分熟
☐ 七分熟
☐ 全熟

vic·to·ry [ˈvɪktərɪ]

名 勝利
同 success 勝利、成功

英英 an act of defeating an enemy in a battle or competition

例 The **victory** of the war brings the general honor.
戰爭的勝利帶給這個將軍光榮。

☐ 三分熟
☐ 五分熟
☐ 七分熟
☐ 全熟

---

vid·e·o [ˈvɪdɪo]

名 電視、錄影

英英 the system of recording or broadcasting moving visual images

例 I watched **video** tapes when I was little.
我小時候會看錄影帶。

☐ 三分熟
☐ 五分熟
☐ 七分熟
☐ 全熟

---

vil·lage [ˈvɪlɪdʒ]

名 村莊

英英 a community in a rural area, larger than a hamlet and smaller than a town

例 There are not so many people in the **village**.
這村莊裡面沒有太多的人。

☐ 三分熟
☐ 五分熟
☐ 七分熟
☐ 全熟

---

vi·o·lin [ˌvaɪəˈlɪn]

名 小提琴
同 fiddle 小提琴

英英 a small musical instrument with four strings and a body narrowed at the middle, played with a bow

例 I learned to play the **violin** at five.
我在五歲就學小提琴了。

☐ 三分熟
☐ 五分熟
☐ 七分熟
☐ 全熟

---

vis·i·tor [ˈvɪzɪtɚ]

名 訪客、觀光客

英英 a person visiting a person or place

例 We provide slippers for the **visitors**.
我們提供了拖鞋給訪客。

☐ 三分熟
☐ 五分熟
☐ 七分熟
☐ 全熟

---

vo·cab·u·lar·y [vəˈkæbjəˌlɛrɪ]

名 單字、字彙

英英 a list of words used in a particular language or in a particular sphere

例 We have to learn the **vocabulary** of this lesson first.
我們要先學這一課的單字。

☐ 三分熟
☐ 五分熟
☐ 七分熟
☐ 全熟

---

vol·ley·ball [ˈvɑlɪˌbɔl]

名 排球

英英 a game for two teams in which a inflated ball is hit by hand over a net

例 I love to play **volleyball**.
我喜歡打排球。

☐ 三分熟
☐ 五分熟
☐ 七分熟
☐ 全熟

---

vote [vot]

名 選票
動 投票
同 ballot 選票

英英 formal indication of a choice between two or more candidates or courses of action; to give a vote

例 I didn't **vote** for the candidate.
我沒有把票投給這候選人。

☐ 三分熟
☐ 五分熟
☐ 七分熟
☐ 全熟

🎧 **Track 269**

vot·er [votə]

名 投票者

英英 a person who votes or who has a legal right to vote in an election

例 The media predict that the **voters** will change their mind.
媒體預計投票者將會改變他們的心態。

☐ 三分熟
☐ 五分熟
☐ 七分熟
☐ 全熟

Ww

waist [west]

名 腰部

英英 the part of the human body which is below the ribs and above the hips

例 She showed me the tattoo on her **waist**.
她給我看她腰上的刺青。

☐ 三分熟
☐ 五分熟
☐ 七分熟
☐ 全熟

wait·er/wait·ress

[`wetə]/[`wetrɪs]

名 服務生／女服務生

英英 a man or woman whose job is to serve customers at their tables in a restaurant

例 The **waiter** is polite.
這服務生很有禮貌。

☐ 三分熟
☐ 五分熟
☐ 七分熟
☐ 全熟

wake [wek]

動 喚醒、醒
片 Wake up 叫醒

英英 to cause someone awake from sleep

例 My mother **wakes** me up every morning.
我媽媽每天早上都會叫我起床。

☐ 三分熟
☐ 五分熟
☐ 七分熟
☐ 全熟

wal·let [`wɑlɪt]

名 錢包、錢袋

英英 a pocket-sized, flat, folding bag or sack for money and plastic cards

例 I lost my **wallet**.
我錢包掉了。

☐ 三分熟
☐ 五分熟
☐ 七分熟
☐ 全熟

wa·ter·fall

[`wɔtə⋅fɔl]

名 瀑布

英英 a cascade of water falling from a height, formed when a river or stream flows over a precipice or steep incline

例 The **waterfall** is beautiful.
這一座瀑布很漂亮。

☐ 三分熟
☐ 五分熟
☐ 七分熟
☐ 全熟

wa·ter·mel·on

[`wɔtə⋅mɛlən]

名 西瓜

英英 a large melon-like fruit with smooth green skin, red pulp, and is full of watery juice

例 I love to eat **watermelons** in summer.
我喜歡在夏天吃西瓜。

☐ 三分熟
☐ 五分熟
☐ 七分熟
☐ 全熟

W

---

wave [wev]

名 浪、波
動 搖動、波動
同 sway 搖動

英英 a ridge of water curling into an arched form and breaking on the shore

例 I stand at the beach just to watch the **waves** on the sea.
我站在海上就只是為了看海浪。

☐ 三分熟
☐ 五分熟
☐ 七分熟
☐ 全熟

---

weap·on [ˈwɛpən]

名 武器、兵器

英英 a thing designed or used for inflicting bodily harm or physical damage in fighting or hunting

例 The country invented some strong **weapons**.
這國家發明了一些很強的兵器。

☐ 三分熟
☐ 五分熟
☐ 七分熟
☐ 全熟

---

wed [wɛd]

動 嫁、娶、結婚
同 marry 結婚

英英 give or join in marriage

例 My friend will **wed** in August.
我朋友要在八月結婚。

☐ 三分熟
☐ 五分熟
☐ 七分熟
☐ 全熟

---

week·day

[ˈwikˌde]

名 平日、工作日

英英 a day of the week other than Sunday or Saturday

例 We work hard on the **weekdays**.
我們在平日很認真工作。

☐ 三分熟
☐ 五分熟
☐ 七分熟
☐ 全熟

---

west·ern [ˈwɛstən]

形 西方的、西方國家的

英英 situated in, directed towards, or facing the west

例 Gay marriage is legalized in many **western** countries.
同性結婚在許多西方國家是合法的。

☐ 三分熟
☐ 五分熟
☐ 七分熟
☐ 全熟

---

wet [wɛt]

形 潮濕的
動 弄濕

英英 consist of or containing with liquid; to make wet

例 The towel is **wet**.
這毛巾是濕的。

☐ 三分熟
☐ 五分熟
☐ 七分熟
☐ 全熟

---

whale [hwel]

名 鯨魚

英英 very large marine mammal with a horizontal tail fin and a blowhole on top of the head for breathing

例 **Whales** are the largest animals on the earth.
鯨魚是世界上最大的動物。

☐ 三分熟
☐ 五分熟
☐ 七分熟
☐ 全熟

---

what·ev·er

[hwɑtˈɛvə]

形 任何的
代 任何

英英 one or some or every or all without specification

例 I will do **whatever** you say.
你說什麼我都會照做。

☐ 三分熟
☐ 五分熟
☐ 七分熟
☐ 全熟

🎧 **Track 271**

---

wheel [hwil]

名 輪子、輪
動 滾動

英英 a circular object that revolves on an axle, fixed below a vehicle to enable it to move along or forming part of a machine; turn in a wide circle

例 The truck has six **wheels**.
這輛卡車有六個輪胎。

☐ 三分熟
☐ 五分熟
☐ 七分熟
☐ 全熟

---

when·ev·er

[hwɛnˈɛvɚ]

副 無論何時
連 無論何時
同 anytime 任何時候

英英 every or any time

例 Tell me **whenever** you need some help.
無論何時，當你需要幫助的時候儘管告訴我。

☐ 三分熟
☐ 五分熟
☐ 七分熟
☐ 全熟

---

wher·ev·er

[hwɛrˈɛvɚ]

副 無論何處
連 無論何處

英英 any or every place

例 You can contact me with a cellphone **wherever** you are.
無論你在哪裡都可以用手機連絡我。

☐ 三分熟
☐ 五分熟
☐ 七分熟
☐ 全熟

---

whis·per [ˈhwɪspɚ]

動 耳語
名 輕聲細語
同 murmur 低語聲

英英 to speak very softly and lightly using one's breath rather than one's throat

例 The girl **whispered** to me.
那女孩在我耳邊耳語。

☐ 三分熟
☐ 五分熟
☐ 七分熟
☐ 全熟

---

who·ev·er

[huˈɛvɚ]

代 任何人、無論誰

英英 any person who

例 Don't ask **whoever** to help you.
不要隨便請人家幫你。

☐ 三分熟
☐ 五分熟
☐ 七分熟
☐ 全熟

---

wid·en [ˈwaɪdn̩]

動 使……變寬、增廣

英英 to make wide or become wider

例 The government decided to **widen** the road.
政府決定要增寬道路。

☐ 三分熟
☐ 五分熟
☐ 七分熟
☐ 全熟

---

width [wɪdθ]

名 寬、廣
同 breadth 寬度

英英 the measurement or extent of something from side to side; the lesser or least of two or more dimensions of a body

例 What's the **width** of the road?
這條路多寬？

☐ 三分熟
☐ 五分熟
☐ 七分熟
☐ 全熟

wild [waɪld]
形 野生的、野性的

英英 living or growing in the natural environment; not domesticated or cultivated

例 Be careful of the **wild** animals.
小心野生動物。

☐ 三分熟
☐ 五分熟
☐ 七分熟
☐ 全熟

---

will·ing [ˈwɪlɪŋ]
形 心甘情願的

英英 ready or eager to help

例 I am **willing** to help you.
我心甘情願地幫你。

☐ 三分熟
☐ 五分熟
☐ 七分熟
☐ 全熟

---

wind·y [ˈwɪndɪ]
形 多風的

英英 marked by or exposed to strong winds

例 It is always **windy** in the fall.
秋天總是很多風。

☐ 三分熟
☐ 五分熟
☐ 七分熟
☐ 全熟

---

wing [wɪŋ]
名 翅膀、翼
動 飛

英英 a modified forelimb or other appendage enabling a bird, bat, insect, or other creature to fly; to fly

例 The **wings** of the birds are long.
這種鳥的翅膀很長。

☐ 三分熟
☐ 五分熟
☐ 七分熟
☐ 全熟

---

win·ner [ˈwɪnɚ]
名 勝利者、優勝者
同 victor 勝利者

英英 a person who wins

例 Who's the **winner** of the game?
這場比賽的勝利者是誰？

☐ 三分熟
☐ 五分熟
☐ 七分熟
☐ 全熟

---

wire [waɪr]
名 金屬絲、電線

英英 a thread or slender rod of metal

例 The **wire** is too old.
這條電線太老舊了。

☐ 三分熟
☐ 五分熟
☐ 七分熟
☐ 全熟

---

wise [waɪz]
形 智慧的、睿智的
同 smart 聰明的

英英 having the ability and knowledge to make good judgments

例 The **wise** man can always give you a solution.
這位智者總是可以給你解決方案。

☐ 三分熟
☐ 五分熟
☐ 七分熟
☐ 全熟

---

with·in [wɪˈðɪn]
介 在……之內
同 inside 在……之內

英英 inside the range or bounds of

例 I will come **within** an hour.
我在一小時以內會到。

☐ 三分熟
☐ 五分熟
☐ 七分熟
☐ 全熟

---

with·out [wɪˈðaʊt]
介 沒有、不

英英 not accompanied by or having the use of

例 I can't live **without** you.
沒有你我就不能活。

☐ 三分熟
☐ 五分熟
☐ 七分熟
☐ 全熟

W

Track 273

---

wolf [wʊlf]

名 狼

英英 a wild animal that is the largest member of the dog family

例 The **wolves** ate the chilcken.
狼群吃掉了雞。

☐三分熟
☐五分熟
☐七分熟
☐全熟

---

wond·er [ˋwʌndɚ]

名 奇跡、驚奇
動 對……感到驚奇

英英 a feeling of surprise and admiration, caused by something unexpected or unfamiliar; to cause surprised

例 I **wonder** why you love her.
我好奇你怎麼會喜歡她。

☐三分熟
☐五分熟
☐七分熟
☐全熟

---

won·der·ful
[ˋwʌndɚfəl]

形 令人驚奇的、奇妙的
同 marvelous
令人驚奇的

英英 extremely good or remarkable

例 It is a **wonderful** project.
這是個完美的計畫。

☐三分熟
☐五分熟
☐七分熟
☐全熟

---

wood·en [ˋwʊdn̩]

形 木製的

英英 made of wood

例 The **wooden** desk is heavy.
這木製的桌子很重。

☐三分熟
☐五分熟
☐七分熟
☐全熟

---

wool [wʊl]

名 羊毛

英英 the fine soft curly or wavy hair forming the coat of a sheep, goat, or similar animal, especially when shorn and made into cloth or yarn

例 I need a **wool** sweater in the winter.
在冬天，我需要一件羊毛毛衣。

☐三分熟
☐五分熟
☐七分熟
☐全熟

---

worth [wɝθ]

名 價值

英英 equivalent in value to the sum or item specified

例 The **worth** of the book is more than you think.
這本書的價值比你想的還高。

☐三分熟
☐五分熟
☐七分熟
☐全熟

---

wound [wʊnd]

名 傷口
動 傷害
同 harm 傷害

英英 a bodily injury caused by a cut or blow; to harm or hurt

例 The **wound** is deep.
這傷口很深。

☐三分熟
☐五分熟
☐七分熟
☐全熟

Yy

yard [jɑrd]

名 庭院、院子

英英 a small piece of land next to a house or behind a house, usually used for growing plants

例 I park in the **yard**.
我把車子停在院子裡。

☐ 三分熟
☐ 五分熟
☐ 七分熟
☐ 全熟

---

youth [juθ]

名 青年

英英 the period between childhood and adult age

例 The development of a country is related to the quality of the **youth**.
一個國家的發展跟青年素質有關。

☐ 三分熟
☐ 五分熟
☐ 七分熟
☐ 全熟

Zz

ze·bra [ˈzibrə]

名 斑馬
名詞複數 zebras, zebra

英英 an African wild horse with black-and-white stripes and an erect mane

例 **Zebras** live in Africa.
斑馬住在非洲。

☐ 三分熟
☐ 五分熟
☐ 七分熟
☐ 全熟

Y
Z

語研力 E071

精準7000單字滿分版：
初級基礎篇 Level 1 & Level 2

完美六邊型緊扣式架構，會考、全民英檢初級都能輕鬆過關！

作　　者	Michael Yang、Tong Weng ◎合著
顧　　問	曾文旭
出版總監	陳逸祺、耿文國
主　　編	陳蕙芳
執行編輯	翁芯俐
文字校對	莊詠翔
美術編輯	李依靜
法律顧問	北辰著作權事務所

印　　製	世和印製企業有限公司
初　　版	2022 年 09 月
出　　版	凱信企業集團 - 凱信企業管理顧問有限公司
電　　話	（02）2773-6566
傳　　真	（02）2778-1033
地　　址	106 台北市大安區忠孝東路四段 218 之 4 號 12 樓
信　　箱	kaihsinbooks@gmail.com

定　　價	新台幣 349 元 / 港幣 116 元
產品內容	1 書

總 經 銷	采舍國際有限公司
地　　址	235 新北市中和區中山路二段 366 巷 10 號 3 樓
電　　話	（02）8245-8786
傳　　真	（02）8245-8718

國家圖書館出版品預行編目資料

精準7000單字滿分版：初級基礎篇Level 1&Level
2／Michael Yang、Tong Weng◎合著. -- 初版. --
臺北市：凱信企業集團凱信企業管理顧問有限公
司, 2022.09
　　面；　公分
ISBN 978-626-7097-24-3(平裝)

1.CST: 英語 2.CST: 詞彙
805.12　　　　　　　　　　　　111012527